THE GIDEONS

HARD OAK PRESS

Copyright © 2010 Jeffrey M. Hopkins
HARD OAK PRESS
ISBN: 0984567321
ISBN-13: 9780984567324
www.hardoakpress.com

"The rich man also died and was buried. In hell he lift up his eyes, being in torments and saw Abraham far off with Lazarus in his bosom. The rich man cried and said, Father Abraham have mercy on me, and send Lazarus that he may dip his finger in the water and cool my tongue; for I am tormented in this flame. But Abraham said, son remember that you in your lifetime received many good things and likewise Lazarus received evil things: but he is now comforted and you are tormented. And beside all this, between us and you there is a great gulf fixed, so that they which would pass from your thence, you cannot, neither can they pass to us, that would come from thence."

Luke 16:22-26 The Gideons

"Those who are wretched shall be in fire: There will be for them nothing but the heaving of sighs and sobs. They will dwell therein for all time that the heavens and earth endure, except as Allah wills, for Allah is the sure accomplisher of what he plans. And those who are blessed shall be in the Garden. They will dwell therein for all time that the heavens and earth endure, except as Allah wills, a gift without break."

The Qu'ran 11:106-108

"Immortality is a bitch."

Dr. Robert S. Tanner

I have seen it in the gulls that scream, hop, and beat feathers against the violent gusts that drive the choppy waves, a vain search of land and brief respite from the torrents of torments. They soar from rocky outcrops to search for desolate islands to lay their eggs. They search for a bit of food to warm the vicious tear in their bellies. But for a moment, then their bellies are empty again. They cry at their fate. They have cried the same cry for eons.

I have seen it in the mass of colliding spermatozoa. The blind will of ejaculate. These blind bumpers rushing forward in time, just a beginning, seeking their goal. They seek creation, even if they are thrown into the dirt. Onan's pure flowing water has dried. It has died with him, now as fecund as a tree in the middle of the desert.

I have seen it in the battles of men. From the commanding general dressed in golden armor, cresting the hilltops, to the pitchfork-wielding peons smashed by their comrades for being too slow and weak. I found great delight in the crashing of armor against armor. I reveled in the formations of men marching towards each other, with swords and spears glittering like hope in the sunshine. Those brave, honorable men! In the end, I laughed at their dead faces. How they hope against the darkness! At Galgema I watched the bloody waves wash ashore carrying with it the Persian viscera. What remained unconsumed by the teeming fish in that unknown depth found its fortune with my bleating brothers, the gulls.

I have seen it in the swirl of galaxies. Their collisions destroy unmentioned and unknown planets. They are smashed to the dust from which they garnered their formation. No tears are shed for them. The universe cries for no one. Its continuity was set in motion by a mere will to be. A blind purposeless will.

I have seen it in the beings that rose from this nothingness to spread themselves amongst the purposeless stars. They followed their own notion. They made the will their own. They set it to purposes sometimes grand. They chose to live. They are the ones that fortune blesses: these creatures with freedom. But it is their choice! How we envy them. Unlike the gull, they wield pens to set form to the ages. They give purpose to the blind will of the universe. They are the owners of destiny. I have no favorites among them. All are blessed equally that they are even alive. No one is in charge.

On the Blue Planet, 4th Prelate Bumpous Zanz, The Mashgool

A pair of eyes sunken in a large skull fixated on the little ones from the safety of a windblown tree. The sturdy pine reached like a skeletal fingertip and pointed past the forest to the heavens above. The big cat waited on a branch that cradled its taut, muscular frame. It took in the sweet air a wisp at a time. The warmth of the little ones smelled like a nectar.

Her eyes rested on one slower than the rest. She watched its movement, fixating on the strangeness of the slow little one's gait in comparison. She heard the air fill its lungs with each tender breath and heard the thump of its tasty, little heart.

The little one was unaware. The cat waited. Once the little, lopsided one separated from the bigger ones, it would be time to strike. Time to leap down from the tree. Time to grab it up in a violent instant and dash up the tree again. Time to hear the screams and hoots from the ones below. Time to feel the terror from the little one caught in its powerful jaws. That is, until she closed her jaws and the long silence came after the initial crunch. Time to taste the sweetness again.

But not today. Still the fantasy overtook her as she stretched in the perch of her home. She had eaten a deer just minutes ago, and its guts were settling into her own. It was slow and weak and better off dead.

The little ones passed by her unaware. She watched them and licked her lips. Sleep's fingers began to massage her brain. She napped, and her mind flickered with images. In her dreams she chased deer in tall grasses. They darted back and forth like a perpetual motion machine. But she caught them. She breathed relief as she tasted their sweetness.

*

In the forest lay the Congregation. The main building was cylindrical with concave edges. It was covered in vines and could not be seen from the air or a horizontal distance unless you already knew what you were looking for. It laid in the forest like it fell to earth randomly--a discarded masterwork of Heaven. It was made of metal, which never could have come from the bowels of the earth or the labors of men. To its occupants, its origins were heavenly. They found it intact. They did not build it. The Father had built it for them and rewarded them for their goodness – so said their teachings.

Most of the cylinder was underground. The cylinder was immense to the men and women who made it their home. It was powered by a means unknown to the occupants. Strange lights shone within it, which the occupants used to worship the Father, their creator and sustainer. The Congregation men constructed buildings made of heavy stone as dwellings for the women and children. The men lived underground--completely separate--in their barracks. They thought that too much time spent around weakness would make them weak; this was no world for a weakling. In accordance with this notion, the sexes lived in strict separation from each other. This was the way of life in the Congregation. This was their religion.

*

From the time he first had memories, Isaac played with his brothers near the Congregation compound. As they grew older, they grew more adventurous, and they began wandering into the forest. The forest stretched across his horizon and surrounded everything he knew. The women who watched them told them from their infancy onwards that the forest was a dangerous and *evil* place. His older brothers paid the women no heed. They walked bravely into the forest. Isaac followed them. They crossed the invisible line that separated the known from the unknown. It was a line of sunshine, which cut into that dank, dark place of nightmares.

They ran amongst the fallen trees and tore into them with sticks; the ones saturated with decay broke open easily. They laughed at the long legged spiders and crickets that scurried out of the danger of the open air into the tiny holes and crevices that riddled the logs.

Jesse was their leader, a seventeen year old young man, who did not have to try hard to impress his younger brothers. His frame sprouted muscles without much work, just like the grasses that grew from the empty spaces on the forest floor. A richness of life flowed through his veins, and a self-assured smile was omnipresent on his face. Baruch, the middle child, was headstrong and eager to show off for his older brother. Isaac, the youngest, dragged along like a burden, slowing them down. They had to take Isaac along wherever they went. Jesse and Baruch could not leave the perimeter without him. The Congregation Elders forced this condition on them, and they resented it with every step.

Jesse punched a hole in a rotten log with the sharpened end of a stick. A small, purple lizard darted into the sunshine. It blinked rapidly and its head pivoted on its neck as it searched for threats. Isaac trapped the lizard under his hand. He yelled for Baruch to come and see. The squirming, purple beast fit delicately between his thumb and index finger. Jesse and Baruch gathered around their younger brother and looked at the purple marvel in his hands. The terrified creature made their eyes grow wide with wonder. It squirmed and kicked its legs to escape. Isaac's hand tickled under its onslaught, and he laughed.

"Give it over, Isaac," Jesse said.

"No I caught him. He's mine," Isaac said with his child's logic.

"Come on now, Isaac. Give him over. I just want to see him. Don't you say no to your elder," Jesse said with a look so stern it made Isaac melt.

Isaac looked at the little lizard as it blinked its large, yellow eyes and pivoted its head wildly. He begrudgingly handed it to his older brother. Baruch squealed with delight.

"Are you gonna smash him Jesse? I wanna see its guts!"

"No! If you're gonna do that give him back!" Isaac screamed.

"You're always wanting to smash them, Baruch! Nope, no smashing today," Jesse quipped with authority.

"What'r you gonna do with it then?" Baruch asked with his eyes wide and full of awe for his older brother.

"I'm gonna see if something I heard is true or not," Jesse said.

Jesse walked slowly to a hillside dotted with trees that stabbed through a shroud of yellowing moss like a small child clawing through a blanket thrown over its face. The suckling roots from hundreds of trees jutted in and out of the moss like sinewy limbs in a life or death wrestling match. Baruch and Isaac eagerly followed their older brother and hugged his hips like a worn, leather belt. Jesse searched out the contours of the hill until he found a small hole about the size of his fist in the maze of roots. A plug composed of errant sticks and bits of moss interwoven with grey silk covered the hole. The plug had worn away at its edges, revealing the utter darkness beneath.

"You boys go and get some rocks that you can stack. Make sure they are long and flat. Build me a wall around that hole," Jesse said with his arms crossed. The lizard had stopped squirming and seemed to be asleep, perhaps faking death in hopes that the big smasher had grown disinterested enough to free it.

"Why you want us to build a wall, Jesse?" Baruch asked.

"You'll know once it's built. Now do it! Don't ask questions of your elders!" Jesse screamed to Baruch, who ran off immediately to comply with his brother's order lest he receive a beating that night.

Isaac stayed near his idol and watched Jesse as he paced back and forth, one hand in his burlap trousers, and one keeping the little lizard in its prison. If only Isaac were bolder, he would rescue the lizard. He walked next to his brother and kept his eyes on the lizard the whole time. Isaac wore the cassock of a monk, complete with a small hood and pouch in the front. His older brother wore the trousers because he had been put to work in clearing the forest for the Congregation's fields; all capable young men did this to train their bodies for the trials they would endure. It was all a big secret, which Jesse would find out about soon enough. Isaac was not aware that Jesse had stopped his pacing. He glared at Isaac and asked of him, "Are you going to follow me everywhere?"

The words hurt Isaac. To the older boys he was useless: just a small boy who was cursed from birth. Isaac looked down at his deformed foot. He did his best to drag it behind him, but he could never keep up. He was useless. Isaac looked at his older brother who shook his head from side to side to remind the little, useless one of his place. Jesse was unrelenting in his assault. He began to point at the foot and smile. There was a vindictive smile on his face, like Isaac had wronged him. Isaac did wrong Jesse and he did it day by day, just by virtue of his happiness. Jesse carried with him the questions that everyone in the Congregation asked of Isaac. *Why should a boy who will never become a man of our people be so happy? He's useless. He's a hungry mouth, kept alive by the old woman. Soon he'll be a full grown baby. He'll have the body of a man with the capabilities of a baby. Useless. At best the congregants think him an idiot. A smiling, perfectly harmless, idiot.* Jesse stared at Isaac and kept up his smile. Then he dropped it like he had just received news that someone died.

"What, Jesse?" Isaac said, unsure of why his older brother stared and said nothing.

Jesse laughed, "I'm sure you know what, little brother."

Isaac grimaced to avoid crying. He turned from his older brother who continued his laughter. Shame sparked in Isaac's heart and leapt from his chest into his cheeks, starting a fire that radiated upwards through the roots of every hair on his head. A tear formed in the corner of Isaac's eye. He did his best to suppress it. At the very least he did not want Jesse to see him crying. He shoved it down into his storehouse stomach where his feelings would fossilize into stone. He looked to his brother and then turned to shuffle away, dragging his foot behind him.

"Get out there and get some rocks, Isaac! You got arms for carrying don't you! Don't be useless!" Jesse threw one last javelin at his defenseless, little brother, which struck its target square in his heart.

Isaac backpedaled and turned to stumble away from the barbed insults, moving towards the sounds that Baruch made as he splashed around the sparse puddles of a drought-licked creek bed. Isaac sat on the ground and watched as Baruch jumped up and down, soaking his trousers. Isaac laughed and clapped at his brother's antics. Baruch stopped and smiled at him. In his arms, he carried two flat rocks covered in slime and mud. The stream had been wearing the rocks down since the Father traced its path on the planet with his mighty finger. Isaac wondered as he looked at them, *were they ever whole? The Father aims at perfection. Why is everything being worn down to dust?*

Baruch built a pile of rocks, but he was not in a hurry to take them back to his taskmaster. The day was young, and there were plenty of games to be played. Isaac crept down the eroded wall of the stream bank by holding onto the roots of saplings that lined the bank. The roots thronged over the water and stretched themselves so thin that by the time they kissed the surface tension they were thinner than a human hair. As he made his way down the steep bank, Isaac grasped at the woody parts and his feet kicked over the decaying debris of generations of plants that lived, fornicated, and perished in the sunshine.

In order to seem that he had actually done work, and therefore please his older brother, Isaac picked up as many rocks as his arms could carry from the piles that Baruch had strewn on the stream bank. Isaac selected flat rocks that fit together well. Baruch carried the remainder in his arms. Jesse approved of their choices when they returned, and they both beamed with pride.

"Stack those rocks neatly, boys. Make a nice wall for my new friend here! Nice and tall with flat surfaces! Make a prison for our little friend. We don't want him to escape his fate," Jesse said and held the purple lizard up to the sun, much like an Aztec priest did with an obsidian dagger before plunging it into a virgin's heart.

Isaac made sure that the rocks fit together tight and the space between them did not even allow a finger to pass through to the other side. Baruch entered the fray, but threw his rocks on Isaac's well-manicured wall. Isaac shook his head and straightened the wall out, smoothing the gaps with mud. Jesse inspected the wall, and Baruch asked him no less than fifty times the identity of the mystery about to be revealed.

Baruch shouted like a woodpecker, "What game is it, Jesse?"

Jesse looked up from his inspection. The wall was ready. It would hold the lizard and not allow for an escape. He climbed a rock so that he towered over his brothers. It gave him the appearance of being very powerful. In a booming voice he said, "This isn't a game. It's life."

Immediately, he hopped into the dried leaves that looked like little hillsides against the trite Jericho wall. The leaves crunched under his feet like he was a colossus. Jesse bent over at the waist and said, "Now the gift to our Father: our sacrifice of blood and water. The cycle is cruel for the weak. For the strong and blessed it is gentle. May our great hairy king prosper for another day!" He ceremoniously released the lizard and laughed from his belly like he had just gotten away with some horrible crime. Isaac gasped, totally unsure about what he was about to witness. Baruch's head pivoted between his older brother and the enclosure. Unsure of how to act, he settled on mimicking Jesse's confident detachment.

The lizard darted for freedom, but ran into the rock wall. It attempted to scramble up the wall but could not get a grip on the slimy edges. Its head darted as it searched for an exit.

"What exactly are we watching for, Jesse?" Baruch inquired.

When children anticipate an event, the wider world ceases its machinations. All eyes came to rest on the lizard as if it were the only entity in existence. Isaac's eyes rested on the beating of its tiny heart. It seemed just a mere vibration just beneath the skin's surface. Isaac stooped downwards to get a better look. He now bowed over on his knees with his hands on top of the coliseum and his head about a foot above the terrified reptile. The lizard was absolutely still, its reptilian brain sensed something lurking. Webs of fear paralyzed it. Isaac felt pounding in his eardrums. A single drop of sweat beaded and ran down his forehead. The deluge had begun. Sweat now ran in rivulets down his face. His muscles tensed, and he felt the overwhelming urge to defecate. Thousands of insects screamed for their mates in the crowd. His brothers paced impatiently. Baruch breathed spasmodically, a shrill whistle erupting from his nose each time he inhaled. Baruch stopped his pacing. He snuck in close behind Isaac and breathed near his little brother's ear. Each puff of breath that hit Isaac's neck cooled it slightly. The drops of sweat evaporated before another one ripped from Isaac's pores to meet the cooling breath. Time stood still. It stood still for no one. The forest plane bent towards life and continued. Movement.

Baruch gasped, "What's that?"

A single, hairy leg ruptured through the trap door covering the hole and tapped the ground. Another hairy appendage followed. The spider sensed a sure meal and safe exit. It shot from its cobweb home and pounced on the lizard. It grabbed the lizard with its forelegs and flipped it onto its back, exposing the soft white underbelly. Isaac shrunk backwards in horror. He opened his mouth to scream but nothing came out; the cry sinched in his throat like the wail of a rotten convict swinging from the gallows. Baruch caught Isaac in his arms and forced his head downwards to watch the spectacle. The lizard let out a tiny cry, sharper than a baby whimpering for milk. It was the weak sigh of being resigned to a fate, giving up, but edged with the horror of being eaten. The spider sunk its fangs into the lizard's chest and injected a dose of venom. The tiny reptile thrashed its legs against its hairy persecution. Isaac began to sob.

Jesse shouted at him, "Stop crying, Isaac! It's nature! It's just Mother Nature! Take her in. She ain't pretty like the fairy tales those ladies have been telling you. She's an old, bitter hag with no front teeth. But she doesn't stop smiling does she Isaac? She doesn't stop ever."

Baruch laughed like a manic automaton wound by his older brother. After thirty seconds in the spider's embrace, the lizard's legs fluttered at random—kicks of a past escape vainly rehearsed by its hind brain. The kicks diffused into twitches. Then everything smoothed out. The lizard lay completely still. Dead. The spider dragged the lizard without ceremony into its balmy, black tomb.

"What's happening to it?" Isaac yelped to Jesse with eyes as big as a calf's miserably separated from its mother.

Jesse smiled at his two brothers while Isaac stared at the little hole, imaging the horrors that were playing out inside. In his mind, the hole contained the greatest evil imaginable. He wanted to do something, but he lacked the courage to reach his hand inside and stage a rescue.

"Simple boys. The little critter is being eaten," Jesse mocked, not ceasing with his smile, granted the somber affair. He turned his back on the boys and explained, "Little brothers, these creatures in the forest, they aren't like us. They don't grow their food like we do. They don't raise up animals to slaughter. They hunt, kill, and eat each other."

Isaac struggled against his desire to remain silent. There were questions that needed to be asked, and he was going to ask them. He stammered at first, then found the courage he needed. "What's happening, Jesse? Tell us. You didn't tell us what's happening to the lizard."

"When the spider bit the lizard, it shot poisons inside that's gonna turn its insides into water. Then the spider's gonna just drink the lizard up. All that's gonna be left is an empty lizard skin. No bones, not anything inside. I don't know, the spider might even eat the lizard's skin if it's hungry enough. I mean when the skin decays, it stinks. Who wants to live in a stinky hole?"

"But, Jesse, why?" Isaac asked.

"You're always asking why, little brother. These things in the forest, they all eat each other. If they aren't eating each other, they're eating the plants. Other animals eat the animals that eat the plants. It's ongoing. The rule is eating and being eaten. You know...sometimes a person like you or me wanders too far into the forest. I don't know...maybe to gather fruits or something. Maybe firewood. The animals snatch us up, too. They have to eat each other or they die. Don't you worry...we humans are different though. We're what's called the 'ception to the rule. We grow the food we eat. We raise up the cattle for slaughter. The Father helps us grow it up by making the sun shine. Making it rain. Making sure the cattle don't get sick and die. Making sure his people do well in the world. We're the lucky ones, Isaac. All the others are on their own."

Jesse climbed up and began pacing back and forth on his rock: his granite podium in his church of infinite bliss. Sensing there would be no response, Jesse took a few deep, sententious breaths. Then he continued preaching the good word to his little brothers.

"Nothing...no man...no creature is above the law, little children. That spider in the hole...he might get eaten by a little, trifling worm."

"No way, Jesse. That spider's too big. How could the worm catch it?"

"There's a stinging wasp like the ones that build the big paper nests on our buildings, only this wasp doesn't live with other wasps. It lives in a mud house and it's solly terry."

"What you mean solly terry?"

"It's a solly terry wasp. It lives in a mud house in the ground. All alone. No family."

"Just like the spider then?" Isaac remarked.

"Yes. But stop interrupting your elder, brothers."

The boys shut their mouths. To incur the wrath of an elder male would result in a terrible punishment for them; it would be violent and not soon forgotten.

"When this solly terry wasp meets up with the spider they start to fight. The spider might bite the wasp, but it won't feel it. It's *a moon* for the poison that the spider has. The *moon* protects the wasp from going to sleep and dying like the lizard did. On the other hand, if that wasp stings that spider, that spider's gonna get real sleepy. It's gonna fall asleep and not be able to wake up. And just like that, the wasp builds its home by digging a big hole in the ground. It drags the spider down there and buries it."

"Jesse! Where does the worm come from?!" Baruch interrupted with a high pitched squeal like a baby pig ripped from its sow's teat.

"Shut it, Baruch! If you interrupt me one more time I'm not gonna spare you the rod! I'm getting to it. Be patient."

Jesse continued his sermon to his now passive audience. "Little brothers, the wasp lays its baby on the spider while it's sleeping. The spider wants to wake up, but it can't. It can't move. The baby is like a chicken egg that hatches this little worm. The little worm takes bites from the spider. Little bites. Just little nibbles like those mice that steal the grain that spills in the storehouse. It eats and eats and eats, and nibbles and nibbles away at that spider until it's all eaten up, 'cept for its hairy coat which the little worm makes into a blanket against the cold. The baby worm gets real tired from its big meal and goes to sleep in the soft spider blanket. It sleeps for months, little brothers. It changes during this sleep. It grows legs and a head. It stops being a worm and starts being a wasp like its mother. When it's all changed it digs out of the hole and flies away so it can find another spider to lay its baby on."

Isaac looked at the hole. He thought of the lizard. He felt sorry for the lizard, getting its insides sucked out right now. Before he caught it, the lizard was running free in its log home. Burning shame ravaged his face: punishment for the role he played in arranging the lizard's grisly death. A solution presented itself to him: something to balance out the world that was thrown off kilter for him. He desperately wanted a wasp to find this spider and kill it. He announced it to his brothers.

"Maybe we can find a wasp like that around here and catch it to kill that *evil* spider," he said proudly.

"The spider isn't evil, Isaac. An animal's only evil if it kills one of us. If it kills a human, it's evil. Otherwise, it's just being an animal," Jesse said with his arms crossed like a holy seer.

"It's awful and disgusting! Let's find one of those wasps, Jesse. Come on!" Isaac said, starting to walk into the forest alone.

"Get back here, Isaac. You can't find one here; they don't live around here," Jesse said.

"Where do they live then?" Isaac said.

"In the desert. A place with no trees, only sand and rocks," Jesse said.

"How do you know about it then, Jesse?" Isaac asked, cutting the bone right to the marrow.

Jesse was silent. The two boys stared at him, burning for an answer. Who told him about such wonders? Baruch had enough. Was his idol a hack? A phony? A liar?

"You made it up!" Baruch screamed.

"No, damn you. My earthfather told me about it."

"That's impossible!" the two younger boys shouted in unison.

"You haven't ever talked to your earthfather!" Baruch said half full of shock and half jealousy. His voice peaked to its crescendo, "You haven't ever seen him either! It isn't right…and it isn't allowed. None of us know our earthfathers!"

Jesse stretched a smile across his handsome face that was as coy and devious as that plastered on a statue smuggled from a temple to the earth God, Caesar. He spoke in tones designed to inspire fear in his lesser brothers: punchy and syncopated like a chop to the neck. He breathed in between to sate his rising anger's call for blood.

"I did once. I saw him. I did. He even talked with me. He was all dressed up in a red robe with gold writing on it. I'll tell you what. He looked real important. He pulled me close and whispered in my ear. You know what he said?"

Jesse had captivated the two boys.

"What did he say?" asked Baruch and Isaac, answering Jesse in unison.

"He said that he was my earthfather. He was real handsome and real strong. See the resemblance?"

"Nah, you're ugly!" Baruch scoffed.

Jesse paid him no heed. He did not pausing a moment in his storytelling, "He knew how to fight and was the leader of all the men in the Congregation."

"How do you know that?" Baruch said, his eyes green with envy.

"My mother told me after he left. She told me I'd be just like him."

"I don't believe you. Where's your proof?" Baruch said.

"I don't care if you don't believe me, Baruch. I know its true. Anyways…when he got to talking to me he set me on his knee and pulled out this book with pictures in it. It had a picture of the Wasp in it. Then he told me that the Father gives all creatures their due; the Father puts berries and nuts on the ground for the creatures to eat up. The Father creates other creatures on the surface to eat the creatures that gather up the berries and nuts. That way nothing gets out of balance. My earthfather told me that the only 'ception to the rule is man, like I told you two before. We've gotta work by the sweat of our brow in this world, or we've got nothing coming to us. We gotta be strong to defend the weak. As men, we gotta protect the little children and women from other men. We gotta do unto them what they want to do unto us," Jesse heaved and stared blanky ahead like he was traversing the distance to his misty childhood.

"What happened after that?" Isaac said.

"My mother came in the room, and he just stopped talking. Mother and him stared at each other for a minute or two, and he just left like there wasn't anything between them. They didn't talk. He said one last thing to me. He said we'd see each other again when I became a man. I haven't seen him since. That was going on twelve years ago."

Not to be outdone by his younger brother in the contest for Jesse's affection, Baruch formulated a question that burned his brain and shot forth from his gullet without much thought to buttress it.

"What do you mean he showed you a picture? Just what amongst the Father's people is a picture?"

Jesse paced on his rock and answered Baruch, "It's like one of those paintings that the women put on the wall of the ancient ones, so we can remember and celebrate them."

Isaac interrupted, "Or the paintings that they do of the special *Gideons* stories on the walls so the children and stupid elders can understand what's happening by seeing with their eyes instead of their mind."

Jesse laughed. "Yeah, like those. Like the pictures of all the Prophets that are up on the walls of the community dining room."

Baruch interjected, "Oh, I know! Like the paintings of the girls who died making the babies come, like those paintings of the babies gettin' cut out of their mama's womb…just like you, Isaac," Baruch said with a look of vengeance directed towards his little brother.

Isaac's cheeks flushed. He tried to pay no attention to Baruch's insult. He finished his brother's lesson for him, "Only this picture, it's of something real. Not all done up and fake like a painting, it's the real animal."

"We've got paintings of cows and horses, Isaac!" Baruch said, trying to stab Isaac in the gut.

"No, Baruch. Isaac's right. It's different than a painting. It's real. It's like you took the real bug and flattened it on a page. My earthfather told me he's seen thousands of books like the one showed me," Jesse said.

"Where'd he see them?" Baruch inquired.

"He's been far out into the world," Jesse said with a smile. "He's been far from here."

"No one goes anywhere, Jesse! It's too dangerous!" Baruch exclaimed.

"You're wrong. It's the women that never go anywhere. My earthfather's been places. I believe him. He looks like he could fight a mushworm and win. Do you believe me, Isaac?"

"I do, Jesse," Isaac said.

"What about you, Baruch?"

"I don't know, Jesse. I really don't know," Baruch said.

Jesse laughed. His chuckle seemed to shake the rock he stood on.

"You're just being jealous, Baruch. You know everything I tell you is true."

"No, it's not," Baruch said, looking downwards.

"Even if you don't believe me, you both gotta promise not to tell anyone what I've told you. Especially those women."

"You're always making us promise, Jesse!" Baruch sighed.

"Promises are between men, little brothers, so the world doesn't discover their intentions and make tools of them," Jesse said.

"I don't want any more promises," Baruch sighed.

"Look here, Baruch. It is important. If you don't promise, I won't play with you anymore. Never again."

Baruch and Isaac looked at each other. The prospect of their brother abandoning them was too much. Individually they swallowed the golden nugget of truth deep into their bellies and swore not to reveal it. A minute passed between the boys before they realized that the sun no longer shot slivers of golden light through the timber. An old woman cawed for them to come eat supper from the edge of the forest. They followed their grandmother from the edge of the forest into a squat stone building and through the

Congregation bowels and into a dining room where the rest of the children ladled fatty beef soup into their mouths with long metal spoons.

*

The Congregation's crude stone buildings sat like rotten teeth in the jaw of a giant with the metallic cylinder as their focal point. Each day in the forest, nature did its best to join the stone buildings back into her fold. Bright green ivy tendrils crept into the stone like cancerous death into an old man's bones. The work of men, if neglected, could be undone in just a few short seasons. Crimson clad men gathered weekly to hack at the creeping vines with short swords otherwise used to hack enemies to pieces. They denied the vines a foothold on the many buildings that made their homes. After the destruction of the vines, they took to scraping moss and lichens off the stone surfaces.

The Congregation was not a welcoming place to the uninitiated. If you bumped into it at random, it had the appearance of being quite sinister. People beyond the forest sought its destruction, this the children did not know. They slept in their beds at night in peace because the men protected them. The mothers at the Congregation raised the children in a communal setting. Meals were eaten in community. They played games together in community. Each mother had one child of her own. Some mothers raised the children of women that died in childbirth. Each woman maintained a humble home, full of love and free of violence. The men never came around, not even to say hello. The Congregation's women did not consider this a defect. They never felt abandoned. This was the best way of life for them, because the men had to prepare for war constantly. Children never asked questions about their fathers. Fathers were immaterial: donors of sperm. Even if the boys and girls wanted to see the men, they could not. It was prohibited. The men lived lives apart in a single barracks, deep within the metal cylinder. Like outcast warriors, they lived simply, with and for each other. They worshipped in the way that their ancestors taught them. Their worship consisted of complete subservience to the Glorious Mother. She was the Congregation matriarch: the mouthpiece of the Father. To disobey her was tantamount to disobedience of the Father. Disobedience was punished with death, or even worse, the offending person was cast out of the Congregation to wander the dangerous world alone, an ostracized Cain.

Each night, the women held fellowship with each other inside the Sanctuary, which was completely off limits to children. The nightly happenings were the subject of much debate between the boys and girls; each had his or her own theory as to what happened behind the mysterious metal doors that guarded the church from trespass.

Prior to entering the Sanctuary, women dropped their children off in the Congregation's nursery. It was a room bereft of any decoration. In this room, the Elder Mother held her court. The old woman told all of the children from the time they were very young that she was their grandmother. They called her Granny out of love and respect. She had the position of an educator in the Congregation hierarchy. She taught the youth the ways of the Congregation and prepared them for their eventual joining. In the ignorant bliss of youth, the children often grew prone to distraction. To combat this, she used her knowledge to entertain and amaze them, holding them in rapt attention until her lessons were learned and internalized.

Tonight, like usual, she began her nightly sermons by telling the Children that their Father was everything, their reason for being, and their source of sustenance. The children nodded their heads in agreement, still lost in the trifles of their day at play. She issued the children a warning.

Granny said, "Boys and girls," and thrusted her hawkish nose towards the little ones like she was about to gouge their livers out, "it is the highest crime for you to go against the intentions of the Father." Their eyes grew wide with alarm. "For if you go against the Father, you go against us all, and if you go against us all, you will be lost and alone in the great big *evil* world." When Granny said the word evil, her face puckered like she had sucked all the juice out of an unripe lemon. In her mind all the wailings of the forest animals and the slippery machinations of men that had been given that label through any age, were equally repugnant, stored in the same drawer of all things that shared in filth and decay.

To the children, Granny was old. She was one of the ancient ones. To youth, whose cares did not amount to much more than forest adventures between chores, she was at least as old as the massive trees that surrounded the camp and as ancient as the paintings dabbed onto the cold stone walls of all the buildings that surrounded the cylinder.

Granny gathered the children into a semicircle and lit one of the blackened soy candles so that the light flickered underneath her jaw line and shot shadows over the furrows that covered her face like a manicured field of grain. In the candlelight, her face took on the shape of a treeless draw in the forest where flowing rainwater took its liberty to wash all the seedlings down the hillside to their doom at the base of massive, ancient oaks. The lines emanated from her forehead and spilled like a waterfall to her jowls, which hung loosely off of her small-boned chin. As she struggled to form sentences under the mounds of flesh that formed her face, her chin darted in and out with each utterance. Her face remained stationary like a stone, only the tiny island point underneath her brown teeth moved when she spoke. Her voice came out in squeaks, sometimes little grunts that got caught in the rolls. The children had to move in close to hear.

"Listen, children," Granny began saying to them as they huddled around each other, gripping their neighbors from fear of what she might say. Tonight she told them a story they had not heard before.

"The world of men was not always as it is now. There were once more of us. Much more. For every tree that surrounds us there were maybe…two…no, four men," Granny began, looking upwards to Heaven as if to ask for help for the multitude she imagined. Blank, faceless billions.

"What happened, Granny?"

Granny turned and looked to her rear as if to see if she was being watched. She singled Baruch out from the crowd of children and pointed her long, skeletal finger at his face. He turned pale as a ghost. The old crone's memory was fading. Her stories came strung in strange loops that circled around themselves. She recalled more data each time she entered the loop.

"That was the Forbidden Time, my children. This is the time that is blotted from all the memories of men. I do know what has been passed down by the Elders, children," she wheezed.

"Granny does not tell lies to her children….I really think that a person had to be there at the time to know exactly what happened," she coughed. "The only thing that *I do know* is what my grandmother told me when I was your age, in this very same place, about…oh…eighty years ago…and my grandmother, Elder Mother Ruth Pharisee…well, I mean, she wasn't even there in person. Her grandmother, Elder Mother Rachel Walled, had to tell her…and she wasn't there children. Her mother, the first Elder Mother of the Congregation, Elder Mother Mary Walled, she was actually there, and from what she says it was a most a most horrifying time children. There was worse hunger than comes in the summertime when all the crops are planted and your bellies are screaming for the harvest. There was bloodshed. There was a war, fought amongst men, like war had never been fought in the world. Millions…no…maybe billions perished."

The children stared at their beloved Granny in horror. She realized the effect she had on them.

"Children, don't you worry about that time…we've lived in peace for generations in our blessed Congregation…," she stopped midsentence and changed thought like a spirit had flipped a switch in her mind. "Then my grandmother told me that her great-great-grandmother…that is Mary Walled, children, the matriarchal Elder Mother,…the first of all the Elder Mothers in my fine and illustrious line…. She could not speak about what happened to her during the Forbidden time without becoming totally hysterical…foaming at the mouth…twitching…and thrashing her limbs…her small, frail body heaving on the ground…why the women around her had to summon the men to tie her to her bed for days on end until she recovered fully and came to her senses. You know, children, all the while the men screamed to her not to tell the children. They then gave her a tea from a plant that grows in the middle of the forest, which made her sleep for days. The name escapes me…Sellinum…? Salynum…? Sullybin…? I forget…my mind is old and tired." The old woman slumped down defeated and rubbed her temples with her hands.

"What happened during the Forbidden Time, Granny? Tell us!" Baruch said, half his intention being to get over the fear she had built in the group and half to break the spell the old woman held him in each time she stared him down.

The Elder Mother paid the boy's pipings no heed, as if they came from a small songbird perched on her windowsill in wait of crumbs. She was not dissuaded from the jumble of thoughts that stumbled through her mind. Her gaze became fixed. Her normally waxen, pallid face took on a healthy, rosy glow, and her hands stopped twitching. To the children, suddenly she appeared to be in full control of her thoughts.

"Mary Walled…my great-great-great-Grandmother's name…the first Elder Mother of the Congregation…and a very wise and truthful woman. We owe much to her. She is the one who rescued *The Gideons*. She is the one who made all the Elder Mothers swear an oath to protect it. She made us realize its infinite value for the survival of our people. Her painting is in the place where we dine at night children…I am sure you have all seen it."

Isaac thought to the creepy flaking painting of the old spinster in the main dining area. Her eyes stared plainly ahead, wide and full of vinegar. It was like the painting followed you while you walked and pierced your soul to read your innermost thoughts. Her face was long and thin – ugly, almost. It was painted and repainted constantly to prevent it from flaking to nothing. Much like nature wanted to blot out her memory, but only Granny's order preserved it.

"When the First Elder Mother was young, she lived in a house near a group of other houses…all similar in nature…she lived near a large building…where children went to learn how to read books…and write books…and be good. It was called a school by the Ancient Ones…it was this school where she took refuge when the dark days came. Before her fits…she would talk about it…there was no real warning. One day the skies turned black with ash, like the world's biggest volcano erupted. The oceans, lakes, and rivers turned blood red and started to dry into chunks of clay. There was absolutely nothing to drink on the surface of the earth. That's when *they* came, children. She told us that was when the Angels of God came to the Earth and judged all the sinners to eternal damnation and burnt them on the surface of the earth with hellfire. My Great Great Great…uh…Great Great Grandmother…she was a good woman, a woman devoted to the Father…that is why she didn't get taken up with the rest of them. The rest of humanity…the other men and women who weren't burned up in the Father's furious judgment of the wicked…they just got *raptured up*. They were taken up, taken to live with the Father in his House in Heaven, where they live to this day…watching us…watching the *spare ones*…those really good ones that the Father left remaining on earth to try and make a new start of things. We are the *chosen people,* my children. Never forget that."

The children looked to each other with wild eyes. Only Jesse seemed unperturbed.

Baruch asked, "Granny, if Elder Mother Mary Walled was a good woman…wouldn't the Father have wanted her to live with him? Why didn't the Angels take her to live with the Father in Heaven?"

Granny's brow wrinkled, and she smiled deliciously like she was a cat that caught a field mouse in the community grain, "Asking questions will get you in a lot of trouble one day Baruch. You know that you are best served if you listen with your ears and speak nothing with your mouth until you fully understand the truth. If you must know…the Angels came to her while she was sleeping and told her to take flight. She took shelter in the basement of the school. She was chosen as the first Elder Mother of the Congregation and chosen by the Father for this role she was to play in humanity's future."

Baruch buried his face in his lap. Isaac could see, even in the crude candlelight, how red his cheeks had become. Isaac interjected for his brother's defense, "I don't know. Maybe the Angels took the people they raptured up to burn in the fires only after they showed them the everlasting joy of Heaven. It would have been a better punishment for them. Maybe all of humanity was wicked, except for us."

Granny smiled to the boy and said, "Show the people what they would miss and trick them into thinking they did good. That way they knew what they were missing when they got burned up and sent packing to Hell. When you've seen the best of Heaven and you've heard the angel's beautiful voices…then are told you have to leave because you aren't quite good enough…the pain of loss is more real. I agree with you Isaac, but that isn't how it happened. You said, I don't know, but we do know. We have what's been passed down to us. You get that 'I don't know' out of your vocabulary boy. We do know…*we do know*."

Granny smiled at the boy. He was beautiful and perfect in every way, except for that damned foot of his. She remembered the bits and pieces that she could recall from his traumatic birth. The nurses had to open his beautiful mother, the Glorious Mother of the Congregation up with a knife. The damned child wouldn't come out naturally. The

16

cord around his neck, him choking for air as his mother lost all her lifeblood on the altar top. How the boy screamed and wailed when he breathed his first breath. Such a powerful voice, but so small and weak. His damned foot, bent and broken as if the evil Angel Lucifer grabbed him by it in the womb.

Their Granny looked lost in a trance. Her distant gaze met Isaac's glassy blue eyes, which stared plainly ahead, with long, silken strands of hair partially obscuring them. A tidbit of knowledge floated through her mind and was sucked up by her awareness. It brought a smile to her face. *The Father sees fit to mix the best and worst together in one human being. That is the Father's way, only accomplished by him. It is beyond human comprehension.*

Granny smiled at him, then recalled what made her get lost in thought. It shot from her mouth like water under pressure released from a spigot.

"This boy is smart, children," Granny announced. "May the Father bless and keep him, and may he be delivered from the sufferings of that dreadfully warped limb of his. The Father willing, my boy, your foot will get better. Let us all pray for his foot, my children."

The children bowed their heads. Isaac burned with shame. Questions unanswered from the time he could first remember thinking began worming their way through his brain. As his grandmother talked, the worm casts grew thicker and thicker, clogging his senses.

"Father, the boy has been given a great mind, but his body is weak. You are perfect in every way. Let the boy share in your perfection. In your name we pray," she looked up from her ruminations. She shook her head as if to clear the cobwebs from around her neurons and announced, "Have no fear, children, everything your Granny has told you will be made clear as you grow older and join the adults of the Congregation. After your Joining Ceremonies you will be in complete understanding of all our mysteries."

Isaac swallowed hard and stared at his shoeless foot in the candlelight. As the light flickered, he could make out the twisted bones and off color skin that stretched over his useless appendage. He was about to explode, but Baruch broke the silence.

"Granny, tell us what the Congregation does during the nighttime that we spend with you."

"No, here's a better question. Why aren't you with them, Gramm?" Jesse said.

Granny cackled like a crow with its beak reared back in warning to other crows not to invade its territory. "Good children do not ask questions, Jesse. Good children wait patiently until it is their turn. It is my function in the Congregation to raise you children up on the right path. I ensure that you are pure enough to join the adults of the Congregation. You do that by following the right path. Do you know what the right path is, Jesse?"

"To follow the ways of the Elders. Follow everything they have proscribed us to the letter," Jesse said with a smile on his face.

Granny nodded to him, but remained silent. The smug look on his face troubled her. She stared. In the candlelight she could not make out his face. His tall, muscular frame spilled out of the semicircle of children. His work in the fields had done the man quiet well. She had been told and thought it right that right when a boy is becoming a man, it is best for him to learn the ways of the fields and forest. It is best for him to exhaust himself during the day by waking early, working all day long in the burning sun, and retiring after the sun goes down to eat his supper, regain his strength, and get to bed. That way, the boy with the body of a man and the mind of a boy does not allow his man's body to get him into trouble on account of his boy's mind not understanding the rules of the community. She spoke, "So, Jesse, what do the Elders say about children asking questions of their Elders?"

"It is not allowed, Gramm, but then again…I'm no child," Jesse said.

The Elder Mother let loose with a surprised chortle but immediately suppressed it. It sounded like she tried to prevent a sneeze. She buried her retort in the soil of her mind. Her age had taught her that outbursts like this were best handled with caution or they could spread. The boy had the capacity to make her look foolish. As the teacher, all she had with the children was her credibility. She glared at Jesse and then replaced it with a kind smile, for the child did not know what line he was treading with her. She'd have to keep both of her eyes on him until the time of his Ascension.

Two boys had grown restless in waiting for the lesson to continue and now played with each other. At first, they lightly motioned to each other. Then the game continued with each lack of response on the Elder Mother's part. One boy pinched the other, and the play fight began to grow like a flame in dry leaves. Two other children took notice and began laughing: annoying sounds of unconstrained youth. Jesse turned to them and yelled, "Alright, you two, this isn't the place!" The children looked up startled and red like ripe tomatoes. They shut their mouths and obeyed. Great booms came from Granny's hands clapping together.

"Our Jesse's gonna have his Ascension soon. You're gettin' all ready for the Joining. No more children's games for you, young man. No more babysitting these little ones."

"I know Granny, I can't wait to get out amongst the men and leave these child's games behind."

Granny used this as a point of education for the rest of the children who looked to Jesse like he was some sort of god, an idol sitting among them, who descended from the heavens above to grace them with his presence. She pontificated, "Jesse's gonna leave us soon, children. Look at him. He is an adult in form, and the Elders will come callin'. In two weeks time you will no longer see your older brother here amongst the children. He'll go and join into the Congregation, just like all of you will once you reach the appropriate age."

A small girl with blond hair like a sunbeam and blue eyes piped up, "What's the 'propriate age Granny?"

"My dear, I joined the Elders at the age of fourteen. That's when I was betrothed to the Father. Prior to that I was with my mother minding to the business of cooking and mending, and one day the Sanctuary was opened up to me, and I saw my first Joining Ceremony."

"You saw it, Granny? You mean you didn't have one?"

"The Joining Ceremony is not for the Elder Mother to participate in. She merely makes sure the candidates are able to be joined to the Congregation. The Joining Ceremony is the mandate of the Glorious Mother. She runs it. I just decide who participates. That was my first Joining Ceremony. My grandmother had died and passed the tradition onto me. It skipped my mother because my grandmother didn't find her worthy…but that my children is neither here nor there…well, Rachel, you're getting bigger and bigger everyday. How old are you now?"

Rachel looked at her face and became lost in her wrinkles, as if she had shrunk to miniature and was weaving her way through the crow's feet and over the sagging cheek towards her grandmother's crusty mouthpiece pursued by the thought that she, too, would fail the test of gravity and be hunched over and scary. She stuttered, "I…I…I'm nine, grandmother." She supplemented her naivety and youth by counting on her fingers.

Granny laughed like a jet of gas escaping from a bog. "Well, ten is a fine age, but you're still too young to join with the adults and serve the Father, Rachel. Wait a good two or four years."

"How will I serve the Father, Granny?" the young girl asked bashfully.

"You'll serve the Father by having many children, Rachel. I do not think that you will be selected the Elder Mother when I depart this Earth. That is reserved for very special girls, Rachel. And while you are very special in your own way, I do not think that you could have *my position.*" The last two words came out like a hiss.

"But, Granny, I'm too young to have children now, right?" the girl said and looked to her sisters for any hint of explanation.

"Yes, my dear. Soon you won't be too young," Granny chuckled.

"Granny, how will I know?"

The old woman paused for a moment unsure how to answer. She leaned forward as if she was about to say something and then retreated as if she were unsure how to say it. She did this several times before Jesse lost his cool.

"When you girls are ready to have babies you'll know. I've seen it before when I was just a boy. One of the girls, couldn't a been older than twelve up and started dripping blood everywhere like her insides got ripped out. The blood came from down there…."

"That's enough, young man. You may look like an adult, but you are no adult yet, my boy. That is up to me!"

Jesse laughed and continued, "Then she up and stopped bleeding about four days later. A day after that the women came and got her, and she hasn't been seen since."

Granny wanted to lash at him again. She wanted to sink her fangs into his soul. He was so perfect, but without any sort of control: always willing to thrust himself into the world without a thought. He was just like all the men. Big. Dumb. Loud. Unthinking. He would fit in with the adults. Perfectly.

"You're an observant one, Jesse. You know, you like to question things, too. You children, it would be for the best if you just forgot about your older brother, Jesse. In case you haven't noticed before, your older brother gets confused sometimes. He would do best to mind his chores in the gardens and leave being wise and brilliant up to the Father. Now Rachel, you listen here…when the time is right, you will know. The Father will show you. His angels, they will be sent unto you. You will come to full awareness with their miracles. After this, my children, you will be ready for anything. You are part of a most special people my children. You are the chosen people of the Father. The Father watches and protects us. No harm will ever come to us as long as we are in the Father's favor."

Isaac stared at his gnarled, useless foot. It protruded from his rough cassock like a whelping puppy that wandered too far from its mother, unsure of which way it wanted to go. The bones meandered through each other like a braid with no rhyme or reason to it at all. To everyone in the Congregation, the foot was the work of the Devil. His older brother, Jesse, was preparing for his trials, glowing in the attention he received from all the other children, but mocking them at the same time in cool condescension. Isaac looked to the girls, who also seemed to know their place. Even his brother Baruch knew what would come in the future, so the question burned in his mind. Had the Father come to them already and told them their future? Why was he being left out? What was the matter with him besides his foot? Why, if he was special and created by the Father, did he have the awful, perverted foot? He glared at it. When he was a child, smaller than the smallest one present at the lesson, he said a prayer before he went to sleep for the Father to cure him. He went to bed full of hope that his foot would change overnight. If the father could raise Lazarus from the dead, if he could part a sea and drown the Pharaoh and his men, it would be easy for him to cure twisted bones and make him whole. He prayed until he sweated and shook. And each day the foot greeted him like a nasty reminder of uselessness. As he grew older he stopped praying about the foot and started saying prayers for those around him. But the question burned in him. It shot from his mouth like a volcano.

"Grandmother," Isaac said, interrupting the old woman's meanderings. She looked up to him, ripping herself from the hard fought and barely established thoughts.

"Yes, my dear?" she croaked.

"How will I serve the Father, Grandmother?"

"What, Isaac?" she said alarmingly, unsure if she heard him correctly.

"Grandmother, everyone here knows what they will do when they get older. How will I serve the Father?"

The Elder Mother looked to him with her foggy eyes and smiled. She had a faint vision of wonderful feats and wretched trials, which jumbled in her mind like a deck of cards scattered to the wind and disappeared as soon as they came to her. She smiled at Isaac.

"My boy. You will come to know that when it is decided. Never you mind that right now, Isaac. Enjoy your youth. We may come to talk of this, you and I. But right now it is time for our readings."

"Who decides, Grandmother?"

"My boy. That is really up to the Father. But never mind that now, Isaac. Listen to the reading."

*

The Elder Mother wrenched her hand inside her tattered burlap robes. Her hand rummaged through her robes like a rat searching out warmth under her saggy, folded flesh. Her face wrinkled in disbelief as if she lost it. She had misplaced the book several times, but it always found its way into her hands again, through what she determined was divine providence.

One time Jesse found *The Gideons* in the latrine, where Granny had been exorcising the demons from her body. When he returned it she made him swear up and down that he would tell no one that she misplaced it. She glared at him until her hand came to rest on the warped and cracked imitation leather cover. Her bony hands closed around it, and her heart leapt for joy that she had maintained the holy book of their people for another sunset. She ripped *The Gideons* from between her rough rope belt and the sweaty, elderly flesh where it sat precariously balanced. She held it out to the children who marveled at it.

She began to unwind the coarse hemp twine that held the book together, and the ancient book creaked like an old man getting up out of bed in the wintertime. She spoke to them in her rehearsed solemn voice, usually reserved for the funeral rites she presided over, "My children, I will now tell you a story from *The Gideons*." Her fingers trembled as she carefully turned the thin acid-eaten brown page carefully to avoid it ripping free of its moorings. In the past she told the children that *The Gideons* was the most precious book in existence. It was more than a mere book – it was a treasure: no mere book, but the most precious thing in all existence. It was the printed word of the Father delivered to the Ancient Blessed Ones. They were now the custodians of *The Gideons*, it having been entrusted to generations of Elder Mothers. And the book had survived wars and trials and tribulations.

Their grandmother began to tell the children a story about two brothers that had gotten into a fight because they were both doing their best to please the Father. Only one brother thought that he had been displeasing to the Father. Isaac heard the story when he was very young. One of the brothers was a successful farmer of grain, and the other brother was very successful at raising livestock. When the two brothers thanked their Father for their success by burning sacrifices to the Father, the results of the fruits of their labors, the plant farmer became jealous and upset that his brother's sacrifice of a lamb may please the Father more. Isaac's mind worked ferociously as his Grandmother read the lines to the children in her voice that creaked from her lips like a tiptoeing corpse.

"Cain said to his brother Abel, let us go into the field…." She leaned forward in the candlelight, her eyes straining to read the fine print of the Gideons, "when the brothers went out into the field, Cain attacked and killed Abel, he slew him with the scythe that he used to harvest the wheat." The old woman looked to Isaac because she felt his eyes were burning holes right through to her soul.

"Isaac, my lovely boy, you know what a scythe is, right?" Isaac shook his head no and continued staring ahead eager to hear the remainder of the story.

"When you begin working in our fields, Isaac, when you thresh the winter wheat, when you gather it up, you will use a scythe. It is a large curved blade, like half-a-circle with one small piece missing. I asked you this, because I am wondering, Isaac, do you know what the purpose of the scythe is?"

Isaac started to shake his head no again but he shot out with the correct answer, "I guess…well I think…it was made to thresh and harvest wheat!"

Granny clapped her bony hands together, which barely made a sound. She chuckled, "Yes, it was, my boy, but it was employed to an ill purpose when Cain killed Abel with the scythe that he should have used to earn his livelihood. Instead of contently harvesting his wheat as the father had ordained and given him the talents to do, instead of fulfilling his purpose, that purpose which the Father intended for him when he was created, he took something good and used it for its unintended purpose. He killed his brother. He committed an act of *evil*."

The children stared at their Grandmother with wide, open eyes at the word she just uttered.

"The Father gives each of us talents children. Some of us are made to be good farmers, some of us have beautiful angelic voices, and some of us are as strong as a bull," saying that, she looked over to Jesse without thinking, "And some of us have minds like a wolf," she looked to Isaac and smiled. "We all aid in the creation, my children, by serving in the position in which is chosen for us."

"Who chooses for us, Grandmother?" Isaac said, thinking about what role he might play when he got older.

"It is chosen by the Elders of the Congregation."

"But do they choose? Or does the Father make each of us specially for a purpose like he made Cain?"

"It comes from both sides, Isaac. You are made special and the congregation realizes just how you are special and chooses your role for you."

"Then why did the Father find favor in Abel and not Cain? Why was he made to be better? If the Father is just, then why isn't the world just? What is jealousy, Grandmother, but a feeling that comes from the horrible inequality of the world?"

"But you did not let me finish the story, Isaac. Will you let me finish the story? Or perhaps you know how it ends because you have such a good memory, and I have told it to you children hundreds of times."

"Yes, Grandmother, I know how it ends."

"Then tell us, Isaac. Tell us all how it ends. Or do you want to read it from The Gideons yourself, my boy?"

"I can't read, Grandmother. You know that."

"I do, Isaac. Then tell us how it ends."

"I don't remember exactly, Grandmother. I think that the Father killed Cain for killing his brother Abel."

"No, my dear. Killing a murderer brings the earthly torments to a sudden end. The demons that haunted him in life can no longer bring torment. Sure he will be burning in the pits of Hell, but that is no lesson to the people who remain alive. No my dear, it is much better to let the murderer suffer alone. You see, my children, the Father is wise. The wisest. The most high. He knows just exactly what will bring each man to his lowest point in this life. He knows what will lower him to the level of the smallest, most insignificant worm."

"What is that, Granny?" Jesse asked in a deep voice that sounded like the rip made by the first tear into a log by a hacksaw.

The Elder Mother ignored the question for a moment and buried her nose into the small tattered book and read aloud, "Killing the brother greatly offended the Father, and the murderer was forced to wander the earth, living like an animal for the rest of his days. He was separated from his people, his land, and from all of his natural abilities to make the food grow from the ground. He was forced to wander all over the world, never finding a place to rest, and it is said that he continues to wander to this day children."

"Where!?" Isaac asked.

"Just wherever there is strife and violence and unease, he will be there children, but he doesn't make the trouble, he just watches what he helped to create."

"What did he help create, Granny?" Isaac wondered, with his hands held close to his body as if to shield himself from the upsetting and frightening words, which poured from his Grandmother's mouth.

"At the very beginning, children…what was created, what was good and solid and set up by the Father was in the process of disintegrating into parts. What was once a strong family and strong bonds were under danger of being broken into pieces – to falling into pieces and then nothing. Some will say this is the natural way of things. Where people had safety and security and each other, there were always those who wanted to see it dashed. There were those who chose, only because they could choose, to go against the way things had been set up by the Father. They went against the Father's intent. Cain was meant to be a farmer. It was what he had talent in. His brother was meant to raise up the animals using the grains that Cain grew. They were meant to have a partnership and to work as one unit, just like we do. But when Cain looked somewhere outside of this partnership, he saw that it was all unfair."

"What wasn't fair, Grandmother?" Isaac said.

"The partnership wasn't fair to Cain. In the Father's wisdom the partnership was perfectly fair. It wasn't fair to Cain because he saw himself as an individual. He didn't think about the fact that Abel's sheep only became fat by eating his grain. He only looked at the end result. He stared long and hard at that sacrifice of grain, and that sacrifice of the young lamb, children. It was displeasing to him--his sacrifice of grain. He only thought about himself. He took his own thoughts and feelings and put them into what the Father was thinking. He thought he knew that the Father was upset with him. For a person to know what the Father is thinking, one has to be the Father! That's impossible!" Granny said.

"But we have *The Gideons*, Grandmother," Isaac said with a smile.

"Yes we do, my boy. But just what are you getting at."

"We know what the Father is thinking because *The Gideons* was written down. Cain never knew what the Father was thinking because he didn't have any *Gideons*. If he's in *The Gideons* what sort of way was he supposed to know that what he was doing was wrong?"

"Well, my boy…."

"Yes, Granny? Jesse interrupted. The Elder Mother looked at each boy like she was stuck in a tennis match, unsure of who would assault her next.

"Did Cain have a *Gideons*, too, that maybe had some other story about some fool doing wrong that he could learn from?" Jesse asked.

"How did the Father punish Cain for doing wrong when He used him as an example in the book He wrote and gave to us men so we wouldn't do wrong?" Isaac said with a blank look on his face.

The Elder Mother turned red and breathed deeply through her nose to keep from exploding. The children could see her frustration because the candles that had burned down to their holders suddenly went out. The pale moonlight that circumvented the flaws in the thatch roof made the circular rafters appear as a giant wagon wheel. Granny folded the pages in *The Gideons*, and rewrapped it in its complex binding of hemp twine. The room went absolutely silent as the children anticipated their release.

"Isaac, you stay right here. The rest of you children run back to your mothers and get ready for your dinner!"

The children scampered off like a warren of rabbits that had been upset by the presence of a ravenous snake. Isaac stood alone with the Elder Mother. His prospects filled him with dread. There had to be some good reason why she would make him stay after with her. His mind drifted towards the worst possible outcome. He became fixated on one eventuality. She was going to punish him for speaking out of turn.

She walked toward him and bade him to stand up. She grabbed him by the hand as he was getting to his feet.

"My boy, I am going to show you something." And with that she bade him to follow her, dragging him by the hand.

Isaac remained silent. He searched for something to say. Her bony claws gripped his wrist like a tight shackle.

"Don't you want to know what it is, boy?"

"No, Grandmother. I trust you will show me something good."

"Ahh, now you are silent, my boy. Before you couldn't wait to share your expertise with everyone."

"I am sorry, Grandmother."

"Don't be sorry, boy. You said your peace."

"Am I in trouble, Grandmother?"

"Trouble?" she said looking back to him with a wide smile. "You are the furthest degree from being in trouble there is, my boy. I intend to reward you."

"With what?"

Her thick sandals clopped to a halt on the stone floor. She leaned down and stared into his eyes.

"Your Granny has something to tell you and something to show you that you must not tell the other children about. Now, boy, you've always been a silent thinking one and that is why I favor you most of all the children. I do, Isaac. I do. You of all the children, Isaac, have the most to complain about, but I've never heard even a mouse squeak of a complaint from you. When I heard you asking what's going to become of you when you get older, I got to thinking. That damn fool trouble-making brother of yours gets to be a man. But you're going to be limited. You're going to be kept back by that damned foot of yours."

Isaac turned red and his cheeks burned with shame.

"Don't be ashamed, boy. You know the Father never gives us more than we can handle. Now I know that you've got the mind to do great things. But that damned foot of yours. Our men are physical beings, Isaac, and you just won't fit in with them. That's the devil's work."

She parted a curtain and pulled him by the arm down a dimly lit corridor that he had never set foot into. None of the children had ever thought to pull the curtain that lined the wall and see what lay behind it. Isaac smiled to himself that he was getting to see something the other children would have to wait for. The corridor was lined on both sides with thin oak benches. He tried to look to the end of it, but was unable because the lighting was so poor. His Grandmother spoke quickly to him, like she was nervous about something. She pulled him by his arm.

"If a child never speaks evil, a child will never do evil. That's what my mother told me when I was just a girl. She told me that if a child hears nothing but complaints from its mother, the child does nothing in life but complains. It's like the parents plant seeds in a child's soul. Bitter seeds of discontent. These seeds sprout into plants that sew all sorts of other seeds in other people's souls. Don't you think that is true, Isaac?"

"Grandmother, I don't want to trouble anyone, I don't want to make problems for anybody. That's why I keep to myself."

"Boy, you will never make any problems for your Grandmother. I love you with all my heart. More than all those other children combined. I'm telling you that you're the most precious child here. Do you remember how we almost lost you when you were little?"

As they walked, Isaac walked back in his memory as far as he could, past the time he first ventured into the woods with his brothers, to his first memories of staring at the tiny particles of dust that danced in the sunbeams that poured through a small hole in the wall near his bed. He remembered how fascinated he was with the dust particles. They were like little worlds, disturbed by the currents of his warm breath: floating wonders in front of his eyes, but with a breath, they were gone. He snapped back from his youthful fantasy and answered his elder with a shake of his head no.

"You wouldn't have, my dear, you were just a small little baby. 'Bout a year after your mother died, you caught a bad fever that stayed with you. We prayed and prayed and asked the Father for His blessings but all you got was sicker and sicker. I don't think our prayers were working. There you were this little gray baby in the center of this prayer circle, with all of us women praying at the same time; all praying for the Father to intervene and save you. We were all praying and singing, and when it reached its loudest point, you know the time when the intervention usually occurs, you just up and stopped breathing. Boy, you stopped breathing for maybe a full ten seconds. The ladies around you started screaming and crying. Your mother just died only a year ago and here you were about to die, too. It was too much for all of us. We had just about given up. But then, like the miracle you are, you up and coughed and started breathing again!"

Isaac looked at his Grandmother with wide, horrified eyes. It was the first time she told him the story.

"Grandmother, I…I died?!"

"Only for a second, boy, but the Father saw fit to kick your soul back into you because you started screaming like a newborn. It was like you just came back to life again."

"Well the prayers must have worked then!"

"They did, Father be praised, but I also secretly sent some of my attendants out to the forest to find some herbs my mother taught me about. Now, boy, these herbs marked you, they made it easier for the angels to find you. Then helped those angels save you. Father be praised."

"Thank you, Grandmother. I owe my life to you," Isaac said.

"I've watched other babies your age die from that, boy. Countless babies. You're a special one, boy. You need to remember that."

"Did you mark the other babies, too?"

"No, son, it wouldn't have been appropriate. We had to rely on prayers for them, but of course the Father just saw fit to snatch them up to His bosom. For some reason the Father wanted you to remain with us. You're special, boy, you need to remember that."

"I will, Grandmother. I won't ever forget."

"You had best not be forgetting, Isaac."

"I won't, Grandmother."

She smiled at him and patted his head in approval.

At the end of the corridor they came to a metal wall. It was slightly bluish gray metal, unlike any Isaac had seen before. Whoever had put the metal wall there probably took a long time to do it and was very strong. It seemed to be one solid piece with a single ridge about seven feet off of the ground. His grandmother looked confused, like she was uncertain of why she had led him this way.

"Granny, you were going to show me something?"

His Grandmother paused for a moment and then a look came over her face as if she had found an old friend in a crowd. She smiled and chirped, "That's right, I'm going to show you something now!" As soon as the smile crested on her face it dropped to a look of deadly seriousness and she said, "Now, Isaac, you promise me. This has to be our secret. I mean, if you as much as tell your brothers and sisters about this place I'm going to take you, there will be huge trouble. You can't tell anyone about it."

"Okay, Grandmother. I promise," Isaac said with an innocent smile pasted on his face.

"Now, follow behind me," she said.

She walked to a wall that appeared just like the other walls they had walked past.

The old lady hobbled up to the far end of the corridor and put her face about an inch from the wall.

"Now, where is it?" Granny inquired with a look of consternation, her brow wrinkling as she struggled for recall, scratching her head with her hand that looked like a piece of leather that had been waterlogged and then promptly thrown into a blast furnace to dry off.

Isaac's eyes followed her every move, but he dared not intervene in her ordeal for fear that the sudden psychical shock of having to scold him would make her forget all together about the wonders she was about to reveal. He kept his mouth shut, but the anticipation was gnawing inside of him like a worm slicing its teeth through sweet and tender apple flesh as it burrowed towards the warmth of a sunny day.

"Ahh yes…it was…right…around…here," she said as she held her hands outstretched, carefully spreading her legs apart so as not to fall on her back as she reached. Isaac gasped, and his heart began to gallop out of his chest. What wonders was she going to show him? The old woman found a nook high on the wall that she placed her fingers into.

"Now, if I can just get a grip on this," she mumbled slowly to herself as if offering up a benediction for strength. She lost her foothold and went tumbling, remarkably bracing herself from landing on her side with her walking stick. When she looked back to Isaac, she appeared more hideous than ever, her thin white hair streaming like moss hanging delicately from dead trees in the forest. The small amount of physical exertion caused the old woman to pour sweat from her head, which trickled in large streams that followed clumps of strands of her hair from the roots down to the terminus, down to her scratchy, white burlap robes. She pointed over Isaac's shoulder.

"Boy, go and fetch that bench over there."

Isaac complied and began shoving the oaken bench with all of his might. It wouldn't move.

"I'm not strong enough, Grandmother," Isaac said.

"Nonsense, boy, it's just held down by the sap. These are fresh cut benches, honey, the wood wasn't allowed to dry. Just give that bench a good shove and it'll come up, hurry now!"

Isaac tried again, but the bench wouldn't move. He lowered himself to his hands and knees and looked at the blobs of sap that ran down the surface of the oak bench. He touched the sap with his fingers and stuck them together. He wrenched his fingers apart and smelled them. The smell reminded him of something fresh, like the deep forest. Isaac sighed and became frustrated at his weakness. He thought about his stronger older brother, Jesse, and how easy he could move the bench. The moment Jesse flashed through Isaac's mind, he thought of what Jesse would say to him. He would call him a little wimp who was better off left at home. He would say that Isaac did not deserve to see the wonders that Granny wanted him to see. An anger rose inside of Isaac like a magma under pressure breaking through the cone of a dormant volcano. He took a deep breath to temper it, and hit the bench with all of his might, driving it from its moorings, and sending it squeaking against the rough stone ground. The bench slid as if it were lubricated by thousands of tiny ball bearings.

"Let that be a lesson to you, boy, if you have faith in yourself and faith in your Father, all things are possible for you."

Isaac continued to push the bench until it was flush against the wall.

"Now, boy, climb on up there and see if you can't reach what Granny had her fingers on."

Isaac stood on his tiptoes and felt along the ridge. His fingers came to rest on a protrusion that was about an inch higher than the rest of the ridge. He could not feel a seem between the protrusion and the remainder of the ridge, just a smooth gradation.

"Okay, Grandmother, I have it."

"Now, push, boy, push with all your might!"

Isaac pushed down and the metal wall folded inwards, the center collapsing first in a wave that pulled the rest of the wall with it. Isaac gasped. He had never seen anything like it. Behind the wall was a stygian blackness. Isaac was enraptured, and moved to enter the dark recess.

"Wait, boy!" Granny yelled. "It's darker than midnight in the middle of the forest in there. Rushing in without your Granny will only make you lost when you run into the walls and turn back on yourself. Let me be your guide, boy. I'll show you the way through this corridor."

His grandmother grabbed him by the hand, and together the two entered the darkness.

*

As his grandmother pulled him by the hand, the rope belt around her midsection became loose. The slack caused *The Gideons*, which was stored against her undergarments in a special pocket, to work its way free. It fell and its brittle pages hit the ground in front of her feet without a sound. The next step she took, she kicked it further into the darkness. She stopped briefly, uncertain of her ability to remember the way, but rather than be an old disappointment, she pulled her most precious grandson forward in an attempt to remember the path she took the last time she used the hidden entrance to the Sanctuary.

"Come with me, my boy, I've walked this way many times. I know the way, I assure you."

She did not sound too confident. Isaac breathed deeply, scared for his life, unsure if each breath would be his last.

*

The Elder Mother shuffled along the smooth metal walls, feeling her way by fingertip in the darkness. Isaac noticed that the air, which was normally moist, was now dry and stale smelling. His Grandmother pulled him to the right, and then dragged him quickly to the left. The air grew staler and the temperature was becoming unbearable. His Grandmother farted audibly as she shuffled along the wall and the smell of rotten vegetables mingled with sweat pervaded the corridor as the old woman dragged Isaac along behind her. The smell passed quickly like the heat. In the thick of it, Isaac nearly opened his mouth to complain, but reminded himself that he had to act like an adult now.

As the pair inched their way down the corridor, Isaac's fingers turned white from his Grandmother's crushing grip on his hand. Suddenly, with each step forward they took, the ambient light increased. This is another wonder that Isaac had never seen. He looked ahead but the light did not seem to fill the entire corridor, but only the small section where he and his Granny stood. Isaac could not see any source of light. In his world candles gave off a flame, which gave off a light which could be seen in the pitch black of the forest. With each step they took in the corridor, the luminosity increased all around them, but not to the front or rear of them. He could see his Grandmother and make out her robes. After a few paces forward, the light went from a dim, barely perceivable glow to as bright as the morning sun. Had the lights suddenly turned on from pitch-blackness to its present state, Isaac surely would have been blinded.

He looked at the walls of the corridor. They were made of a dull gray metal that appeared at its surface to be moving and changing form like the surface of water in a pot. He felt no heat from the walls and reached out to touch it. As his hand approached the surface of the wall, Granny screamed and grabbed it with her weathered claw.

"No, boy!"

Isaac gasped and pulled his hand from her grasp.

"No! No! No! Don't you touch a thing in here! Nothing's as it seems!"

"What do you mean, Grandmother?"

"That wall is so hot that it would singe your hand off faster than if you stuck it in the blacksmith's coals." The Elder Mother's eyes were wide open and bugged out of her head. Isaac could see all of the tiny veins that ran from the outer rims to the surface of her clouded irises. They were mixed with fear and anger.

"How would I be able to explain to everyone that you got your hand burnt off up to your elbow?"

"I don't know," Isaac said, thinking about holding his mangled foot to the wall.

"Don't touch anything. Do you understand me?"

"Yes, Grandmother," Isaac put his hands into the front of his cassock and held his hands together like they were glued. Isaac looked past his grandmother into the murky blackness that lay just a few feet in front of them. He wanted to ask his grandmother how the lighting in the corridor worked, because it conflicted with everything he had ever seen in the world, but before he could bring expression to his thought, she stole his words.

"We're almost there now, boy," she said.

Isaac swallowed down hard the fear that was crawling out of his throat, trying to goad his vocal chords into a scream. He took a deep breath and banished the prickly worm down to dwell with the butterflies in his stomach. Begone. He reminded himself to show no emotion. Eventually he would learn to harness the feeling of fear when it clawed its way to the surface, but now choking it down only made him want to vomit. With each step the fear became more intense, until it finally gave way to expression.

"Uh…grandmother, where exactly are you taking me?" he said, barely audibly as the two came to rest at the end of the passageway facing a door that was as black as the passageway behind them. As she answered his question, he looked at the door. The surface was mirrored and he could see his reflection. When he moved closer, the door began to pulse between having a perfectly reflective surface and frosted black surface that Isaac could see nothing in.

"Go ahead, boy, touch this door, this one isn't hot," she said and snapped her fingers at him to hurry up and complete the task.

Isaac reached forward, but when his fingertip came within an inch of the door, he felt sharp resistance. No matter how hard he tried, he could not touch the black surface.

He tried with his palm, then his fist. Nothing worked. His grandmother looked at him and chuckled.

"I told you, boy, nothing here is as it seems. What this place is, is the evidence of the Father's mastery over the merely natural." She pointed towards a small indentation on the door where it met the gray metal wall. "Touch the door here," she ordered.

Isaac touched the door at the indentation. The solid black door began to flicker like a flame of fire running out of fuel, pulsating between solid and gaseous form.

Finally, it flickered so fast that the door disappeared. When they saw the sunlight streaming from the room of the grand chamber, Granny ushered Isaac into it by pulling him by his shoulders. When they were through the door, it reappeared solid. Isaac pulled away and tried to touch it, but his grandmother fixed his attention on something else with her words, "Honey, just look at this."

Isaac turned around. Sunlight poured in from a hole in the center of a room that appeared enormous to him. If he had several duplicates, and they stood on each other's shoulders, it may take one-hundred to reach the hole in the ceiling. Words would not come to his lips. It was what was hidden to the children. I was what the adults made as their own secret place. It was the Sanctuary. His grandmother did not need to explain it to him, but she insisted with a tapping of her walking stick on the metal floor. It sounded like a piece iron being cast into a deep cauldron and reverberating as it bounced off the sides.

"Why did you bring me here, Grandmother?" Isaac asked, listening for the echo. "This is our Sanctuary, boy. You wanted to see it one day. I know you did. The only thing that holds you back is that nasty leg of yours. If anyone deserves to see this, you do. Not that awful brother of yours, Jesse."

Isaac remained silent because he did not know what to say. He was taught never to question one of his elders. His grandmother continued her soliloquy, pacing back and forth.

"Isaac, precious little Isaac. There is so much you don't understand about your people or the world for that matter. The Sanctuary is the most special place in the entire world. The Sanctuary provides us a direct link to communicate with the Father. We ask Him all of our needs, and the Father provides for them in full. He even provides us more than our fill from His bounty. We ask the Father for his blessings, and they are showered on us. We beseech Him for a bountiful harvest and our storehouses are overflowing. We ask Him for healthy children and our women never cease producing them from their wombs. You see, Isaac, healthy children are our evidence that the Father has blessed us. Many people doubt the Father's magnificence whenever a child dies, or in your case is born…eh…deformed. In fact, it quite reeks of the Evil One's works in this world," she said walking towards the far wall of the Sanctuary. Isaac was lost in the distance between the immensity of the place and his child's mind in processing it all. The wonders made him gasp with each new sight he took in.

His eyes caught the first glints from the convex wall ahead of him. It was covered from floor to ceiling with a mosaic made of glittering rocks of all shapes and sizes. The mural overlooked the entire floor of the Sanctuary, stretching across the sloped walls like a jeweled valise on an endowed woman. It depicted men locked in a fierce battle. Naked men, faces twisted in horror recoiled and ran with their arms flailing over their heads, pursued by men wearing suits of armor, with jutting protrusions throughout their carapaces. Each mosaic man in armor towered over the panicked masses, and each had a circular halo of the shiniest white pebbles around his head. A single man, who Isaac surmised to be the leader, was depicted the largest. He stared off into the distance pointing a long slender finger that followed you wherever you went. From his other hand, he shot azure and ochre gemstone flames onto the screaming hordes. They burned en masse, skin and hair melting amidst piles of what looked like skulls littered the diamond layered ground. The two haloed men at his feet appeared to be laughing, smiling, as they levied destruction.

"What you are seeing is when humanity was raptured up, my boy. Those men, they aren't men, that's the angels of the Father distributing His holy justice on the land. Those terrified peoples are the masses of evil humanity being cleansed from the lands and judged in the holy fire. They are judging them with the might of the Father's Crucible…you see there…in the hands of the largest angel," Granny proclaimed, pointing at a black pyramid shaped object, spitting fire.

"The evil…the haughty…the prideful…they were all burned up…those who were not destroyed were purified…their bodies made glorious…they went on to live with the Father for all eternity in his house in Heaven."

"It did happen then, Granny! The Father did rapture everybody up."

"Those weren't just stories I tell you children," Granny said with a musty cough that creaked from her like the door opening to an ancient tomb. "Your grandmother was getting you prepared."

"Why are we here then, Grandmother? What's our point? If all the good folks got raptured up, and we're good people, how come we remained here?"

Granny turned and mumbled to herself, stroking her chin with her gnarled hand, before she turned to Isaac and said, "Boy, you've got such an inquisitive mind. What ever will we do with you? Honey, we are just like the people in *The Gideons*…the lost children of Cain…like the man that was forced to walk the earth forever in search of a home, but who would never find a home because he had cursed himself. We were spared, boy. Somehow we were spared. We were spared by the Father to fulfill the Father's plan on Earth."

"What is the Father's plan? Why does he need our help?"

"No one really knows, my boy. It is a mystery. But listen here, boy, it will come to fruition. Nothing can stop the Father. The Father is like the tree that grows in the mountain's crack. He spreads himself over all the rocky surfaces and outcrops. The small seedling grows into a mighty tree and ruptures the mountain asunder. The Father has big things in store for you, Isaac. I do not think they are in this place my son. I have had dreams and visions about you. I've heard the Angels whispering about you, boy."

She spun around to the mural and bowed before it like something had taken possession of her body. Her eyes closed and she concentrated very hard, with such intensity that she began to shake, and her voice became a stifled scream, "I was told to bring you here, Isaac. Told to bring you to the Sanctuary. The people here are ignorant of your importance. You shall lead the people to unity, you will show them the right way instead of them clawing and scratching and eating each other's young like rats in a filthy sewer. You will lead us to our home."

As soon as the words spilled from her mouth, she descended back to earth from her heavenly trance. The crone looked at Isaac. Her milky eyes had an otherworldly look to them, like she penetrated his soul with her gaze. She lowered her head like she was taking guilty pleasure in witnessing the execution of a capital criminal, and her voice became somber and full of grit, "But you will have to suffer much before the plan is revealed, my Isaac, the terror of all terrors awaits you, boy…terror more terrifying than all the loosened bowels of all the battlefields of men…but such is the way with a chosen man of the Father. You have read it in *The Gideons*. You will join these chosen men soon."

"I don't want to suffer, Grandmother."

"No one human wants to suffer, my boy, but you will have to. We are sent into this world to suffer. Your success is all in how well you bear your sufferings that the Father allows for you, whether you turn out well or not. You will not be dealt more than you can withstand. You are like a bucket in a deluge, my boy, floating with holes in the sides, the Father will only give you so much to fill you up, not so much that you sink into the murky black depths. You will overcome it all, my boy. I know your path will be difficult, and I wish I could tell you where your trials will begin, but I can't. The Angels don't tell me that. They just tell me to be looking out for you…but the trials are coming my boy…they are coming."

Isaac thought to change the subject, but his Grandmother's prophetic smile held him fixed. He looked past her to the podiums and indentations in the floor. The podiums appeared to be well worn through the ages.

"What happens in this Sanctuary, Grandmother, and why am I not allowed to see it?"

The hunched woman chuckled again, partially at herself for revealing the secret place and partially because she knew that it would add to his innate curiosity. She wanted to tell him. The urge to tell him everything boiled within her, but she tamped it down, smothering the spark of rebellion that glowed within her.

"I'm sorry, Isaac. That, my boy, will have to remain a mystery to you," Granny said with a peevish smile that melted off her face into a frown. The old woman turned from Isaac and pointed at the mural. "Do you see the largest angel, my boy?" she said in excitement. She pointed to the largest angel, who pointed outwards and whose yellow eyes and steely blue finger followed you wherever you moved. "Do you see his eyes?"

When Grandmother directed his attention to the eyes, he noticed that they seemed to have a glow to them.

"Yes, Grandmother, the big eyes that look bright glowing yellow?"

"Yes, my son, those eyes…please come with me now, I must show you something before we depart from here."

She pulled him by the hand to the wall underneath the mural and he could see that the mural was composed of individual gemstones fixed in place with a resinous substance. She stopped at an area that was lightly decorated with gemstones, right underneath the monstrous feet of the largest angel. She knocked three times with her hand, and Isaac's ears were met with a hollow echo that sounded like a child hitting an overturned cauldron with a wooden spoon. She pried upwards on the wall to reveal a panel no bigger than Isaac's hand. She placed her hand gingerly inside the hollow, her face contorted to a grimace as if she were in pain. After a second the wall retreated backwards like a wave of metal pinched from the center and dragged backwards by a giant hand, each collapsing section, smaller than the one that dragged it into the opening. There was no sound of mechanical movement. Isaac gasped as the passageway opened, black as death, the wonders of the Sanctuary incomprehensible to his neophyte mind.

"Come, my boy," she beckoned him.

The two entered the passageway, and the woman groped her way into the opaque chamber. She dragged Isaac by the arm as the doorway rescinded to close without a sound. The lights in the room came on slowly, but like the hallway, Isaac could not detect a source. In front of them lay a flat surface extending at a forty-five degree angle from the surface parallel to his feet. As soon as she crossed from the flat floor onto the angled surface, they were whisked to the top platform effortlessly. The entire two seconds he traveled, he did not feel like he moved at all. There was no sound, no whirring of gears. It was amazing, but not as amazing as what he was about to see.

She pulled him to an alcove that had small fragments of lightly glowing crystals on the walls, giving the appearance of a starry nighttime sky. Two spherical, translucent crystals emitted light one after the other. When one crystal was dark, the other glowed at its brightest.

"Those are the eyes of the angel, my boy, if you couldn't tell. Look out of them and tell me what you see," the woman said to him with a smile on her face. Isaac noticed that when either crystal glowed its brightest he could see through his grandmother's skin, past the wrinkles and veins, down to her bone. He closed his eyes to the apparition of her ghostly face and attempted to look through the crystals. He stood on his tiptoes, but could not quite look through them.

"Grandmother, I'm not tall enough!"

"Nonsense, boy, step up to them."

Isaac followed his Grandmother's command and took a step up the wall. As he did, the wall responded to his footsteps by sloping gently, carrying his weight. He did not feel himself being lifted towards the ceiling, but suddenly was at the requisite height. When he put his face against the stones, he wondered what the bones under his skin looked like, but the thought ripped from his mind and was replaced by the sights on the Sanctuary floor.

When he stood in the Sanctuary, everything had the color of dull gray metal. Through the use of the stones the entire Sanctuary seemed full of activity, full of life. Brightly colored flashes of light traced their way along every inch of the floor and walls below. Packets of light shot along the lines with a rapid randomness and spiraled along their pathways. It throbbed with energy and life. Each podium seemed to be a focal point of the light packets. At each podium's terminal end, the light packets amplified into a regular pulsing flash that didn't seem to shed any light on anything in their surrounding vicinity.

"What is it, Grandmother?" Isaac said with his voice full of wonder, like a child first gazing at the sun.

"This place, this is how we communicate with the Father."

"How, Grandmother?"

His grandmother froze in thought and finally spit out, "Well it isn't for small children such as you to know about."

"If you can't tell me then, I mean, do we tell the Father?"

"We don't tell the Father anything, my child."

"He tells us things?"

"Yes, the Father tells us things."

"What things?"

"Well, for instance, how the Congregation can go about getting the world back into order."

"   You mean, after all the people got raptured up, right?"

"Right."

"Well what does the Father tell us to do?"

She paused again for thought, "He tells us to stick to our ways handed down to the ancient ones and follow everything in *The Gideons* to the letter."

"And if we follow everything in *The Gideons*, what happens then?"

"Then He'll come again, my boy, the Father will come again and we'll all be saved."

"How long have we been waiting, Grandmother?"

"Not long son, not long. The Father came the first time boy, and He'll come again."

"Grandmother?" Isaac questioned, still staring at the organized confusion on the sanctuary floor.

"Yes, Isaac."

"Grandmother, do you think the Father will come back?"

"I do, Isaac. I believe that with my whole heart and my whole mind. You could say I believe that with my whole being."

"Why?"

"The Father said He would come back, and the Father always keeps His promises. We must have Faith, boy."

"What else did the Father promise?"

"He promised the first rapture, and it happened. It is fact. The question for you Isaac, is do you believe that the Father will come again? Do you believe all that your Grandmother tells you and all of the stories from *The Gideons*?"

Isaac did not respond to her immediately. He looked out the window to the pulsating activity. A better question forced itself to him.

"Grandmother, who built our Sanctuary?"

"It was given to us by the Father, Isaac."

"So the Father taught us how to build it?"

"No, Isaac, we did not build it."

"Where did the Sanctuary come from then?"

"The Sanctuary fell from Heaven, Isaac. We found it. We know it was created by the Father."

"How? How do we know the Father created the Sanctuary? If we just found it?"

The woman paused and scratched her chin. "Look around, you. This is too beautiful and perfect to be the work of men. Isaac, we live in buildings of brick and stone made by the sweat and labor of men. This is something not of this world. It is divine. Does not a building have a builder, Isaac? This beautiful creation, the Sanctuary, has a creator! The Father made it for us. He showed us where to find it. He told the Ancients about its location and revealed it to them. He showed them the way. Just like He showed the Ancients the secrets of *The Gideons*."

"But who made the mural, Grandmother, the scenes of the angels rapturing the people up?"

"We made that, my boy, over all the generations back to the beginning when the Father led the Ancients here. The Father gave us the Sanctuary, Isaac, we only decorated it to remind us of all that happened to our people."

Isaac stared at his Grandmother. The glow shone through her, and Isaac thought he could see her very soul. His words lodged in his throat and stumbled from his mouth like a bloated pig that gorged itself on fermented forbidden fruit.

"I've...I've never seen anything like it."

"I know, Isaac. I know. It is proof of the Father's magnificence. And proof of his glory. You are special, Isaac. That is why I showed you the Sanctuary. Otherwise you may never have seen it. You know you were born imperfect. You are valuable because you were born amongst us, the struggling righteous ones of the land. If you were born to the savages that live beyond these walls, they would not have let you live amongst them. They surely would have left you out in the woods alone to be eaten by whatever animal happened along."

Isaac's stomach sank as he imagined himself being torn to bits by wild dogs, their sharp ripping teeth tearing into his flesh. He thought back to the lizard, seized by the spider. It angered him. He shot back against the vision.

"What makes me special?"

"Your imperfections make you special, Isaac. Your foot, it makes you slower. It makes you weaker than the other boys. Our elders, especially the men, will never tolerate you amongst them."

"Maybe I don't want to be amongst them."

"You needn't worry about that, boy, you don't have a chance. Our men are physically strong and powerful. They have to be to survive in this world. They would never accept you."

The woman rested her weathered hand on the young boy's shoulder and looked at her leathery skin in comparison to his warm youthful glow. Even in the light of the pulsating stones, everything about him lived. Jealously nosed its way into her consciousness, but she flipped it down her gullet and choked it down like a bird would with an earthworm blindly escaping from the rain soaked earth. She looked at the boy's foot. The glow revealed his crisscrossed bones, snaking like a parched, knotted tree root. She patted him on the head in an effort to assuage the look of sorrow on his face. Suddenly she felt very stupid. In her awe of the place and at showing it to him, she realized that they had spent too long a time there. They would be discovered if she did not lead the boy out immediately. She grabbed him by the hand.

"Isaac, we must flee this place. We can't be caught in here," she said with a pause. "That would be very, very bad for us."

She tore him from the fascinating window and dragged him the hand through all the twists and turns. Isaac did his best to remember them, and he had a prodigious memory, well honed from his time spent in the woods with his brothers. As the two entered the darkened corridor that led to the entrance to the fascinating place, Isaac's misshapen foot brushed gingerly against *The Gideons*. The boy did not feel the book against his skin, but heard a slight sound of the pages rustling. He wanted to tell his Grandmother to stop, but dared not open his mouth out of respect for her insistence that they leave. He had never seen her act in such a directed manner before. Usually she bumbled and stumbled confusedly through her days, but now she moved with forthrightness that he had only seen previously in his older brother, Jesse, as the man-child fearlessly bushwhacked his way through the forest during their adventures.

When they were back in the children's area she brought her face down close to his. Her breath smelled like boiled potatoes and wild leek stew that had been left in the sun to fester for a week. Isaac cringed. She vomited forth her dire warning to him.

"Not a word of this to anyone, boy. If you tell anyone what I showed, your life could be lost. Not a word to anyone. Promise me!"

"Yes, Grandmother. I promise you," Isaac said. "I promise I won't say a word."

"You are the best, boy. Your grandmother loves you best out of all the children. Don't ever forget that. No harm will ever come to you, if you just remember that...."

"Yes, Grandmother. I will remember."

That night Isaac went to sleep and his dreams were filled with visions of wonders. The next day, as the sun rose and his brothers readied themselves for their daily toils, he conquered the urge to tell them, piecemeal. He remained quiet. Like nothing happened at all.

Jesse marked the time remaining for his ascent to manhood with notches whittled into his bedpost. The notches grew so numerous that they weakened the bedpost in places and put his bunkmate, Baruch, in danger of crashing to the floor below. When Jesse watched his two younger brothers playing their childish games, the care-free smiling happiness of his youth slowly gave way to ennui. The blank stare on his face befit an adult of the Congregation and watching his brothers squeal on the floor like children annoyed him. While they played with carved wooden animals that he used to enjoy, he didn't mark the slightest upturn at the corners of his lips. His lips were more concerned about other matters. He looked out into the blackness of night. It was calming: a balm for him as he attempted to set his wandering mind to rights. The nighttime forced him to make a decision. It was time for him to do his wandering through the forest alone. The forest was dangerous at night -- *for children.* When he walked through the forest alone he was not afraid. Besides, she was waiting for him. He could feel her warmth all around him, guiding him through the will o' wisps and rips and pangs of conscience that snagged at him like thorny branches. What he did at night in the wilderness with her, it was wrong. It went against everything he was taught. But Jesse did not care. He looked to his brothers and their annoying childish games.

"The bear takes the wolf and eats him!" Isaac laughed as he crashed the crude wooden animals together.

"But the wolf bites the bear by the neck!" Baruch yelled as he pulled at the coarse bristles that made up the bear's fur, trying to detach the bear's head from its body.

"But the bear chomps the wolf in two!" Isaac exclaimed, laughing.

The trees tamped out the burning sun as it slid beneath the horizon, and Jesse's burning forced him to leap up out of the chair. Without a word to his brothers, he bounded out the door.

"Where's Jesse going, Baruch?" Isaac questioned.

Baruch stayed silent, but he had a look of worry applied like a makeshift bandage to his face. He knew what was happening.

"Where's he goin', Baruch? We aren't supposed to leave at night!"

"That rule's for us children," Baruch said.

"He's not an adult yet."

"He told me he's got chores."

"No one does chores at night, Baruch. You're lying to me!"

Baruch's face glowed scarlet in the candlelight. Isaac was unsure if it was the reflection of the candle, or if his brother was enraged. He found out shortly. Baruch punched him in the arm, hard. Isaac gasped and winced.

"None of your business, little boy. You pay attention to your toys."

"I'm not a little boy."

"You are. You're a little boy."

"You know, Baruch. You know what Jesse's off doing."

"So what if I do? You can't know. It's not for children."

"What if I went and told mom that Jesse left?"

"You wouldn't dare."

"Where's he going?"

"Don't know," Baruch said with a smile.

"You do, Baruch! Tell me!"

"Why do you care? He just went for a walk!"

"Why didn't he ask us to go?"

"Because he doesn't want to be around us anymore. Can't you tell?"

Isaac thought about it. It was true. Their older brother grew more distant by the day with every single notch he carved from the post. It was like a piece of his affection for them fell by the wayside, like the pieces of the post that just gathered dust underneath Baruch and Jesse's shared bed.

"He thinks we're children, Isaac."

"I'm not a child," Isaac said.

"You are. You don't know where he's going. I do. Jesse told me not to tell you 'cause you're a little kid."

"I'm not a little kid," Isaac said with a sneer. Rage boiled within him. If his brother said one more word, Isaac was going to punch him square in his nose. He readied his fist. He waited for Baruch to open his mouth. He thought, *if I punch him in the mouth Baruch will just get mad and really beat me.* It happened all the time like that. Isaac tried to stand up to Baruch, but Baruch only beat him down into the ground and reminded him he was a little boy. But he wasn't a little boy. Grandmother showed him that he wasn't. She showed him the Sanctuary, and like that, it flew out of his mouth like a diseased insect straight into Baruch's ear. It flapped with rage and spite and barely eclipsed a whisper over the noise of the crickets outside.

"I saw the inside of the Sanctuary, Baruch. You didn't."

He couldn't believe what he had done and prayed his brother didn't hear, but Baruch was onto him like a lion.

"What did you say, Isaac?"

"Nothing, Baruch. I didn't say anything."

"You did. I heard it. You said you went into the Sanctuary."

"I, uh, I," Isaac prattled.

"Who took you, Isaac?"

"Grandmother."

"Why did that crazy old lady take you, of all people, to the Sanctuary?"

"Because I'm her favorite. And I'm an adult!"

Baruch laughed at him. "You aren't an adult. She's just old and senile. She probably thought she was taking me or Jesse."

"No. She meant to take me!"

Baruch grabbed his arm and twisted it.

"You know how to get in there, Isaac?"

"Maybe."

"You're going to take me there."

"No."

Baruch punched Isaac in the arm, *hard.*

"Ow. Damn you. I can't take you."

"You're going to take me, Isaac."

"I told Grandmother I wouldn't tell anyone."

"I'll tell Granny you told me that you went into the Sanctuary. I'll tell her you took me."

The gravity of Isaac's error began to crush him like a heavy stone laid upon his chest. He started to cry.

"You can't, Baruch. You can't. She said I might die if the adults find out."

"Maybe I want you to die, Isaac," Baruch said with a sneer.

"You can't! Baruch, you can't!"

"You're going to take me there. You're going to show me what its like."

"We can't go tonight, Baruch. You know the adults are there," Isaac whimpered.

"You know what they're doing? You better tell me."

"No. Granny took me when it was empty. Its really nice inside," Isaac sobbed.

"Can't you just wait, Baruch? Can't you just wait to see it when they let you?"

"No, Isaac, I can't."

Isaac thought for a second between his baby tears. He took a deep breath; then Isaac did what any grown up would do in the situation to get what he ultimately wanted. He attempted to compromise.

"Okay. I'll take you. We'll go tomorrow. But tonight you have to take me to see what Jesse's doing."

"I can't. Jesse told me it's not for children, Isaac. I already asked him to go along. Jesse wouldn't let me go!"

"But we're not children! Do you want me to take you to the Sanctuary or not? Don't you want to see what Jesse's up to? You don't know really. He could be lying to you."

"He never told me what he was doing."

"You see. He doesn't want us to know. Don't you want to know, Baruch?"

"I do. But he can't find out."

"We'll just see what he's doing and come right back."

"We'll have to spy on him."

"Let's take some lanterns with us," Isaac said with a smile. His tears were gone, replaced by the tingle of mischief in his stomach. Baruch grabbed his lantern with a slight chuckle. If Jesse was going to be called up to join the adults soon, he would have to get used to playing with his younger brother alone. And this would be their first adventure.

The brothers, Baruch and Isaac, set out with lanterns in hand to find their older brother, somewhere in the forest. They had never been out alone before, especially at night. Isaac walked behind Baruch, deferring to his older brother in the tradition of their people. Baruch swung his lantern back and forth as he walked, casting death black shadows from the gnarled bark of the trees ahead of them. The deep instantaneous shadows formed by Baruch swinging the lantern like a pendulum made the trees appear to Isaac as if they had grotesque faces. From the side of them, the lantern made light reflect off a pairs of eyes. The owners screeched and dashed into the blackness, sending shockwaves of fear through Isaac's stomach. He watched Baruch's feet, frightened to look ahead and trusted that his older brother knew where he was going. He kept reassuring himself in his mind that this was a good idea and worth whatever danger it involved. The boys did not speak to one another until during the journey. Isaac thought that Baruch was as scared as him, but did not see any fear on Baruch's face when the two stopped at their first decision point: a stream that cut through their path like a knife wound. Thick cobwebs bunched between the juvenile trees, the tops of which came to their head level. Gossamer dandelion seeds with attached floating tethers dangled like ripe fruits in the bunched silk littered with gray insect corpses. When they stopped underneath them Isaac stood far away, deathly afraid that a spider, like the one that devoured the lizard, would jump from the tree in search of a bite of boy flesh.

Baruch ambled forward with his head down. He was talking to himself, like he always did when he got confused.

"I remember that Jesse told me he would be going across the stream and picking up another trail. But did he pick up another trail before he made it this far?"

He continued on unimpeded in his soliloquy before Isaac interrupted him.

"Baruch, if you're lost, we can just go home."

Baruch turned his lantern on his younger brother, setting his face aglow like a demon.

"No, you wanted to find him, so we're finding him."

"But, Baruch, I'm scared."

"Oh, you're scared? I thought you were the big man who got to see the Sanctuary? Well I'm not waiting for you, little boy. No damn way. Now you can either follow me or get home yourself. Now it's that way," he said pointing at the forest behind them.

Isaac looked. Home was a distance away and even though he could probably make it there, he would be even more scared than right now. He sighed. His brother had won.

"Okay, let's keep going."

"I thought you'd come to see it my way, Isaac."

The boys continued walking until they reached the creek. The ground at their feet was soft and spongy, and the air was heavy and cool, smelling of partially decayed vegetable matter.

"How deep is this stream, Baruch?"

"I don't know, brother. I'll measure it," Baruch said reaching for a moss covered stick thrust from the water's edge. He grabbed the stick and tried to budge it. Grunting, he yanked on the stick with both hands. He did not see the serpent move from its hiding place underneath the hollow bank. The brown snake struck with a flash. Baruch felt pain and screamed. Isaac brought his light just to see the enormous snake with the triangle head release his brother's hand and splash into the water. It soon disappeared on the water's surface into the distance.

Isaac rushed to his brother's aid, kneeling down beside him.

"Baruch, it's a Mocha Assassin!"

"No, it can't be."

"There aren't any other snakes out here."

"It burns!"

"We have to get back."

"No, we can't. They'll wake everybody up. They'll find out Jesse's missin'. You gotta go get Jesse, Isaac."

"Baruch, I can't."

"Isaac, you have to!"

"I can't, Baruch. We have to go back."

"Isaac, you can do it. Please, I can't move. I have to sit still so the poison don't get into my bloodstream too quick. I have to sit here."

Isaac started to cry. Tears streamed down his face as he looked at his brother, Baruch.

"Father damn you, Isaac! Now grow up. You need to be strong now. Isaac, you always told us you were a man, now prove it. You go get Jesse. Otherwise I'm a goner for sure. Go! There isn't time."

Isaac stared ahead into the blackness. He held his lantern in front of him at chest height.

"Oh, Father no…," Baruch moaned.

Isaac did not hear his brother's second lamentation because he had splashed through the water up to his waist and come out of the creek on the other side. When he got over the water's sudden chill, he started screaming his older brother's name and running headlong into the forest. He didn't know where he was going, but it couldn't have been too far past the creek. His mind flashed to what their Grandmother told them when she took them on her nature walks. She pointed out all the dangers of the forest to them as a warning, lest they wander away from the Congregation. Like most of the Congregation buildings, the greater forest was also off-limits and full of horrible animals and even more horrible people. One time, she pointed to the stream with a look of menace in her face and told them of the stream's horrors. Snakes. They would bite you and you could die in an instant and your dead body would fall in the water to be eaten by little crayfish a bit at a time. And no one would ever find your body. The snake was the Mocha Assassin. He remembered it spilling from her lips. The most feared snake in the forest. It lived near the water's edge killing frogs and fish and the occasional person who wandered too close.

"Jesse!" Isaac screamed running until he heard his heartbeat pounding in his ears and his lungs were about to explode.

That day their Grandmother told him that the Mocha Assassin's venom would burn a hole in someone's heart if it entered their bloodstream.

Isaac hobbled through the forest like a screaming madman trying to scare the nocturnal animals into the light of day.

The Mocha Assassin's victim will experience a horrible pain beyond anything men are capable of withstanding...like the fires of hell itself are burning the insides of his veins out...and the venom will, children, burn a hole straight through the victim's heart. Isaac remembered how his Grandmother's face looked. It was hideous and contorted like she had eaten something putrid, and she tapped her oaken walking stick on the ground in front of her.

He imagined his punishment as he ran. It was best to have his heart explode and be eaten by all the animals of the forest than go back there, but his brother was in trouble and it was time for him to be a man.

He remembered Grandmother's talks. They always ended with her repeated proclamation of doom for any child that strayed too far from the Congregation. *Lest you be eaten by animals and preyed upon by the apostates of wicked tribes, it is best to stay within the confines of the Congregation, children! It is best to stay within the confines of the Congregation!*

He screamed for his older brother again, "Jesse!" His shrill cry rang hollow off the mess of trees that surrounded him. A few tears formed in the corner of his eyes. If anyone was going to save his brother, Baruch, it had to be him. Twigs snapped under his feet as he shambled in the direction of randomness that he took. Branches tugged at his shirt and scraped his tender, young skin. He clawed through them like an animal trying to break the confines of a cage. As he ripped through the underbrush, his lame foot carried huge clumps of undergrowth with it. Hook encrusted seed pods clung to his clothing at every turn, and insects darted to meet the invading fiend. Isaac bent down and tore the vines from around his feet. Their juices and sap green stained his hands. Isaac cocked his head and listened for any sound of his brother. Far away he heard what sounded like mismatched animals having a fight; the air permeated by a low growl echoed by a scream. The growling animal was clearly winning. Isaac did not walk towards the sound, he was drawn to it and the slow rolling of insect legs rubbing against insect thoraxes provided the background noise. The incessant call, broken up by rhythmic high and low pitched din of the animals fighting. It seemed that they said, 'Let us finish our lives in this musty day and never see another evening.' Spindly legs gyrated against coxcombed thoraxes calling each other to the perpetual dance.

"Jesse!" Isaac screamed in the direction of the animals fighting.

He walked towards them. The sound grew more intense. A dense thicket of proud upright trees thrust before him. The animals were fighting there. Isaac rushed forward as fast as his gimp could carry him and burst into the clearing with his lantern in front of him.

If his thoughts were on his brother, Baruch, those thoughts were dashed. There were no animals to him in the clearing beyond the proud erect trees. It was Jesse lying face down, propping himself up with his muscular arms. Underneath him was a woman. Her legs were wrapped around his brother like she was trying to keep him in place and he kept trying to get off of her but she drawing him back down. He brought his lantern up to her face, which contorted in a look of pain each time she drew his brother down, but she bore a smile. She opened her eyes and screamed at Jesse.

Jesse looked up blinded by the lantern.

"Who the hell?"

He jumped to his feet, naked, and tackled Isaac. As they tumbled to the ground, Isaac wailed, "Jesse, it's me!"

Jesse, naked from the waist down straddled Isaac and screamed, "What the hell are you doing here?"

"Baruch and I had to find you...I wanted to go back...he dragged me out here...I didn't mean...."

"Where is that little bastard?"

"He got bit."

"He got bit by what?!"

"A snake bit him down by the stream. We were gonna go back, Jesse, honest. But when he got bit I had to come find you. The adults would have found you were gone and a whole lotta questions would have happened for you."

"A whole lotta questions are going to happen. Father damn you two! Where is he?" Jesse picked himself off of Isaac and helped his brother up. Isaac's lantern slowly burned out as the woman got up and stood by Jesse. She nuzzled Jesse, but he pushed her away.

"I gotta go, love. I don't know when I can come back."

"You will come when you come. I will be waiting for you."

She turned to Isaac and reached into a purse bag that was around her waist. She rustled through it and pressed a small piece of wood and leather into Isaac's palm. He could not see it, but it felt like it was cut in the shape of a man.

"This will help your brother."

Jesse kissed the woman and told her goodbye, then dragged his brother by the hand back to where Isaac told him Baruch lay by the stream's far shore. Isaac caught Jesse looking back several times to where he left the woman, but when Isaac looked back his eyes would not penetrate the infernal darkness. He wondered if his brother had the capacity to see in the dark – something he was not born with – something he had also been robbed of at birth.

"We're walking too slowly, little brother. Get on my back, I'll carry you," Jesse said.

Isaac obediently climbed and grasped his hands together around his brother's massive shoulders. If only he could be that strong one day, everything would be right in the world.

As Jesse walked, each step he took smashed the twigs and vines at his feet like a man breaking a bundle with his hands without straining. Isaac clasped his hands around his brother's neck and held the small totem the girl gave him between their bodies so that the top of it stuck out and Jesse saw it.

"Isaac, get rid of that thing. Whatever she gave you, throw it away."

Isaac protested, "No, she gave it to me to help Baruch."

"You think that thing is going to help Baruch? You're stupider than she is." Jesse said gruffly as he ripped his legs through the undergrowth trying to find a deer trail in the midst of the tangling vines and saplings. Isaac discovered that he was actually quicker than his brother Jesse in navigating the mess of plants and trees, because he was smaller and could shamble right under them without ducking. He let Jesse's comment slide, but he did not drop the figurine.

"Isaac, it's stupid. Get rid of it."

"If you think she's stupid why were you meeting with her? What were you doing with her?"

"I was helping her gather firewood, Isaac."

Isaac laughed, "Like that? I didn't see you had any firewood. Plus why would you gather firewood at night? Wouldn't you want to during the day so you could at least see the firewood?"

Jesse breathed deeply. Isaac could feel his lungs expand beneath him. Jesse said in his slow manner of saying things before he was about to explode and destroy something, "Never you mind what I was doing, boy."

"Tell me, Jesse."

"No, I can't tell you. You'll find out when you're older."

"Tell me what you were doing with that girl back there. It looked like you were wrestling her to me. What, did she steal something from us? You were trying to get it back?"

"I was helping her gather firewood, that's all you need to know about it."

"But, Jesse...."

"Isaac, shut it!"

His fuse was burning quickly down to the point were there was no shutting off his anger, and Isaac knew what the response would be, however Isaac's curiosity was overflowing. If there was something new in the world that was unexplained to him, he had to know the reason for it and what it was called by the adults.

"You looked like you were wrestling, Jesse."

Jesse set Isaac down on the ground. Isaac used the opportunity to put the figurine into his belt. He had it behind his back, and tied it quickly there, hiding it beneath the leather strap.

"Listen, Isaac. You can't know what happened back there. It's one of those things you have to discover on your own when you're an adult."

"I am an adult, Jesse."

"No, you aren't, and you're never gonna be an adult unless we get to Baruch. I'm tired of carrying you. You need to lead me to where you both were."

Isaac looked at the surrounding forest. It all looked the same to him. The screaming and fornicating insects diffused any sound of the stream behind their blanket of sound.

*

The forest responded in kind to the upset in the delicate balance of the ecosystem. The denizens that acted as its eyes, its nose all of its senses – came alive to the stimulus that the three nighttime encroachers forced upon it. One, a large gray she-wolf exited her den when the first smells of delightful distress met her flared nostrils. She nudged her pups back into the sunken chamber that was formed out of an uprooted tree and root system hollowed by larvae, which long since took flight to lay their eggs at the base of other trees. The she-wolf sternly implored her youth to return underground with a few well placed nips of love at the scruff of their neck. She nudged them, *the forest has eyes for young ones: like we eat so can you be eaten, too, my children.* She nudged them and bade them hide, just as her mother nudged her. The pups yelped and flopped back into the earth to cuddle and share whatever body heat they could muster.

The wolf stretched her hindquarter. Steam shot from her mouth as she breathed deeply, prepping her muscles for the hard work. She listened back to her children for the slightest murmur that would excite a snake or other devourer. Her children were quiet, just as she instructed them. They would only yelp upon her return, eager for the food and future life she would bring them.

She stretched once more and fixed her gaze in the direction of the tantalizing scent: suffering animal mixed with fear; the forest was thick with it. She exploded into a full sprint. The small branches parted way and grasses quaked at her approach. She let loose a snarl as the memory of fresh blood and flesh and the memories of the comforted snoring of her children impelled her forwards.

*

"What were you doing back there, Jesse?" Isaac asked as he attempted to find where he last abandoned Baruch to find their older brother.

"Point the way, boy," Jesse retorted angrily.

"I'm no boy, Jesse. I'm sick of everyone calling me a boy."

"Because everyone thinks you're a boy, Isaac. And you are a boy."

Isaac had burned to the end of his fuse. He realized his own curiosity would get him nowhere with his older brother, so he just came out with it.

"Grandmother doesn't think I'm a boy. She showed me the Sanctuary!"

"That's bull. I don't believe you."

"I found out before you. I know what it looks like."

"I don't care. You had to sneak in. I get invited in next week."

"But I know what it looks like."

"So. It's not like you're ever going to get to take part in any of the ceremonies in there. So what if you've seen the Sanctuary. You'll never know why it's special."

Isaac recoiled. His brother was right. Anger flashed through Isaac, searing his limbs with wrath. With his hands around his Jesse's neck, he wanted to strangle him. Isaac tensed up, but could not even bring himself to try. Jesse would have killed him. Still, Jesse was right, it was nothing to have seen the inside of the building. He had to see the ceremonies. But Grandmother would never go for that. She would never take him to see those. Especially if she found out that he told someone. And now he had told both of his brothers and broken his promise to his Grandmother twice. She would never let him see the ceremonies. Isaac wanted to sit down. He looked to his immediate right and noticed the place where he stopped and ripped the vines from around his legs. They lay there in the moonlight like a clutch of dead snakes.

"I stopped here. Here's where I cleaned the plants from my feet," Isaac turned around trying to remember which direction he came from.

"You little idiot, look."

Jesse pointed towards the underbrush. There was a very distinctive trail that Isaac had blazed right through the middle of it.

"We'll follow this," Jesse said with an air of superiority that was impenetrable to his little brother's attempts at recognition.

*

The scent of struggle at the molecular level permeated the air and found her nostrils. With each step the scent of struggle grew stronger until it was an overwhelming urge rushing her forwards. The sinews in her legs tensed and exploded, catapulting her five feet in a single stride. Her heart pumped warm blood to her eyes, which were fixed like telescopes on the horizon and at her goal. The lips cemented into a snarl: a fleshy span of bridge across her sharp, devouring crevasse of a mouth. The tongue wagged like a propeller through the empty spaces that weren't filled with the pointy teeth engineered for tearing, disemboweling, and ripping, but also comforting, bringing warmth for hungry pups sleeping satiated in the hole. She would silence their cries, but for an evening until she was called to repeat her hunt again.

*

Isaac looked towards his brother with a frown across his little face. Jesse pointed approximately ten meters to the right of the broken up vegetation that Isaac had struggled through, to reveal a well-worn deer trail that had probably been used for centuries by the animals as they roamed the forest in search of food and back to the stream to drink. Jesse placed Isaac on the ground, sure that he could now walk for himself.

"All you have to do is open your eyes, Isaac. The best solution is often in front of you," Jesse said, less the teacher and more the preacher.

*

The she-wolf burst from the underbrush onto the stream bank. She spied her quarry. A clumped small one, with little brown hair, lying near the stream, barely breathing, maybe sleeping; regardless, it was separated from the big ones. It was not an injured deer or rabbit it had to wrestle from the paws of a fierce wolverine. This little one had no sharp horns or claws. Nothing to make it hurt. The she-wolf gingerly walked up and smelled it, tasting the air and steam that poured from the little one's lungs. The stream rushed by like the bright, tasty blood in the little one's veins. As the wolf approached, its head bowed to the earth out of respect for the human it had come across. The smell, still pulsing with life, was much different than the carrion she was used to gathering in the forest, not a half frozen deer, not the old ones that the winter killed. To what did she owe her fortune to find the tastiest meat of them all? And this one without the sharp tools or loud hurters that the other ones carried. Her mother taught her, just like she taught her children that these animals screamed when you stole one of the little ones. When you came out of the forest and grabbed one of them in your jaws, the big ones screamed, the long haired ones shrieked, the ones dressed in your own skins, the skins of your kind, chased you into the forest until they found your den. Then they killed you and made coats of your skin, and a hat of your head, and they wore your teeth around their necks. And they took your children…they took them…*leave the two legs alone, those are more trouble than they are worth…the only animal that does not follow the rules of the forest…if you eat you must expect to one day be eaten.* It is better to hunt the deer and not sneak into the place where the two legs live. It is better to eat a thousand frozen rabbits than arouse the two legs' anger.

She smelled the small one again. A twinge of fear straddled her waist as she gave the little one a nip. It did not move. Not even a shudder. All she heard was the cries of her children. She smelled the little one again. The meat was fresh, but something odd flowed through this one. She smelled again. It smelled delicious with a twinge of the vile. It was mixed with the snake, the animal that slithered through the grasses and was hated by all the other animals. It smelled of the snake, the intruder, the sneak, and a killer of babies. Against all that she knew, she grabbed the little one by the foot and began to drag it into the underbrush towards her den. The other wolves would have chastised her, but she was hungry. Where were they now to feed her? Where were they to feed her babies? They had run her out of the pack, alone and pregnant. Left her to fend for herself. They hoped and prayed for her death by throwing her away. She backed up and dragged the little one towards her babies. Her hunger convinced her. *It was good.*

*

Isaac turned red with shame. He looked towards the ground only to see his brother's feet gallop ahead to the deer trail. He did not want to be alone, so he tried his best to catch up with Jesse. Jesse ran up the deer trail, dodging the tree roots that skirted either side of the trail, erected in place by the massive oaks that clustered on the banks of the stream, dipping their taproots into its life. He disappeared from Isaac's view as he passed over the crest of the hill and began his downward descent towards the stream bank. Isaac dragged his useless foot behind him and grew winded as he reached the hilltop. He tripped at the top of the hill and landed on his knees. He was slow to pick himself up, out of his exhaustion, until his older brother's screams fractured his self-pity.

Jesse's screams sounded like when the baby cow is born and its mother is not the first thing it sees and the cold world rushes in on it while the steaming placenta still hangs from its neck.

*

The wolf tensed. The smell of two legs was all around her. A big two leg bolted from the trail and was on top of the gray wolf before it looked up from its easily gotten feast. The wolf recoiled and bared its fangs. The food was too good to abandon, and the babies were starving. She would have to fight, and her hair stood on end: a reflex action to make her appear larger. She put her paws forward to defend against the big angry one. She snarled which usually sends the two legs running. The big angry one did not run away; it kept coming. It screamed like it meant to fight. The wolf sunk her teeth into the little one's foot and tried her hardest to drag it deeper into the underbrush, towards her den, hoping the big angry one would give up.

*

Isaac trudged down the hill, muttering to himself. He was not going to waste his time chasing Jesse. Jesse knew that he was bigger and stronger than everyone else, and he did everything he could to show off for anyone who would listen. Isaac felt that he did his part for Baruch by sending the alarm to their savior. He would just continue on his way home and let the hulk, Jesse, carry Baruch home. Isaac felt that he would just slow them down. He was sick of Jesse reminding everyone about how special he was: how big and strong and perfect he was. Jesse could go and be with the adults. He and Baruch would find their own fun. They did not need their dumb older brother anyway.

Isaac placed his hands in the front pocket of his burlap robe against a sudden chill. As he walked down the hill dragging his leg behind him carefully, lest he tumble head over heels to the bottom, a thought came to him, which he tried his best to beat back. He secretly hoped that his older brother Baruch, Baruch the tormentor, Baruch the one who picked on him so much – Isaac hoped that he would die so that Baruch could never pick on him again. Isaac beat the thought back into the recesses of his mind and tears started to flow down his face. Though fall was just approaching, the coming winter wind blasted off his face and froze his breath in his throat like an icy death grip. Suddenly he felt as if a piece of himself was missing, as if he lost something very near and dear to him, but he couldn't quite call up. It was as if he had a hole in his very heart that nothing could fill -- not even the Father that his grandmother had told him would be with him wherever he went. The tears continued and lifted themselves up to a miniscule sound that echoed gently off the massive trees, deaf to the spectacle that took place around them that blindly stretched their arms toward the heavens to embrace the rising sun. The cries were high pitched and alone like the call of a bird to its mate. The tears dribbled off of his chin and only a salt trail remained after they dried in place. Only Jesse's screams reminded him that the time to feel pitiful had long past and pity was only allowed in the confines of the Congregation.

The boy began dragging his leg behind him, relying more on the force of gravity to carry him down the hill; it was rather that he floated, carried not by a will of his own. And then he saw it. It was like he came across the scene of a murder, or fell into a painting with broad gray and black knife strokes tinged in blood red. It did not happen in front of his eyes. In the rising sun he saw that his brother Jesse had an unconscious Baruch by his arms, holding him with a strained look in his face and bulging veins. Jesse's white-knuckled hands gripped tightly around Baruch's forearms, struggling in a life and death tug of war with a huge, gray wolf that had vicious blood in its eyes and both of Baruch's feet in its mouth.

"Help me, Isaac, don't just stand there!" Jesse screamed at the boy who appeared in the clearing with a face as white as the snow that would soon to be falling. "Father damn you, get over here!"

Isaac was too scared to move. His feet felt as if they were frozen in place, taking root and driving into the soil. Ice crystallized in his veins, and he was unable to breathe. His brother's face was as red as the rising sun that leaked in jagged edges of crimson through the pine trees.

"Isaac, get your ass over here now!" Jesse screamed, taking his eyes off of the snarling wolf for just one moment to look at his terrified brother.

The wolf used the pause to readjust its grip on Baruch's foot, letting a snarl slip out. After a moment's rest, its mouth was back around the foot with its teeth nearly coming together.

"If you don't hurry it's going to bite his feet off, Isaac!"

Isaac shuffled, impelled by a force beyond himself that yanked him to his older brother's side. He grabbed one of Baruch's arms from his brother and locked himself into their brutal tug of war. Jesse started working a large stone from the muddy clay stream bank with his foot. He kicked water from the stream onto the stone trying to release it from its sticky prison. He brought his foot up and brought it down hard, slipping off the stone's wet surface. His heel caught and the stone came loose, falling into the stream.

"Hold him, Jesse!" Isaac said. He took his cue from his older brother and darted along the stream bank. A large black piece of obsidian jutted upwards from its clay moorings. Isaac got on his hands and knees and pushed on the jagged piece with all of his might. The black glassy rock lost it's anchoring from the silt shore and came loose. It was light and sharp in his hands. He brought it to his brother, who looked to be nearing exhaustion. Jesse looked to Isaac and said, "You do it, Isaac! I'll hold onto Baruch, but not for much longer."

Isaac took aim at the wolf's head. He heaved the stone above his head and looked at the wolf's broad forehead. He looked below, to its eyes full of their nihilistic blackness. Isaac brought his aim to right between the wolf's dead eyes and he heaved the stone from over his head at the fur and flesh target. The stone flew from his hands, tumbling in the air. The momentum caused Isaac to tumble forward onto his face. The wolf yelped and Isaac raised his head to see the wolf stumbling backwards, dazed from the blow of the heavy rock. Jesse leapt forward and kicked the wolf in the head. It yelped again, this time more shrilly than after the first blow. The wolf sank to its haunches. Jesse grabbed the glassy black rock in one hand. He held it high above his head over the wolf.

"Jesse, let it go!" Isaac said on his hands and knees.

"No, brother! Once an animal has the sweet taste of a human in its mouth it can't forget."

The wolf's eyes fluttered briefly. She thought back to her den, through the mists, the chirping of birds, and the buzzing of random flying insects. She tried to run back to the cries of her hungry little ones. She tried to run but her legs wouldn't work.

Jesse brought the stone down squarely on the wolf's head. There was a brittle crack followed by a dull crunch. To Isaac, it sounded like the hulls of wheat under the heavy millstone as he fed wheat through to be crushed into flour for bread. The wolf dropped dead like a branch fallen from a rotting tree. Its black eyes glazed over and reflected the silhouettes of mossy birch trees as the last of its breaths escaped from its lungs.

There was no time to gloat over their victory. Jesse picked Baruch's body up and listened for any breathing. It was faint and he may have only imagined that Baruch's lungs were taking in air as Jesse held his brother's clammy, cold body against him. Jesse started running, whipping past the trees as they shed the first leaves of fall in preparation for the coming of long desolate winter. The boy shambled behind his older brother as fast as he could.

Unlike all the other life of the forest, the humans thought they were the exception to the rule. Did they not accumulate and store over the year to survive the winter? They stored fat on their bodies and food in jars on their shelves. They put on warm blankets and animal skins against the deadly winter chill. The trees dropped their leaves and retreated within themselves, just as the men and women go indoors to sit around the fire and plan the spring's planting. The bear crawls into its burrow to enter stasis, not feeding, but burning the fat that he gained by eating the entire preceding year. The snakes, much like the one that bit Baruch, slither into underground caves to be with thousands of their kind, cold-blooded, sleeping close to each other for warmth. Like the other animals, the humans worked all year to prepare for the winter months. They prepared, or they died. Life was as easy as that.

The women of the Congregation were in full preparation for winter, stockpiling their food stores into neat clay pots, carefully filling them to the top before they put the hot beeswax seal on them to keep the hungry field mice and scheming insects at bay. The women sewed the animal skins that the Congregation boys had butchered after raising them for two full seasons. That day, the only thing out of the ordinary was when the young man and his brother burst into the dining area during the morning meal carrying their ailing middle brother screaming about snakes and wolves.

The stronger of Dam Ruth's two boys, Jesse, carried Baruch's nearly lifeless body past the marble monstrance where the women gathered flour to seal in clay containers with timid beeswax. Dam Ruth screamed when she saw her middle child sprawled on the floor, and she begged her oldest son and her adopted youngest son as to what horror happened to him.

Isaac delivered her worst nightmare between teary sobs, "Baruch got bit. Bit by a snake, momma."

Their mother sprung into action with no time to mourn, for Baruch still coughed and struggled to hold onto life. "I'll go get the Elder Mother," Dam Rachel yelled and ran off down a darkened corridor in search of the one woman amongst them that had to know a cure for snakebite. Soon the entire congregation was taken over by a peculiar hubbub, buzzing frantically like a wild bees nest invaded by marauding ants crazed by honey.

Jesse dragged Isaac over to the corner where they could be obscured by the shadows and hidden by the chaos of the women.

"Where is she? Where is the Elder Mother?!" The women yelled to one another as they fanned out through the corridors searching for the healer and shouted their muffled reports from the various halls and venous passageways, seeping in like blood returning to the heart through valves plugged with clot. As the time passed, the rate at which the shrieking women returned and exited like a flash of drab color slowed, because they were honing in on the Elder Mother's location. The women's arrivals and farewells were punctuated with the sound of their footsteps: hard leather on harder stone like a drum roll. The only constant was their mother weeping over her stricken child, wailing long and slow, stopping to breathe in between sobs. She returned to him after the first alarm and now held his head to her chest, his cold and limp body in her lap, legs spread around him like when she gave him to the world in birth. Baruch's breath was coming barely, if at all; each timid sip of air he took increased her panic, and soon she shook like a sapling in a hurricane.

A nondescript woman, talented in her culinary approaches to feeding the children, but thoroughly histrionic in her attitude to plainness, stumbled from the kitchen carrying several loaves of long bread for the evening meal. The loaves obscured her vision, but when she heard the commotion and exhortations of panic for the old woman's whereabouts, she shouted the solution over the tops of the ryes, marbles, and wheats, "She's in her chamber in bed! Quite sick! She's been there for nearly a week you know!" No one did know. They really only called upon the Elder Mother now when they needed her for a ceremony. An emergency of this nature had not manifested itself since a kick from a recalcitrant mule brained Dam Russell's four-year-old daughter.

From the shadowy corner, Jesse and Isaac watched their mother as she cradled their brother. The candlelight illuminated their frames in its unhealthy, flickering glow and gave form to her despair. Baruch seemed to be at peace, and the sweat on his brow reflected the candle's dying flame. The warped wax candle staves above him oozed pure randomness, melting and cooling into stalactites that dripped to cover the wrought iron candelabra that fastened to the high arched ceiling by means of a long hemp rope.

Isaac focused on his mother, and the tears started to well up in his eyes. He did his best to suppress his urge to cry, but it escaped from him in a whimper: the last cry of a dog that wanted to be let in from the cold but was tired from continual rejection. He felt the stern gaze of his older brother and a sense of shame washed over him, setting his cheeks on fire. His burning spark of his brother's reproach struck him like he was dry tinder. Isaac looked up to his brother and Jesse shook his head in disapproval. Men were not allowed emotion in the Congregation. The men were taught that only the Congregation's females were supposed to blubber at setbacks. Whatever the men did outside of the congregation, they were accountable to themselves only. Their conscience was their only brake. In the forest the men were free. Among the trees they could laugh, stomp their feet in rage, huff and puff and feel as if they were the owners and inheritors of the planet. When they returned to the confines of the buildings were they lived, learned to worship, and pray to the Father, they were accountable to each other. As a boy about to be a man, Jesse had to enforce to his junior that he was supposed to be stone faced at all times. That was what they were taught; it was the way things were.

Emotions were weakness; emotions clouded your judgment, and judgment was all that a man in the Congregation had. His logic was his shield and sword. It was up to him alone to make it as sharp and piercing as possible. His logic guarded him from being battered and buffeted by the flowing stream of time that ground all in its path to muck. It was the goal of every boy of the Congregation to serve his great Glorious Mother in the Council for Defense and Raids. To be one of the men! If he honed his logic, it would serve him well on the Council. To be the Master of the Council, that was the goal of every boy. But first, he would have to remove any vestige of weakness from his face, and with the weakness, emotion. He could feel it inside. Expressing it was forbidden.

Isaac tried to avoid looking at his mother holding his brother. He tried his hardest to avoid it, but like a child who peers through a keyhole into a room that he has been told not to enter upon pains of death, he glanced at his mother's crying. Just a glance, from the corner of his eye, and he looked away quickly again. The pain welled up within him. Sympathy. Concern. Human emotions. He wanted to share her grieving and cry with her. He wanted to run to her and sit by her side. He wanted to remind her that she still had a child that was living. No matter how much he tried to sit there like a rock in the darkness and tell himself he could do nothing for her, he looked again at his mother, and the tears started to flow down his face. He looked to his brother Jesse, who glared at him like death was a better outcome than crying. Isaac stopped his tears like jabbing an iron pickaxe into the base of an enormous cistern overflowing with rainwater. The tears slowed to a trickle, but the pressure behind them built. Tears meandered down his face to his upper lip, pooling on the underside of his nose. There they were dammed, until their numbers were sufficient enough to send them blindly mining the path of least resistance down his face. His cares, lubricated by the waters of emotion washing over him met his will to resist halfway. He turned the corner. The pickaxe dislodged. The cistern emptied out the bottom fed by gravity. Isaac wailed out loud.

"Stop making like a woman, Isaac!" Jesse scolded him.

Isaac would not look at his brother, but instead stared blankly ahead at some cobwebs. One, amongst all the random gossamer threads, was freshly made. He traced the threads to their source, and a tiny brown and white spider about as big as his fingernail laid still as death a few fingers above the floor.

One of Isaac's tears fell from his nose and struck the web, causing it to shudder. The spider bolted into action as if it had captured an unfortunate insect. The tear beaded and was kept a perfect drop of spherical sadness by a combination of the surface tension and the web's natural waterproofing. The spider stopped halfway and waited for further vibrations from the victim. It felt none and hunger forced it to continue its investigation. It crept slowly to the orb. As it shambled, the spider's legs vibrated the web lightly with each step. The perfect sphere pulsed as if it had a heart beat. The teardrop dislodged from its electrostatic anchor and slid down the thread to rest at the spider's feet. It peered at the sphere as if gazing into an alien universe. It spent its life indoors away from the annoyances of drops of dew and rain. It drank the fluids from the gray bodies of victims, but few had fallen into its web. The teardrop's moisture was a gift from a God unknown. The spider sipped from the surface of the teardrop until it was consumed. It sprang silk from its abdomen and repaired the damage the tear wrought on its home and livelihood like a well geared machine.

"I said stop it, Isaac," Jesse admonished his younger brother.

"I can't stop crying, Jesse. I'm scared. I think Baruch's gonna die."

"Are you scared for Baruch, or are you scared for yourself?"

"I'm scared for him. He doesn't look good at all. I don't think he's going to be okay."

"He should be okay, but I don't know. It looks bad to me," Jesse said as he gazed towards his mother gently cradling Baruch.

"Granny will be the ultimate judge of whether he can make it or not. Hopefully the women find her soon."

52

After he made his utterance, a panic arose in Jesse as a vision flooded his mind of the old woman entering the room, full of fury at being aroused from her prayers. She would begin questioning the boys, with her face twisted with accusations of negligence, and his little brother Isaac pointing his finger at Jesse and telling their grandmother everything that he saw Jesse doing in the woods. It was Jesse's fault that Baruch got bitten. Jesse was the one that went out at night and the young boys were just following him. And why did Jesse go out in the woods at night? Why did he give up his purity and sound judgment for a few minutes of grunting out in the forest? It felt good. It felt right. Why did he find her gathering strawberries and what was it she showed him how to do? The first time was all he needed, after that he was hooked. He began to do it like he had been doing it his entire life, like he had been made to do it. He couldn't imagine the horrors the Council of Defense and Raids would subject him to once they got his confession. And what would they do to Isaac? The boy didn't have a chance. His thoughts turned back to himself. In a panic the thoughts shot back to his younger brother. He knew what action to take. The boy was smart and Jesse knew he was loyal. Jesse knew that Isaac would listen to him and would follow his reasoning without question. He would follow Jesse into anything. Besides, if Isaac wouldn't agree, there was always the use of force.

Jesse pulled his brother close to whisper into his ear. Isaac resisted and tried to pull away, but Jesse's grip around his neck compelled him to listen.

"You know, Isaac, they are going to want to know what happened. I'm telling you right now you can't speak a word of what you saw in the forest, little brother," Jesse's words were mixed with just the slightest tinge of panic in his timbre.

"I can't lie to them, Jesse."

"No, Isaac. You can lie to them, and you will lie to them, little brother. Otherwise you know what will happen."

"No, I don't. What's going to happen to you?"

"Don't play stupid, Isaac. You know they won't let me join them. I have to join them, Isaac."

"They are going to know. Besides, I don't want you to leave. If I tell them, you'll be able to stay with us. You'll still be able to play with us."

"No, little brother, you don't know them. You don't know what you're a part of. You have to promise me, little brother. You just forget about everything you saw after you came to get me. You can't say anything about it."

Isaac's face went blank while he thought. Jesse had a look of grave concern in his face that Isaac had never seen before. Isaac's ran his hand through his hair, thinking. The fears that he felt last night about telling his brother Baruch the secrets that Grandmother showed him in the Sanctuary lay dormant on the floor with his stricken brother. They were replaced with a slight fear of having revealed the secret to Jesse as well.

"If you don't tell anyone I told you I went to the Sanctuary, your secret is safe with me."

"And your secret is mine to keep, brother," Jesse said with a smile.

The older man pulled his younger brother in close and whispered into his ear everything he would have to tell them. It was best to get their stories straight now than to fabricate them extemporaneously.

"Isaac, you're gonna say that we were playing out in the woods in the early morning and Baruch ran off and got himself bitten by the snake. He wanted to play a trick on us and he got himself into trouble. He's a troublemaker, Isaac, they'll believe us."

Isaac was always searching for third possibilities, or ways that disregarded the other paths that his brother had already thought of.

"What if Baruch comes out of it, Jesse? What if he gets better? What will we say then?"

The notion struck Jesse as strange: that of Baruch getting better. "What do you mean, Isaac?"

"I mean, what if Baruch comes out of it and tells people a different story. Say he starts talking? He starts saying that you ran off in the middle of the night, and we only wanted to follow you and see what you were doing. Say he says that he knew you were meeting a woman off in the woods?"

Jesse's expression soured. "It doesn't matter, Isaac. If we have the same story they'll believe you and me. Everyone always believes you, Isaac. Baruch will be called a liar."

"I'm not going to say anything about you seeing the Sanctuary, brother. I will keep your secret. I will tell everyone something about you though."

A seed of doubt fell into the fertile soil of Isaac's mind and took root. He enjoyed watching his brother Jesse squirm. Even though he loved him and worshipped the ground he walked on, it was still nice to see the perfect one nearly brought low. Of course Isaac would support his older brother, but what he said next really brought closure to the whole artifice.

"Isaac, listen to me. I know you're a hero."

"What do you mean, Jesse? What did I do?"

"I know you killed the wolf that attacked Baruch. It wanted to eat us all. Even I was scared. The wolf was fierce and hungry. It would have dragged Baruch off and eaten him if it wasn't for you. Sure I helped. But you killed the wolf."

Isaac's face lit up with joy. "You'll say that, Jesse?"

"Yes, I will. From now on you'll be known as Isaac the Wolf Slayer."

"You promise, right, Jesse?" Isaac asked with a cherubic look of hope.

"Yes, Isaac, I promise you."

Isaac embraced his brother, and it lingered. The rest of the people in the room were too focused on their dying brother to pay them any heed. The women continued scurrying around until a great calming force entered the room. The Elder Mother hobbled in carrying her long walking stick. Her withered hands were ensconced in woolen mittens against the chill, though the fingertips were threadbare from years of use. The women settled into one corner of the room, huddled together in a chorus of prayer. When the Elder Mother saw Baruch she yelled, "Oh, my dear boy!"

The brothers broke their embrace and watched the scene unfolding before them. Grandmother bent over the boy, trembling, and held his sweaty head into the light.

"My dear, dear, dear boy, what has happened to you?" She implored.

"He's on fire!" some of the women wailed in unison.

"I must find the proper verse to recite," the Elder Mother said. In her mind she thought she placed *The Gideons* in her belt loop. It had been some time since she looked at the tome, having been sick for weeks. She reached her hand inside her belt loop pocket and found it empty. *Why, that's strange,* she thought to herself, wandering through her mind as to where she could have left it. Then she didn't remember seeing it anywhere. Her wanderings left a sick empty feeling in the pit of her stomach.

"My Father, I don't have *The Gideons*," she said in a soft voice to avoid alerting anyone to her error. "I don't have *The Gideons*," she said louder. Dam Ruth looked up from her dying child, "You must have it! He will die without it! He will die!"

The women in the corner began buzzing like a nest of fierce hornets that had just been pelted with rocks by an unruly child.

The Elder Mother backtracked nearly in a panic, "Don't you worry my dear, eh...I just left it in my hutch at the foot of my bed, you know the cedar one that keeps the moths away...just right where I always put them. I just forgot this time...."

"Grab *The Gideons*!" The women shouted in unison and departed, dashing towards the Elder's quarters. Granny's face calmed, she was sure *The Gideons* were there. She looked at Baruch who did not appear to be breathing very much at all.

"You must hold on, Baruch, you have to wait. You have to stay with us until your Grandmother uses *The Gideons* to deliver you from the evil you suffer from. You must stay with us, boy."

She reached down and touched his sweaty forehead again. His skin felt like the fires of Hell. He was being slow cooked to death. The serpent's poison was probably burning a hole into his heart. The Elder Mother turned and yelled down the corridor, "Make haste, children! Bring me that book!" The remainder of the time she waited, the Elder Mother paced back and forth tapping her walking stick on the ground.

The women returned shortly with exasperated looks on their faces. "We couldn't find it!"

"That's nonsense. If it wasn't in the cedar chest, I had to have left it on the table next to my bed."

"We tore your room apart and searched it so that not even a bookworm, let alone a book, could escape us. We swear to you, it's not there."

"Well, dear Father. My goodness. I will just have to perform the healing ritual without its aid."

Dam Ruth began shrieking. "My boy is going to die!"

"No, he won't! I have the ritual memorized," the Elder Mother said with a hint of reproach in her voice.

The Elder Mother reached with her bony arm, and with a strength that seemed unnatural for a woman of her advanced age, she ripped the mother's arm from around her ailing son. She pointed her finger towards the wall where the other women stood murmuring amongst themselves and looking with sideways glances. Dam Ruth obediently took her place amongst the other women, shuffling her feet and walking crook-backed and defeated. The women welcomed her with open arms and each took turns consoling her, telling her not to worry, that all would be good with the Father. He was in good, experienced hands. But their faces were still marked with worry because the old woman was without her instrument. She had misplaced the cornerstone of their society. What should have been treated with utmost care and concern was lost by her. If she couldn't remember the passage to deliver the boy from the snake bite, Baruch was doomed.

The Elder Mother looked to the women and sighed. All of their eyes were on her and their burning glances singed her ego. If she failed, the women would blame her and hold her age and infirmity against her in the eyes of the Glorious Mother. The Glorious Mother would poison her image when she communicated with the Father, and the Elder Mother could be robbed of her very life. She had to perform now and perform well.

"My Father, who dwells in Heaven, Your name is praised; Your glorious name is praised throughout the world as the source of all goodness. Deliver you good creation from its suffering. Deliver us from the evils of this world to which we are bound. Grant me the wisdom to cure this precious child through your workings."

Some of the women in the corner began to sob. They sounded like a great flock of water birds, echoing each other's warbles with more elaborate warbles and caws designed to outstrip the other's grief with their own. By far the most talented crier was Dam Ruth.

The Elder Mother continued, "The Father provides us the sustenance of our lives and keeps our enemies at bay. He protects us against the Firmament of the wild, evil world in which we find ourselves. Like our ancestors whom He harvested up, the pure unbroken winter wheat of the plain, we seek His discerning hand. We seek His judgment upon us, His deliverance from our cares."

The old woman raised her head towards the ceiling as if she were looking for a hole to Heaven. With her arms outstretched, her fingers spaced close together, her hands forming a knife edge, she brought her hands against her knees several times with violence.

Isaac and Jesse had never seen their Grandmother behave in this way, but she looked like she had done this several times.

After she thrust her hands against he bony pelvis five times, their Grandmother nearly injured herself. Her bones were old and brittle. She decided not to hit herself nearly as hard in the future when the ritual called for self-castigation.

"Father! Deliver this boy from his suffering!" she said as she brought the knife edges down into her pelvis gingerly. She raised her arms to the ceiling again and formed the knife edge with her fingers. This time she paused slightly, as if she were gathering her strength.

"Father, I implore you! Deliver this child from his suffering!"

She brought the knife edges down into her pelvis like she was kneading her hands into the coarse dough that the women of the Congregation used to bake bread. She did it for effect, as her hands and pelvis were throbbing with pain now. Tears streamed down her face, because Baruch was not moving.

"Father! This child must live!"

She brought her hands down once, twice, three times, each time diminishing the force of her blow even further, looking to see if the admonitions had any effect on the boy's condition. Baruch remained perfectly still, at peace. His chest no longer rose and fell in a struggle for life.

"You must save him!" Granny screamed bringing her arms up again for another blow to her pelvis. "You must save him!"

She hit herself harder. She brought her arms up and flung them into her midsection, nearly taking the wind out of herself. Tears began streaming down her face at her futility. The boy remained completely still: white as snow.

"My Father! You cannot abandon Your child!"

She brought her arms down against her pelvis so hard that she doubled over and fell to the ground sobbing and screaming, *"The Gideons*…my Father…I need *The Gideons!"*

The women in the corner room ran to the stricken child beating their chests and wailing. No one comforted the Elder Mother, who lay in heap next to Baruch's corpse. One of the younger women felt the boy's neck for a pulse. Her fingers were met with absolute tranquility.

"He is dead. The boy is dead!" She said with much bravado to the crowd.

*

The remainder of the day, instead of preparing the Congregation for the winter time, the women prepared Baruch's body for transport to the Sanctuary. In a room apart from the children, the women anointed the body with fragrant oils, while they sang sorrowful hymns to themselves.

Isaac listened to the women from outside the barred door, but was not allowed in. It was not right for children to see the dead. He thought back to how Baruch had tormented him unceasingly, but he was sorry that his brother was dead. Soon Jesse would be taken from him, too. He thought of his future. He would be all alone with his mother. He had to be strong for her. He had to take care of her now, until it was his turn to be an adult. But these people wouldn't let him. It was his damn cursed foot. The swirling in his mind began. He had to make up for his foot. It was impossible for him to get a new one. His mind kept whirling, gaining new energy as he went back to the original thought, back to thinking about his foot, back to the catalyst. He started pacing back and forth at the front door. Each time he passed it, he wanted to knock. He wanted to knock and announce himself to them. When was Jesse going to give them the good news that he had killed the wolf? Was it even important now that Baruch died? Would they care? Isaac only knew one thing; they had to pay attention to him!

He grew tired of waiting to tell his mother and Grandmother the exploits of the day. He wanted to tell them how he killed the wolf that was trying to drag Baruch into the forest and eat him. The dust storm of his wants met up against his natural quiet and restraint, which took all the energy out of him. The dust storm settled to coat all of his memories and hopes in the fine grained blackness. He started to sulk back to his room. As he walked, the thought crossed his mind, *Maybe I will just leave them all, and they will all be sorry. They will all cry over me like they are crying over Baruch right now. Only I'll be alive and living somewhere far away from them. Having my own adventures.* Isaac got into his bed, and the tears flowed from his eyes uncontrollably. He cried in silence. It would be easy to leave them. He cried for his brother, Baruch. He thought again, that all he had to do was walk out the door. He looked over to Jesse's bed through his translucent teary curtains. Jesse left a few hastily stuffed sacks of potatoes in his bed to throw off anyone glancing into the room. They were too bulky and would have come off like an obese version of Jesse. It would never pass for him, even in the darkness. Isaac rose and ran to his brother's bed. He adjusted the potato sacks so it looked more like his brother.

Jesse was in a pantry rummaging. He filled a sack full of breads and salted meats for his lover. The Congregation had more than enough food and the miniscule portions he stole would not be missed. He made haste because she would be waiting. He stopped and looked in on his younger brother who appeared to be sleeping. He turned to go and Isaac called out, "Jesse, please be careful."

Jesse stood in the doorway and waved to his little brother. "I will, Isaac. I will be back before the morning. You sleep well," he said as he turned to go.

Jesse slipped out of the children's quarters bound for his forest meeting place. He carried the bag of food over his shoulder, and it bounced up and down as he strode off powerfully, with the excitement rushing from his head, filling his lungs, and burning straight down to his midsection with each step that brought him closer to his desire.

*

The room where the women were wailing was converted many generations ago in the past from a kitchen that had been used to prepare communal feasts to its present function of storing the dead until they could be transported to the Sanctuary for the ritual. The Elder Mother sat in the nook of a corner window, ostracized from the rest of the preparations. She watched the younger women and paused briefly to gaze out the window at the forest. That night, while the preparations were coming to a close and the women were drying the remainder of their tears, the Elder Mother looked out the window with sleepy eyes. Then she saw it. It ran across the field toward the forest from the children's quarters. In the moonlight she swore she witnessed a hunchback galloping off towards the forest. *Just what was that?* the old woman thought to herself. She blinked once, and the figure was gone, leaving nothing but the obscure black and white shapes protruding in the darkness. *Its my damned old useless eyes*, the elderly woman thought. She pulled her face from the window, and thought, *I have to talk to those children tomorrow and find out just what happened in those woods. Things aren't making sense anymore.*

The position of the Elder Mother was invaluable to the Congregation. She was not beautiful enough to have ever been the Glorious Mother, but she was wise, which befit the role of the Elder Mother. She was a good teacher to the children, but she noticed that some of the women started looking at her with scorn. *The Gideons* had been passed from one Elder Mother to the next since the beginning of their people, and now she had lost it. But perhaps the hunchback stole *The Gideons*? Perhaps he had been lingering in dark corners of the congregation for years stealing things that were left out. Stranger things had happened in her life. Still she knew that she made a mistake. A little boy died because of her negligence. She had to make up for it. In the morning she would question the children about what had happened in the forest. She would start with the little lame one first. He was her favorite. He loved her with all of his heart and would tell her anything she wanted to know. It would have to happen in the morning. Now she was tired and longing for her bed.

Isaac woke in the morning as the sun crested over the tightly bunched forest trees. He sat up in his bed and began to stretch, looking over to his brother's bed to see if it was filled with a potato sack or if his brother had returned during the night from his wanderings. Isaac was relieved to see the potato sack thrown into the corner and his brother sleeping in the bed with his muscular arm thrown over his eyes to shield out the sunlight. He snored, intermittently mixed with sighs and moans.

Suddenly, the door to the children's quarters slammed open. Two large men dressed in red robes with looks of murder on their faces burst into the room. The taller man had dark brown hair and wore a purple sash intermeshed with golden thread across his chest. The shorter of the two had hair as black as midnight and about two days growth of a beard. He was carrying a large bucket of water. Isaac gasped. He had never seen a full grown man; his brother had always been the closest approximation. Two more men dressed in bright red stood at the entrance with their arms crossed. One of them looked into the room with the same vacant look of *I'll kill you if you speak.* The tall man brought his finger to his mouth to tell Isaac to be quiet and whispered, "We've come to gather your brother to join us, it is time for his days of struggle." He then nodded to the smaller man, who raised the heavy bucket chest high and poured it our over Jesse.

"Wake up, little brother!" the man screamed.

Jesse jumped from the bed naked with his head drenched, drops of water dripping down his face and cascading down his genitals. He drew his fists, looking for a fight. He knew from the very beginning that he had to fight. If he didn't fight they might think him soft. The small man drew a dark black club from his waistband and held it shoulder high, tossing it from hand to hand, goading Jesse in striking him. Jesse feinted with his left hand and struck the man with a powerful blow that sent him reeling onto the balls of his feet. He moved in to knock the man down when the large, powerful man grabbed him in a bear hug with his massive arms.

The man laughed as he crushed Jesse against his chest, "Got some fight in you, boy? That's good. You're coming with us though. You've got no choice."

The color started to depart Jesse's face as he continued kicking his legs in an attempt to escape.

"That's it, my boy," the man said. "Not so tough now are we? Don't worry my son, you soon will be."

Jesse's eyes rolled back into his head and the enormous man dropped him to the ground. "Cease!" he yelled to the two men at the door.

The men left their posting at the door and bundled Jesse into a large burlap sack and carried him out the door. As they walked out the door, the enormous man flashed Isaac a smile as cold as steel left outdoors in the wintertime and said, "Mind your mother, son."

Isaac stared at the man's dead black eyes, too scared to talk. He listened to their heavy footsteps as they ran to the hallway and heard the door to the outside open and then slam.

His grandmother entered the room with her walking stick in hand. She had a curious look on her face, as if she had to tell Isaac something of great importance. But the look melted the closer she got to the boy's bed. As she walked forward, she tapped her stick on the stone floor and the tapping echoed off the walls.

"My boy, you do know what happened this morning, right?"

"The men, they came to get Jesse. But, I don't understand," Isaac said.

"It is not your place to understand, but you must know that you will never see your brother, Jesse, again."

"I am alone then," Isaac said and started to cry. He had not fully grieved for his brother Baruch, and now his brother Jesse was taken from him. The shock and violence of the morning struck him like a heavy boulder dropped onto the parched earth.

"Don't cry, Isaac. You mustn't ever cry. It is our way."

"I'm alone now, Grandmother. I've lost Jesse. I've lost my brother, Baruch."

"Well you are alone boy, but there will be other children for you to play with."

"I don't want to play with the other children. I'm sick of playing with children. I want to be a man."

"I'm afraid that is impossible, my boy. The men, you just saw them. They will never accept you."

"You will stay with the women and help with the children."

"What you women do is boring to me. I want to have adventures, Grandmother."

"I'm sorry, my boy, but you weren't made for adventures. This world beyond the walls of the Congregation, you don't understand it. It's not a place for either women or a boy with impairment. It's a nasty and dangerous place full of rogues. Everywhere is at war, my boy. If you're going to survive, you'll have to stay with us women."

"I don't want to…."

"You must, Isaac. Now enough about that, I have to talk to you about something. Get dressed and come to my chambers."

"Yes Grandmother, as you wish," Isaac said.

The ancient woman rose from sitting at the edge of Isaac's bed and shuffled out the door, tapping her walking stick on the floor ahead of her as if to feel out the divots of the stone lest she trip on one of them. As she departed, she looked back to the child whose face was red with shame.

Isaac sat in bed thinking. He stared at his feet underneath the covers. He stared hard at the wider fuzzy shape and attempted to move his feet in unison. The smaller foot made wide swathes under the gray woolen blanket. The larger foot barely budged. He looked at the feet in disgust. *Why do they allow me to live then? If I'm so awful why did they allow me to live when I was born? They should have just pitched me out into the forest.* He looked to his feet again, and a thought crept into his mind that he never felt before; it was utterly foreign, but it struck him like a bolt of lighting. *I want them all to die, then I will be able to live in peace. All of these people that judge me everyday that think I am freak, I want them to die. Just like I wanted Baruch to die. It happened.*

He shuddered and beat the thought back from his mind, scolding himself internally for thinking it. Then, he felt very guilty. He wanted to remain in bed all day long, but remembered that his Grandmother requested him.

He put his coarse burlap clothing on and fastened his leather shoe. He put the leather bag that the women had fashioned for him over the monstrosity, or the sight of his foot may have made them all sick to their stomachs. He shambled to the Elder Mother's quarters. As he walked, the forgotten totem that Jesse's woman had given him became loose in his belt, and the twine unwound all the way to the floor. The little leather man dragged behind Isaac for the last two steps before he came to his Grandmother's door. He grabbed the heavy knocker and pounded as hard as he could.

When his Grandmother opened the door, she saw Isaac, with his face still red with shame at what he had thought. She believed that the discussion they had earlier was still troubling him.

"You aren't still upset at what we talked about, are you? Are you troubled by Baruch's passing, honey? He is in a better place, dear."

"I'm not upset, Grandmother. It is the Father's will for me. It is the Father's will for Jesse. It is the Father's will for Baruch. No one can argue with the Father's will."

"Oh you are so wise, my boy. That is why you have always been your Grandmother's favorite."

"I know, Grandmother," Isaac quipped with a face as blank as a snow covered plain.

"You know? What kind of way is that to talk to your only Grandmother? You should thank me, my boy."

"Thank you, Grandmother," Isaac stated monotonously with the same blank stare. He looked at the wall past her shoulder to avoid staring into her eyes.

"Isaac, I'm very concerned about you. I'm concerned that so much has happened to you in the past few days that you may not be able to handle all of the changes you've witnessed."

"I'll be fine, Grandmother. If this is what the Father planned for me, I'll accept it."

"That is the thing, Isaac. I want to make sure you've been following the Father's will for you. Why do you think the Father has heaped all of this suffering on you right now? You haven't done anything recently that you wouldn't want the Father to see you doing, have you?"

Isaac searched his memories for anything he did that might have offended the Father. The only thing he could think of was being born with the lumpy misshapen foot, but that was not his doing. If it was anyone's fault, it was the Father's fault.

"My boy, I talked to your brother about what happened in the woods. He told me the reason that Baruch died."

Isaac piped up with the concocted story, confident that Jesse had stuck to their plan, "Baruch ran off by himself, and we told him to stop playing games; we told him to come back."

Isaac looked at his Grandmother for any reassurance that the story he told matched what his brother Jesse said. He did not receive any, because the lady continued looking straight into his eyes. He continued talking, "Last we heard was Baruch screaming and hollering. I don't know how the kid ran so fast ahead of us. We had to skirt a big briar patch before we found him."

"Yes, Jesse mentioned something about a big briar patch, too," the old lady said, and brought her wrinkled hands up to her chin to scratch it.

"We got up there, and Baruch was on the ground and there was this wolf on him trying to grab him."

"My goodness, what did you boys do?!"

Isaac smiled, realizing it was his chance to shine, confident that his brother told her that he killed the wolf. It was his chance to be a hero.

"We fought the wolf, Grandmother! Jesse hit the wolf hard, and it got stunned, and I smashed its head with a rock!" Isaac said, smiling at his Grandmother, waiting for a sign of recognition. He wondered if his Grandmother would spread the news around the Congregation after their meeting. He was going to be a hero. He looked in her face for a sign of amazement but there was none, only cold calculation.

"Isaac, when was Baruch bitten by the snake?"

"It must have been before we got there."

"Were there some stream near this briar patch you found him in, Isaac?"

Isaac paused, thinking.

"Were there any sort of puddles around?"

"What do you mean, Grandmother?"

"Water, Isaac! Why are you having difficulty with this question, Isaac? Either there was water there or there wasn't!"

Isaac spit out the answer, "Yes, Grandmother, there was a stream right there. I think Baruch tried to cross it when the snake bit him."

"That's strange, my boy. Your brother Jesse told me that Baruch was behind the briar patch and the snake that bit him was one with a rattle tail."

Isaac gulped in nervousness. The two hadn't thought about their story in that amount of detail.

"Yes, Grandmother, it probably was one with a rattle tail. I didn't see it. Maybe Jesse did."

"Do you think your Grandmother is stupid, boy?"

"What?" Isaac asked in shock.

His grandmother leaned forward in her chair to look the boy right in the eyes. She stared hard at him.

"Do you think your Grandmother is stupid?"

"No, I don't, Grandmother," Isaac said, the nervousness rising in his tone of voice.

"Then why do you keep lying to your Grandmother?"

"I'm not lying."

"My boy, you are lying. You know you're lying to me. Why are you lying to me?" she asked still leaning forward. "I have been the Elder Mother of this Congregation for nearly seventy five seasons, my boy. How old are you?"

Isaac thought for a second and said the number, "Fourteen."

"That means that your Grandmother has been performing the duties of the Elder mother of this congregation for a full sixty years...uh...sixty one years before you were born."

Isaac fidgeted. The string began to work its way from his belt.

"Who taught you about the Mocha Assassin snake, Isaac?"

"You did, Grandmother."

"Do you think that I don't know what poisoning by a Mocha Assassin looks like? Do you think I don't know the difference between the bite marks of one snake and the next? Do you think I haven't treated little careless boys who were bitten by the rattle tail snakes?"

Isaac wanted to run from the room, but he had nowhere to go. He had to face down his Grandmother. "I suppose you know the difference, Grandmother."

"I do, Isaac."

"What sort of snake was Baruch bitten by, Isaac?"

"I don't know, Grandmother. I didn't see the snake."

Anxiety caused Isaac to rock back and forth in his chair. His motion caused his Grandmother to concentrate on his hips, and she noticed the small bit of twine wrapped around his belt. Her face remained calm. Then her expression began to change, and her mouth twitched a bit. She took a deep breath to try and dissipate some of the steam that was building in her. The breaths did not help. She exploded.

"Just what is that?" she screamed.

"What, Grandmother?" Isaac said in shock.

She ripped herself from her chair and grabbed the bit of twine. Isaac saw the twine and his heart sank. She began following it to its source; hand over hand followed the twine.

"Just what is it you've got tied to you, boy?"

"Nothing!"

"No you've got something tied to you."

Isaac bent over trapping her arm. He fished the tiny man from beneath the chair and held it in his hands.

"Damn you, boy, let go of your Grandmother's arm." She adjusted her cloak from the battle and smiled at him. "Give me what you have in your hands, boy," she said.

She pried his fingers apart easily because he did not put up any resistance. The tiny leather man fell into her hands.

"Just what the hell have you got here?"

She looked at it and gasped.

"Where the hell did you get this, boy?"

"In the woods."

"Dear Father, boy, where in the woods?"

"Jesse told you about the wolf, right?"

"Boy, tell me where you got this?!"

"Grandmother, what did he tell you?"

She laughed, "You kill a wolf, boy? Why, you couldn't crush a nit from your bedding!" She looked to the small totem man again, "He told me he fought while you cowered behind the briars like a child."

"No, Grandmother! I stunned the wolf and he killed it! That's the truth! I didn't run and hide, Grandmother! I didn't!"

"You tell me where you got this, Isaac!" She said holding the evidence in front of him.

Isaac looked as stupid as a convict who had saved the executioner time by volunteering to help him sharpen his axe at the whetstone.

"You tell your Grandmother the truth. Don't be like your brother, Jesse. Don't be a liar. You tell your Grandmother where you got this and what happened."

"Jesse went out into the forest in the middle of the night, and Baruch and I followed him."

"Yes, where did he go?"

"He was way ahead of us so we had to catch up to him. But we got stopped at a stream. We looked for a place to cross the stream, and that's when the Mocha Assassin bit Baruch." Isaac began to cry, "It jumped up and bit him. I started screaming for Jesse. I tried to get to him as fast as I could Granny. I swear I did!" He broke down further into tears.

The Elder Mother soothed the boy as best as she could, with reassuring tones, "I know you did, grandson. You have always done your best."

"Where did you find Jesse?"

"I found him in a briar patch. He was with a woman."

The Elder Mother sat forward in her chair. Her jaw dropped.

"What where they doing, Isaac?"

"Jesse was wrestling her. They were both naked."

"Really?" his Grandmother said, her cheeks starting to glow with rage. "How long did they wrestle for?"

"They stopped when I came."

"What did she look like?"

"She was pretty, I guess. She wore animal skins."

"Animal skins, how gross," his Grandmother said.

"And this woman, she gave you the little leather man?"

"Yes, Grandmother."

His Grandmother shook her head, breathing deeply, trying to clear her mind of the images that flooded through it. She put the leather man in her pocket.

"And then when we returned to Baruch he was getting attacked by the wolf, and I threw a rock and hit the wolf in its head, and Jesse killed it...that's the truth, Grandmother."

"Yes, I know, my boy, that's quite enough. You're free to go."

"You believe me?"

The Elder Mother was concentrating so hard on blotting the imagery from her mind that she forgot how she convinced her Grandson Isaac to speak the truth to her.

"Yes, your brother told me the same things last night."

Isaac looked at her crossly but her head was down.

"When did you talk to him, Grandmother?"

"After you went to bed, my dear," she said with a smile.

Isaac started to back out the door, not taking his eyes from the woman. Jesse went out on his escapades the night before, there was no way the old woman could have talked to him. Isaac was starting to feel sick at how easily she had duped him. He looked at her. He would never allow himself trust her again. The people who actually loved him in the Congregation were slowly being whittled away to none. Still he had one last question for her, which he asked with a hint of malice that she did not detect, "When does Jesse become a man, Grandmother?"

"Oh it depends, Isaac."

"On what?"

"If he passes the men's tests, but he probably will. He probably will."

"What tests do the men have?"

"I don't know; that's for the men to know. It will take a few days at the most, then everyone will go to his Joining Ceremony."

"Everyone but me."

"Yes, Isaac, you and the children."

"You'll go?"

"Yes, my dear. I have a surprise for your brother, Jesse," the old woman said half paying attention, half lost in her plans for the future. All she knew is that it had to be big and dramatic. Her favorite Grandson had helped her more than he could possibly know. Her head remained downwards, staring at the table, with visions flashing before her on the wood grained surface. She was so lost in thought and plans that she did not notice her grandson storm out of the room dragging his useless foot behind him.

Jesse awoke bruised and bleeding from one eye on the edge of a circular room. A single beam of sunlight streamed through an oculus. His head ached like the smash of a blacksmith's hammer against molten steel. He took a few deep breaths, and the oxygen in his lungs alerted his mind to how much pain he was in. He shook from his head all the way down to his behind. Jesse blinked twice to adjust his eyes to the dim light. He was naked.

In the dusty haze he saw he was only one person among a very large number of young men, all in various states of consciousness. Some moaned and tossed about on the metal floor. Jesse recognized a young man that he used to play with before Baruch and Isaac were born. The young man was kept very sheltered by his mother and not allowed to go off adventuring in the woods. He was much smaller than Jesse, almost Isaac's size. He looked more a boy than a man about to undergo the trials.

Jesse touched his old friend, Robert's, naked torso. He shook it gingerly and received no response. He shook him more vigorously. Robert exploded backwards like he was being jabbed with a spear. His face was covered in welts and bruises. The men who escorted him to his trial had a bit of fun with him, given his small stature.

"Stop touching me!" Robert screamed into the darkness.

"I was just waking you up," Jesse said.

Robert looked around like a timid, little mouse trapped in a corner. His breathing was short and rapid like the heartbeat of a shrew. He reeked of fear.

"Where are we?" Robert asked.

"No idea. Are you scared?"

"Yes, aren't you?"

"No. You shouldn't be scared; we're here to become men."

"I miss home."

"Your mom kept you indoors too much. Now you can get out and have adventures."

"She took care of everything for me."

"Too much of everything."

"I miss my home. Don't you?"

"I'm here to be a man. My home is nothing to me now. Taking care of the home is for the women. We're men. We're here to take care of the women."

"I guess. You know where we are?"

"We're underground. I think it's the training area."

"Let's wake the others so we can get started," Robert said.

The young men did not know right then, but they would soon wish that they let everyone sleep off their bruises and pains.

One of the captives screamed for his mother when the pair woke him, making the other young men giggle. "Quiet down," Jesse ordered them.

The boy, with caked blood on his forehead and a busted, blood spattered nose that screamed *I told you so*, started muttering to himself as he regained consciousness. It started off barely audible and slowly grew into a crescendo. The stress of the morning had already overwhelmed him. "What did I do?" he repeated to himself over and over rocking back and forth. Jesse looked to the other young men, who were now huddled together warming their naked flesh, in the light that poured through the oculus, clutched together like a nest of baby mice, sheltered for a moment from the fear that pervaded them. Only one remained in the darkness: the boy rocking himself and shitting himself and now screaming to himself.

"Dear Father, please help me…oh, what did I do?"

His voice kept skipping out of the darkness. The young men implored him to come into the light. "Get over here! You didn't do anything, just come over here into the light with us!"

"Father, we are all going to die down here!"

"Shut up! You don't know that!"

"We're going to die down here! Just like him!"

The chamber flooded with a bright light. All the young men shielded their eyes. The light dimmed and the young men saw that the entire circumference surrounding them was lined with men dressed in long crimson robes. Each man had a large hood covering his face. Some of the men had beards that jutted beneath their hoods: black and pointy. The screamer gasped and scooted on his ass toward the center to join the rest of the young men. The screamer was correct that someone had died. He passed by the naked body of a young man that did not move. Whoever the young man was, the rest of the men could see only one thing: his head had been bashed in.

Two robed men stepped forward: one was the biggest of the group, and one undoubtedly the smallest. When they stood together, the short hunched man fondly looked up to the other man as if the big man was his master, and he was just a dog on a leash.

The big man spoke, "You are all going to die down here unless you realize that you are no longer individuals."

The short hunched man paced back and forth. The young men could see that his face was awry, for when he turned to the right it appeared he was smiling, and when he turned to the left, his face was contorted into a vicious snarl. He spoke in a voice that modulated in its pitch randomly, like the voice of a madman.

"My little ones, do not listen to the big man," the little impish man said as he paced toward the big man. "You are all miserable little weaklings and will perish just like your friend!"

A spotlight shone on the corpse of the dead boy. His head looked as if it had taken a blow from a heavy mallet. Blood and brains painted the ground in front of him. The children in the crowded center gasped. The spotlight faded. The little imp paced towards the area of the room where the light butted up against the darkness facing his body so he spoke out of the side of his face fixed in a smile.

"You boys will all die like your friend here, who was so weak that he did not even take the first step into manhood before the weakness overtook him."

The big man spoke with his arms crossed in front of him in mocking restraint, "Do not pay attention to Sambus. Look at him: this deformed little troll. He's only here to goad you into quitting, and mind me, young men, *if you quit, you will die.*"

Sambus turned to the young men so that his full countenance with the facial harmony of mocking happiness and repulsive abhorrence stretched across his scarred lips.

"My children you will die, because you are weaklings. None of you will survive. This is the most pathetic group of boys I have ever seen. We would have done better to look outside the Congregation for warriors, maybe bought some of the children from the neighboring villages, rather than test you."

"Do not pay this mutant any heed, men. Whatever he tells you, do not believe him. You are of us; you are the fruit of our loins. You are the strongest young men in the world. Believe that, and you will prevail."

Sambus retorted, "Take a look at your friend, little children. He is peaceful now. His troubles are over. His brains have leaked onto the floor. He will not have to struggle any more. Don't you want to join him? Don't you want an easy death over a life of pain and hardship? That is what you are looking towards when you join us, children. You are best to choose death."

Sambus turned so that his face was contorted to a smile, "When the sunlight departs and you are surrounded by darkness, and your spirit wanes with your last hopes of any future, and your own children are crushed under the boots of your enemies in front of your eyes, and your women impaled by their long spears, then you will know what it is to suffer. My children, my precious little children, you have not even begun to know suffering."

The large man took his turn, "My sons, you must suffer now so that our people will never know true suffering as Sambus described. You will suffer now so that suffering can be overcome and mastered in the future. You will suffer as men so that your sons can have a place in the world."

The imp took his turn, "No. No. No. I have said no, never, to you three times. You will fail. Your kind will become extinct. You will not even live on in the songs sung by your women who will be singing praises to their new men, used and run through by whomever wants to have their turn. They will become wide open fields for plowing. Whomever wants to sow their seed will have a go," while the imp said these words he licked his lips and made short then long thrusting movements with his hips, "Your children, burned in piles, will scream in agony for their fathers who were overcome by fear: you, their cowardly fathers, who shit themselves in the face of the enemy and were slain. No one will eulogize you, for no one ever laments the weak. You will rot under the burning sun."

The large man, the voice of calm, the master trainer, the Head of the Council for Defense and Raids breathed heavily as if he had a tremendous burden to bear. He looked at the mass of naked youth in front of him, clinging to the order of sunlight and each other and told them, "The trials of your young lives will begin in a few minutes. In these trials you will decide your future. Will it be a short future or a long future marked with glory and honor? You will distinguish yourselves, but know that you must work together in order to be victorious."

The imp rebutted again, for the voice of doubt creeps into the best-laid plans and intentions after the fact. "You are all alone. You must fight and struggle alone. Your comrades will abandon you. Your fighting will be futile. If you wish, when the lights come on, you can arm yourselves with whatever weapons you can find. These weapons will be dull and useless and offer you no aid in your defense. You will find them in the barrels, which will thrust up from the floor. If they ever come."

The Council Head laughed heartily at the little imp and flashed the young men a calming smile, he raised his arms to them as if welcoming them to the fold. "Pay this wanton fear no heed, arm yourselves, and battle well, my sons. The battle cares not for outcomes; you either fight until you die or your enemy dies. It is the simplest thing in life. Fight like you are dead already and you will know no fear."

The robed men departed in silence through a passageway that closed behind them. The oculus in the ceiling began to close, and the sunlight dimmed slowly as if a great solar eclipse were happening. In the huddle, panicked grimaces overtook faces painted red with the fading sunlight. At the periphery there was jostling and pushing to remain in the light. Unyielding fear gave way to screaming. The cover clanked and ratcheted shut with a dull thud. All was black.

Blackness. Jesse felt the warm but shivering bodies of his fellow combatants all around him. He did not know if they were cold or afraid. He felt nothing. No fear. No anticipation. A glowing Sambus walked toward their huddle tossing a large dagger from hand to hand. When the light flickered, Sambus flickered. When the imp came within striking distance, Jesse swung with a haymaker that should have sent the little man reeling, but he connected with air. The force of his blow caused him to lose his balance and fall on the floor. Laughter erupted in the room. Disembodied laughter cacophanied off the metal walls.

Sambus spoke, "You don't think I'd be so foolish as to be in there with you, boys? I am in the safety of my control room. What you see is my image. I will watch you from here and offer you my advice. The test is about to begin." The little imp crossed his arms, and a look of anticipation came over his double-edged face. "Arm yourselves, my little ones! Make haste!"

The floor opened in front of them and a barrel sprung forth. The young men huddled around it and Jesse began passing out swords to the men who fought and clawed at their chance at a weapon.

Jesse heard scurrying from the passageway, which opened before them. Several pairs of red eyes penetrated the blackness, like pinpricks in the fabric of Hell. Jesse breathed hard and tried to calm himself. Some of the other young men had seen the eyes. They shuddered as the demon of fear stroked their minds with its barbed fingers. The smell of shit hit Jesse's nostrils. One of the young men was now lying on the ground in the fetal position. He had already been conquered and had given up. He rocked back and forth, and the liquid crap ran from his ass to his legs.

"Get up, man!" Jesse screamed to him.

Destroyed by fear, the boy did not respond. Some of the other young men looked at the terrified boy on the ground and started to breathe heavily. Jesse could hear that when they exhaled, they carried some of their growing anxiety with them in the form of a cat-like whimper. With each second of the red eyes staring at them, the fear grew. Someone had to take charge of the situation, or panic would spread and cripple the entire group.

"Lock arms!" Jesse ordered them. Only a few of the young men complied. "Father, damn you! Lock your arms together!" More of the young men moved into line with renewed sense of purpose. They joined arms to present a larger shape to whatever it was lurking in the passageway. The light above them flickered, and the scurrying came to a halt. Jesse looked down his line. The boys still breathed hard, but their intensity seemed directed more outwards toward their unknown enemy than inwards upon themselves in terror. Robert looked at Jesse, and Jesse nodded to him that they were now ready for anything.

A giant rat exploded from the passageway with murder in its starved red eyes. It bounded toward the center of the room brought on by the smell of easy flesh. It stopped for a moment at the quaking child on the floor and called to its fellows.

The boys screamed to each other, "Kill it!" It was too late. Three more of the giant rodents shot from the passageway and landed on the terrified child. He came out of his catatonia only to scream before the starving beasts ripped his guts out. The third silenced his scream by gnashing his throat with such vigor that the boy's head flipped off into the black distance trailed by a geyser of blood. The rats set about greedily stripping the flesh of the meatier portions of his body. They arched their heads in the flickering light to force to meat down their gullets. It was eat as fast as you can as much as you can, the rule of ratdom.

When Jesse was four years old, his mother told him a story about a rat that broke into the Congregation nursery. The woman watching the babies sat in the next room and thought the child was fussing. She only ran in to check when the baby screamed like it was being parboiled. The black monster covered the little one's precious face and it was too late. The child's face was chewed. The Elder Mother did her best to save the babe, but *The Gideons* did not work. The filthy rat's mouth had poisoned the child's wounds, which crept into its bloodstream. Jesse was terrified of rats until the women launched a campaign to hunt down rats and destroy them. Jesse accompanied the women as they opened up the dark places and surprised the nursing mothers. He laughed when they drowned the rats in barrels of rainwater. He giggled when his mother told him to smash the babies, pink and naked like a fat man's fingers, between a pair of flat rocks. When he pressed the rocks together the popping sound made him laugh with joy. He was no longer scared of rats, and these rats were no different.

"Take them!" Jesse shouted. He advanced towards the gorging rats weighed down by boy flesh.

The other young men followed him, raising their swords and screaming in imitation of their leader. Jesse ran upon the first rat, which was too content on eating to see the sword blow aimed at its head. Jesse sliced the head from the rat with one blow, and its body shot upwards in shock and bounded a few feet towards the passageway on muscles twitching in randomness.

"Hit their heads! They come off easily!" Jesse yelled to the rest of the warriors who charged forward flung by a new force. Robert kicked one of the rats in the midsection and slashed its spine with his sword, crippling it. The rat attempted to drag its useless hind legs back to the passageway but another one of the invigorated young men pierced its skull with his sword and impaled its brain. The other warriors paired up to hack and slash the rats to bits.

Sambus reappeared again with his arms spread wide. "One of you has fallen, my little children. A boy succumbed to fear. I am sure his death was not pleasant for you. My children, you saw that dying was easy. It stalks and hunts us for all time and comes in the end uninvited." He turned to the side of his face, full of joy, a smile bent sickeningly upwards toward Heaven.

"Why fear your eventual end? Embrace it! Prepare for it! Take up arms against it and master it! Dance with it. Make love to it! In time you will find it is nothing."

With that, the imp disappeared. The young men breathed hard, sweat dripping from their naked bodies. The lights flickered, and they were accompanied with the sound that another passageway was opening.

"What is it?" The young men asked in unison. The passageway folded backwards, and the black depression erupted with a deep, throaty roar.

"It's a cat," Jesse said. He had seen one of them before in the forest, dead from old age. Maggots and flies covered its body.

"It's a big fucking cat. We have to fight together on this one," Jesse said.

The cat trotted from the depression and stared at the group of young men. Its mane was full and flowed down from its head to the center of its upper back. The cat smelled the air and lowered its body slowly. Its face fixed into a snarl. It roared at the group of two legs, looking for a way to split their force. Its yellow eyes fixed on one of the smaller ones, one that was shaking audibly, on the far right flank of the bunch. The big cat fixed its focus on the little one. The little one was breathing hard and panicked. The cat could smell the fear from its pores. Split decision. The cat sprang and covered ten feet in the bound. It brought its heavy paw down on the boy's face, splitting his spirit from his body and knocking him across the room. The massive paw separated the vertebrae in his neck, and his head wobbled on his neck like that of a chicken swung around like a rock sling. The cat followed the dead boy just long enough to ensure the smell of life left his body. The feline was well fed and not interested in eating. It only wanted to kill its tormentors. It killed not out of hunger, as was its mandate, it killed out of hatred.

Jesse ran headlong at the cat with his sword raised, and other young men followed at his heels. The cat took up a defensive position waiting for the two legs to get closer. Jesse stopped ten feet from the cat, unaware that the other men were behind him. They collided with him pushing him forwards towards the beast. Jesse pointed his sword downwards, extending the tip towards the cat. The cat let free a great roar and leapt to greet the mass of youth. They met midway in a violent clash. A shriek erupted. The cat grabbed Jesse in its massive paws and carried him the distance. Its momentum carried them past the brittle prickles of swords the other men held. They did their best to slash and hack the beast as it flew past them. The cat's body landed with Jesse underneath it, and it shrieked like a woman grabbed suddenly by the hair. Sure that Jesse was crushed, the other men ran towards the lovers' embrace. The cat was motionless. In the flickering light, they could only make out Jesse's face, covered in thick red blood, as he struggled to breathe under the cat's crushing weight. The cat's enormous head lay to the side of Jesse's making him look like a little doll.

"Get this big bastard off me," Jesse wheezed.

The young men ripped the cat to the side, groaning as they strained to move the dead bag of muscle and bone. The great cat's dead body gave way a flood of blood that rushed from its pierced heart, coating Jesse in its bright, ferrous stench. Jesse picked himself up and limped away with his sticky sword at his side. The young men cheered their champion, amazed at what they had seen.

Sambus' projection reappeared, flickering like a candle flame before it achieved a degree of stability. Sambus displayed his happy side and clapped his hands to applaud the young men in their struggle. "It appears there is a champion among you boys. Well, champions are soon laid low. A poison arrow felled Achilles. Life sees fit to grind

Everests to foothills and dry massive oceans to salty deserts. We will see if this boy here survives or he just follows nature's path. But mind you, children, nature does not wait. She does not take time off for the weak ones to pick themselves up again. Nature is a cruel and vicious bitch! All she wants is to snuff you out. She is the mother that denies her babe the teat out of jealousy. She is the woman that scorns her lover for another because his manhood does not please her. She is death packaged in the radiant colors of a rainbow. On her surface lies beauty soft and inviting, but this beauty has jagged edges underneath waiting to crush your bones and grind them into a fine powder. You are fuel just to keep herself going. You are the grease of her machine. Your death is her lubrication. She delights in each of her victories."

Jesse shot to his feet. He grimaced through his pain and took a deep breath, "Someone shut that freak up!"

Sambus' projection burst into a peal of laughter. He paced back towards the center of the room where his hologram flickered and then disappeared. The third door folded upon itself like an accordion and the metallic slats retreated, revealing the passageway. The young men, shivering and naked, but clothed in the courage that budded from the slender branches of their limbs and taking root in their hopes for overcoming their ordeal, joined arms when they first smelled the foul smell reminiscent of latrine that farted forth from the depression.

Sloshing. They heard a slow rhythmic sound, like a farm laborer dragging an overfilled sack of potatoes on the rough ground, then through a series of progressively deeper puddles, the sound of trickling water as an afterthought. A hulking shape, undulating, rippling flesh with slimy dripping mouthparts edged with grotesque tentacles, thrust itself forward from the hole in anticipation of a meal. It sensed fifteen delicious morsels. All it sought was warm nutritious flesh. Eating was its prime function in life. Its other secondary function was to leave a trail of concentrated flammable sulfur smelling shit behind it.

Jesse's granny told him of the mushworm just once, when he was the tiniest boy just able to comprehend things like a child, motivated by fear alone. He was a precocious little boy and with no brothers to play with, he often snuck into areas of the Congregation that he was not welcome. His grandmother told him that behind one of the many doors he opened he would find a mushworm. And the mush worm would suck him inside the room and eat him up. His grandmother did not tell him about the life cycle of the mush worm, but he was in perpetual fright of it, terrified for a period of a week as he darted from bathroom to bed to hide under his covers, always sniffing the air for the presence of the mushworm. To Jesse she was an eating, gaping mouth and a shitting anus, nothing more complex than that. Jesse asked his Grandmother why the Father would see fit to create such a monstrosity and she reminded him of the two headed goat that killed its mother the following spring and wouldn't eat but both heads bit each other and fought over food until the poor creature died of starvation. Like all creatures, the mushworm had a divine purpose. When driven from its hole, humans could get at the mushworm shit, an excellent, albeit stinky fuel, which would burn for days on end. When driven from its hole, the mushworm got aggressive. Its bloodlust was unquenchable. It hurtled forward devouring whatever flesh it could roll over. This is what the young men faced. This female mushworm was out of its element. It was starved and pissed off.

It slurped up slowly, lurching, leaving a slippery slime trail of half shit half mucus behind. The young men tried to cover their mouths when the smell hit them. Sulfurous oxides burned their nostrils and eyes. The worm slopped forward. For the young men, breathing too much meant passing out. For the worm, they were easy morsels.

It undulated, its guts visible through its transparent, keratinous shell. The young men darted to its flank, slashing and swinging their swords wildly. Their weapons clanged off its hard carapace. When the worm sloughed forward, a gap in its armor appeared. The young men hacking at its sides attempted to slab the worms tender flesh when it shot forward, but it contracted, pulling the rest of its hulk with it, closing the gap as fast as it opened. It blindly flung its barbed tentacles at the darting objects: the young men who jumped like fleas from a dying dog. It sensed the food in proximity to its mouth and thrust its head in that direction. It failed to capture anything, narrowly missing Robert who dove out of the way. The worm grew desperate and writhed its body. The lower half thrust violently against the metal wall, trapping the three wildly hacking young men beneath against it, squishing them. The worm pulled away, and all that remained of the youths were bloody skin bags with no shape other than the protruding bones that jutted out randomly from under mangled flesh. The worm thrashed and undulated again. It lassoed a young man's leg that was careless in avoiding the reach of its tentacles. Being dragged towards the meat grinding gullet, the other young men grabbed him by his arms as he screamed. The massive worm's strength proved too much. It sucked the youth inside its mucus-lubricated mantle and his cries disappeared. With a taste for blood the worm lassoed the lion carcass and dragged it into open black mouth. Its tentacles formed scoops, and it scooped the mucus-wetted dried blood by the bucketful into its mouth. The tentacles fell upon the rat corpses and the bone bag children. They thrashed, scooping up the mucus and body pieces until the floor of the place was spotless.

Jesse's Grandmother taught him that the mushworm was put into the world to clean up the battlefields of men who were willing to march directly to their deaths without second thought. The Father made men and placed them into a beautiful paradise, but they rebelled. They subdivided and analyzed the paradise. They assigned names to things. They assigned values. They assigned prices. Some things became good. Other things became evil to be annihilated. Some groups of men took it upon themselves to do the annihilating of other groups of men. And why not? They were never content. The good and evil would keep bubbling up in their minds and attaching themselves to the world of the living like a transparent, invisible glue. No, they were never content. They strived. They spread their kind across the surface of the paradise. They thought it was good. They made messes that festered and polluted the paradise. And in the End, Father be praised, the Father decided to rapture them up, the men, the messiest creature of all creation. And the great annihilator, the mushworm, was there to make the surface of the earth as clean and pristine as the dead surface of the moon.

When the great worm was sated with all the carrion and boy flesh it could hold, it withdrew. It pulled itself backwards, no longer thrashing its tentacles, but rather it was calm and content like a newly suckled baby. As it withdrew into the darkness its tentacles vibrated rapidly and it belched a fine mist of acrid gas that drifted slowly to the ground and settled as a fine dust that soon disappeared.

Sambus reappeared with a smile on his face. Five young men remained out of the original fifteen. Usually only two or three were left alive, but now the final battle would be very entertaining for the dwarf and his brothers in arms. When Sambus placed his bet in the control room, he placed his three diamonds on the tall, muscular lad who tried to punch his hologram. The man child was sure to win out. The next monster they would face was the most fearsome yet.

"My boys, I must regretfully say that only one of you can be triumphant in our little endeavor. One of you will join us, the remainder of you will be sent home to your mothers. That is, if you survive, of course."

A barrel of weapons of all shapes and sizes erupted from the floor, and the blunt skull crushers clanged off the sharp cutting edges of swords and knives.

"There is limited time for you to choose your weapon! Make haste!" Sambus said with a laugh, and then flickered to nothingness.

The five boys stood around looking at each other with expressions of mordant surprise on their faces. Jesse grabbed a heavy hammer.

"You heard the freak, grab a weapon, brothers! Whatever this is, we're in it together."

Three young men grabbed sharp rapier swords--perfect for stabbing through the guts of anything that came through the passageway. Robert grabbed a hammer much smaller than Jesse's but with a claw on the opposite side of the flat iron smashing face. The two stood some distance from each other as they waited for the door to fold in upon itself, and whatever lay behind it to rush out.

It seemed that at least a minute went by and the door had not opened. Jesse expected to be in the fight for his life with whatever starving and tortured animal these men had captured in the forest to test them with. They all breathed deeply, staring at the door, waiting desperately for it to open. Waiting for whatever would come through, so they could end its life and get on with theirs.

Sambus appeared. "My children, out of the lions, the rats, the mush worms, one creature is more fearsome. Do you know what it is?"

The young men stood fast watching the door, not paying any attention to the little imp's hologram.

"Nothing? No one wants to answer? Okay. Children, get this through your thick skulls, the most fearsome creature is man. Of course, after this test, we will see how thick some of your skulls really are," Sambus said with a vile laugh and disappeared.

The boys stood there, waiting for the oncoming army to charge through the passageway. The passageway opened. Instead of darkness there was light. An exit! An iron grate shot up from the ground and covered their hopes. The crimson hooded men, brandishing spears lined up at the iron grating. Sambus was in the middle of them.

He screamed to the boys, "All right! Get at it, you fools! Only one of you can come out of there alive!" The lights dimmed suddenly. The three boys with rapiers set upon each other after a slight delay, stabbing each other wildly, screaming in the darkness. Jesse leapt in the middle of them and brought his hammer down on two of their heads in quick succession. The third boy dropped his rapier and ran to the gate screaming. The men stabbed at him with their spears. He turned around and ran right into Jesse's hammer blow. The men cheered wildly.

Jesse paced towards Robert, gore stained hammer in hand and eyes fixed on one thing.

Robert stepped backwards, holding his hammer weakly. "Jesse, you can't do this. We knew each other as children."

Jesse kept coming forward.

"Jesse we're friends."

Jesse's eyes were glazed over, and he heard nothing but the miniscule squeaking of a mouse.

"We don't have to play their game! Don't!"

"Robert, you heard them. We must," Jesse said without a hint of emotion.

Jesse raised the massive hammer and brought it down towards his playmate's head. Robert tried to deflect the blow but his hammer shot from his hands under the weight of Jesse's onslaught. There was a sound of metal force connecting dully with flesh. It would have sickened Jesse, but all he heard was his heart in his ears and the cheering of the men at the gate. The boy crumpled to the floor under the man, motionless. The Crimson Guard, the Council for Defense and Raids, his new family, called him to come to the gate and receive their congratulations.

Jesse walked triumphantly through the iron grate that the applauding crimson robed men opened for him. The men formed a line and urged Jesse forward. Sambus handed Jesse a golden brooch emblazoned with a trefoil seal, three circles intertwined, representing infinity and his pledge of brotherhood forever to his comrades.

"Place the seal on your chest, pin side down," Sambus ordered him. Jesse complied and Sambus jumped up and punched him in the seal so that the pin jabbed into his chest muscle.

"Time for you first scar, man!" Sambus screamed with a maniacal laugh. "Get on down the line; you're not a boy anymore!"

Each man, in turn, punched Jesse in the chest hard and each nearly knocked the wind out of him.

"You're one of us now, no longer a boy," said a red bearded man missing an eye. Each punch felt like a nail being driven into his heart.

"Stay in line, man!" said the large man that had addressed them in the arena, serving as Sambus's counterpoint. He punched like a sledgehammer, knocking Jesse backwards.

"We're in this together, my man," a slender man with a dark beard that covered his entire face except where there was a jagged raised scar from a knife wound. Jesse looked in their eyes as they congratulated him, trying not to show a hint of weakness. They had all been through the same trials and were marked with scars, missing fingers, patches over gouged out eyes, and gaping smiles formed from punched out teeth. All together there were about two-hundred and fifty of them. They ranged in age between young or just a few years older than Jesse, to very old. The Council Leader stood at the very end of the line and greeted him with a bear hug, picking Jesse off the ground. Jesse recognized him immediately. He looked into Saul's large blue eyes and saw the man that he last saw when he was a small child. Jesse thought he was looking in the mirror at a much older version of himself. White hairs streaked through Saul's black hair and beard, and he wore a bear pelt over his traditional red robe. The man whispered in his ear, "It is good to have you with us, son." After that brief bear hug, the affection between earthfather and son ended, and Jesse was just another soldier under Saul's command.

Sambus handed Jesse his red cloak and a short double edged sword, approximately three feet in length.

"Now pin the cloak to your body with the brooch, and may your blood mix with the fabric of the crimson cloak and may your blood and the blood of your brothers be bound forever. Repeat after me."

"I will trust my brothers and act so that they may trust me."

Jesse repeated, wincing as he extracted the trefoil brooch from his chest muscle. The blood flowed freely from the wound and mingled with the red cloak, now around his shoulders.

"I will protect the women of the Congregation."

Jesse repeated, wiping the sweat from his brow.

"I will follow all the orders of the men appointed above me."

Jesse repeated, standing tall in front of the dwarf who both smiled and sneered uncontrollably.

"All praises are due to the Father and his fount, the Glorious Mother."

Again, Jesse repeated, and the men cheered.

"The women of the world shall be freed; this is the will of the Glorious Mother!" Sambus said.

All the men in unison shouted, "The women of the world shall be freed! This is the will of the Glorious Mother!"

Sambus began his speech to the collection of men while Saul looked at them all, stoic, his face like a Roman statue, marbled with confidant poise and assurance.

"Our young brother now joins us. According to custom he will be baptized in fire, steel, and blood. Prior to his enrollment, he was just a boy. Now he is a man. Tonight he will come to know just what manhood means. We will offer him no quarter. We will not hold his hand or his sword and lead him into battle. He will fight, and he will do his part, just as all of us have done in the past. Should he fall in battle, he will not be honored, for honor dwells with the living. Honor comes from the wounds that have healed and scarred over.

Saul took over the speech with his booming voice, "Honor lies in your arm that you lost suppressing the wicked Magicians of the Lower Swamps, Eli." Saul pointed to a tall slender man whose amputated arm was covered in coarse leather, so that only a stub showed. "It is in your ability to kill the enemy with one arm, and honor comes in the axe blow that damaged your face Sambus! You survived and lived to fight another day!"

Sambus bowed to Saul and continued, "It comes from the women that you free from their taskmasters. It comes from the women that we make part of the Glorious Mother's fold. This is the plan of the Father. He said to be fruitful and multiply when He created the heavens and the Earth."

The men nodded in agreement, and a slow rolling murmur, like a wave, rose up in the crowd. It was time for a mission. This was how they always began. Besides eating, sleeping, and training to fight, the men fought. Everything else was honing their skills for the inevitable mission. Saul addressed them, "This very morning as dawn breaks, we will pour into the Valley of Rimbleton. We will make those boys of Rimbleton feel our might. You all know your duty, brothers. You are to make them fall to our swords and spears. Not one of them can be spared. As for the women and girls, you also know what to do."

"We agree! It is understood!" The men screamed in unison.

"Prepare yourselves. We will depart when the moon is highest in the nighttime sky."

Jesse made to follow the other men to the barracks, but Saul grabbed him by his shoulder. He whispered into his son's ear gruffly, "My son, you must remember the oath you swore to us. You are now a man."

Jesse pulled away and nodded to his earthfather silently.

An air of joy swept through the barracks as each man took time preparing his weapons, sharpening and stowing them in leather scabbards. The younger men then aided the older brothers in preparing their own. Sambus sang with a voice sweeter than his face, half humming to himself, gaining in intensity until all the brothers joined in with him. The rhythm of steel on whetstone was his accompaniment.

"Stalking through the woods during daytime warm and fair, I came upon a beautiful woman with flowers in her hair, I followed her to her home without making any sound, that night I ran the men deep and laid them on the ground, my sister freed, my sister freed, her hands are now unbound, my sister freed, my sister freed, my sister freed without a sound...."

Jesse imitated the movements of the men surrounding him. When it was his turn, he brought sword to whetstone. The sword shot off bright sparks of superheated metal from the cutting edge. Saul grabbed his hand and adjusted the angle at which Jesse held the blade, so that it was more acute. "Like this, son," he said looking Jesse in the face.

After a minute the sword was sharp enough to slice soft bread without crushing it. Saul nodded with approval and helped Jesse to don his armor. The two laced up their leather boots in silence. Then, like the other men before them, they applied the wetted ashes of birch trees to their faces so they were totally blackened. Jesse broke off the wet charcoal and wiped his face and hands with it. He smelled the smoke and ash as he spread the camouflage across the ridge of his nose and underneath his eyes.

The men formed a line and began marching silently through the woods. The moon glowed in the sky at its crest, high above them. Sambus lead the way through the underbrush, which skipped and glanced off their sinewy muscles and tugged at their crimson cloaks. Sambus darted ahead, using his small size to get underneath the low hanging branches without impediment. Occasionally, he heard something ahead and would raise his hand to tell them to halt. He stood with his hand outstretched and palm facing them, listening intently to the surrounding woods. During the trial Jesse wished him death, but now he felt a strange liking towards the little man with the hideous scar on his face. Content that there was nothing stalking them, Sambus motioned the men forward. As they walked, Jesse kept his eyes on the man in front of him, and he appeared only a dark bulky shape in the low light. Jesse became like a walking dead man; his only intention was putting one foot in front of the other, unaware of where they were going.

All Jesse could hear was the crunch of debris beneath his feet and the breathing of the men to the front and the rear. Sambus attempted to take the most direct route to their quarry, but tonight his mind was attuned to other things. With each step, the bulge in the front of his tight cassock grew. Sambus shamed himself when it started to protrude and chafe on the coarse burlap, but they were getting close. He could smell the dying cooking fires of the village. As the smell got so thick that he could tell the people that evening ate potato and leek stew, his breaths came in near pants that trickled out of him with each lusting heartbeat. Sambus led the men up a hill, pulling at the wispy juvenile trees, threatening to pull them up by the roots.

"This way, my brothers," Sambus whispered. "On the top of the hill is our vantage point from which we will strike when the time is right."

Jesse clawed up the hill behind the men, digging his boots into the churned up mud and ripping at the vines hanging from the trees for support. His sword hung from his belt like a burden begging for release. His spear lightened in his hands, and he moved without a sound. A faint metallic taste blossomed from his lips as he breathed deeply, and the hideous swarm of butterflies flapped towards his heart. He longed to scream out. The baboon of rage gnashed at the firm cage of his heart, but the silence of his brothers kept him in the line, thrusting up the hill. When they came to the top, the crimson warriors lay prone, watching the sleeping village below.

The houses were nearly all of uniform size and shape, and in the dim light of the rising sun, they appeared hastily constructed, as if they were only temporary for the people that inhabited them. A few dogs milled about the village nosing into the huts and eating scraps from pots at cook fires.

Sambus rose to his feet and observed the line of men. They were all fit and eager for a fight. The young apprentice even appeared to be made of steel, laying there with murder in his eyes. Sambus longed for the high-pitched screams of the women as they ran the men through, followed by the squeals of delight as they stopped mourning their dead husbands and greeted their liberators with open arms.

Saul gave the order to charge in a throaty growl that bounced across the helmeted heads of the men who lay nearly on top of each other, their spears protruding past the crown of the hill and pointing at the damned village in the valley below. With spears raised, the men roared to life and flooded down the hill as fast as their legs would carry them, their arms raised above their heads. A dog stopped its scavenging and raised its head, barking once: a howl, which ended in a whimper as its head left its body. The men separated and flew from hovel to hovel in pairs. One man ripped the front door off its thatch hinges and the other pounded inside and slashed the men of the house to bits in their leafy beds. Once the men and boys were dispatched, they bound and gagged his bride and dragged her to the center of the village, kicking and trying to shriek, but it only came out as muffled warbling. A boy ran through the clearing between the women that were collected there. He managed to make his way to the periphery of the village before and of the raiders saw him. Saul shouted over his shoulder to the collection of troops who were bringing the last of the captives to the center, "Fools, one of the boys is escaping!"

Jesse and two other men readied their spears and hurled them at the child with all of their might. The boy dashed like a field mouse behind a mud and grass hut. The spear clanged off the rocks behind him. The second bashed through the hut and the third, Jesse's spear came closest, but all missed him. The boy ran into the forest. He ran as fast as he could until his lungs could no longer keep up with his muscles' demand for oxygen. He did not want to meet with the spear throwers close up. He ran until his legs would not move and collapsed into a shelter made of two fallen and rotten trees that had once been magnificent oaks full of choruses of songbirds and host to hundreds of gray squirrels.

The remaining nomads were doomed. Their only weapons the tiny contingent of men left alive could muster were crude implements better suited to digging up roots and tubers than cleaving a man's skull. The hollering of the nomadic men was soon replaced by death wails and blood gurgling screams. When the Congregation men entered the homes and found the babes quaking under their beds, if it was a boy they stabbed it once viciously. Girls and women of age they dragged to the center.

When the justice of the Father was fully meted unto the men of Rimbleton Valley, the raiders stood at the center with their collected prize. The women sat looking at them, sobbing with wide open eyes. Saul walked triumphantly up and down the line of captives holding a walking stick that he retrieved from one of the hovels. It belonged to a weak old man who dwelled in the largest of the houses, and who thought himself a chieftain of sorts, but was now lying in pieces on the dirt floor of his grand home. Why did he not train the men how to fight them? His three wives were bound and gagged at Saul's feet. One showed that she was with child, probably four months along, just starting to get big. Saul waggled the stick at her. The women around her trembled, unsure of what the proclamation by the terrifying bearded man meant. The expectant mother's face went pure white. Saul waggled the long blackened stick at each of the women with gray in their hair and breasts at their waistlines. The women were of no use to anyone but taking care of the children and supporting other women in their birth pangs. He stopped in front of a poor soul with stringy matted hair on her head. He eyes looked like black, blank slits, and her ears bent outwards at the tops and bottoms, like the Father had pulled her ears taut against her head in an attempt to keep her from shooting out of her mother's womb to pollute the world. They treated her as a sort of holy fool, a soothsayer of sorts, but Saul did not see it and waggled the stick at her, too.

"Scoop them up, Sambus. You know what to do," Saul said grabbing his son, Jesse, by the shoulder and walking with him. Sambus followed behind them and tugged at Saul's cloak. He pointed to one of the women that Saul did not select. She had hair of a raven and green eyes. She sat with the rest of the women, and like them, her clothing was in tatters.

"Look at her. She's a looker."

"Yes, those eyes could pierce through a man."

"Those milkers. Look at them, Captain."

"Aye. They're like two moons," Saul said with a smile.

"Such a skinny little miss, too, it's unnatural," Sambus echoed.

Jesse watched the men with curiosity. Sambus had a look of pleading in his eyes.

"Boss, why don't you point the stick at her, and you and I can take her to the outskirts."

"No, it isn't proper, Sambus."

"Come on, boss. Why look at the boy here, he wants a go, too."

"It's not proper, Sambus."

"Boss, you can point the stick at anyone you like."

"I can, just not her."

"Why not? Only you and I and the boy will know about it."

"She'll be the Glorious Mother's, Sambus. It won't be any other way."

"Oh, the Mother wants her, does she?"

"That's our orders, Sambus. We'll follow them or go home dead."

"It's already decided then?"

"I didn't choose this, Sambus. She did."

Screams of women ripped from the edge of the clearing.

"We can't take them all in."

"Aye. We have to take the healthy ones, the beautiful ones. That's what the Glorious Mother said."

"The beautiful ones, yes," Sambus muttered with a twinge of spite.

"She wants them all to herself."

Screams and grunts poured into the center of the small encampment.

"You know what they say, Sambus," Saul proclaimed with authority.

"The Glorious Mother knows best," Jesse boldly stated before Sambus could answer.

"Yes. She does, boy," Sambus muttered.

Jesse could not tell if he was happy or full of rage.

The men waddled back to the center exhausted, and their swords trickled bright red, which was wiped invisibly on their crimson cloaks before preparing the captives for the long march back to the Congregation. The women wailed through their gags. They wailed for their dead men to save them. With each step from the thick black smoke of the burning Rimbleton valley encampment, they began to accept their fate as a woman in the world of fierce and violent men.

Word escaped the male barracks and found its way back to the Elder Mother. It was passed through her loose network of spies from mouth to ear of the women at the margins of their society: the undesirables who served as her entourage. The Glorious Mother had her own entourage full of the most beautiful women born to the mothers of the Congregation. These women were absolutely off-limits to the men. The Elder Mother's entourage moved freely enough to be able to meet the men clandestinely in the forest for sharing information and bodily fluids. The two women, the young and vibrant Glorious Mother, and the old and decrepit Elder Mother were locked in a mortal competition for the attention of the female Congregants. While the Glorious Mother was the fount of knowledge from the Father, the Elder Mother had control of the children and could influence them according to her whim. Until recently, she also had *The Gideons*. Word reached the Elder Mother that Jesse passed the trials and would be joined to the Congregation in a matter of a day. The Elder Mother plotted her saving grace: a miracle that would overcome her blunder in misplacing *The Gideons*. She had her spies looking for that, too.

The Elder Mother told Isaac's mother of the planned Joining Ceremony in her private quarters and the woman was so elated that she ran back and told her youngest adopted son the news. The news came to Isaac as a sudden ejaculation of joy from his mother's mouth.

"Isaac, your brother, Jesse, is now a man. He has passed his trials!"

Isaac did not look up from his toys that he had arranged on the floor in battle formations. One army greatly outnumbered a second army, and he was about to mouth a trumpet for the larger army to charge and rout the smaller one.

"Isaac, don't you care that your brother has succeeded?"

"Mother, did you have any doubt about him?"

"Why, no, Isaac, I didn't!" She said getting slightly angry with him, but holding her voice to a minimum.

"Then why are you so overjoyed? Wouldn't you take it as just another thing that Jesse's great at?"

"Don't be jealous, Isaac."

"I'm not."

"You sound like you're burning up inside."

"Can we just not talk about Jesse anymore, mother? I mean, he's gone."

"Not yet he isn't. He won't have the joining ceremony for another day. The men at this very instant are returning from a far off mission."

"What did they do?"

"I don't know. Beats me. I'm not a man."

"What happens at the Joining Ceremony, mother? You've surely been to one before."

"I have. But I'm not telling you."

"Please, Mother, tell me."

"No, Isaac. It isn't for children like you to know."

"I'll find out, Mother."

"How, Isaac? No one is going to tell you."

"I don't know. I'll think of something."

"Well you only have a day to think of something, big boy, because the ceremony starts at sundown tomorrow."

"I'll...I'll...," Isaac stuttered trying to find the words to tell her what he was planning. Isaac glared at his mother who smiled back at him.

"Don't be mad, honey. The Father saw fit to take Baruch from you and me, and now he's seen fit to elevate Jesse to be a man."

"What does he see fit for me?"

"The Father wants you to stay home and keep your mother company I guess, I don't know. I can't speak for the Father, dear."

"Well, it's a damn awful place for me to be in."

"How dare you talk about me, your mother, like that."

"I wasn't talking about you, mother, I just need to grow up!"

"Well in order for you to grow up, the adults have to accept you, and in order for the adults to accept you, first you have to pass the adult trials and have your Joining Ceremony."

"Whatever. I'm stuck here with you, I guess."

She hugged him. "And is that so bad, dear?"

He did not respond, but smelled the oil in her cassock and felt the warmth from her breasts on his face.

That night when Isaac went to bed he began questioning the world around him. His grandmother had always called him a curious boy. It was a detriment wrapped up in the guise of a blessing from the Father. The blessing was that he was a precocious youth. The detriment came in the fact that the society into which he was born was given to rites that precocious men would consider strange. That is why the Congregation kept these rites underneath the ground, shielded by cool metallic walls in the Sanctuary and away from the eyes of the children. If someone unwanted by them witnessed the rites, they would lose their authenticity. They would lose what made them special. The rites would be for everyone and not just the initiated. The children were kept obedient by the promises that they would one day reach adulthood. The children hadn't a clue as to what adulthood meant. They only knew that it had been inculcated from the first time they could remember and that reaching full maturity as a member of the Congregation meant taking part in a Joining Ceremony in the Sanctuary. If the only truth they saw was the ugly, obese, heaving and sweating truth, when all the baubles and gemstones of youth were removed and the long flowing silk dress of its serenity, were also removed, would adulthood still be desirable?

Isaac could not go to sleep. His thoughts plowed through the fertile soil of his mind, tilling up vast tangles of wild vines that flowered and bore the hanging fruit of desire. When he dreamed, he was running through an open field towards door standing up on its own. He stopped at the door. It did not appear to be supported by anything. He did not want to do it, but he opened the door and saw wonders that would make him forget the sunshine and rainbows and all the idylls of his youthful folly. He woke with a start. He leapt from his bed into the sunshine streaming through his window. He would position himself. He would enter the Sanctuary and go to the place that Grandmother showed him. He would steal in, quiet as a mouse, and watch the wonders that Jesse would experience. No one would tell him that he could not know the secrets of his people. That night he did not sleep.

He stared into the darkness until the first glow of morning. He put on his musty cassock and tied the rope belt around his midsection. He thrust his hands into the gaping front pocket against the chill of loneliness in his room. He tied the makeshift boot around his hideous foot, glaring at it for a moment before he hid it from the world in shoddily tanned pig leather. He placed his other foot gingerly in a supple, fur-lined shoe. Carefully, Isaac snuck past the rooms of the other children, not making a sound. They slept peacefully in their beds with their chests rising and falling like a metronome, the steam exploding from their mouths and then trickling down the sides of their angelic faces like an obstructed waterfall. Isaac smiled as he walked past the rooms. He imagined they were dreaming of playing with their heavy oak wood toys or listening to a lesson from their Grandmother out of the book. He often dreamed of *The Gideons* as a child. They were vivid dreams. The dreams were of walls tumbling down. Rapes. Massacres. Death stalking the land. Plagues. Destruction. Locusts. The Roman soldiers in their shiny helmets and crimson capes. The dancing women. The Father's hand in it all. The burning bush. The man, Abraham. The wanderings of the doomed man, Cain. Joseph sold into slavery by his brothers. The man, Moses. The people wandering in the desert. Hunger. Unquenchable thirst. The Promised Land. The destruction of the wicked cities of the damned: Sodom and Gomorrah. Lot. His wife as a pillar of salt. Job. His sufferings. The boy David destroying the giant with a rock and a sling. Baby Jesus. The wanderings of the man. His disciples. The cross. Pain. Misery. Coming back to life. The Revelation. The Angels in Chariots throwing lighting. Death. Destruction. Plagues. Locusts. The final battles of men. Mushworms. The darkness. In his dreams it had all played out over and over again. What the Father had intended for all men came true. It was written in *The Gideons,* and it came true--every last word of it. But, there was nothing in *The Gideons* about him or Jesse or any one else of his people. It happened. All of it!

His grandmother lied to him! She lied to him! She was the one who told him about *The Gideons*. She was the one who told him to always tell the truth. His Grandmother lied to him! He walked towards the secret entrance to the sanctuary, and each time he stepped with his useless foot, an old cross voice implored him to stop. It felt like his conscience, only it used the sneering voice of his Grandmother. Isaac laughed to himself and easily broke the thread of doubt that threatened to pull him back to the safety of his bed. The urging to stop came to its greatest when Isaac came to the area where Grandmother taught the lessons from *The Gideons*. In his mind he devastated every one of her arguments that he should be a good boy and just go back to his bed and forget all the nonsense of wanting to see the Joining Ceremony. He used her nagging voice to make himself angry, which helped him push the bench to grab onto the lever. He pulled the lever and the wall folded open, black and ominous inside. He scooted the bench back to its original position, careful that it was in its original moorings, lest someone get smart to his crime. He entered the doorway, and it closed behind him. He was now in the blackness.

He remembered it was fifteen steps to the first turn. He began to count them out. He should have turned at the eleventh step, but he took two more. He walked into the wall, and fell backwards onto his ass. He shuffled on the ground towards the right, sure the turn was there, and his knee brushed against something. He heard the rustle of papers as he withdrew his leg and felt the object with his hand. His heart leapt out of his chest. It was the book! *The Gideons!* He had found it! He picked it up and put the precious book in his pocket. After the ceremony was over, he would turn it into his Grandmother and redeem himself. He would be a hero! But was it really *The Gideons*? He pulled the book from his front pocket and put his nose to it; it smelled like the middle of the forest, wet and earthy. He returned it to the safety of his front pocket and continued in the darkness, now doubly excited, both by what he was about to see and by the hero's congratulations he would receive after he returned the book. But what if they asked where it came from? Isaac thought as he lumbered through the darkness to the hallway where the light performed strange wonders.

In the lighted hallway, he pulled *The Gideons* from his pocket. He never had his hands on it before. The cover was completely black, scorched as if it had been tossed in a great fire. A small worn golden stamp glinted from the bottom right corner. *THE GIDEONS*. The name had survived the fire to be proclaimed throughout the generations to follow. It was as if the Father himself had made the name of the book indelible. Most of the pages survived; the fire had burned the boundaries of the pages, wiping out some of the first sentences of paragraphs, but those bits and pieces were filled in with his Grandmother's imagination.

Even if his grandmother lied to him, she couldn't lie to everyone about his discovery of *The Gideons*. Isaac would wait until the mealtime and announce that he found it; just to make sure that everyone knew. Then he would be a hero. All of the children of the Congregation would then be safe from the forest Mocha Assassins. They would probably even let him join to the adults. His Grandmother would be overjoyed.

His thoughts stopped as he entered the Sanctuary. There was a slight humming sound as he crossed into the large room. It filled his head as he slinked to the secret side stairway that would take him to his vantage point over the entire ceremony. When he was sure that the door closed behind him, he walked up the stairs, slowly, with the urge to run back to his bed growing in him with every step. When he got to the viewing room behind the great golden-jeweled eyes of the Leader of the Angels, he looked at the wonders below him in the chamber; the flickering of millions of lights surged through every inch of the Sanctuary. It spoke peace to him, and the terrors in his stomach subsided. There was time before the ceremony. He looked to the Sanctuary floor and went into a dream-like state while watching the patterns of lights pulsing like a nervous system. He breathed deeply, and the dreams in his mind played like a kaleidoscope as sleep ran off with his consciousness.

The brilliant flashings woke him. He looked through the great diamond window and saw the Sanctuary chamber awash with life. Hundreds of women dressed in white linen robes filed into the chamber to a drum beaten by a child dressed in golden robes. A woman whose beauty made Isaac gasp, with jet black hair, a nose that descended to a sharp cruel point, and cheekbones that began so far on the side of her face that they seemed unnatural, led the file of women. On Her head She wore a golden circlet crown. Even though he had never seen Her, She had to be the Glorious Mother, their leader, and their fount of communication with the Father. Isaac was taught that through Her all future prophecy was revealed. In Her dreams and visions She entered into dialogue with the founder of the universe. The Founder, the Father, the Lord of Life, the Builder, the Blessed One, the Holy One, revealed His wisdom to Her in chunks. She spit it from Her holy mouth, and whatever words flowed through Her caused a frenzy of vibrations in the crowds of assembled women.

In the short time that followed, Isaac would come to realize painfully just what he was part of. He would learn the system that birthed him. He would come to see what he could never participate in. He would see the boundaries of his one and only life thrust before him; he would come face to face with his lack of any choice. Just as he had not chosen to be born a miserable cripple, dependent on others for his sustenance, and just as he had no choice in the matter of his birth, he would come to witness the truth of his conception--he would witness it, and he would be horrified.

The women formed a circle around the periphery of the Sanctuary, interlocking arms that they alternately raised and lowered to the rhythm of the pounding child-beat drum. The Glorious Mother spun around on the raised central platform and hurled Her long black hair outwards as Her momentum carried Her in faster and faster revolutions. The platform underneath Her feet glowed brighter with each revolution until it appeared white hot to Isaac. The women gasped in unison, and it sounded like a tidal wave about to break on a distant shore when the Glorious Mother began to float upwards toward the towering ceiling. Isaac stared at Her mystified as the raised central platform shot off bright pulses of light which hit off of her sanctified body, glowing all of her bones and sending packets of light from Her eyes, nose, and mouth which were wide open transfixed in a sanguine mixture of pain and ecstasy.

Unsuspended by hooks or tassels, She floated upwards. She swirled in the air like a child's top, and then descended. When She reached the platform with Her tiptoes, the twirling stopped, and the Glorious Mother opened Her mouth to deliver the information that descended to Her straight from the wisdom of the Father. Her head was bowed, and She shook in exhaustion. Her bosom radiated the last energy out of Her nipples, and it flowed back into the vast collection of shimmering lights that tickled Isaac's eyes and sparked his sense of wonder.

She spoke in a voice full of compassion and wisdom. "My children," She said.

In unison they replied, "Yes, Mother, speak."

"My children."

"Yes, our Mother, we are prepared for your wisdom."

"My children."

"Yes, Mother, we are ready for the wisdom of the Father, inform us."

"It is the year of our Father, and our Father's year shall be very productive for us. We have already begun our expansion past the confines of the forest. The Father wishes us to expand our influence far past the forest by the end of this year. The Father has told me to dispatch our warriors to scout the entire distance of the river. The Father has informed me that there is a settlement up the river that seeks to destroy us. They are sharpening their knives and spears for us even as I deliver this message from the Father upon you."

Some of the women in the crowd began to shriek hysterical high pitched and piercing wails for mercy from the Father.

"Do not despair, my children. Our warriors will make short work of their men. More of our sisters will join us."

"Bring them in, Mother! We want to meet our sisters!" Some of the women from the crowd cried.

"Soon, all of them will join us. Soon all of the women will be our sisters. Just today the men have returned with our sisters from the Valley of Rimbleton. I spoke with each of them, sisters. They told me they desired to join us. They told me the horror stories of their captivity. These women have revealed to me that their men forced marriages they did not desire upon them. Their fathers gave them to these men because these men claimed ownership over the entire settlement. The fathers of these men claimed ownership, and their fathers before them claimed ownership. It was quite a queer way of life. But now it is gone. Children, two of our new sisters were betrothed to a useless man well over the age of sixty. He was weak and graying and useless our men put him to death and saved these women. These women are to be joined to us, children."

The four women were marched into the Sanctuary by the group of warriors, with Saul at their head and Sambus bringing up the rear, his head staring at the bare rear of the last woman. He did not take his eyes from her round buttocks even as the assembled women cheered and screamed for their new sisters, whose faces were plastered with panic. The woman in the rear started to fidget and made to run, but Sambus slapped her back into the line. The Glorious Mother glared at him, and he genuflected deeply to Her. Saul stopped at the foot of the podium and bowed deeply to the Glorious Mother, who nodded to him and raised Her hand like an empress.

"We know what a man does for a woman, right, my sisters?"

"Protects the women!" the assembled crowd roared.

"That is correct, children. They do not enslave women. They protect them. We all know that only the Father is the creator, owner, and maintainer of all! No man can claim ownership over any piece of the world. My children, if no man can claim ownership over a mountain, the squirrels in the trees, or even a minute blade of grass, how can he claim ownership over a woman?"

"They cannot!" the Congregation women shouted with faces of fury. The men stood in silence with their muscles flexed, clasping the captured women's ropes that tied their hands in bondage.

"Our new sisters revealed to me that if they did not marry these men that they were forced to marry, they would have been cast out in the wilderness to fend for themselves. They were forced to think they were dependent on these men."

The women of the circle cried out in horror, "It is the opposite, Mother! The opposite! It has been revealed by the Father!"

"They were forced to bear children to these weaklings. They have already told me they find our men more desirable. Our men are champions."

She nodded to Saul, but his eyes did not leave the fixed position of attention that he was in. He only responded by clenching his jaw to the Glorious Mother's words.

"My sisters. My children. These women -- they long to join us. They long to join the Congregation."

The men unbound them, cutting their ropes with sharp swords. They removed the gags from their mouths and blindfolds from their eyes. The sight of the rough men that killed their husbands caused the women to shriek hysterically. The men stood still. Sensing their nakedness, the women then began to cover themselves with their hands. The sisters moved to comfort them and offered them the same flowing white robes that they possessed. They forced the white linen over the curly black hair of the women, and others whispered comforting words to them. Soon the women were pacified, but it could have been a state of shock taking over them. Their eyes were fixed on the Glorious Mother who ordered Saul to take his men from the Sanctuary and prepare the Champion to join the women to the Congregation.

As the men departed, the assembled women reached frenzy, as if they were gas particles in a room under steady heat. They raked their hands through their hair and down their bellies through the white robes. They screamed to their Glorious Mother, "They must join us! It is good, Mother!"

"Is this what you desire, my sisters? Is this your wish, my children?"

"It is, Mother! It is good!"

Their Mother leaned forward with Her hand on Her hip and pointed Her long, outstretched finger at each of them, fixing Her gaze on each of Her children for a moment, just enough to take the glare of their dark eyes into her own aqua blue vision. They were all witnesses for the ceremony. She answered them with a smile from Her crimson lips, "Yes, my Children, it is good. It is the will of the Father, made manifest through us."

*

In his hiding place, Isaac breathed heavily. Just seeing the girls and women in their pure white robes that barely obscured the form of their bodies and the drape of the thin white cloth forced the feeling of the shamed lusting warmth from Isaac's face straight down to his loins. He began to swell. A hint of nausea hit his stomach when it swelled. It was for pissing out of. He did not understand what seeing the women almost naked – breasts hanging out in a few instances – was doing to his body. He did not understand, but he only knew that he wanted to smell them. He wanted to smell their hair and feel their bodies against his. He wanted to feel their thick hair as it streamed through his fingers and pull at its kinks. He wanted to rub their shoulders and touch their breasts from behind. He wanted to feel their soft lips on his. Feel their nipples between his fingertips. He wanted to pull the girls close to him. Feel their sweat on his chest. A memory flashed to his consciousness, or was it a memory of a memory? He had seen his adoptive mother naked. She was drawing a bath, standing partially obscured by steam, and he peeked his head in the door. He watched with delight as she dipped her feet past the surface and splashed to test its warmth. His mother caught him in the mirror on the wall in the small oval that did not fog completely. She recoiled and kicked water at the door screaming, "Get out of here, you little monster! It isn't proper!" His glee froze into shame, and he ran and hid under the covers of his bed. He was afraid she would tell everyone. He was afraid she would tell his Grandmother who held a powerful sway over him. He worried for days, but she did not discuss the subject again. At nighttime he pulled the covers over his eyes, but could not blot out the memory of pendulous tits and the hair that ran between her legs.

*

The girls that were called to participate in the Joining Ceremony were the strongest of the Congregation. The others had succumbed to pestilence, coughing and hacking their way to oblivion during the sweltering summer, or perishing when the cold and wailing winter winds cold took them. They died before reaching maturity: the age when they were ready to have children and the Elder Mother inspected them. She determined if the gentle flowers were ready for the buzzing and probing bee. At the hands of the wrinkled, dried up old crone their evidence flowed from them. Upon seeing this evidence they were forced to give up the trappings of childhood. They were ready to bear children, qualified for adulthood. They were forced, just like *The Gideons* had taught them, to be fruitful and multiply. They were forced to fulfill their duty in life, much like the sun is forced through compulsion outside of itself to burn and generate the light that feeds the crops that feed the animals that feed the people that wander on the surface as dazed and bewildered beings, not comprehending much other than their own survival and good intentions. The women hadn't a choice in the matter. Even their champion was chosen for them. Studded to them for passing his test, he won the title of the youngest bull in the barracks. He had taken on all challengers and came out on top. Even Jesse had no choice in the matter. He would have come out on top no matter the trial, for that was how he was made.

The Glorious Mother was the first to fully disrobe. Her white robe slid slowly off Her shoulders, pulled by Her two attendees who smiled at Her glistening caramel skin. She breathed deeply against the chill in the Sanctuary, and Her nipples swelled at the thought of what she could expect. Her breasts perked outwards and separated slightly as She inhaled. She stepped out of the robe gracefully, but powerfully just as She slid out of her mother's womb nineteen years ago. The Glorious Mother raised Her arms above Her head and pulled at Her long raven hair. Her fingers parted through Her hair and down the side of Her body, resting for a moment on Her broad hips. She arched her back and stretched, thrusting Her breasts forward; She shot Her arms out to the side. She pointed one finger at the group of captives, but they did not know what to do. They looked at Her and each other, mesmerized by Her presence.

"In order to join, you must be initiated," the surrounding women said as they directed the four captives to the four platforms that formed a circle around the central platform where the Glorious Mother was now kneeling. There were more captives than four, but only these four were deemed beautiful enough to be vessels for the Father. The other captives were parsed out to the Elder Mother to watch over the children. They would not take part in the Joining Ceremony.

*

Meanwhile, the champion paced back and forth in the holding chamber. The men did as much as they could to clean him up and tossed some oily resin on him that smelled like prairie flowers after a summer rainstorm. Sambus made him drink a dark green concoction that smelled like a mixture of dung and rotting flowers. Jesse winced when he brought the gnarled gourd containing the mixture up to his lips. Sambus encouraged him by saying that it would help Jesse pass his final test. Jesse breathed through his mouth and refused to drink, but Saul nodded to the rest of the men who grabbed Jesse and held him to the ground. Saul told him that the Glorious Mother was a very demanding woman, and he had better drink his strength up. Sambus jammed a funnel into Jesse's mouth.

"Damn you, child, this is for the best, so drink up!" Saul said as he poured the hot liquid down the funnel into Jesse's throat. Tears dribbled down Jesse's face as the disgusting rot shot down his gullet. From there, the drink entered his stomach and bloodstream. It dilated his lungs and blood vessels. It made his heart pound and his eyeballs feel as if they were going to explode from his head. All his rage at the men for holding him down evaporated into one all consuming need.

*

The captives were disrobed and bound to the platforms surrounding the Glorious Mother. They were bound so their legs were spread and they were totally open and defenseless like lilies of the valley on a purple spring morning. The writhed and screamed at their bondage like the bad slaves of Egypt.

Isaac gasped in his hiding place. He hid his eyes. For Isaac, in all of his conversations during the walks and talks with his brothers in the forest, in all of their speculations as to what the world meant and what being a man would mean to them once they reached that pinnacle, nothing prepared him for what he was about to see.

The Glorious Mother called to Her children from Her prostrate position, "Release our champion." The cry echoed through the crowd until it came to the women closest to the enclosure where Jesse paced back and forth like a tiger in a zoo. Jesse lunged out making the women nearest to him shriek with a combination of fear colored with pleasure. The man exploded from the enclosure, unsure of what to do, wild and erect from the concoction his brothers forced down his throat. The women goaded him towards the first captive: a wild red haired Boudicca beauty queen with skin the color of milk. Tattoos that covered her arms indicated her former position in the hierarchy of her destroyed tribe. Jesse seized her by the hips, putting two hands on her buttocks and thrust forward. She arched her back in a vain attempt to escape. He went crashing down on top of her three times before his testes coughed up their potency in spurts. The women surrounding the semicircle applauded him with shrieks of joy.

The concoction worked its magic as Jesse caught his breath. He was ready again after one minute passed, aided by the gorgeous aides of the Glorious Mother who were dressed in golden sashes with circlet crowns of golden stars in their perfect hair. Her aides stroked and teased his cock with light feathers, then pulled him by his arms forward, as he mindlessly shambled after them up to the next captive. Jesse mounted her and plowed her fields to the chorus of her screams.

Isaac closed his eyes to the scene. He wanted to run, but his exit was blocked, and he was trapped. Even though he wished himself away, he kept opening his eyes to see if the charade was over.

The third captive received her entrance ticket to her new home in the same fashion as the first two. Jesse wiped the sweat from his forehead and followed the ladies-in-waiting to the fourth girl, who was the youngest, but the fairest of the captives. She was smaller than the rest and strained under Jesse's weight. His face reddened as he thrust in her, and the ladies in waiting restrained his full vigor by holding him back with leather straps they fixed around his waist. He struggled against them like a great whale struggling against the annoying harpoons of puny men. He lunged forward to impale her, staring at the look of pain in her eyes. One of the ladies-in-waiting whispered in his ear, "You must save your energy for the Glorious Mother, you must please her champion, or your life could be forfeit."

As he thrust in the captive, he glanced up at the Glorious Mother's face. She watched him with a smile. It was perfection. No skin or bone or hair out of line. She was without flaws. The Glorious Mother looked at him longingly and licked Her lips delicately with the triangular point of Her tongue. Jesse tasted the sweat from above his lip and emptied his soul into the little one. He stretched his back, and the ladies-in - waiting cleaned the blood from his midsection with buckets of water and soft towels. The champion kept his eyes on the Glorious Mother, and Her blue eyes called him to come and climb the platform and have his way with Her.

It stood at attention and pointed the way. He grabbed onto the platform's edge and pulled himself up, the muscles flexing in his back to the oohs and ahhs of the women in white. Behind him there was first a murmur in the crowd like a wave gathering momentum. Then there were screams. Shrieking.

Isaac took his eyes from the centerpiece of perfection, the pole of magnetism to which all the people in the room were attracted, and saw the crowd parting ways like the sea parted for the old man, Moses, in *The Gideons*. It parted for his Grandmother who entered the room like a poxy slave entering a banquet of aristocrats. The gasps and shrieks from the women could not drown out his Grandmother's voice which screamed and pleaded to the Glorious Mother, "My dear! My dear! You must stop the Joining Ceremony! This man is not fit for you! He is not fit!"

The women around her tugged at her oily robes, only they ripped at her with a slight deference, afraid to touch her with any vigor, lest they catch her age. The Glorious Mother looked up and wiggled to the side of the bull that struggled to mount Her. She leapt to Her feet like a gymnast and stood over Jesse. He stared upwards at Her naked flesh with a look of beggary in his eyes.

"What brings you to the Sanctuary, Old Mother? Is not the playpen your domain?"

"This ceremony most stop, I beseech you. I have evidence that this young man has been polluted by the world outside these walls."

"What do you mean, mother?"

"This boy is a criminal!"

"What evidence have you for this young man's crimes?"

The Elder Mother turned to the assembled crowd, which would act as the jury in this queer courtroom: a jury of the true power wielders in the Congregation. Power is mistaken to be a measure of strength, but power only points out the center of activity of a people. In an ant colony, it is the queen. In the Congregation, it was the Glorious Mother. All wills were bent towards the Glorious Mother's own, because the guide of Her will is the Father in Heaven. The Elder Mother knew she had to make her case solid, and she had all the evidence she needed.

"My sisters," she said addressing the crowd, "You all know the incident, where the boy, Baruch, was bitten by the snake and succumbed to its venom."

The women nodded that they had heard of the happening. Some looked to the Glorious Mother to take their cues. If they screamed out too soon in judgement of the man, it may upset the others. If they applauded at the wrong time, a time judged as wrong by everyone in the crowd, they could lose the Glorious Mother's favor. Everything was dependent upon her. She answered the old crone with the cold vigor of youth, "And what of this incident, mother? How does this constitute evidence against the champion?"

"This boy is not a champion; he is a horrible sinner, Mother: a criminal amongst us!"

The crowd buzzed, aghast at her accusations. She had already spoiled the course of the ceremony with her prattle. "What of it?!" The assembled women shouted at her as if they were pelting the Elder Mother with stones.

"Now hear me! Now hear me! This young man has been sneaking like a misbegotten snake through the grass into the greater forest and coupling, yes, you heard it correctly, *COUPLING* with one of the tribal women! Not of our congregation! A savage!"

The Glorious Mother turned red with a growing rage. There was a slow collective gasp that boiled up from the women in the crowd.

The Elder Mother continued in her diatribe against the man, "He violated all of our tenets even before this sacred Joining Ceremony, and even before his full assumption by the men of the Congregation. He had not even been tested by them, and he was already testing the local fare out in the forest!"

The Glorious Mother paused for a brief moment and glared at Jesse, who lay underneath Her feet, staring upwards at the prize between Her thighs. Time had dulled the concoction and Jesse's manhood was wilted slightly to the left, resting on his thigh like an oak uprooted and blown over in a tornado. The Glorious Mother stared at his face, and then looked at the crone who paced in front of the podium demanding an answer.

"You are serious, aren't you, mother?" The Glorious Mother said to the old woman.

"I am," the Elder Mother snapped.

"You have made accusations against this season's champion of our people. What evidence have you against this man?"

"She has nothing!" Jesse yelled from underneath the Glorious Mother's legs.

The Glorious Mother glared at him and screamed, "Shut it! Your donation has already been made to this cause! If you speak again, I'll have that magnificent oak cut off and fed to the hogs."

Jesse smiled at her, and his face was written with the confidence that she would not touch him.

The Elder Mother stretched out her hand. Inside it she held the amulet she retrieved from Isaac. "This, my women, this is an amulet of the vain and wicked Boorsin people. You all know the heathen and irreligious Boorsins. Well, I retrieved this amulet from this boy's younger brother, Isaac."

"The little bastard lies!" Jesse screamed.

"Father damn you, if you don't shut up I will feed the hogs your baby makers, too! Now you'll shut your damn mouth if you know what is good for you!" The Glorious Mother screamed at Jesse.

*

In the observatory, Isaac swore that he would kill his Grandmother the first chance he got. He would poison her soup with a weed from the forest that would end her life painfully. He would then apologize to his brother and explain to him how the old lady tricked him. As he looked on to what was happening below him, tears streamed down his face.

*

"The little bastard lies, does he? The little bastard told me that he and Baruch only left the Congregation to look for you."

"He told you he killed the wolf, right?"

"Shut up!" The Glorious Mother said. "Shut up! Shut up! Shut up!"

"Did you hear that, women? This man said that the little lame boy killed a wolf! Why, isn't that just the funniest thing you ever heard? He told me that you both came up with a story to say that he killed the wolf. How could you be so foolish, Jesse? No one will ever believe that that weakling could ever take on one of the wolves of the Forest," the old woman said laughing.

The assembled women looked at each other, puzzled, and then looked to the Glorious Mother who stood over the man with a smile on Her face. Droplets of laughter pattered from Her throat and spewed from Her mouth. Her breasts bounced up and down as She belly laughed with Her hands on Her knees, staring at Jesse's face. The laughter was contagious, and soon all the women were laughing whether they thought it funny or not.

Jesse yelled, "Isaac did kill the wolf! He did!"

"Oh, dear boy, do you really expect us to believe that?" The Elder Mother screamed as she nearly doubled over in pain from the spasms that all the laughing had caused.

"My boy! That's hilarious!"

"I'm no boy. I passed all the tests. I'm a man now."

"No, Jesse, we decide when you are a man. And you are no man!" The Elder Mother said. She looked up in reverence to her superior, afraid that she stepped down the wrong line of questioning.

"That is right, Mother? Correct?"

The Matriarch nodded Her head, and shot a squint-eyed grin to Her champion, showing no teeth. The cackling all around Her grew quite annoying. Her midsection burned like the fires that cleansed the dead winter fields of the remnants of a vibrant green spring. The Glorious Mother looked at Her disgraced champion and felt a drought coming on. It would have been delightful to join with him. Her yearning manifested itself in a single shake of Her head from side to side, mocking Her disapproval. The Glorious Mother looked askance at his hands and traced the profile of his body to his chest. Just a simple tuft of hair graced the valley between his chest muscles. She traced the veins on his arms and his hands--those hands that were almost on Her body, the strong hands that looked as if they were chiseled by the hands of the Father. Sadness welled up within Her like the last breath of a drowning Ophelia. He was so young, strong, and reeking of the future. The future was about to be crushed for the sake of the past. Their intercourse flashed through Her mind for a moment. All of the eyes were on Her, burning Her flesh with their jealousy as he seared through Her. She heaved underneath him tugging at his buttocks until they both exploded and felt the breath of the Father in their souls at the creation of the new life. She came to, sucked from the kernel of the fantasy by the old annoying crone who was busy tapping her walking stick on the ground in judgment. The old, tired, dried-up cunt would have to have her way. The Glorious Mother looked to Jesse, and a newfound rage boiled up inside her, with all the cackling and squawking, laughter and riot in a place normally reserved for holy erudite ceremony. It was as if a bunch of apes had been let in uninvited. The Glorious Mother's color changed from tan to one as red as a rhubarb stalk. The little bees with their buzzing and waggling had profoundly disturbed their queen, and She was no longer the center of attention and power; it was no longer Her teats being milked, it was the withered dried up bile filled teat of the Elder Mother. The Glorious Mother looked right at the old woman as if she were staring through her, like her existence were wiped from the records of all birth, and screamed like a banshee above the hubbub, "Everyone quiet now! The insolence crested above Her heavy voice and she tried again, this time screaming in a voice powerful enough to shatter glass, "Everyone quiet now!"

The wave broke. A few trickles and droplets of laughter remained, but the sisters now knew that the Glorious Mother meant business. A few random jibes, like flies trapped in a house searching for escape, were all that remained. All of the fixed stares in the room were back on their center of attention: the nexus of power. If anyone would allow the soon-to-be-dead woman speak, it would come with her permission.

"Elder Mother. You will speak now, and then you will depart back to your book and your children. Bring your charges, but come closer to the center, for everyone present must hear you."

The Grandmother paused, then waggled her long gnarled walking stick, pointing it a Jesse. She walked forward through the crowd slowly. As she parted the sea of women, she tapped the walking stick gingerly on the ground ahead of her. The Elder Mother held the little man amulet out in her hand. "I retrieved this from Isaac. It was given to him by one of the witches from the Boorsin people. The same people who threaten our territory on a daily basis. The same people who want to smite our religion and replace it with their own wicked ways. This witch was the woman that Jesse met in the woods for ill purposes."

"Why would the witch give the boy, Isaac, the amulet?"

"Why, she told him that it would help his brother, Baruch, out. These are a queer people who believe that their amulets and talismans have an effect on the world around them."

"That is a queer belief."

"The truth is though, Mother, that these amulets do influence the world, but in ways that are evil." when the Elder Mother said the word of curse, she pursed her lips like she was about to vomit.

"The talisman was the reason for Baruch's death. It corrupted him. I could have saved him. I remembered all the correct passages from *The Gideons*."

"You didn't have *The Gideons* though, did you, woman?" The Glorious Mother said.

"I had the verses memorized, Mother. I have said them enough."

"And what has your success ratio with these verses been, Mother?"

"What do you mean?"

"Out of all your cases. How many of them have survived?"

"Well, I used *The Gideons* on the boy, Isaac, when he was deathly sick, and he was saved. I used it on some of the women who would have succumbed to childbirth, and they were saved. I also used it on some infants with success."

"But some of the time *The Gideons* failed right?"

"Yes, you didn't save them all," Jesse echoed from beneath the Glorious Mother's legs.

"Be quiet, damn you!" The Glorious Mother said to him. Jesse looked up to the Matriarch with a sheepish grin and shut his mouth.

"Yes, fool, I'm making the accusations here. How dare you insinuate that *The Gideons* isn't the cornerstone of this people, how dare you," the Elder Mother said full of rage for Jesse.

The Glorious Mother interrupted, "But, my dear Mother, *The Gideons* isn't the cornerstone of this people, I am."

The Elder Mother stared at the young woman not knowing what to say. All the women around her heard what the Glorious Mother said. In another time, it would have been blasphemy, but *The Gideons* was gone. The Elder Mother had lost it. How could she lose something so important? The Glorious Mother smiled at the Elder Mother's sudden loss for words and said, "Please, our Great Grandmother, please continue in your accusations of this young man."

"Yes, Mother, I shall," the Elder Mother said and began pacing back and forth like a pious executioner waiting for a bitter axe. As she spoke, she waved her free hand to illustrate each point. "Jesse, it is apparent that you and Isaac concocted the story. You tricked the young boy into agreeing with your version of events by claiming he killed the wolf that attacked Baruch after he was bitten by the snake. You concocted the story together, and you promised to support him. The boy told me all about it, and also told me about the reason you went into the forest alone at night."

Jesse's face turned bright red like a beet washed of all the soil that anchored it to the earth. He coughed out a weak response, "It isn't true, Grandmother!"

Granny stopped her pacing and now dangled the amulet in front of Jesse's face.

"But, my son! We have the amulet. I found it on the boy!"

"He found it in the forest somewhere! I don't know where he got it from!"

"Jesse, was it really for healing? Or was it something to remember your lover by?"

His lover, Roxanne, had treated him like a king and begged him to leave his wicked people behind and come to the forest where he would have a choice what to do with his own life. Jesse's eyes darted to all the angles of the room, looking for a door. They darted over the bodies of the women, to the captives that he had just inseminated. He looked up to the Glorious Mother's blue eyes for some sense of acknowledgement. She now covered Her vagina with Her hand so he could not see it and Her breasts with Her arms when he looked at Her. It was like he was a foreigner. He realized that his only escape was the truth. He was the Champion. What could these women possibly do to him? He would tell them the truth and demand to be made an exile from them forever. He would go to her, to Roxanne. When they lay in the leaves, he used to look into her eyes and felt he was looking into the deepest portions of his own heart. When he had thoughts of her, he drifted and swirled, buoyed by his highest hopes and carried by the currents of passion. His mind passed from the Sanctuary through the forest, and he saw her in her settlement, mending baskets, skinning animals; he saw her completely free. He longed to be with her. This Glorious Mother was no Roxanne. She was nothing but a hobbyhorse whore who had been ridden and rammed by all the men in the Congregation. She probably even offered Herself up to the little freak, Sambus. A voice called to him from deep within his own mind. It told him to reach up and grab the Glorious Mother by the throat, and in one swift move, crush the passageway that allowed Her to breathe. If he did that, all of these women would bow to him. He contemplated the action for about a quarter of a minute. Then he came out with the words, "Isaac is a liar."

"No, my boy," his Grandmother said. "You are the liar. Isaac never lies."

Jesse stared at the Elder Mother with murder in his eyes. She smiled back at him, thinking him capable of doing anything. He lay prostrate at the feet of the Glorious Mother, ready to grab Her by the throat the first moment he could. It would be a righteous coup d'état.

Isaac squinted through the crystalline angel eyes to see what his Grandmother held in her hand. He saw the little wooden figurine, and his heart sank. He watched as Jesse's body leaked the ruddy color of lust, turning white with fear and then growing red again.

Isaac knew that Jesse ran up against the unyielding walls of his lust. His lust had caged him like a tiger and taunted him at the same time like a man with a cattle prod. Jesse judged women to be weak creatures in need of protection. This was his final mistake. When he jumped to his feet and grabbed the Glorious Mother by the throat, pandemonium broke out in the Sanctuary. Isaac could see from his vantage point that the Glorious Mother had no fear in Her eyes. Instead there was that crimson smile that showed Her perfect white teeth.

The men stormed into the Sanctuary that was normally off limits to them. Previously, they performed their role in the ceremony of delivering the offering of captives to the Glorious Mother, and abandoned the women to their champion. This was unprecedented, that a champion, instead of just doing the deed and mounting the Glorious Mother like a good boy, should seek to murder Her with all of Her loyal subjects as witnesses.

The Glorious Mother brought Her knees straight into the young man's naked testicles so hard that the men storming the crowd of women would swear for months afterwards that they heard a sickening pop. Jesse collapsed off the platform and onto the floor where the men had to shield him from the women wishing to tear him to pieces.

"Now is your chance, my brothers!" Jesse said meekly. "We can be kings!" Without a word, Saul jumped onto the platform like a jaguar and met the Glorious Mother face to face. Jesse cowered underneath them shaking from head to toe and then broke before his superior like a blood red wave crashing on the shores of a long forgotten atoll. Whatever confidence he had melted from his body, because Saul had embraced the Glorious Mother in his massive arms and glared at Jesse without a hint of forgiveness in his eyes. Jesse tried one last out with the man.

"Earthfather, I did well, right?"

"You do not know what you are dealing with, boy. This is the way it has always been since the beginning. We can't allow some boy to come in and mess that up."

"Why does it have to be this way? It's just what we're told. Roxanne, she taught me different."

"It's the truth, boy."

Nothing stirred in the massive man's face. Not even a matchstick spark of understanding. There was no miniscule sum of agreement. Saul's mouth ceased moving. It was a blind and final routine. What had been built was infinitely more important than his upstart child, his errant boy, his strong but foolish boy. Jesse was sired from his own Joining Ceremony and forgotten, until he noted the resemblance. What did it matter? Jesse was just another man. He was just another brother in arms, just another slave. Saul looked out on the crowd of women as he held the Glorious Mother in his arms. They had the faces of angels. He had known many of them in secret meetings, in glances exchanged and in sweaty forest liaisons under canopies of shame with the light of the moon in her eyes and the dripping, burning lust that began in his stomach and leaked into sharp barbs down his spine. The women taught the men unfulfillment of these lusts. They were taught to use it to murder. They were schooled in enslavement to the women's ends. They were taught to kidnap. They were taught to murder. They were taught to slay their enemies. They were taught to chop other men to bits. They were taught to grind their farms and white bones into the shallow, brown earth. Saul looked at the boy and then thought of his life. He thought of all he knew: his life up to that point in time. His existence was nothing but conflict. All of his hopes and dreams were wrapped up in the Congregation and the woman that he held in his arms shaking. Saul looked at Her and she nodded Her head to him with a blank stare on her face like nothing had happened. The choice She had made was settled with a brisk flick of Her wrist. The Champion would have to die. No man was allowed to put his hands on the Glorious Mother.

Saul knew his son, Jesse, was not an aberration. All of the men had secret lovers in the woods. It happened all the time when the pressure became too intense. Sneaking off into the woods was a favorite pastime. Jesse's crime was that he was discovered. Saul looked at the old crone that sat knotting her useless fingers together like she was kneading a wholesome wheat bread. He envisioned himself throwing a spear right at her. It would hit her square in that repulsive face of hers and tack her to the wall. Saul knew that that action would be the end of everything known and the start of the great uncertainty. He looked out over the crowd of female faces again, most round and beautiful. They would all be his. They would all submit to him. He looked back to the Glorious Mother as if choosing between them. The thrust of his will ripped through him, but his muscles did not respond. All he was aware of was complete submission. Saul was a great leader, but he was not a man who destroyed greatness.

The Glorious Mother looked at the man with apprehension, "Why do you hesitate, Saul?"

Saul dared not respond. He jumped from the platform and landed on Jesse. Jesse squirmed to get away, but Saul did not relent. The boy attempted to kick his legs into the man's chest to push Saul off. He tried two times, the second being weaker and more timid than the first. Saul brought his elbow up to Jesse's throat and pressed down with all his might, blocking his son's frantic gasping. Saul looked toward the crowd of women who all looked pleased, holding their arms at their sides. Soon, Jesse lay still.

*

Isaac covered his mouth to avoid screaming. He stood shaking in horror at what he had done. To him, a boy of an innocent nature, this was entirely his fault. He had brought death on Baruch and now his older brother. He would be alone in the world after everyone cleared out of the ceremony. He cried but could not pull himself away from the eyes, lest he miss something.

*

After Saul killed his son, he looked up to the Glorious mother, who did not miss stride in Her ceremony.

"We have witnessed the Father's justice carried out," She said with no hint of emotion, only Her usual bravado.

The women in the crowd murmured. Saul shook his head in disgust. He could not control himself and gathered the rest of the men around himself, walking through the exit. Saul broke into tears in the darkness, but did not utter a sound.

The Glorious Mother called to them, "Men! We thank you for our new sisters!"

The men did not turn back, but had other matters on their mind. After Saul choked back his tears and scolded himself internally for almost losing his bearing, he told the men they had other missions to plan. In order to overcome any mounting grief in his heart, he needed missions. There would never be a moment's rest for them. If they weren't venturing outwards, thrusting into the unknown, gaining new captives and sisters, the men were useless.

The Glorious Mother delivered her speech to the adulating sycophants. "Even though we just tried a criminal, and he was found guilty by his actions, this boy was one of us."

The women nodded in affirmation.

"This boy, this dear...sweet, *misguided* boy...though he was a criminal...deserves the proper respect in death that all of our guardians are accorded."

At Her words, the women began talking amongst themselves -- some debating, some questioning underneath their breath, trading furtive glances with one another and back to their matriarch -- but none dared question Her wisdom.

"My sisters, he shall be enshrined like all the other heroes that fall in battle. After all, he was one of our guardians, even if for a short time."

Beyond Jesse's outstretched body, the Elder Mother stood surrounded by her circle of helpers and adjutants. They whispered quietly to one another, sensing that there was now a grave problem between the Glorious Mother and their mistress, the Elder Mother. The old woman in charge of the youth had let them run amuck. One transgression was all that was pardonable. If the Glorious Mother were made aware of any more, one in her cohort would replace the Elder Mother immediately. But as all things in the Congregation went, replacements were never bloodless; there was always some kicking and screaming to accompany them.

The Elder Mother appeared to have grown more disheveled as Jesse's trial went on. Since its conclusion, she had not received even as much as a wink from the Glorious Mother. The paranoid thoughts flapped in her brain like bats startled by light streaming into their comfortable cavern. She thought to how many funerals she had seen. How many men had the Congregation sent to their deaths in the forest? Hundreds? Maybe thousands? But what good were the men after they had coughed up their seed? No good whatsoever. It was best to have the men doing what the men did best: Committing acts of violence; but not toward the women!

A door opened in its usual fashion, and three young girls emerged. All of the congregants' eyes were on them. The girls were darker in complexion than the rest of the women and looked to have come from fierce backgrounds. In her left hand, each girl carried an object. The tallest of the three, who stood in the center as they marched into the sanctuary, had her hand covered by a metal cone. The Elder Mother recognized the cone immediately as the Father's Crucible from which the holy fire was released onto the evil peoples of the world during the Rapture time. The girl to the left of the tall girl, a small little girl with curls that draped to her shoulders and a sturdy frame, carried a disk made of metal about the size of the breadth of measure between a full grown bull's horns. The disk looked heavy from a distance, but the small girl carried it with ease. The third girl, portly, who looked as if she had been baked by the sunshine, carried with her a set of tongs, silver in color, with several layers of cloth wrapped around the handles. They stopped in front of the podium where the Glorious Mother stood. She began Her oration with a somber reflection.

"The Ancients founded the Congregation at this very site. In founding it, they broke with the past and discovered their future within its ruins. In accordance with their traditions, the traditions handed down to us, we inter our dearest brother, Jesse. May he shine on for all the future generations, a pure and unspoiled diamond, with the facets glimmering in the light of a new day."

The tall girl carried the father's crucible to the base of the podium. There she stood over Jesse's body and raised the Father's Crucible towards him. The point of the cone began to glow and became white hot, illuminating the eager faces of the women in the crowd. The Glorious Mother called to the child, "Do the Father's will."

The girl nodded silently and thrust the cone at Jesse's corpse. A white-hot orb shot from the tip without a sound and coated Jesse's corpse in light. The corpse did not move, but became blindingly bright. The women surrounding it shielded themselves from the light, but felt the warmth on their skin, which was pleasant like bare breasts in the summer sun. The hissing began like a teakettle about to blow steam, which took a second to congeal into a whine, slowly losing pitch as the fiery inferno reached its maximum then began to abate. In the process, Jesse's body shrank in a uniform manner until all that was left was a glowing nugget the size of a newborn baby's fist. The nugget took on a shade of violet, then blue, cooling to orange, and red until it finally had cooled to the clear glimmer of a large uncut diamond.

"We have witnessed the Father's will, sisters. Now our sister in waiting will memorialize the container of his soul. In so doing he will be one with the Father."

The portly girl clasped her tongs in both hands and retrieved the diamond from the ground. The small girl placed the disk on the ground and stood on it. She held her arms to her sides to keep her balance.

Isaac dare not open his mouth. Instead the horror of witnessing his brother's death tunneled through him like a voracious worm sucking up the soft and tasty bits, lapping at the remaining shreds of innocence that clung to his soul like a babe at the breasts of a flabby woman. He ran his fingers over his face to block out what he just saw. The images were burned into his brain by visions as hot as the plasma that destroyed his brother's strangled body. Isaac scanned the ground where Jesse's body lay for anything that could bring him back to flesh and blood. Nothing, not even a scorch mark, remained.

Warriors who fell in battle to the slings and arrows of the enemy were burned down into bigger diamonds than the thirty carat, uncut diamond his brother became. Children such as Baruch weighed in at about ten to twelve carats when the funeral was over. All the members of the Congregation went into the mural when they died. They were all a piece of the puzzle: a memorial to the world that perished and burned because of humanity's wicked ways. Isaac watched as the small girl floated upwards on the disk to place his brother's diamond into a suitable bare spot.

The girl floated up and spied the perfect location for the diamond. It would go into the eyelid of the largest angel. She readied the diamond in her hands. When she passed near the eyes of the angel, her eyes met Isaac's.

Isaac gasped. He backed to the farthest dark corner.

The girl screamed downwards, "A spy! There's a spy in the Sanctuary!"

She shrieked like a bird shot met in flight by a hunter's arrow and lost her precarious balance. The crowd beneath her gasped as the girl fell from the floating disk. The sisters dashed to get out of her way but the area she fell into was too crowded. She landed fully on two of them and kicked another with her feet as she came down. The disk crashed and banged off the floor like a coin tossed idly onto a tavern table by a drunk. The diamond struck the metal floor and bounced twice before it nestled hidden into a crevice at the base of the Glorious Mother's podium. The tiny girl jumped up from the bloodied and unconscious fat women that served as her pillows. She pointed to the angel's eyes, and screamed again, "There is a spy! A little spy in the Sanctuary!"

Women around her began shrieking and pointing upwards towards the massive angel as if it had come to life and was spraying its fire on them.

"My Father, get it out!" Granny screamed with her the best anger she could possibly fake. She knew who the spy was. Immediately she began planning her defense.

"Thrust open the doors! Find this little rat!" the Glorious Mother ordered.

The minions complied. Isaac sat in the darkness, rocking back and forth, waiting for the inevitable.

Isaac's heart felt as if a large clutch of maggots hatched and began burrowing through his ventricles, drowning in his blood in a writhing search for oxygen. Sweat poured from his temples as he rocked back and forth. He looked for a way out of the room, but found none. As his possibilities pinched to nothingness, his breathing increased until it was out of control. Hyperventilating, all he heard was footsteps on the stairs and screams. But he could not tell if they were screams of agony or of delight. Suddenly, their hands were all over him, tearing at the musty hem of his cassock. Their sharp fingernails scraped into his face and gouged his pudgy cheeks. He kicked at the first few and screamed as he quickly lost his will to resist them. The women dragged him down the stairs and his head bounced off each step. The women took their turns kicking him in the darkness. They sneered at him as they dragged him down the long hallway. Two women held each of his legs. The rest spit and slapped his face in turn.

When they dragged him into the Sanctuary, he looked up and saw his Grandmother at the center of her clutch of followers. Isaac looked at her and began to sob. His Grandmother's complexion took on a ruddy tone that looked as if all the blood had descended from the upper jagged peaks of her leathery skin into the deep valleys of her wrinkles. She pulled the woolen mittens from her hands, and the light blue vein pipes that skirted over the tendons and sinew and pithy bones throbbed with a hidden rage. As she approached Isaac, her stride became more purposeful. By the time she traversed the short distance between them, he had vomited on the front of his cassock. She leaned down and whispered in his ear.

"You poor, pathetic, little boy," she said.

"Grandmother, I am sorry."

"Don't be sorry, boy. What's done is done," she said with a smile on her face.

"But mind you, boy, if you value your life in the least you will not say a word. I will talk on your behalf. Grandmother knows best."

The shock of his capture numbed Isaac into agreeing with her even though he knew deep down she was nothing but a lying old bag of bones.

She stood up and began smashing her walking stick on the floor to quiet the women who booed and hissed and clucked like hens terrified by a marauding fox. Each time the Elder Mother smashed the floor with her stick little shards of wood went flying and the crowd of women grew more and more quiet. Soon, it was so silent in the Sanctuary that you could only hear the sounds of Isaac's little whimpers; he sounded like a puppy looking for its mother in the dark.

"Just what in the Father's wonder do you think you're doing here, boy? Why did you come to this ceremony without an invitation?" the Glorious Mother asked.

The Elder Mother spoke before the defendant got a chance, "Mother. Now I believe the young boy was merely curious."

"Curious? My boy, you were curious? Why did your eyes get their full share?"

"I didn't watch most of it."

"Oh. So you didn't like watching what happened?"

"No I didn't see it."

"He did not see it, Mother," the old woman said.

"Guard your tongue, Grandmother before I have it plucked, squirming, from your mouth!"

The Elder Mother stumbled backwards, aghast, "Why I have never...," she muttered to herself.

There were chuckles from the women standing in a circle witnessing the scene.

"You didn't like watching me, boy? You didn't like these?" She caressed her breasts with Her hands allowing the nipples to poke through Her outstretched fingertips.

Isaac looked at them and couldn't help but feel warm.

"I didn't watch, Mother. I swear it."

"So you don't like what you see, then?"

Isaac remained silent. The Glorious Mother smiled at him like She could crush him under her foot at any time.

"Why didn't you see...what's your name?"

"Isaac, Mother."

"Isaac, what possibly could have distracted you from me."

"I couldn't stop crying after my brother died."

"Why were you crying? You killed your brother."

"No, mother. The big man killed him."

"Yes, my boy. Saul strangled your brother. But, didn't you ultimately kill him?"

"It's not possible," Isaac moaned.

"Didn't you tell your Grandmother what Jesse was off doing in the forest?"

"I guess I did."

"I know you did. And then your Grandmother, she told me, and I ordered Jesse to be killed because he was a criminal."

"How do we know if someone is a criminal, boy?"

Isaac stared at the young woman that paced in front of him. He then looked to his Grandmother who motioned for him to keep his mouth shut. The Glorious Mother paced in front of him like She were a tigress drooling for a piece of easily gotten meat.

"How do we know if someone is a criminal? Are you hard of hearing, boy!?"

Isaac did not make a sound. He closed his eyes and wished himself to another place. The Matriarch stepped forward until She was standing over Isaac.

"Answer me, damn you! You stop acting like you can't hear me! You had better answer me you little freak...."

"I don't know, Mother!"

"Are you angry with me, freak? Sharp tongues are easiest to dull in isolation, boy!"

"No, Mother, I'm just scared."

"We know that someone is a criminal after they have been tried for their crimes. But before that, we have to know that they committed a crime. You know what that requires, freaky boy?"

"No, Mother, I don't."

"It requires someone willing to tell. Someone who is willing to tattle and spread the tale of what they saw!"

"But the boy did you a service, Mother!" the Elder Mother said with an ample helping of hesitation in her voice.

"Yes. We thank you, Isaac. We thank you for tattling on your brother Jesse and ruining this year's Joining Ceremony. We don't know why you told, but you did. Everyone, show our little freak brother our appreciation!"

The entire congregation broke into chortling cheers and clapping that sounded like a deluge of searing fiery arrows hurled at Isaac by the taut biting bows of a powerful army. When they struck, they pinned him to the ground under the weight of their insult. The uproar died down when the Matriarch motioned her arm.

"This brings us to your crime, Isaac."

"My crime, Mother?" Isaac said as he cried.

The Elder Mother darted between the two, thrashing her cane in front of her. "The boy committed no crime! He was only curious!"

The Glorious Mother's face reddened with rage. The Elder Mother had already ruined Her day, and now she was trying to play defense for this little rat. There had to be a reason why she cared about him so much. "He's just curious, Grandmother? Just curious? I'd say this boy knows many things that he has no business knowing."

"Mother, I just wanted to see my brother…."

"You wanted to see something you had no right to be part of!" the Glorious Mother said.

"Why doesn't this boy have a right to be here?" the Elder Mother asked.

"Because we don't want him here!" the Glorious Mother said.

"That doesn't mean he has no right, Mother."

"Who has rights and no rights, is up to me alone," the Glorious Mother said.

What slipped out of the Glorious Mother's mouth froze the room around Her.

"Which brings us to how the boy found out about the Sanctuary in the first place, how did that happen, Grandmother?"

"Oh, I don't know. He's an inquisitive boy. He discovered it somehow."

The Glorious Mother stood over Isaac and pulled on his little arm, picking him up until she cradled his head against her bare breast in an awkward embrace.

"My boy, my precious, little boy, how did you get it in your mind to come and look at this place?"

She stroked his hair with her free hand, parting it from his sweaty brow. She looked directly into his face.

"Come, boy, tell your Mother. Who told you about this place?"

Isaac thought and looked to his Grandmother for a split second. The Glorious Mother watched him break his gaze and look at the old crone, and it made Her madder than a feral pig fenced in.

"I discovered it myself, Mother."

The lie he told shattered whatever restraint the Glorious Mother held towards the old woman. The Glorious Mother pushed the boy hard onto the ground. She grabbed the Father's Crucible from the young girl, who screamed when it was wrenched from her grasp.

"You had better tell me the truth right now or you will join your brother, Jesse!"

"Wait!" Granny screamed.

"Isaac, please, tell me. Did you like anything you saw today?"

"No, Grandmother, I didn't like any of it."

"None of it, boy?" the Glorious Mother said, holding the Father's Crucible at Her waist.

"Are you telling the truth to us?" the Elder Mother asked him.

"No, I hated every bit of it; it was just plain insane."

"Okay then, boy. You can leave us," the Glorious Mother announced.

"I can leave? I can go back to the children?"

"Yes. But stay for now, boy," the Glorious Mother said with a bitter smile on her face.

The Father's Crucible glowed brighter than the sun in an instant. Isaac screamed and shielded his eyes. He expected to feel only a momentary blast of pain, and then he would be with the Father in Heaven. He wondered if they would put his diamond into the wall to be enshrined with heroes, or if they would just chuck it into the forest to be picked up by some animal attracted to shiny objects. The blast traveled over his body. It singed his arms and set the burlap at the edge of his cassock ablaze. When he reached up aghast to put out the flame he saw the intended target. His Grandmother only managed to scream the moment the orb, hotter than the sun, struck her. As the biologic matter of her corpse burned away, fat sputtered into hydrogen and oxygen. The carbon congealed by forces unknown into a small red-hot diamond that fell to the floor with a tinkle right behind Isaac's bare ankle. He could feel the heat from the diamond on his foot.

"Pick her up, damn you!"

Isaac put his hand near the diamond to grab it by he felt it would burn the flesh off his hands if he touched it.

"Pick her up, Isaac! Pick your dear Grandmother up!"

"No."

"No?"

"No. It's too hot!"

"Are you refusing your Mother, Isaac?"

"No, I'm not refusing you. I won't touch it; it's too hot," Isaac said in between sobs.

"But, Isaac, you must pick her up. She's our parting gift to you."

"What, Mother?"

"Our parting gift, Isaac. You see, you're leaving us today."

"I don't want to leave."

"But you see, little boy, you must. The only person keeping you here was your dear departed Grandmother. Now that she's gone, there's no real reason you should stay either."

"I can stay. I promise I'll be good!"

"No, my boy, you really should be going."

"Where will I go?"

"My boy, that is up to you. There's a great wide world out there. I'm sure you'll find your way through it. You are a smart little sharp-tongued boy."

"I don't want to go!" Isaac screamed.

"No arguments. Sharp tongues are best dulled in isolation, boy. Grab your dear Grandmother up and go! Or I will have the men take you by force. Go boy! There's the exit!"

She pointed to a doorway that slowly opened in the front of the Sanctuary behind the triple podiums. Through the doorway, stairs led up. The light in the stairway flickered a strange orange as if it were lit by candlelight. Isaac sobbed and grabbed the diamond up with a hand covered in the cheap burlap. He looked to the Glorious Mother for any hint of reprieve in Her eyes. Isaac saw nothing but hate and self-assurance. He placed the warm diamond in his front pouch next to *The Gideons*. He reached down and picked up the little man amulet that his grandmother flung on the floor. As he started to walk out the door, the women began to shriek at him. They cackled like their beaks were bonded with glue and all the sound was coming from their chest cavities. In their eyes, he could see they wanted to tear him to shreds. They held off from ripping his guts from his body, because they knew that exile from the Congregation was a fate worse than death. He was about to become a vagrant, one of those horrible cursed wanderers from *The Gideons*. When he climbed the stairs toward the sunlight the women shouted curses upon his name.

"We hope you die out there boy!" they screamed in unison. "The beasts will make bread out of your ground down bones!"

Isaac did not look back at the shrieking ninnies as he climbed into daylight. He trudged up the stairs like a man defeated. *Damn them to hell*, he thought. *May the mushworms pick all of their bones clean.* He imagined bears and wolves invading the halls of the Congregation and ripping the terrified women to shreds. As he thought that, he started to cry. *The only person that was going to be eaten by beasts was him. The members of the Congregation had each other. He was now alone in the world.* He made the first step into the wide world alone and the forest that surrounded seemed cloaked in a resplendent shade of woe. The door shut on their derision behind him, solidly and metallically with an empty clunk.

He carried *The Gideons* in his front pouch, the words printed in black and white on the pages that he could not read, for he had never been taught. The scorch marks covered the ancient tome as if the book had been burned in an ancient fire. It rescued for some reason. He put his hand on *The Gideons* and his hand came to touch the diamond that was his grandmother. He pulled the small stone from his pocket and thought about tossing it into the underbrush, but he put it back in his pocket. He looked back to the metal door and listened intently for any stirrings within. The only sound he heard was infernal silence of a crypt and the cawing of a raven in the woods. He stopped his tears and reminded himself of the stories that his Grandmother taught him from *The Gideons*. Whatever would happen to him was now up to the Father. He gulped his fear deep down, banishing it past the frolicking butterflies, and took the first step of a journey into the great unknown.

Isaac grew up following his older brother, Jesse, into the woods. He had trudged four-hundred paces before he realized that he had no idea where he was going. Should he find people? Would they be friendly to him or would they kill him and leave him to rot in the sun? The farthest he ventured into the forest was the clearing where he saw his brother Jesse with the woman. By the time he made it there, the sun had fallen down like and old peasant man wobbling on uneasy legs to a bitter rest.

The forest was no place for a boy at night. The shrieks of madmen and angels haunted his moonlit shambling. He knew only one thing: that he could not stop walking. He wished he was fearless like his brother, but every step forward came with a pinprick of doom. He headed in the direction of the burning out sun, hoping to find the river. In one of their lessons, his Grandmother told him that people of all sorts tended to dwell along the river, because it enabled them to fish for food and get water to drink. She told him that the only type of river people didn't live along was a stagnant one. That quickly became a swamp, and the only life in a swamp held death daily in a sweet embrace. When the water collected in little pools and the fish flopped in frenzy and fought one another in their vain attempts to breathe, it was time to pick up your settlement and move. His grandmother told him that industrious people, like the people of the Congregation who were the best and smartest people to grace the world, dug deep holes into the Earth to find hidden caverns where water bubbled clean and pure. As Isaac passed by a stream feeding the river he sought, he shed a single tear, because it reminded him of the stream where Baruch met with the snake. In the moonlight, the surface obscured the speckled green and yellow trout from the wily intentions of men and raccoons. They sat floating a foot above the mucky bottom with mouths open to receive their holy communion. When a hapless insect fell from the tall grasses into the pools: it had but one thought. To escape it beat its wings to break the surface tension. The trout ascended to the surface. Schwup! The green bottle fly became one with the cosmos in the cold, wet gullet, and the trout darted back to the safety of the creek bottom.

His Grandmother told him that in years past, men fashioned insects made of fur and bits of metal in order to catch the fish. When a fish bit into the phony insect, a sharp metal hook sunk into its jaw. The men caught the fish, not for food, but for the mere sport of it. Unlike the animals, men did not have to spend entire days storing food for the future days when the cornucopia ran dry. The men did the things they enjoyed with their time. They were not forced to bow their heads in prayer and contemplation. His Grandmother told him that men had too much time on their hands and they went wicked. That's why the Father punished them. That's why they got burned up. The art of fishing was lost with everything else when the angels of the Father descended upon the Earth to exact their punishment.

Isaac continued along the stream for at least one thousand paces. His legs felt like two big bags of grain that had ruptured. He could go no further and stopped to rest at a tree that was wrenched from the earth by a storm. It now lay on its side, dangling its root-like fingers into a deep pool like a sad woman washing mud from her hands. A pang of hunger started in Isaac's stomach like a small seed. As he sat by the stream listening to the fish eat their fill, his hunger grew into a veritable redwood. He watched the surface of the water as his stomach screamed to him. Isaac wished he could see enough to catch the trout, but no amount of wishing could turn the earth around from its course of mindless revolutions. Before sleep overcame him, he said a prayer that he would eat as soon as he woke up in the morning. He cried a bit before sleep took him. He knew the days of getting up from his nice warm bed and going to eat a hot breakfast with the other children were over. Sleep took him in the tall grasses and rotting mulch underneath a sap coated pine tree.

As Isaac slept, he dreamed a terrible dream. In his dream, he stood over the forest, tall as a giant, with his head in the moist clouds. With each step he took he heard the trees underneath his feet crunch and snap like the brittle bones of elderly women. The animals that were crushed under his feet sounded like the little peeps of mice caught in traps with no chance of escape. He thought, *why can't I stop walking? What is driving me forward?* A voice from the heavens poured over him like a waterfall. *You must not stop walking and you will not stop walking. You will walk until you can no longer walk. Just as the spider sings no dirges for the half eaten fly, you will sing no dirges for yourself. You are what you are boy. Do not decry the destruction. It is written into your being.*

Isaac shrank to his normal size but kept shrinking down past the level of the grasses that blow over in the slightest wind, down past the level where ladybug act the terror of aphids that sip the sweet nectar of roses. He shrunk down to the level of spheres and clouds of particles. Down to the level where everything in existence was vibration, a great cosmic thump. All around him was nothing but the fuzz and buzz and hymn of eternity.

He woke as the trees whipped at his face and scraped flesh from his cheeks. A great throaty cat growled behind him and chased him through the underbrush. He could only feel the burning of his lungs and his pounding heart beating its bass drum in his ears. Louder and louder its rhythm grew until he realized it was a dream within a dream, his primal fear of being eaten ran rim shod through the reptilian part of his brain. He shrieked as the cat pounced and sunk its fangs through his eye socket and then he felt nothing.

He awoke in the middle of a large plain. The grass was stunted and wispy, growing up in small patches like the hair on a balding man's head. Isaac put his hand on his face, and it stung. A blood-red sun framed the silhouette of three crosses. A man hanging from the center screamed in pain. Isaac crawled forward to get a better view and was stabbed in the palm by something sharp. He looked at his palm and saw that a large diamond stuck from the wound. Blood trickled from the clear, faceted sides. As Isaac got to his feet, he noticed the hill was made of diamonds of a very uniform size and shape that reflected the blood red sun. As he climbed the hill, the diamonds shifted and spilled downwards making his ascent difficult. Isaac's legs burned with muscled rage by the time he got to the base of the crosses. Two of the men were dead, rotting, pecked by crows. There was no smell. The third man looked at Isaac and begged him for water. He said, "I thirst."

Isaac apologized because he had nothing to drink. The man stared at him with sunken eager eyes, saying nothing more. Isaac asked him, "Are you the Father's son that I've heard about?"

The man answered, "No. I am just a common thief whose only crime was stealing bread for my children's hungry bellies. Well, among other offenses."

"And who are they?" Isaac asked.

"You mean the two corpses?"

"Yes. Did you know them in life?"

"They were kings, loved by men."

"But they are dead now, rotting in this blood red sun?"

"Crucified on a hill of riches, Hope died first and Charity followed."

"But who killed them? Who put *you* here?"

"They came willingly. But I was dragged."

"And what is your name?"

"I, my boy, am Justice. When the men turn wicked and anarchy rules, I am put to arbitrary purposes by anyone with Power. I was brought here to kill my comrades and make sure they were good and dead before I returned to my so-called masters. This was like shutting off the sun. For when they were nailed to the crosses, I being bound to them, was also bound."

"And you can't get down?"

"Not till the world is put to rights."

"When will that happen?"

"When you become what you are."

"And what am I?"

"You are the poorest beggar of us all. Nothing is asked of you and nothing is given you. You are the ruler and the ruled, the measure of all men. You are a toothless dying beggar like me."

The resplendent diamonds at his feet shifted uneasily. A great cracking sound came from beneath their feet.

"Oh dear," the crucified man said.

The edifice came crashing down and Isaac felt himself falling into free space. As he drifted, the diamonds fell around him like snowflakes, each one having been so unique that another one would never be like it in the world. All were perfect individuals. But that was in their human life, before they were burned up by the Father's Crucible. When he hit solid ground, he awoke with a raging tear in his belly, screaming at him to satiate it.

Isaac trudged for miles past the brambles and tangles that clawed their way into the chaotic void, forming their majesty on the bitter earth. His legs burned with fire as his mind began to settle on one overarching eventuality that he had previously been in complete denial of. His fear began with a small seed, tossed into his soul by the out of control hunger in his belly. Now, it mimicked the brambles he fought his way through, but still he walked forward, heeding the voice in his dream. He walked forward, driven by the knowledge that if he did not meet others of his own kind soon, he would most likely die in the wilderness. Phantoms loomed behind every bush that he skirted. Snakes were there to strike at his ankles. The bright white lilies with greenstalks gently whispered his doom and the hope that their root systems would find nourishment in his bones. They would see another sunrise with the warmth of the sun on their outstretched hands. The dew that condensed on their faces would water the flies that laid maggots on Isaac's corpse. As he trudged forward, his fear grew. Would he perish? What would happen to him? He placed his hand on *The Gideons* and thought of the other men who were cast out of their families and homes, impelled by the Father to do magnificent things. They did not know it at the time that they were bound for greatness. The men merely answered a call from the Father. These men survived no matter what, and if they died, their message lived on, though diluted to the dull faced men and women that surrounded them, following their every move, poking and prodding the Prophets with eager fingertips. Isaac put one foot in front of the other. It was all he could do, until he heard the familiar sound coming from a clear pool of stream he had been following to the river. *Schwup!*

Isaac kneeled at the edge of the pool and watched the fish dart to seize their prey: small flies that chanced the waters edge until they embraced the surface tension. They struggled, beating their wings against the water and alerted the brutes lurking beneath. Isaac watched the fish flickering underneath surface. They rose when the flies fell into a point where they darted to the surface splashing. Isaac raised his hand so it was parallel to the water's surface and timed his slap just right. Schwup! He slapped the water and the fish floated, stunned. He grabbed it in his hands, excited at his catch. It was slippery and fat.

Isaac turned with the fish against his midsection. He gasped and dropped the fish into the dirt. It flopped vainly for its watery home. A wild looking man wearing animal skins and brandishing a spear tipped with sharpened metal scraps stared at him with eyes filled with fury. He was sweating. His chest heaved. The cloak he wore at his shoulders looked like a mosaic of pieces of fur from every animal in the forest. Nine more men, each dressed similarly emerged from the surrounding brush. The fish flopped again, drawing the man's attention to it. He thrust his spear forward, causing Isaac to fall down. All of the men laughed.

"Who gave you the right to fish in the waters of the Forest People?" the wild eyed man said as he stepped forward towards Isaac, pointing his spear downwards at Isaac's bare chest.

Isaac hurried and grabbed the trout and threw it back in the water with a splash. It floated on the surface, showing its painted rainbow side and then rushed to the bottom.

"I was hungry. I didn't think the fish belonged to anyone."

"They do. The fish in the stream belong to the Forest. And the Forest belongs to us. So you see, the fish in the stream belong to us."

"I didn't know that the stream belonged to you. I mean, you didn't put a sign up."

"A sign? Everyone knows this part of the Forest belongs to us. The stream is in our part of the Forest, so it belongs to us. This is our home, and you are trespassing in it."

"I didn't mean anything by it. Just show me the way out of your home, and I will walk that way. I don't want any trouble."

"I would do that, but I can't. You see, you're in the Forest, too. And everything in the Forest belongs to us. So where does that leave us?"

"I don't know."

"Sure you do. It's basic. Besides, a weakling like you will never make it out of here."

"You mean, I belong to you?"

"You're very bright. You figured me out. So I'm thinking you should come with me now."

"I can't."

"You have no choice."

"Impossible!" Isaac yelled and made to run from the men, but they easily overtook him after hooting and hollering enough to alert all the deer in the Forest that there was a large contingent of human beings walking through the forest to hunt and kill them. The man threw Isaac to the ground and sat on top of him while the other men searched his front pockets.

One of the men had a knife scar across his face and reeked of onions. His hair was as black as rot and longer than the others; it matted across his scalp and seemed to be styled in a spiral around the crown of his head by the natural grease he exuded from his pores. He ripped the diamond from Isaac's front pocket. He brushed his hand across *The Gideons* but didn't think it valuable.

"Squirrel, why, look what I've found!" He held the diamond up for another man, skinny with bowed legs to see. Soon all the men stared at the diamond with mouths gaping open, cavities and broken teeth pointing like signposts to their lifestyles. The man sitting on Isaac snatched the diamond from the black haired man, making him turn bright red.

"Damn you, Rooster! I found that! It's mine!"

"No. No, Crow, I'll be taking that," Rooster said with a chuckle.

"Damn you!" the black haired man named Crow said in disgust and turned to walk off into the forest by himself. "Damn you, Rooster! I won't bear it this time! My hand touched the stone first! It's mine!"

"That's the old way, Crow! Remember, I own everything in the forest, and this was in the forest!" Rooster said as he laughed.

Rooster held the diamond up into the sunlight and could see the trees through it, their green making it appear an emerald.

"Beautiful," one man, a powerful looking red haired beast said to his leader.

"Perfect!" The smallest of the rough men exclaimed.

"She's bright and clear as a winter's morning," Rooster said.

"It shines like the stars, boss, let me see it."

"No you can't see it, do you think I'm a fool? It shines like Deer's eyes," Rooster said, putting the diamond into a pouch around his neck.

"You're right. It does. It shines like that slut's sweaty breasts when she's ridden every man, boy, and beast in the forest!" The red-haired man proclaimed exuberantly.

'You're wrong about her. She's only mine, and I'll keep her. She'll love me if I bring her this. She will agree to marry me for sure."

"She just might. A beauty for a beauty! And you'll get all of her, you ugly dog, Rooster."

The black haired man exploded from the woods like a tiger in full bore charge. Raven ran directly at Rooster with his spear leveled and a scream in his throat which he did not hurl until he was upon the big man. He flung his spear and released his voice at the same time, bringing Rooster to his knees. The spear stuck out of his chest like a signpost pointing the way to Hell.

"Mother of the Woods!" the men yelled in unison as their leader sank on his knees, further and further downward until he fell over. Rooster looked down at the spear shaft in shock.

"You've...you mushworm fart...you've k...k...killed me...."

"Right I did! And you deserved it!" Crow yelled at him, standing over his bloody body.

"You damn traitor, may you die in your sleep, catch the worm that grows inside you while you shrivel and die, you bastard wolf child of a whore. May your children rise up and chop the berries from your bush...," dark maroon organ blood shot from his mouth and plugged his stream of insults. He died looking upwards at the treetops.

Crow danced around his opponent.

"No Rooster, you're dead! I survived! You're dead! You Rooster, you died! I'm victorious!" He said dancing around Rooster's freshly minted corpse with all the glee of a child celebrating his first steps.

The other men stared bleakly at their fallen leader who was now turning ashen gray. Crow had a look of joy on his face like he had drunk too much wine. He plucked the diamond from Rooster's pouch and held it to the light. He said looking through it,

"Now I'm the hunt leader, men. You know the rules; you'll do what I say."

The men dropped to their knees around Crow. Some of them grumbled under their breath, but it was the way of their people. Crow challenged Rooster. Rooster must have thought that the smaller man was bluffing. It did not matter how Crow carried the challenge out, just as long as it was made.

Isaac watched the scene unfold before him with his hand on the Gideons. These savages could never find it. They wouldn't know what it was and would use its brittle old pages to start a fire. His hand brushed up against the small wooden man. The woman that had given him the amulet dressed like these men, so Isaac figured that he would show them the amulet out of hopes they would treat him better. He held it out to them. Crow saw it and leapt to his feet with his mouth gaping wide open.

"Where did you get that!" he screamed

"This doll? I just found it out in the woods here."

"That's no doll, boy, that's what a Forest woman gives her man before he goes off on the hunt or raiding. It protects him from his enemies. It brings him home safe and promises her to him for the entire length of the hunt."

"Did Rooster there have one?"

"No. Rooster was in love with a woman but he never had the courage to talk to her. So he was never given the caringtotem, which allowed me to kill him," Crow laughed.

"Where did you find that, boy?"

"Near my home."

"If you found it near your home it must have been dropped by one of our men near your home," Crow said and turned to look at his men. "Have any of you been near this boy's home?"

"Where does he live?" One of the men called out.

"Where do you live, boy?"

"I don't live anywhere. My people got rid of me."

"Why?"

"I told my people I didn't like their ways, so they told me I could leave. But that's only after they killed my brother and my grandmother."

"Why did they kill your brother and your grandmother?"

"It was my fault. I interrupted a ceremony, and they had to pay for my sins."

"Your people sound very strange."

"They are strange. Probably just the strangest people in the world."

"Well, do you know anyone else?"

"No."

"Well you can't make it here out on your own boy, you can come with us."

"I will hunt with you. I know the forest pretty well. My Grandmother taught me everything about it before she died."

Crow laughed. He doubled over in a great belly laugh that soon proved contagious and had his men laughing on the ground rolling over each other in a quest for oxygen to fuel their outbursts.

"A woman taught a man about the forest? A woman taught a man about the forest!" Crow yelled in disbelief.

"Only men know about the forest, boy, and the women stay at home."

"Then I'll be a man with you then, because I know all about the forest."

"Impossible. Not with that foot you won't."

Isaac stared down at his foot and a wave of shame washed over him. He felt at that moment that he would be carrying the burden of his deformity until his dying day. If there existed a way out of this he would gladly take it.

Before the hunting party departed, Raven retrieved his spear from Rooster's still warm corpse. Isaac looked into the face of the dead man as he passed by, his eyes were fixed straight ahead in a worried stare. Isaac thought about what Rooster might have been thinking in his final moment. Was he afraid for himself, or the future coming after him? Was he thinking about the woman he loved and how he would never get to show his love for her? Was this a look of bitter regret? It seemed just silence and nothingness to Isaac.

"Are you going to bury him?" Isaac asked.

Crow turned red and stared at Isaac with his coal black eyes.

"No. That isn't our way. In life we're masters of the forest, and when we leave this life we go back into the forest. The animals will pick his bones clean, the foxes and wolves will eat his guts for supper until they all have their fill, and in the end Rooster will become just a tiny part of everything. Only the forest and the forest people will remain to continue on."

They continued walking and Isaac said, "I apologize for my ignorance, but what happens to his soul?"

"What?" Raven asked.

"His soul? What happens to it?"

"What is that?"

"The part of him that is missing now that he is dead."

"He's just dead."

"Oh."

"What are you getting at kid?"

"I'm just saying that part of him is gone now."

"What part? All his arms and legs are there, he just has a hole in his chest where I ran him through, and his blood ran out on the ground."

"But we have souls."

"You still haven't told me what that is."

"It's the part of him that isn't there anymore now that he's dead. He was alive and it was there, he's dead and it departed his body."

"That's nonsense."

"It isn't nonsense, the Father made each and everyone of us special."

"Where is this Father?"

The men started to laugh. Crow grabbed Isaac and held him so they were looking at each other's faces. "Look, be quiet about things that are nowhere to be found! We're part of the forest just like the deer and raccoons. We aren't special because we were made special; we're special because we make ourselves special! Stop talking your nonsense."

"But, I learned a different way."

"Did you not say that your ways were strange?"

"I did."

"Then don't question our ways using yours. It will bring you nothing but misery."

Isaac stared off into the distance, and Crow walked ahead of the men. Isaac was firmly sandwiched in the middle, perhaps to protect him from any wild beasts, but he felt more like their captive than anything. He watched the power in the strides of his captors and how gracefully they moved through the ferns and underbrush. With every one of his clumsy steps, his face burned with shame. His foot would follow him for the rest of his days. If he was ever going to become a man, he thought, he would have to hack the bastard foot off and wear a wooden one. At the very least, he could tell strangers that he lost his foot to a battle instead of having been born a freak.

The men carefully wound their way through the paths in the forest that had been carved into the minds of their people since great-great-grandfathers took ownership of the massive wood. As their elders taught them, they would teach their own children. They were careful that the pathways they cut through the grasses resembled the ones made by deer so as to avoid their enemies following them back to their camp. Isaac did his best to follow them, but the fleet footed men kept getting ahead of him. Always, the last man in the line would turn around and glare at Isaac and tell him to hurry up. They reminded him through their exhortations that in the deep woods getting separated meant getting eaten by something hungry and bigger than you. Isaac did his very best to keep up with the men, following behind them just out of reach of their animal skin clothing, walking as fast as his legs could carry him.

By the time he heard the rush of the river over rocks and saw the glow of campfires that emanated from hollowed out trees with trunks that seemed to open up and swallow the night in black chunks, he was exhausted. The group of men had walked several miles. Their women rushed from tree houses to greet them. Each man gave his woman his caringtotem to return to the leather necklace on her bosom and disappeared with her into the darkened recesses.

Crow yelled, "Chief, I must see your daughter!"

A muscular man painted from head to toe in half black and half white appeared from the darkness. In his hands he was holding entrails from one of the deer.

"Now, Crow, you know now is not the time to call for the daughter of the Chief's hand in marriage. You must wait for the appointed time. Not that she'll accept your offer, being you're such a brute. How do you plan on sweetening your offer?"

"I've found a diamond as big as my fist. How do you think that will sit with her?" Crow said holding the diamond up in the moonlight for the shaman to see.

"The girl doesn't care for treasures, Crow. She doesn't care for the things that make men mad with passion and twist their petty lives to naught. Maybe if you had the gift of persuasion you could convince her, but your persuasion lies at the end of a sharpened spear."

"I will win her heart," Crow said clutching the diamond to his breast.

"We shall see," the shaman said laughing. "Now, who is this you have brought to stay with us?"

"Tell him your name, boy," Crow ordered.

"My name is Isaac."

"Well met, Isaac, and what brings you to stay with us?"

"I was all alone in the forest and these people captured me."

"We did not capture you, boy! We rescued you."

"Well, that's neither here nor there. Either way, the child is a guest, and he deserves our best hospitality. I hope you're not as ungrateful as that other little boy staying with us."

"Who is that?"

"Oh, just some child from the forest, seems his village was destroyed and he's the only one who made it out. Can't quite talk to him though; he's too busy ranting and raving like a madman. I just hope you have better manners."

"Okay, Isaac, sleep here by this central fire. In the morning we'll have to decide who gets you," Crow said, fumbling to put the large diamond in his rough leather knapsack.

"What do you mean, *who gets me*?"

"Well you can't just be unattached here. You'll have to join to a family to make it. Tomorrow we'll see who wants to take you in. I really don't. Not much use for a one legged child in my house."

The shaman looked at Isaac's foot and muttered something under his breath. In the moonlight Isaac could see that his eyes were as wide and white as basketfuls of eggs. The shaman stumbled back into the darkness without saying another word.

"Looks like you scared our shaman off too, boy. That guy doesn't spook too easily either. Well, I guess you'll just have to sleep there by the fire tonight. It'll keep the animals from making a meal out of you."

Isaac looked up at Crow, but before he could say anything in response, Crow backed into the darkness, pulling his head into the shadows like a turtle into its shell. Isaac lay down to sleep in coarse animal skins and felt totally alone. The occasional dog snuck up and smelled him with a wet nose and trotted off before he could shoo it away. He could not sleep. The forest around him played out in a symphony of disparate sounds distant roars and grunts that made Isaac uneasy. He started to think back to the safety of his bed and the comfortable blanket his mother made for him when he was a small child. He thought it fitting that his perfect brother was dead; the strong, daring Jesse was no more. He, the defective one, was left to struggle on. If anything, it was the Father's continuing punishment for him: a pre-ordained punishment thought up from before time existed. The worst that could possibly happen to him now was that he would die. He did not want to suffer, and Isaac remembered his Grandmother telling him that death was the end of all sufferings for the good. The good must suffer in the world while the wicked profit, but the good people's rewards are stacked up in heaven like the wicked people's plates of gold are always full on this world. But to die young like his brother, Baruch, without having ever experienced the world, that was sin made manifest. Isaac wondered if the Father put the snake at that location or if Baruch just walked into the wrong place at the wrong time. Did Jesse put the whole turn of events into effect by going off into the woods to wrestle with his lover? If Isaac hadn't been curious as to Jesse's nocturnal activities and felt left out, maybe they never would have gotten to the point he now found himself in. The possibilities darted through Isaac's mind like comets through devastating asteroids of reason. They wobbled in space pulled by forces outside of themselves. Their collisions knocked everything that he knew and took to be the truth, askew. The asteroids collapsed off one another hurtling into deep black space. The strength of his conception of the world lay in his front pocket. He reached in and felt for the comfort of *The Gideons*. It was everything he knew. It was truth. He sighed the burdens from his heart and started to shut his eyes when he saw a flash of movement from apex of his vision.

He gasped and imagined leaping lions in wait to rip his guts out. His mind drew pictures of tigers tearing teeth through tendons and wolves wearing his carcass for a bib. Their mouths were foaming and bloody. What came from the darkness sent a shockwave through his body from his eyes to his throat that escaped in whimpers.

A tall, slender figure of a woman dressed in a shaggy matted fur escaped the darkness of the surroundings into the light of the fire. Her face was divided elegantly by a bright white smile. Her eyes were like obsidian shards sharpened to razors that pierced the flabby bits of your perception and sank straight to a man's soul. Her way was preceded by gasps. She was the woman that surprised you with her presence, as if she stepped from a higher plane of existence into this mired and fallen world. In the shadows, her cheekbones stretched nearly to her brow, which seemed to float like a leaf on a river down to her jaw line and soft pointed chin. Isaac stood up immediately when she approached him.

"You're Isaac?"

"Who…who…who are you," Isaac stammered struggling to find the words. The only women he talked to previously were his mother, some of her companions, and his old granny. None of them came close to comparing to this woman.

"My name is Deer. My name means that I am as graceful and beautiful as the sylvan animals that dart through the trees and munch grasses in peace without making a sound."

"Your name is beautiful."

"Tell me, Isaac, what does your name mean?"

"Many years ago there was a man who had a son named Isaac. This man's name was Abraham. The man spoke with the Father who told him to kill his son, Isaac, in a sacrifice to the Father. He had to kill his son in order to prove his worthiness to be the earthfather and shepherd of the Father's people on Earth for all times. All great prophets must prove their worthiness."

"Did this man kill his son, Isaac?"

"No, he climbed a large mountain with his son and built an altar. He put his son Isaac on the altar and raised a blade to sacrifice him with."

The woman's eyes grew wide, "What happened? Tell me!"

"He stopped."

"Why? He couldn't kill his son?"

"No. The Father sent Angels down to stop him. Then he found a lost lamb to sacrifice instead."

"Strange, but it's an interesting story," Deer quipped.

"What's strange?" Isaac asked shuffling back and forth on his feet, afraid that he may have offended the woman.

"The story of your name; it's quite strange."

"It's not the story of my name. It's a story that actually happened."

"How do you know it happened? Were you there? Did someone who was there tell you about it?"

"No it's in a book."

"What?"

"A book. You know with writings in it. *This book,*" Isaac said as he pulled *The Gideons* from his pouch and held it up to Deer with great pride. He did not originally intend on showing it off but he felt he had to, in order to keep her from walking away.

"Where did you get that? We've found others but they were all just dust and ashes."

"It was my Grandmother's. She's dead now, of course."

"Oh, I'm sorry about that. She gave it to you before she died?"

"No. I found it."

"And the story is true, because it's in that book?"

"Yes. This is the holy book of my people."

"And why does that make the story true?"

"I was taught that it is all true, plus what was written at the very end of the book, it all came true. So...I think that makes it all true."

"What came at the end of the book?"

"The angels of the Father descended upon the wicked earth and destroyed it. All the good people were raptured up to dwell with the Father in his home in Heaven. All the bad people were burned up in the fires and now burn eternally with the Evil One in Hell."

"Okay. When did all this happen?"

"My grandmother told me it happened no less than five-hundred years ago."

"How did your grandmother know besides from what the book says?"

"Her grandmother told her, and her grandmother told her, and her grandmother told her, and her grandmother told her," Isaac said. Deer laughed and shook her head.

"Maybe your Grandmother's old grandmother got things confused."

Isaac shuffled on his feet again searching for an answer. All he could say was, "That's how I know it to be."

Deer laughed and said, "That's not what happened at all. You want to know what my people say? They say that in the very beginning humans were born into a perfect forest. Humans were the only animals that knew they were in this forest. All the others just act out a role. The deer munch grasses and are content with this. The squirrels gather nuts and are content with this. The huge forest that man found himself in stretched over the entire world like a great garden. It was as if there was a great gardener that made sure all the fruit trees were succulent because all the unhealthy trees just died off. These first men had everything they needed and could ever possibly want, but they had to work for it. These humans had everything including the knowledge that they were in this forest. Having everything in the forest wasn't enough for them. They looked at each other and they felt totally alone. They longed for something else. They could not explain this with their words."

"I feel this, too, Deer," Isaac said.

"And so do I, Isaac. All men feel this lack in themselves. It is part of being the animal that is us," Deer said with a slight smile on her lips.

"What happened to these humans?" Isaac asked her.

"The humans soon discovered that they grew old and died. They died when they were young from disease and injury. They were frail, and they knew it. They searched the forest for a cure for all of this suffering they had to endure. Looking around the forest, one man thought there must exist a tree that if a person ate the fruit they would live forever. No injury could touch them and no old age would take them to their death.

Even though the humans had many other trees to choose from, they all sought this tree because of its promise to deliver them from all their sufferings in this world. No men found it ever. They all had their various beliefs about what this tree would look like and how its fruit would taste and what living forever would mean, but no man ever found it. They found trees with fruit that tasted sweet, but it left them unfulfilled. They wandered across the forest and many made settlements at the base of the fruit trees. They fought over them. They gave each little leafy thing a name. The men gorged themselves on the sweet fruits as long as they could. They pissed and shit at the base of the tree and picked it bare before the season was over. Soon they had no more trees to search out and they were content with living around the tree they chose. The trees turned out fruit that was slightly bitter. Each season afterwards, the fruit grew more and more tart. The humans would not depart the base. They longed for the sweet fruits, which soon faded into memory, something to tell your children about. They talked much about the good fortune of their distant ancestors. They ate the bitter fruits to remind themselves of the way things were."

"Ah yes, we have a story similar to this, but it was a woman tempted by the Evil One to eat a particular fruit."

"Just let me continue, Isaac," Deer said with a patient smile.

"Please do; I'm sorry for the interruption."

"Then another man told them they could stop eating the bitter fruit. He showed them that the animals tasted lovely. The humans began to hunt the animals. They gnashed their teeth on the bloody meat and chased great herds across continents. Then one human came up with another way. They kidnapped the animals and forced them into pens, and over time the animals' offspring lost their way. They were content to live in these pens. They were content to be eaten for food by the men. Many of our people say that the animals lost their fear of the men, but in reality they were afraid of everything. They were bred to be afraid of the men and afraid of leaving the men and afraid of not having anything to eat and afraid of ever living on their own. Just as they had claimed to own the bountiful fruit trees, the humans claimed to own these animals. Raising these animals and growing the food for the animals needed vast amounts of land and water. Soon people viewed the old men who owned these huge farms as wealthy. These old men could feed more people in their families. The old men wanted to have large families because they thought it was important and because they enjoyed young women whom they traded like their animals to each other in exchange for pieces of land and animals. The old men needed water and land for their animals so they could keep getting more young women.

The old men did not care about young men unless they were their sons so they sent the young men who were not their sons off to kill the other men who lived in the spaces they wanted. The men bunched in groups to kill the other men and destroy the walls of the cities and rape other young women and pillage and plunder. They got better and better at killing each other over time. They killed each other over the fact that they had killed each other at some time in the distant past. They killed each other over phantoms. They butchered each other like lambs over ideas. They called it attacking and defense. They learned it, and they studied it and passed it down to their sons. They continued doing this until the attackers got so good at killing and the defenders got so good at defending that they killed each other so well with their weapons that they destroyed the planet and themselves in the process. And to think this all started with men who realized something was missing and it would always be missing because they had to die."

"I think that is how the Father separated the good people from the bad people. He had them fight. The good people won out because the Father was on their side."

Deer had a wild look in her green eyes. Isaac could not tell if it was the fire reflected in them or just a fire within her.

"No! No one had them fight. They just wanted to fight. I don't know, maybe they did it to distinguish themselves. Maybe they did it so they weren't just people huddled around trees waiting for fruit to drop. Anyways, Isaac, that's what we believe. It isn't written down like your book, but it is as real to us as the sun and the moon and stars and trees."

"Well, these people, they were created by the Father. Maybe He made them like that, He made them to want to fight. He made them to want young women. The Father did say at the beginning of His book, *be fruitful and multiply*."

"What kind of Father creates a beautiful world and then creates its little destroyers? It makes no sense, Isaac. They decided to be that way. They make the decision everyday. They decided their own doom. They decided to create the world we know today with their weaponry and their contempt for their own lives."

Isaac thought. He had no immediate answer for her. What he thought he believed was now a deal more uncertain in his mind. His mind wandered for a moment as he struggled to come up with something to say to her. His eyes wandered to her feet. Furry moccasins covered her feet and wrappings covered her lower legs. He traced his eyes up to her waist, then her breasts, then her mouth slightly askew as if she were waiting for an answer, then her eyes. An answer came to him that was tied at the very center of his belief, but tied to nothing else.

"They have a choice. The Father made them with a choice."

She was silent. Her lips faded from a smile that expressed hope to an indignant rage that bubbled across her visage like a fatty stew. Isaac thought immediately to please her because he did something wrong. He moved towards her, to just within the space that her breath decayed into the atmosphere and cooled his face instead of warming it. She looked surprised. She backed up a step and said, "I want you to read that book to me."

"I can't," Isaac replied.

"But it's been read to you, right? Can't you decipher it?"

"I can try for you, Deer," Isaac said with a smile.

"Yes, please. I think you're interesting. You know the shaman sent me to talk to you."

"Why is that?"

"He says he's had dreams and visions about you. Strange stuff."

"Like what?"

"The shaman chooses the next chief of our tribe in his visions. Just like he chose my father from among all the men. He says that a boy with one decent leg who becomes a whole man will become a great leader of this tribe and a great leader of humans. He told me that his visions may be coming true, and that I should come talk to you."

"Why?"

"I must marry the next chief of our people."

"I think the man, Crow, wants to marry you."

"I would never have him, not for all the animal skins in the world. The shaman told me his visions. They came during the time of a full moon so we know they are true and correct visions of the way the world will come to pass. He told me that my husband is waiting for me in the center of town, and he will be a young man with an infirm leg that will grow into a great man who will lead all of our people. I want you to come with me, Isaac. But please, for your sake, don't make a sound."

"Where are you taking me?"

"I can't have the future chief of our people and my husband to be out in the cold."

Isaac gasped. He did not believe her.

"Surely you're joking," he said. He had been told he was no good.

Now he was staring right at the most beautiful and perfect woman, like she had stepped out of the forest a phantom and not of flesh and blood. And she was to be his! Time stood still for him as the warmth spread from his face to his chest and shot downward to places quite undiscovered. He looked into her face, and she didn't seem to be joking. She held out her hand to him, and he grasped it. The pair walked off to the direction of his new tree trunk home, fit for impeding royalty.

Crow watched them from the shadows. He watched her perfect form that he desired more than anything in this world melt away into the darkness with the little freak that he delivered into her clutches. If only he had known the Shaman's portents, he would have smashed Isaac's head with a rock.

"But there is still time for that," Crow muttered to himself before withdrawing to the cold dark room of a lonely hunter.

Deer woke Isaac early that morning before the sun came up with a showering of fragrant oils derived from the skins of a forest tree's purple husks that at least one entire hunt perished while searching for. Isaac coughed as the oil coated his face and woke startled.

"What is happening?" he asked her overwhelmed by the smell of sweet flowers.

"The groom should not speak," Deer said and backed out of the room with a great smile on her face. Next, a woman of middle age, only slightly less beautiful than Deer because of the subtle rancor of time tugging at her countenance, tossed two handfuls of red dust on Isaac that stuck to the oil and turned a vivid purple color. Deer's mother bowed at the waist to Isaac and backed out of the room, not taking her eyes from his. The Shaman entered dressed in a shiny metallic suit that reflected the tiny bits of light in the room. He bowed at the waist to Isaac and began to the proclamation to Isaac of the ceremony that he was about to undergo.

"Our beloved chosen one, you will accompany our most humble daughter, Deer of the Ashguri folk, to the center of the trees in the round. And there you will be wed to the daughter of the Forest and given over to the Protector, the blessed Forest Mother. Have you any questions?"

Isaac wiped some of the purple slime from his face and nodded his head to the Shaman that he had no objections. Perhaps his grandmother's visions of him were going to come true after all and all he had to do was leave his people to make his way in the world. His people had stifled him because he was born differently. And now he found himself at the rear of a wedding procession. His wedding. As he stepped through the underbrush, following the train of people that made their way to the circle of trees near the encampment, the pride within him welled up in his chest. For once, he did not dwell on his infirmity but walked with his royal purple coated head held high. The procession passed by Crow and his band of hunters on the side, and Isaac did not even break his concentration to see them glaring at him. The sun began to rise through the massive oak trees and their branches divided the light like a porous filter. The observers tried to stand in the shadows to avoid the glare. A flock of birds exploded from the tree, squawking protests at the human's encroachment. The birds circled in the air above and looked like rainclouds on the horizon. Isaac wondered what to do as the as the wedding procession halted and the people formed a semicircle around the Shaman. In the crowd Isaac noticed a man that was dressed in a splendidly bright suit of armor. He had a chiseled face frocked with scars and looked like he had battled his whole life. He was taller than the Ashguri people, but he seemed at ease amongst them. Isaac's gaze gravitated towards him because he looked so different than everybody else. The man nodded his head to Isaac and bent slightly in his knees: a symbol of respect. Isaac looked next to his bride. She stood humbly and plainly decorated next to the Shaman, her natural beauty enough to secure her place as the proper cynosure of the ceremony. The Shaman spoke in a loud voice so everyone assembled could hear.

"We celebrate the eternal union of our beloved daughter of the Ashguri with this noble stranger."

Several of the observers shot distrustful glances like pithy shafted arrows in Isaac's direction.

"It may come as some surprise to you that our Ashguri maiden chose this young man to be her husband, but the visions delivered to me through the Forest Mother make no compromises with natural course of events. These visions are the natural course of events before they happen and are to be followed without hesitation. The Ashguri maiden and I had long discussions, and she is entering into her marriage with this young man freely. Please come forward, young man."

Isaac stepped from the semicircular crowd and was met with some murmurs that washed over his back. He was very nervous and felt all of their eyes burning into him. Deer smiled as he approached and offered her hand to him. They clasped hands and looked in each other's eyes and were suddenly alone with each other in the universe. The Shaman prattled on about the forest and trees and animals and man being part of a greater cosmic whole, and Isaac was sure that it was very meaningful, but for now he could not take his eyes off his woman's eyes. He could not for a second remove her from his gaze. Even though he just met her the night before, this felt as natural to him as being born.

The Shaman continued his talk to the assembled guests, and then Isaac and Deer kneeled facing each other in the soft leaves. "The two of you are a wellspring of life and a hope and joyful blessings of the cold dark earth. While the earth is dark and rife with shadows you are a light unto the people and your love will be something very beautiful and a hope for the world. Teach your children the ways of the Ashguri, the ways of seeing beauty in the black world, and keep them safe until they are old enough to shelter you in your infirmity. And when you go to your appointed death, as we must all, go with peace and love and the knowledge that your children will keep your promises of the world to come bound to life. They shall not die with you."

Isaac stared at Deer's eyes, but he was not looking at their surface. He stared into the beyond. All his cares up to that moment seemed to melt into the deep infinity of her soul. Her hands were warm, sweaty even, and she smiled back at him. Isaac saw a brief flash of the entirety of the universe, infinity in a second, in her and he knew that this was love. Isaac could not decipher from her expression if she felt the same way that he did, but he assumed it because she looked at him the same way he looked at her.

Isaac realized he did not even know the most basic principles of the way of the Ashguri, but he looked at his wife-to-be and trusted that she would teach him well. His face must have been pained at that moment, for Deer pulled him close and whispered to him, "Do not worry, husband. This will be over soon." Joy dripped into Isaac's soul punching through the barbed shellac of sadness and overwhelming it. His heart melted in an instant and no his past sufferings ceased to stack themselves upon his shoulders. Each thrust of joy felt double-edged to him, the sweetest happiness mixed with the sloughing off of sadness like a snake's skin. The Shaman reminded the young lovers of times of their mortality. The joy would one day come to an end.

The Shaman said, "My young man, like the choice of this Ashguri maiden, your consent is now required. Your being here is not enough; you must proclaim that you will never leave this woman's side unless she sends you off into the wilderness. You will protect her and tame your wild hopes to her best intentions. You will promise to always be a man no matter the circumstance. This is your oath, and your promise to the earth that bore you."

Isaac spoke in a voice that began timidly but grew in strength with his conviction, "It is my promise as a man that I will harness my wild intentions to the better portion of the Earth. My wife will be my center, and I hers," Isaac spoke from inside himself without any cares for anyone but the woman in front of him. Tears formed in her eyes but soon evaporated in the rising sun.

"Now the bride will take her groom to the house of her mother where the marriage will be complete. But first we ask that any challengers to this union, appointed rightfully by the Forest Mother, now abdicate any concerns publicly or forever hold their desires and designs inside themselves."

The Shaman paused for a moment and then said, "Is there no man who wishes to challenge this rightfully appointed union?"

Members of the crowd looked at each other as if they were waiting for someone to speak up. The tall, armor clad man crossed his arms in front of his chest and stared at Isaac with no emotion on his face. The black flock of birds circled in the sky and landed in the trees. Their chatter boiled over into the sky as if they were cheering the newlyweds, but there was no such joy in them.

Crow and his band shambled into the circle from behind the ceremony hooting like a band of glutted brigands cut off from their treasure.

"I've an objection!" Crow shouted. "I've an objection against this sickly fawn marrying the Chief's daughter!"

"Why how dare you interrupt this ceremony and question the guidance of the Forest Mother in these matters!" the Shaman retorted.

The armored man uncrossed his arms and looked like he was ready to attack at any provocation. Isaac and Deer rose from their position and stood next to him. "Right time for these fools to show up," the man said as he scratched his short graying hair. "I wouldn't worry there. These guys are just gasbags upset at their lot in life."

"The Forest Mother will not show you kindness based on your actions today," the Shaman said to Crow who now stood in the center of the circle of trees.

"The Forest Mother has never shown me kindness, and I've gotten along well enough."

"The Chief will hear of this Crow," the Shaman said.

"The Chief! The Chief is due for a date with the worms at any time now. Why he's not even able to come to his own precious daughter's wedding!"

"He has important matters to attend to Crow. Shouldn't you and your band be out on a hunt?"

"We've important matters to attend to, tree lover. Namely, why this young fawn was allowed to marry the Chief's daughter. He's never been on a single hunt, nor has he ever passed any of the trials for belonging to the Ashguri, and he gets promoted right to the top because this old nitwit had a few dreams about a cripple!"

"How dare you insult me that way!" the Shaman yelled, wavering at the last moment.

Crow laughed, "And you people go right along with all this nonsense! Why, this cripple is going to be your Chief soon!"

A few shouted objections to Crow's accusations, but many of the people stood in silent concordance with Crow.

"The whelp should at the very least be forced to perform a trial, otherwise he isn't even a man and can't be married to the Chief's daughter. Why, any man here has more of a right to just take his place at her side," Crow said as he walked up to Deer. Isaac got in his way, but Crow pushed him to the side causing him to lose his balance and land on a knee. "Would you like that, you little flower?" Crow asked her as he reached for her face.

"No. I don't want you. I would never want you even if the race of men were to perish from the planet if I didn't consent to you. Even then, I wouldn't consent to you," she said and backed up.

Crow flew into a rage and raised his arm to strike her but the armored man punched him hard in the chest and caused him to fall immediately into the leaves where he rolled and writhed in pain as if he had no control over his body. His men gathered around him and pulled him to his feet, coughing and hacking against the force of the armored man's well-placed blow.

"Damn all of you. All of you! We are going to Moojtema! We're off to the Last City without you all! We are leaving you and going to save ourselves! You will see! You will all see!"

"You won't make it past the door, Crow. You have nothing to offer them," the armored man said grimly.

"Like you know, you Institute queer! You don't know anything!" Crow exclaimed, nursing his bruised chest.

"I know more than you think, Crow, and this Institute queer man-handled you," the armored man said with a smirk. Crow and his cronies shambled off into the forest shouting bitter curses like the birds that screamed epithets at the happy couple and all their human witnesses.

That evening in the darkness of their hollow she turned suddenly and wrapped her arms around him, pulling him close as she pressed her full breasts against his chest. The intensity of her attack repulsed him at first and he thought she sought to murder him. She attacked again, this time pulling Isaac's mouth forward onto hers. He tried to pull his face away to ask her what she was doing. Her kiss was warm and wet, and he discovered that the locusts nipping through the lining of his stomach headed were south to rampage the wild oats of his loins. She brought his midsection to hers and let it linger there. She whispered into his ear, "Have you not ever been with a woman?"

He fumbled for words and she plugged the verbal leak with a kiss. She put his hand against her naked body, and he felt the gooseflesh of her thighs. Their breathing heightened and their distance between their heartbeats matched the brevity of their short-shared lives. In his dreams she ran through fields of orange flowers that bent as she fluttered by bowing her head in homage to the eternity in her steps. In the distance a mountain jagged upwards, punching granite fists into the sky. She ran ahead of him, bounding through the grass that graced her to her knees. With each stride, the flower petals stripped from their anchor in the cold dark earth to descend like dead butterflies into the dust. Suddenly she was on top of him.

"Get this sack off," she implored him.

"I can't; you're on top of me," Isaac gasped barely able to get the words through his anticipation.

"Damn you, Isaac," she said.

"Help me."

"I'll do anything for you."

She pulled his cassock up over his head and he felt the itchy wool rip against his skin. Now naked herself, she took him in her hand and tugged gently, straddling him. Then it happened.

Warmth and wetness and her breath in his ear, pointy nipples against his face, the thrusting and retreating and the rising moan from the depths of them as she dripped and exhaled, and he felt something rising within him, rising with the tempo of her delightful squeals, rising and stretching over the center of his body. She lunged forward and shuddered against him, and he met her retreat. He thrust one last time against the counterweight rising against him, and the explosion ripped into her.

She whispered these words into his ear, "You are a man, husband."

Isaac held her to his chest and felt her breathing with him and whatever care he maintained for the wild ways of the world melted away. He opened his eyes and looked into her brown eyes, and for the first time in his life, he saw. They drifted to sleep, one being.

*

Isaac woke and there was an empty space in the bed next to him. Light ripped through the dugout's entrance and shot sparkling trailers on the disparate dusts, kicked up by the most miniscule movement. Isaac looked at the implements stacked on shelves in the sunlight. They were all crude and seemed to be fashioned by hand. Many of them he could not discern a purpose for. Perhaps they were only decorations. A woman entered the room with the sunlight behind her. He could not see her at first until she moved closer. Isaac felt the warm absence next to him and called out, "Deer, my wife, is that you?"

The woman came closer and he could see that it was Deer's mother. She replied, "Deer is helping some of the other women out with their chores. You know, just because she was recently married doesn't mean she gets a day off."

Deer entered the hovel amongst the rays of sunshine and ran her fingers through her hair. Isaac stared at her and she smiled back at him. Elsewhere there was cruelty, death, and decay – all the morbidity of the rotting logs of the forest warred over by innumerable beetles, centipedes, and spiders, but to him she just beauty. The beauty burned to his memory with the pearly whiteness of her teeth. He traced ever angle of her frame down to her furry boots. He sighed and stood out of bed to greet her. He now knew the entirety of his life. He would seek her out to be with her until the end of his time.

Her mother shrieked with laughter. In his haste to greet his beautiful wife, Isaac neglected to put on any clothing. Isaac looked downwards and discovered his error. He dove under the covers.

"That's a nice young man there, daughter. He's perfection but for that foot," Deer's mother said with her hands crossed in front of her.

"He's not even close to being full grown, Mother," Deer said.

"I wish you both wouldn't talk about me like I'm not here," Isaac said from beneath the covers where his only his head peeking out.

"Come now, Isaac, you're too sensitive," Deer said.

"I only want to please you, wife," Isaac said.

"For such a young man, he takes to his role naturally," Deer's mother said with a laugh, "But who ever heard of a man trying to please a woman? It seems like it should be the opposite way."

"Yes usually men are all the same," Deer said.

"Yes, they use you for a few moments until they reach their goal and then it's off to sleep for them," Deer's mother said. Then the older woman smiled at the young man coyly and said softly, "You want to please my daughter, son? You'll have to learn how to use that little inquisitive tongue of yours."

"Mother!" Deer said.

"What? I need to learn to talk with her and listen to her?"

"That's important too, young man. You'd best learn the secrets of life from me before these idiot men get a hold of you and fill you with their rot."

"The men think that gifts are the way to a woman's heart. I'm telling you that they are not because the door is already open for you if she wants you, but it is very small and hard to squeeze through. Once you enter, there is no backing out."

"Crow thought he could woo me with a diamond," Deer said with a face that mocked a stupid look.

"That hothead will be the lightning bolt in our dry timber, the death of us all," Deer's mother said.

"I saw him kill the man they called Rooster. Rooster found the diamond on me first. Crow killed him for it."

"That was only a matter of time, those two men hated each other. I guess Crow saw his chance and took it. It's a shame, Rooster was a good man."

"So Crow has your property? You said it was your diamond? Where'd you get it?" Deer's mother asked him with a look of concern plastered on her face.

"I found it."

"It was a big diamond, we usually find the little ones lying about. Were did you get that one?"

"I found it in the forest on my travels."

"How long have you been traveling for?"

"Just a few days."

"Where is your home?"

"My home doesn't matter. They expelled me."

"Why are you a criminal?"

"No. Look at my foot. They had no use for me."

"I hope you don't mind, but when I was picking up the place I moved your clothing and a caringtotem dropped out." The older woman's face became very serious and she said, "Tell me man, do you already have a woman somewhere?"

"No. That was the caringtotem from my brother's woman. He's dead now."

"How did he die?"

"Love killed him," Isaac said from his perch in bed.

"Queer," Deer's mother said shaking her head.

"Love is beautiful and infinite, but when perverted by a people for control it becomes a hideous little slave master. My brother made the mistake of falling in love with a woman and not giving all of his love to the woman in charge of us."

"So they killed him for this?"

"Yes, they killed him."

"Oh dear," Deer's mother said. "Anyways, I've gotten your clothing ready," and Deer's mother handed him a set of animal skins to wear.

"My cassock? What happened to it?"

"I put your old clothes in the fire, they were covered in grime and lice, only fit to be burned," she said with her arms crossed and her head cocked the side as if she were curious to see if she made a mistake.

Panic shot through Isaac. "Oh, Father! The book in my cassock! What did you do with it?"

"The old burned book?"

"You burned it!" Isaac said nearly screaming.

"My love, settle down! It is just an old book. I don't care if you don't read it to me. I've got you now," Deer said.

"It was not *just an old book* – that was the Holy Book of my people!" Isaac said.

"I didn't burn it! I swear I thought about it, but I gave it to the village elders to do with as they pleased."

"What will they do with it?"

130

"I don't know. I'm not one of them! Go and see the Chief," her mother said with a flushed look of embarrassment in her face.

"Yes, honey, we have to go there anyway to announce our wedding."

"You know, there is something else you should do while you are there too!" her mother said. "You should tell them that you demand to undergo a trial."

"Why is that mother?" Deer inquired.

"Well some of the villagers have started to talk about Crow's point, that Isaac has not undergone even the simplest of trials, and he got to marry the Chief's daughter without suffering in the least."

"I've suffered alright!" Isaac said.

"But we don't know that," Deer's mother quipped.

"Come now, husband, we'll go to the Council. We'll get all of this taken care of. Just don't leave, husband."

"I can't, I have nowhere to go," Isaac said and took his wife's hand.

*

The men of the forest departed earlier that morning for their hunt. They were usually gone until they obtained enough meat to sustain their families and the leftovers were thrown into smoking houses tall as a man. Today they were only gone for two hours. They got lucky in that as they crested a wooded hill and descended into a treeless depression they happened upon a gang of deer. They slew the deer one by one with well-placed arrows. The smack of the bowstring against the bow was all the deer heard before the sharp arrows pierced their beating hearts. Some managed to escape with the particular ferocity of this attack seared forever into their fears. As the hunters carried the dead ones, with their hooves tied to wooden poles, their long, graceful dead necks lolled lazily with each step like they were merely sleeping. In their dead eyes, you could see the promise that life once held for them and it looked like they were looking off into the distance. Crow's arms were reaching his muscles' failing as he struggled with the other hunters to carry their quarry back to the scarlet stained ground of the butchering area. As Deer and Isaac passed him, he glared at them, and his knife burned him through his coarse leather britches. If throwing his knife into Isaac's back meant dropping the fresh killed deer into the dust and facing the eternal reprobation of the tribe, he would do it in an instant. He rested the pole, glistening with deer blood and entrails, on his shoulder and grabbed for his knife. He would hurl it into the little bastard and follow it with a hatchet to the head. The thought rose in his head and nearly forced his muscles to respond. He breathed in and readied himself for the attack. Deer pulled Isaac close to her as the happy couple and the hunting party passed each other within swinging distance. Crow stopped when Isaac's back was available to him, but the fantasy melted away like the fat from a charred carcass roasting over a glowing fire. Crow brought the skewering pole down on his opposite shoulder. The murder couldn't be like this. Too many people would know. He would be judged and possibly killed himself. This boy was the anointed Chief among them. No, it couldn't be like this. The boy had to suffer. His death had to be a spectacle for the ages.

*

Isaac and Deer walked through the twisting confines of hollowed out trees and shelters constructed of bark and dried grasses patched together with the thick, mossy mud that coated the forest floor after spring rains. Women nursing infants that cooed and suckled at overflowing breasts shot them funny glances. Isaac tried not to look at the bare breasts, for he had been taught that it was improper to stare at a woman while she was nursing. His grandmother told him that a glance of lust at a nursing woman could spoil the milk in her teats instantly and rob the child of its only source of nutriment. Isaac could not and would not be responsible for a child's death.

His eyes wandered to the men who lay in tall grasses. The men, taut and muscular from a life of toil, lazed about laying on mats in the upcoming sunshine. Their women brought them fruits, feeding them sweetness as the light pouring through the canopy from the semblance of heaven cast shadows on their gruff, bearded faces. Their children, not even old enough to walk, took turns climbing their chest hair to look these beasts in the face. While the children tugged their fathers' hair like a ladder, the men winced playfully. After each tug the children giggled and the brutes laughed heartily, their chests heaving like a bellows stoking glowing warmth in the dark despair of life. When the babe's struggle was finished and it climbed over the barrel chest, meeting eyes in a mortal game of peek-a- boo, they laughed like there was no burden of time – no death hanging over them counting seconds. The rough men patted their sons on the head and pinched their daughter's cheeks, staining them red.

Isaac thought about his life, and it condensed into a fantasy with the breadth of a single thought. The thought came as he looked at Deer's profile and her flat belly underneath her leather leggings. His eternity would not be when he departed this world in death. It would come when his wife's belly was swollen with his child. When her heart screams and birth pangs robbed the sleep of the village and a warm, wet, bloody child came into the world. His eternity would come when his child was walking with him through the forest, tugging at his index finger with a tiny hand, asking questions of the great man, outpacing the storm of fears and nightmares. It would come when he told his children of his many mistakes in life and bade them to do better, constructing the hope that they would not venture down the same paths in their lives. Flash forward. Isaac saw himself on his deathbed, old and worn and gray and hacking against the cold with steam pouring from his nostrils, surrounded by the bright faces of his grandchildren. The ancient man looked to his daughters, all strong vibrant women like Deer had been. He looked to his ancient wife. He looked to his daughter's husbands with their strong arms resting on the heads of his grandchildren. His eternity would not come in death, but rather it would come in what he left in life. He retreated from the vision in his mind and staggered back to the reality of the present. The vision would remain with him though, and he would make it his duty to make certain that his vision matched his actions with his life.

The Chief's lodge loomed in the center of the camp and unnatural sounds reverberated from within the leather and bark covered sloping walls. Isaac heard low masculine voices shouting demands, muffled only by the cries of women. When Deer opened the door, the dull murmur of voices escaped to the greater woods. The sound greeted Isaac's eardrums for only a second before he was encompassed by silence and stares.

Isaac felt nervous at the prospect of meeting the Chief. Their round faces of the sweat lodge inhabitants were on him like spotlights. In the sunlight that streamed through holes in the ceiling, smoke lingered. The room smelled of burning pine needles, a high-pitched stink, combined with the sweat of the occupants. All of the forest elders were naked and sweat washed over their bodies from the coals burning in a central fire pit shaped like a great gaping mouth that barfed heat into the room. Three young boys dressed in supple leather loincloths surrounded the fire pit ensuring that the coals stayed hellfire hot. The child attendants studied Isaac intently with their batting eyes when he entered. The Chief, a massive, fat man, attempted to stand but could not make it to his feet. He remained seated in a comfortable position and rested his flabby arms on his massive belly. Rolls of fat stampeded down his midsection and cascaded down towards the floor like a river rolling gently off a cliff, forming a waterfall.

The child attendants left the room only to bring the Chief plates of food, which he washed down with copious amounts of honey wine poured into a never empty cup. The pendulous breasts of a gorgeous young woman glowed orange and dripped sweat onto the floor from supple brown nipples. Occasionally, the Chief gave her a morsel of food from the wooden plate and allowed his fingers to linger in her mouth long enough for her to suck the grease from them, which she did with fervor. The chief was bearded, and little bits of yellow fat and crumbs collected in this salt and pepper food trap. His tongue darted to the bits of food like the tongue of a fat bullfrog sitting in the swamp shallows, murdering wasps and flies. His beady black eyes, recessed into two enormous cheeks and jowls, had the appearance of being dark tunnels to nowhere in an ominous mountain.

When the pair entered, the Chief took no notice. None of the other elders dared ask the Chief's daughter her business, and they contented themselves with merely talking out loud about the pair, who seemed so odd together. The chatter of the much skinnier elders grew so loud that it punctured the Chief's intoxicated stupor. He raised his head like a contented cow to the pair who patiently awaited some acknowledgement. No one ever came to the sweat lodge uninvited, and no one came without having business with the Chief. Now his drunk was compromised, and he demanded to know the reason. His eyes focused, and he saw his daughter standing in front of him; the look of drunken stupor slowly morphed to a contented superiority. He did not address his daughter, rather his gaze shifted to Isaac.

"Who are you?" the Chief slurred and belched.

Isaac did not speak. He looked to his wife, who shot out with, "Father this is my husband, Isaac. We were married just yesterday."

"Your new husband? He's got such a funny name. Tell me daughter, whose permission did you get to wed this man?"

"Well, Father, the Shaman began telling me about his dreams – dreams of Isaac here and how I am supposed to wed him and how Isaac will be a great leader."

The Chief laughed. It was not a chuckle. His laughter filled the room and drowned out even the snores of the drunken entourage. He raised his voice, "So you did not come to me first, daughter? Why did you not come to me first?"

"Father, you were busy," Deer said holding her ground.

"I am always busy with my affairs, Deer, but you must really come to me first with matters as important as these."

"Father, I consulted the Shaman. He told me it was a wise decision."

"The Shaman? Are you joking? You listened to that insane old man and his dreams?"

"Mother agreed," Deer said.

"Your mother, she is a wise woman, but I fear that she is doing nothing by trying to spite me for my many, in her mind, indiscretions. Your mother did what women everywhere are supposed to do, Deer. Women are supposed to marry up. They are supposed to marry up from their station in life and improve their situation for their children. They aren't supposed to marry gimpy strangers."

"I believe the Shaman's dreams are true. I believe there are great things in store for my husband, Isaac."

"You should know by now, Deer, that our path in life is what we do. Our path in life is not determined by the dreams of an old madman, no matter how charismatic he is. Your mother supports it. I suppose I have no other option but to support it as well."

"You haven't been with mother for years now; you've just been sitting here with your whores."

"Who are you calling a whore?" one of the girls sitting in the sweat lodge snarled like a minx.

"Quiet down!" the Chief yelled at her, "Now, Deer, have some respect for my female friends. They have no place in this world except my protection."

"And I'm sure you and the Elders enjoy protecting them everyday," Deer shot back. The Chief glared at Isaac. The boy's silence angered him.

"Don't you speak, fool?" the Chief said looking directly at Isaac. "It's a fine position you find yourself in, right? Where are you from, fool? You one of those Olden Dale cubs? Maybe from the Dread Lake People? Are you just like that little fool, Rockhead? Were your parents killed, too? Are you going to do nothing but cry all day and not talk to us? Where do you come from?"

"Really, my Chief, my people aren't important. Just know that they do not allow me to remain with them."

"So...great, you're an exile! An ostracized twerp! We seem to attract a lot of exiles in these parts, don't we, men? First we get that little moron, Rockhead, and now we have the other moron, Isaac. How sweet."

"You don't seem to mind if they're female and cute, Father," Deer said snidely giving her father a generous helping of his own venom.

"Damn you, daughter! So I'm told that this whelp is to be the replacement for me? Do you see this little man here?" The Chief said this with a booming voice, so all the Elders woke from their slumbers and stared vaguely at Isaac before they went back to dozing.

"I was going to marry you off to the most successful hunt leader, honey, and now you've gone and dashed all my best plans."

"Father, you won't be disappointed. We came here so that my husband could ask something of you."

Deer motioned to Isaac to say what he had come to say to her father. She goaded him with her eyes. He came right out with it, but it stumbled from his mouth like a one legged infant. "Sir, uh, I am wondering where my book is."

"Speak up, whelp!" the Chief screamed.

"My book, Chief? Where is it?! It was taken from me and I want it back."

"A book, you say? Has anyone seen a book?"

One of the Elders, a man only slightly thinner than the obese Chief, raised his head from the pillows of a large woman's breasts and said, "Aye, Chief. That old burned book. Remember? Your first wife brought it to us but left in a huff after she saw all the young ladies in here."

"Ack. Deer's mother brought a book here? Where'd you put it?"

"It's laying around here somewhere," the Elder said stroking his graying beard while he adjusted his head to sit perfectly between the drooping breasts of another woman. One of the women pulled the book from between her and another woman. Its cover seemed saturated with sweat. She held it up. "This your book, boy?"

"Yes. I will come get it," Isaac said making his way through the sprawl of sleeping and naked bodies on the floor. The bald children minding the central fire pit glared at him as he passed them.

"Not so fast, boy!" the Chief said, "We're going to see if those Institute folks want that book. Toss it here!" The woman complied with her Chief and lazily threw the book to him. It bounced off his chest and slid down his fat belly, coming to rest in a fat roll. The Chief grabbed it up like a treasure.

"Those Institute folks are willing to give up a lot for anything from the past, and especially dusty old books."

"It's not yours to give away, Chief."

"Oh really? Where was this book found? It was found in the forest, right? Everything in the Forest is mine. Everything I see there amongst the trees and everything that passes underneath their leaves is mine! I claim it all. Don't worry, son, your book was given to me to investigate. I did not understand it, so I'm going to give it someone who will understand it. In exchange for a few things, of course."

"Who are you going to give it to?"

"I think I'll see what Cornelius from the Institute can give us in exchange for it."

"I'll do anything for that book."

"You'll do anything? Why is this old thing so important to you?"

"It's the Holy Book of my people. My Grandmother used to read us stories from it."

"You still haven't told us of your people, Isaac. Who are they? They sound quite queer," the Chief said with a look of gross disdain seeping from his fat face.

"I suppose they are strange to outsiders. I don't even understand them. When I was kicked out of the Congregation they told me I'd die out here."

The Chief gasped when he heard the nasty word that trickled innocently from Isaac's lips.

"What did you say? What did you say? Did I hear you say the word, *Congregation*?"

"Yes, Chief. They kicked me out into the world hoping I'd die. But I took their Holy Book with me."

"Mother of the Forest!" the Chief yelled. "Did anyone follow you here, boy? Did anyone follow you here, Spy?!" the Chief screamed.

"What do you mean? I got kicked out!"

Deer looked to Isaac with shock in her eyes. "Love, why didn't you tell me? Why didn't you tell me you're from *those people*?"

"I don't understand, Deer!" Isaac said.

"Guards, Guards, Assassin! Murder! Spy!" the Chief screamed with the timbre of a woman in the throes of childbirth. The burly men that had been lounging outside with their children burst through the door and grabbed Isaac. Stick this Assassin into the menagerie with Rockhead!"

"There must be some mistake!"

"Father, be reasonable! Isaac's not a spy," Deer screamed and cried as she tried her best to prevent the men from dragging Isaac out the door.

"Please, I don't understand! I hate my people!" Isaac yelled as the men pummeled him into unconsciousness.

#

The prison tent smelled of shit and was more like an animal cage than a dwelling fit for a human being; it doubled as the Chief's menagerie. Besides collecting women from the disparate tribes of the Forest, he collected strange and exotic creatures that his hunters captured and brought to him. Just like his women, the Chief liked to visit his animals occasionally, but like all things he touched, they suffered from neglect.

Isaac had been in the menagerie for a day at most and had tried to speak to the other human imprisoned with him to no avail. In the meantime he wondered what prevented Deer from coming to see him. Perhaps she was organizing a way to get him out of his bondage. Perhaps she had forgotten about him and succumbed to Crow's advances. Perhaps her father, the disgusting Chief, banished her much like his people banished him. Why did they react so fiercely when they heard that he came from the Congregation?

There was a cruel cage in the far end of the tent opposite Isaac's straw bed where a ferocious wild dog gnashed its teeth at the wooden slats, barking at Isaac and seeking to tear his throat out for nothing other than sustenance. Small mammals tied to tent pegs screamed in their own voices at the intruder. To them, Isaac was someone there to steal their food and to grab their rotten apples from them. He was someone to starve them until they were skin sacks of bones and leave them to be devoured by their cellmates. Swamp rats fought over the scraps of a comrade that suffered an illness and succumbed in the darkness. They sat on their haunches with bits of flesh hanging from their sharp teeth set in jaws agape at the sight of new blood. They hoped Isaac would free them from their collars that bound them to the tent and make it possible for them to engage in their rat freedoms of pillage and plunder. They hissed and screamed at him with all the terrors of Hell glowing in their eyes.

Next to Isaac lay the boy the Forest people called Rockhead. He lay in bits of straw spilled over from Isaac's bed. Rockhead was still, barely respiring. He lay with his face buried in the stitched leather folds of the tent. He was hiding from the world and the stinky breath of the rest of the animals.

"Tell me. How did you come here?" Isaac asked Rockhead.

Rockhead shivered at Isaac's words. He expected the slap or punch to come, and he seized up his muscles to be able to take the blow. He would take their fists. He would shed tears for no one. He would show them nothing. He would owe them nothing. He would accept their meager food when they brought it and he would wait. He would wait until he was done sharpening the dagger from the piece of deer antler he found in the tent. He would shove it into the guard's neck when he came in to deliver the food. He would watch the bright red blood pour out. He would make sure to perforate the windpipe so the blood went into their lungs and drowned them. They would be unable to scream for help. He would drag their corpses into the forest and escape. He would escape just like he escaped the devils with red capes when they murdered his people.

"Rockhead, how did you come here?" Isaac asked the cowering boy on the floor next to him. It didn't work. It didn't seem that anyone could bring him out of turtle shell his psyche retreated into.

Isaac repeated his questions for two or three days while he waited for someone to rescue him. His belly acquired the same vicious tear that tore through him while he was wandering alone through the forest. He lamented out loud, "Father! I am starving."

"Eat a rat," a voice shot from the blackness.

"What?" Isaac said.

" Eat a rat," the voice repeated. It was Rockhead talking halfway between dreams and waking. He sat up. "You aren't tied down. They are."

"I couldn't eat one of those," Isaac said.

"You get hungry enough you will," Rockhead said, standing up. He nonchalantly walked over to the tied up swamp rats and grabbed one in his bare hands. The rat screamed like a baby. Rockhead broke its neck with one twist and bit its throat out.

"You're more animal than human now," Isaac said to him.

"I've been in here for weeks. See how you act after they abuse you for weeks. No, you'll probably die in here."

"I won't. My wife will rescue me."

"Not likely," Rockhead said as he pulled strips of flesh from the rat and chewed heartily. His face was all puffy and swollen. Isaac wondered if it was just like that or Rockhead had been beaten up.

"What happened to your face?"

"The hunting party led by that black-haired bastard found me out in the woods trapping some birds. They said that I had to pay up in order to trap birds because they owned the forest. I argued that no one could own the forest, and they beat me up. All ten of those bastards punched and kicked me the whole way back to their camp. The black haired sicko said I had a head like a rock. The name just stuck after that. Rockhead."

"But what's your real name? What name did your parents give you?"

"I don't right remember. What's your name?"

"Isaac. Why don't you remember your name?

"That's a strange name. I've never heard of that name before."

"It's from a book my grandmother used to read me."

"Quaint."

"Well, whatever. Why can't you remember your name?"

"My name is dead like my people. I'm sure it will come to me when I'm not so upset."

"What happened to them?"

"We had just moved our camp to a valley, following the deer migrations, and some red cape wearing psychos descended out of the hills and killed everyone."

"Everyone?"

"Well except the pretty young women. They took them. Everyone else got killed. You know what the bastards said about the women they killed…including my mother?" Rockhead said, trying hard to stifle the growing anger inside him. "They called them the useless ones."

"I'm so sorry," Isaac said.

"No. You needn't be. The woods are dangerous. Full of dangerous people. We weren't ready. But I swear by the Forest Mother that I'm going to get back at those Red Devils."

"You say they wore red cloaks?" Isaac said, his mind racing. "What did they do with the other women?" he said trying to see if the puzzle pieces fit.

"Yes. Hundreds of them came out of the hills screaming murder and wearing red cloaks."

"What did they do with the women?" Isaac repeated.

"I saw them lead about four off. The ones they didn't rape and murder right there. The ones they didn't call the useless ones."

"Oh dear Father...Jesse how could you?"

"What?" Rockhead inquired with a puzzled look on his face.

"When did you say this happened?"

"I've been here for two weeks perhaps. I was living on my own in the forest for four days maybe. I don't really remember; when you're living like an animal time doesn't really stack up for you like it used to."

The time frame was right. Isaac couldn't believe what he was hearing. He thought about remaining silent, but it would have been wrong for him to do, a sin against himself.

"I think I know who did this to your people," Isaac said plainly.

"Who?" Rockhead said with vengeance burning in him.

"My people," Isaac said with his head down towards the ground.

Rockhead lunged at Isaac and landed on top of him. "I'll kill you!" he screamed, trying to get his hands around Isaac's throat. Isaac brought his hands up to guard himself and yelled, "No! I hate my people. I didn't do this! They did!"

The words took a moment to sink in and Rockhead breathed hard. This cripple couldn't possibly have taken part in the raid, so he let up in his attack and sat next to Isaac on the ground.

"Do you really hate them? Are you sure you're not a damn spy for them?"

"That's why I'm in here. The Chief heard that, and he wouldn't listen to me."

"Why do you hate them so much?"

"They kicked me out of the Congregation. They killed my grandmother and my brother in front of me. They wouldn't let me...."

"Sick. Your people are just plain sick."

"I know they are, I used to live with them."

"You know where your people live right?"

"Of course -- I know where I am from."

"Could you walk there from here?"

"I'm pretty sure I could."

"Then that's our ticket out of here."

Rockhead stood up, "You have to swear to me. It's my people's way of doing business. You have to swear that we'll see this through to the bitter end, them or us."

Isaac thought for a moment. "If you can get me out of here, I'll go with you anywhere. I need to see my wife."

"Losing faith in your wife already?"

"No. I'm sure her Father, the Chief, has locked her up too. He's quite a hothead."

"You married the Chief's daughter? How? Ahh, nevermind. Well, I suppose four days is good enough time to marry her off to someone else," Rockhead said with a serious look on his face.

Isaac frowned but did not want to think of that possibility.

"I will call for the guards and tell them that we have a proposal for the Chief. But only if the Institute man, Cornelius, is here. He seems to be the only person who can talk sense to the drunken Chief."

"He was in attendance at my wedding. He really put Crow in his place."

"After we deal with your people, we'll deal with Crow. If, Forest Mother, help him, he's married your woman, I'll chop his skinny spear from his body."

"I'll do that myself," Isaac said.

"Isaac, you are a good man. Your body is lacking, but you have the fierce heart of a bear. I see that in you. No matter what creeps out of the darkness of life and tries to devour you, you won't succumb. You won't go willingly. You will fight."

"I've been fighting for much of my life."

"Then we will get out of here and fight some more, but you have to promise me, we're in this together."

"I promise you. We're in this together."

After much negotiation, the boys managed to convince the fat tent guard to take a message to Cornelius who was watching the festivities in the sweat lodge. Cornelius watched the drunken orgies with dispassion, carefully taking notes on all he observed. Cornelius scratched his head in disbelief when he got word that the strange, gimpy boy that washed up in the village and married the Chief's daughter knew the location of the Red Death and would reveal it to him. He had been waiting for this moment for two years, living with the wretched people in their squalor and hoping for some breakthrough. The higher ups at the Institute dispatched him to serve as an advisor to this drunken miscreant and aid him in protecting his people against the Red Death menace. Thus far he had accomplished nothing. Motivating the Forest people to mount any sort of campaign against the Red Death had been futile. They were too disconnected and spread out to form any cohesive military units. Too many tribal loyalties to this chief or that warlord separated them. They were content to hunt, and when the Red Death destroyed one of their outposts or wiped out a hunting camp, they shrugged their shoulders and tried not to think about it. Cornelius's mouth watered when he heard the news from the guard. He thought to tell the Chief about it, but he knew it was best to just convince the Chief that the two captives had something valuable to offer, and that they should be released to then let them tell the Chief the good news. The Chief agreed in a drunken stupor and was quite surprised when he saw the two boys in front of him to discuss their upcoming mission.

The Chief was busy talking to Cornelius, who dressed for the occasion in a strange suit of bright metal armor. It was much brighter than the armor he wore to Isaac's wedding and seemed to have a sheen of electricity covering it that disrupted then coalesced in an instant each time he moved. Everyone's eyes were transfixed on Cornelius as if he were the center of gravity in the room. The semi-naked black haired beauties could not take their eyes off of him. His scarred face was long and angular, capped with a pointy salt and pepper goatee. In the shafts of light that pierced the sweat lodge Isaac could see that his eyes were blue: the color of Sapphire.

Isaac strode to the center of the lodge when the Chief called him and bade him to speak. The sweat lodge smelled particularly musty today as if its occupants had not left for several days. It smelled like a fat man's farts mixed with body odor. The whores in the sweat lodge looked at Isaac with a sense of longing, but they looked at every man with a sense of longing naturally pasted on their eyes like neediness in the cries of a baby.

"I have heard you know the camp of our mortal enemy," the chief slurred to Isaac matter of factly. The chief's eyes lolled around and came to rest on Isaac who stood in the streaming sunlight coming through the roof. The assembled elders whispered amongst themselves and cast suspicious gazes at him; it was obvious they did not trust him fully.

"I do. I aim to show you that I am trustworthy and capable of being married to your daughter, my Chief."

"Ahh! So you want to prove yourself worthy to me? You think this is an adequate test? Do you know what tests men have done in the past?"

"Chief, this may not be an adequate test, but it is the most expedient test we can give this young man," Cornelius said. "All the scouts we've dispatched either went missing or returned with nothing. This child is a godsend to us."

"Speak in a manner I can understand, Cornelius!"

"Sorry, my Chief. As your advisor, I recommend that you allow our young friend here to show us where his people live."

"They are not my people. The Forest People are my people now," Isaac declared. The Elders nearly threw a fit talking amongst themselves.

"Rockhead and I will travel to the Congregation. You just have to follow me."

"It could be a trap! This could have been your plan all along!" the Chief proclaimed, grinning. Cornelius stroked his head, deep in thought.

"No. We won't follow you. We'll give you something to mark your Congregation with."

"I'll do it. But I want one more thing."

"You're in no position to negotiate son," the Chief said.

"I want only what belongs to me. I want what I came with. My book, *The Gideons*."

"Where is that damn book?" the Chief yelled to the assembled Elders. They shook their heads that they did not know.

"Isaac, the book has been delivered to our Institute. Do not worry; it is in good hands. No harm will come of it."

"Why did you take it? It was not yours to take."

"The Chief here gave it to me last night before we discovered what you knew. I'm sorry, but the book is far too important to be left unguarded."

"It's important to me. It's mine. It's all I have to remind me of my *former* people."

"It needs to be shared with the rest of the world, not left under a rock," Cornelius said.

"Promise me I'll get it back when I do this task."

"We will see."

"Leave us! Leave us all!" the Chief shouted to the Elders. They begrudgingly filed through the entrance to the sweat lodge grumbling to themselves at having to leave their women behind.

"If you can do this for us, Isaac, you will be my heir. I will put my full weight behind your ascension to my position after, well, my death. All that you see around you will be yours. We will have a proper ceremony when you return. I will put my support behind you in public. You will have my word not just the word of the crazy, old Shaman."

"I don't know. You can trust me, but I don't know that I can trust you."

"You are still living, son; that's trust enough! I have told Crow he is to leave you alone. I have told him to have no further designs on my daughter."

"Do you think he will listen to you?"

"He had better if he knows what is good for him."

"The bastard's bound for Moojtema, he told everyone at the wedding," Cornelius said, "He's a madman if he thinks he can get in there."

The Chief folded his arms in front of his chest and rested them on his massive belly. "That one isn't right in the head. As a child, he longed to be a hunter. As a hunter, he longed to be a hunt leader. As a hunt leader, he longs for one thing."

"To be the Chief," Cornelius said.

"It's obvious. I want him dealt with," the Chief said.

"It will be done," Cornelius nodded. "Just say the word, Chief."

"Where?" the Chief asked with saucer-wide eyes.

"Best to wipe him out on a hunt. Convince one of the other men to do it. The question is, would they?"

"I think so," the Chief said looking lovingly at one of the beautiful whores who lay on the ground. "They can be convinced," he said with a wide smile. The woman shifted up on her elbow and stared at Isaac as if she were looking through him.

"Okay. It's settled. You and Rockhead will leave at the first light of morning," the Chief said.

"I must coordinate with my higher headquarters and arrange everything with Jacobus," Cornelius said.

"Old Jacobus, how's he doing?" the Chief asked warmly.

"I don't believe he has any complaints. In fact, this new breakthrough will please him greatly."

"Go say goodbye to your wife for the time being, son," the Chief said smiling. "And tell that bastard, Rockhead, he's going with you!"

Isaac departed the sweat lodge and the whores swayed listlessly, propped up on their arms. Cornelius left shortly thereafter to communicate the good news to his higher headquarters. The Chief dozed off on the floor, covered in woman flesh. One of the women, a young girl with hair as black as midnight, woke and carefully made her way to the door. She looked back to the sleeping Chief and did not regret what she was about to do.

Isaac burst into the door of the dugout and did not see his wife. Her mother was there with her hands moving like the legs of a spider spinning silk, stitching clothing.

"Where is Deer?"

"She isn't here, Isaac."

"She left me?" he said with shock.

Deer's mother laughed. "No, don't be silly. She's off gathering berries, but she is very afraid for you."

"Did she tell you this?" Isaac asked her.

"No, son, women know their daughters just like they can trace a line down their own thigh. Our daughters are us. We know what we thought in the past when we were in the same situation. I know what she thinks about you. I thought the same thing about her father. Things now have changed, as you saw in that sweat lodge he's always in."

"I need to tell her goodbye until I return."

"Oh dear, that Chief has you running an errand for him?"

"Yes. It should be simple."

"Nothing in this life is simple. Remember that, and you will go far. You know, I worry about my daughter while you are gone. The new crop of men around here, the ones without steady wives that go off in the forest for long periods of time...too long a time, they're different than any people I've ever seen."

"Your daughter is strong."

"These men don't care about anything but themselves. I don't even know that they care about themselves though. You came in with them! They live to die, Isaac. That's it!"

She paced back and forth holding her sewing in her hand looking at him imploringly. Isaac could see where Deer got her good looks. The mother looked just like her gorgeous daughter only slightly more stretched with time.

"Do not remain long in your travels, if you know what is good for you."

Isaac gave Deer's mother a lingering hug and she told him that her daughter usually picked blackberries in a clearing not far from the village.

*

Isaac walked through the underbrush like a lumbering giant doing violence on all the mouse burrows and insect nests he trampled on. The whole while he walked, he yelled for his wife, hoping she would appear from the dusky orange forest before the darkness of night crept upwards from its tomb. The forest was pure beauty to an observant man, but Isaac had other things on his mind. He missed the moment that may have emanated from the Father as a sign pointing to his future. The sign showed that beauty remains permanently fixed in place while man's restless spirit is destruction.

144

From the corner of his eye he saw his wife standing amongst the thorny bushes. The forest was alive with violence, an offense against this, or a defense against that. Men frolicked in it brandishing sharp instruments to butcher each other and the black bears rasped their tongues against the same thorns that Deer wove her fingers through delicately searching out the ripe, purple berries. The rife possibility of all beauty inside the struggle expressed itself in her caring fingertips. Isaac dismissed it when he saw her make eye contact and saw love. Her surprise solidified into a smile, and they embraced each other like they had not seen each other for decades. She pulled back, and her smile turned to a frown, "I know. You have been released, but you must go."

Isaac bit his inner lip when he saw the tears welling up in her green eyes.

"I will not abandon you, my love. I will return to you. This is my promise."

Deer smiled to him and said, "I will wait for you until the all the animals of the Forest go cold."

"Until winter?"

"Longer. Until the trees drop leaves and never see the first green buds of spring."

He grasped her and pulled her close to him. He kissed her lips and tasted their lingering sweetness, which stroked his uncertainty.

"Do not give up on me."

"The only way that I give up on you is if you give up on yourself."

"That is not possible, Deer. I want you to keep something with you, Deer. I will love you forever, and I will return to you."

"Do you know why I love you, Isaac?"

"No, you have not told me why. You have only shown me so far."

"I love you because you are the most different person that I have ever known. You are a whole individual in this mess of stick men. When I saw you for the first time, it was like the breath of the forest ceased. The world went silent. I watched you in the darkness for a long time. I watched how calm you were. There was not a hint of complaint in your actions."

"I was taught by my people to remain silent in times of strain and stress. It doesn't bode well for a man to go screaming into the night when he is with unfamiliar company."

"There you are, honey, trying to avoid the subject with me again. I know you don't like to talk about yourself, so just be quiet and listen. Listen to everything happening around us."

The two were silent, but not even the calls of insects met their ears. Bland wind sung to them through the trees. Spiny outstretched arms were now nearly devoid of any of their purple or yellow leaves. They piled high on the ground, bedding and warmth for insects that copulated and lay eggs in the leaves that were soon to return to the soil. Isaac seized his wife by her hips and they laughed, falling to the ground. They wrestled each other in the bed of leaves and pierced the silence of the forest with their love. They rolled over each other a few times, and Isaac came to rest on top of his wife against a hard oak tree, ancient, and knotted against the earth. He pressed her to the ground and brought his chest against hers. He stared at her face in the darkness. He traced the beautiful symmetry of her face from her ears to her nose.

"Never give up on me, husband," she said.

"I will not, wife. But, you do the same for me."

Crow watched the pair bonded lovers as they groped in the darkness. The sound carried in the woods, and his ears were well trained from his years of hunting experience. He heard their entire conversation, and the whelp's love for his wife sickened Crow to his core. When the whelp went away, it was his time to act. The whorish girl had done him well, alerting him to their plans for him; but like all the mere things in his life, he gained his advantage with her and cast her aside.

Rockhead and Isaac stood in the sweat lodge with the Chief and Cornelius and listened to the tall armored man detail their part in the plan for dealing with the Congregation.

Cornelius opened a compartment in his armor with the touch of a button and took out a chrome orb in the shape of an elongated egg from the space.

"Your mission, boys, is to take this device and go to the Congregation's location. You will activate the device by twisting it at this seam. You place it at the Congregation, and you get out of there." He motioned like he was performing the action.

"What is that, then? What does it do?" Rockhead asked with a hint of scowl on his face. Really his expression did not change much from indignation and often bordered on rage. Everyone assumed it was from seeing his family butchered.

"This is just a tracking device so we can know where the Congregation is and plan from there."

"So, they're just supposed to take the device there and wait, right, Cornelius?" the Chief asked, seeming more sober than Isaac had ever seen him.

"No. They have to pull the device apart so that it can be picked up by our sensors."

"Then you have to tell them that, then. I mean, you can't expect these children to know that."

"Yes, Chief, you twist the device at the seam and pull it apart. Then you hide it somewhere and get out of there."

"Like run away?" Rockhead asked.

"Yes. Run to a safe distance of about half a mile."

"Why? Is it gonna explode? I don't want to do that. I want to fight these people. Just putting a bomb there is for a coward."

"No. It's just a tracking device. Don't worry. It won't explode," Cornelius said. The annoyance in his voice was apparent now.

"Whatever, Cornelius. You're the scientist with all these gizmos. I'm just giving the orders around here," the Chief said.

"What's going to happen to the Congregation?" Isaac asked.

"Why do you care, Isaac? Do you still care for them?" the Chief asked.

"No. I don't care about them. I just want to know what I'm doing this for."

Cornelius interrupted them. "I think it's safe to say that Isaac has no love for his people. If you're wondering what's going to happen, we just want to visit them and make them stop their raids on their neighbors. We all want to be able to live in peace."

"So you're just going to talk to them?" Isaac asked.

The Chief looked at Cornelius as if he were unsure of how best to answer the question. Cornelius added, "You are from a very secretive people, Isaac. The Institute knows nothing of them. We merely want to introduce ourselves and help the Chief negotiate a lasting peace with them. We will only send our representatives."

"I'm pretty sure they'll kill your representatives," Rockhead said with malice in his eyes.

"How do you know that?" Cornelius asked.

"It's what they do," Rockhead said.

The Chief and Cornelius looked at each other and turned promptly to Isaac.

"What do you think, Isaac?"

"Anything is possible with them."

"Then that will be dealt with if it arises," Cornelius said, and folded his arms across his chest, causing the armor to briefly change color and go back to its usual steely blue.

"Do not fail us, boys. Consider this your first test," Cornelius said to them.

"My first and last test. After this, I will be a man," Isaac said.

"A man indeed," the Chief said before he stood up to search the room for hidden wineskins.

Isaac took the device and several days worth of dried deer meat and placed them in a deer leather knapsack. Cornelius gave him what he said was an ancient bag made of a substance that would not allow water inside. When Cornelius opened the bag for Isaac it made a clicking noise. Cornelius placed the device inside the bag and clicked the bag closed again by squeezing it at the top. There was something scrawled on the surface of the bag in black. Isaac could not read it but was sure that it said something very important. When Isaac got the Gideons back, he would put it inside the bag to keep it safe from all harm. He would never get it taken from him again. He wished that there was a bag big enough to put Deer inside and keep her safe from all harm.

"Please keep my wife safe," Isaac told the Chief.

"Aye, I will keep my daughter safe, Isaac. Just mind your mission now."

"Guard *The Gideons* for me, Cornelius," Isaac said.

Cornelius bowed humbly to him and reminded them once more of their mission. "Keep the device in the safety bag until you need to use it. Don't get the device wet, son," Cornelius said, pointing his finger in the air for emphasis.

"And by all means, boys! Don't get caught!" the Chief said with a laugh.

"We won't, if I have anything to do with it," Rockhead said.

The pair set out into the forest after a restful nap. It loomed like a phantom before them. As they walked they could only hear the sounds of their footsteps and the calls of songbirds that made their homes amongst the ringed trees. The squirrels gathered their acorns and carried them up into nests. Some were buried and forgotten about. The saplings grew tall and spindly until they penetrated the canopy to take great mouthfuls of nourishing sunlight. As the pair walked into the rising sun, Isaac noticed how carefully Rockhead walked through the forest. The boy took small, simple steps as if he were tiptoeing, careful not to step on any green.

"What are you doing?" Isaac asked him.

"I'm walking."

"But why are you walking like that?" Isaac said.

"My people were only a part of all this. It was not ours to ravage with our footprints. I was taught from the time I took my first steps not to make a mark on it."

"I was never taught how to walk; I guess I just took to it."

"I was taught to walk well. You see, look behind you," Rockhead said and pointed the muddy furrow that Isaac's lame leg made behind him. "Someone could follow you for miles with that trench you're digging. Everything you touch, you destroy," Rockhead said to Isaac who paused to stop.

"Ok, Rockhead. I may destroy everything I touch, but if you don't want to destroy anything, how do you eat?"

"Me and my people ate only what we needed, and we stayed hungry."

"Why did you stay hungry? That's absurd. No one wants to be hungry."

"It served to remind us that all of this will end," Rockhead said.

"My people taught me that it all did end already," Isaac said.

"That was only a hiccup in nature's infinite march. If all the human beings were no longer here, all of this forest would remain. It would continue on without even a moment's pause for sadness."

"I was taught that men are to have a dominion over nature. They tame and master nature to their ends and purposes. That is what makes us special."

"That's impossible, Isaac. How can nature have mastery over itself? We are part of nature, nothing more."

"You don't think we're special?"

"I know that I'm just a small part of all this. I can feel the sun on my face. I can smell the rotting oak leaves under my feet. I hear the birds and insects and the wind howling through the branches of trees. I feel it as it strikes against my face. But before my birth, there was nothing for me."

"And what happens after you die?"

"I don't ask questions of things that don't affect me. What do you think?"

"I think I go to live with the Father. I will live forever with the Father in Heaven."

"Why do you want to live forever? We desire to return to the whole. It is only in our children and our children's children down on the line that we live forever. It is in what we teach them and what they carry with them of us."

"Just like you learned how to walk carefully."

"I was taught how to walk by my father and he is dead now. That's it. It only matters who I teach. Each of us is a teacher and student at the same time."

"Teach me how to walk properly," Isaac implored his partner.

"Look and learn, my friend," Rockhead said. He laughed and pushed Isaac's shoulder to show he was joking. "After all, we are in this together, and I can't have you getting us followed."

Isaac and Rockhead weaved a path through the spindly oaks, careful not to interrupt their worship of the sun god. Each of them in time could become a massive tree shedding millions of acorns, as numerous as the dust in the galaxy, spawning from their mates millions more. Isaac watched his friend walk for a moment as he rested on the knotted roots of an oak tree. Rockhead made sure that Isaac was aware of the marks he made with his feet and told him that even though he was lame he could still walk without being detected. From then on, Isaac was careful only to step on the backs of dead things and keep dry dirt under his soft shoed feet. The dead things were separated by spaces of green that Isaac had to leap between. From dead spot to dead spot Isaac leapt, sometimes walking sideways in order to mimic his friend.

They came to a clearing. The ground was brittle and black but overgrown with life in small patches. Little flecks of white paint cropped up haphazardly, not overwhelmed by the weeds. The paint flecks delineated neat compartments with no discernable purpose. Rockhead pointed to the far end of the clearing. The remnants of a massive building with trees coming up through the roof, peeled back metal like a piece of armor perforated by a spear, lay in tranquil ruin.

"What the hell is it?" Isaac asked his friend.

"That's built by the Ancients. Their buildings don't collapse back into the earth. They just stand up and make everything ugly around them. Look at all these plants. They're all warped and yellow and sickly looking."

In the sunlight, Isaac could see glittering glass through the wispy weeds. He bent down and saw piles of diamonds, just like in his dream. He gasped and stood up. He thought of all the people that must have died at this place and the glittering shards of lives lost, like a broken mirror blinded him.

They approached the building. Great twisted pieces of metal and blue shards that would not be consumed by the earth littered the ground. Isaac made out the indentations that were slightly darker than the rest of the bleached white building. These holes, remnants of a sign, where the fallen, giant letters served as nests for birds, as evidenced by the bleach white and gray bird dung that covered the walls. The building was so large it looked to Isaac that it would take at least an hour to walk around.

"What does it say?" Rockhead asked. "Something this big had to be really important."

"Have you not seen anything like it before?" Isaac asked.

"No. But I've never been in this part of the forest before. I've heard there were massive cities where all the Ancients lived, but that they are just overgrown piles of rock now," Rockhead said.

"It must be a sanctuary," Isaac said.

"What is that?" Rockhead said as he looked into the darkness in the building.

"A place where we communicate with the Father. Why else would they have built it to last so long?"

"Do you want to go inside and look around?" Isaac asked.

"It looks destroyed inside."

"Maybe we could find something of use," Isaac suggested.

"We have all we need. We have water and meat to eat. We know how to make a fire. What more do we need?"

"Just let me look," Isaac said, his curious nature getting the best of him.

"I'm not going in there. I'll stand outside. That place looks like death," Rockhead said shaking his head.

"Just don't leave me here," Isaac implored his friend.

"By the trees! Where would I go?"

*

Isaac entered the remains of the building. Light streamed through the hole the trees ripped in the rooftop. Overturned shelves stretched in the distance as far as he could see. Dust floated on air currents, illuminated by the light streaming in from holes on the ceiling. Isaac heard the cooing of pigeons in the distance. He stopped and looked ahead to see if it was worth continuing onwards into the building. Columns that supported the roof were lined with wires that jutted out in random directions. Everything inside was filth and ruin. As he walked into the barely illuminated darkness, his curiosity drove him forward, much like it had forced him watch in on Jesse's unfortunate ceremony. With each step he took, dust kicked up behind him that made him cough.

He came to a shelf where there was a single metal can. Isaac picked it up and felt its smoothness on his hand. He shook it and heard sloshing inside. He found a piece of sharp metal on the ground next to his foot and pierced the top of the can. It coughed out a horrible stench, like the contents had gone bad centuries ago. He gagged and tossed the can into the darkness ahead of him, trying not to vomit. The can clanged off the metal shelves and caused one of them to tip over and crash to the ground.

Pigeons took to wing out of their perpetual fear of death. The flock burst from their nests hodgepodged in the sign on the wall to his rear and flew toward the light streaming through the ruptured ceiling. Isaac heard their rhythmic flapping echo off the walls of the huge, dusty sanctuary. They flew one after another, and it seemed that he was watching the same scene play over and over again, like the world became stuck in a groove, skipping.

Behind him he heard the faint whispers of women. He spun around but all he saw was a flash of movement into the maze of shelves.

Isaac breathed deeply and started to make his way to the light beckoning him to the entrance. He heard the whispers again, this time to his side.

He saw Rockhead's profile in shadow outside the door. His mind screamed... RUN!

More whispers came from just an aisle over; they sounded like birds chattering in a faraway tree conveyed by the gentle breeze. He went very still. The whispers died as the last escaping pigeon broke through the boundary of the sanctuary with the greater world. Its feathers lingered on the air currents and swirled gently round and round as they fell to the dusty floor.

"Gotcha, boy!" came the cry from behind him. Two powerful arms wrapped around Isaac's midsection. He gasped and tried to pry himself loose but could not budge the arms that felt like steel cables crushing him. The assailant let up for a moment to get a better grip. Isaac screamed and dropped to the ground. His assailant was on top of him in an instant squeezing him with legs like a constricting snake. He wheezed to breathe. The two rolled in the dust, and his face and hair became covered in grime as the dust turned to mud when mixed with his sweat. He managed to turn and face his attacker. He expected a man, but came face to face with a black-haired girl. She panted for a moment and renewed her attack.

Isaac yelled to her, "Get off of me!"

She continued thrusting her hand around his throat, and with her other arm, pinned his arms to his side. He kicked his legs outward like his brothers had taught him when they were wrestling. She faltered, and he pivoted so he could get on top of her. He brought his hands upward against his face, and she bit him. He screamed as she tried to close her teeth around his finger. He punched at the side of her head, and she let up biting him just enough for him to yank his finger from her mouth. A jolt of electricity and fire shot from his finger down his arm.

"I'll kill you, bastard!" she screamed at him. His leg spasmed and kicked one of the shelves causing it to crash to the floor. The sound filled up the emptiness and poured into the forest outside like an alarm bell.

He rushed to his feet. The girl pulled a knife from a scabbard and lunged for him. He barely dodged and the two struggled again ripping at each other's fleshy bits like two starving wolves.

Just as Isaac thought his strength would fail him, he saw Rockhead running towards them carrying a length of metal. He came from around the shelving towards her backside and knocked the girl to the ground. She screamed and the knife flew from her hands into the distance. Rockhead raised the length of metal and was about to bring it down on her head when Isaac yelled for him to stop. Rockhead looked at Isaac dumbly and held the metal rod in both hands to menace her with it. She sat up and spat dust from her mouth. She fixed strands of hair that hung down in her face in great sweat streaked clods. She started to sob. "Finish me. Do it, you brutes," she said.

"We won't; you're a girl."

"Just do it. I've failed. I'm no good to anyone anymore."

"Why did you attack me?" Isaac asked her with a gentle voice.

"No one comes into the She-Wolf's lair without permission."

"Is that what the sign outside says? This place belongs to her?"

"No. That's funny. This place used to be a store of sorts many years ago. She brought all of us here when were just little girls. We don't really remember much. Some were just babies."

"What'd you say it was?"

"A store. There used to be a lot of things in here to buy. This place was all abandoned, but the She-Wolf was smart. She found a way into the warehouse, and it was stacked with things."

152

"Like what? Food?"

"No that was all rotted. Just all sorts of stuff," the girl said to them, still looking them up and down.

"Like what was this stuff for?"

"We don't know. We couldn't understand most of it. Just boxes and boxes of stuff we didn't know how to use. The She-Wolf said the Ancients used this stuff to remind them they were alive. She told us the Ancients only wanted one thing in their life, and that was leisure time. So, they had all this stuff to make their lives easier, and it gave them more time to do what they really wanted to do."

"What did they spend the rest of their time doing?" Isaac asked with his usual curiosity.

The girl smiled, "We don't know. All we have here to look at is all this stuff. Everything else just disappeared I guess."

Isaac cradled his wounded finger, which was dripping blood onto the dusty floor. The girl looked to him and said, "I'm sorry, let's get you bandaged up. I'll take you both to the She-Wolf. You seem trustworthy enough."

"She sounds pretty wise. We'd love to meet her," Rockhead said. "Are there any other young women like you about?" Rockhead asked the girl as she turned her back to them to walk away, smiling and winking at Isaac.

"Yes, there are. Twenty of us or so," she said, bidding them to follow with a motion of her arm.

"Miss, if you don't mind, I'd really like to ask you for some bandages, and we'll be on our way. We have something very important to be doing," Isaac said to Rockhead's chagrin.

"It's quite all right; we've got plenty of time," Rockhead said glaring at Isaac.

Rockhead pulled Isaac to the side, out of earshot of the girl, "Just be patient, Isaac, and let us see how this turns out?"

"I've a wife to get back to," Isaac said.

"Oh, your wife will be waiting for you, don't worry, but look at this girl here – if there are twenty like her, brother, we're in paradise," Rockhead said with a smile.

"We can't. There's not enough time," Isaac said, getting annoyed at his friend's persistence.

"Are you two going to be coming?" the girl said, standing in the gaping double doors leading to the warehouse.

Rockhead started pulling Isaac by the sleeve towards the double doors like he was an intransigent boy not wanting to take the take the ride of his life. When they crossed the threshold, the doors shut behind them. Rockhead let go of Isaac's sleeve, and they stared at the girl who was in the center of the room surrounded on both sides by fierce looking women. She had a growing smile on her face.

"Now are you sure you don't want to meet the She-Wolf?" the girl said with a smile.

"No, we really must be going. We have no time," Isaac said.

"You have no choice now either," the girl said.

The women leveled their weapons at them: long tubes painted to look like leaves and trees.

"Come with us, boys," a tall, blonde woman said.

"We really have to be going," Isaac said again.

The tall woman pointed her tube at a box. Her hands tensed around the weapon. The sound of an explosion and flames shot from the end of the tube. The box ripped at the edge.

Isaac and Rockhead erupted in a shared gasp. The woman pointed the tube at them and said, "Next one is at you two. Now walk!"

Their captors led them through a maze of busted up shelving. When they turned to look at the fierce women, the ladies prodded them with knives bound with rope to cheap plastic mop handles. Most of their weapons were ramshackle implements fashioned out of whatever they could find in the warehouse for defense; but the tall blonde's leaves and bark painted tube really scared the pair into obedience. Isaac held his finger to his chest as it throbbed, because his grandmother had told him that it was the best way to prevent little animals from getting in it and eating his flesh off.

They came to a corrugated steel door, which the tall blonde woman opened. She motioned with the tube for them to enter. She glanced back at Isaac and smiled for a brief moment, looking him up and down. Isaac felt peculiar warmth in his body when she did this, like someone opened a window in his soul to the sunlight and then shut it immediately. The woman adjusted her hair with her free hand and repatriated the menacing look back on her face. The floor in the warehouse was littered with busted up boxes haphazardly strewn on the concrete floor. A layer of dust and bits of paper at least a foot thick covered the floor except in the areas where the women walked. As the group went towards its destination, a woman swept dust onto the floor to cover their tracks.

"What's she doing that for?" Isaac asked the blonde.

"You fool, it's the only way to keep the Institute from finding us and taking us away."

"Why do they want to do that?"

"She-Wolf says it's because we all came from Moojtema. The Institute wants to pack us up and study us. It's always causing us trouble. A madman runs it. That's what She Wolf says. It's none of your concern. If She-Wolf wants to tell you She-Wolf will tell you."

"Isaac here wants to know everything. That's what he does," Rockhead said.

"Quiet, ugly!" the blonde yelled, leveling the tube at Rockhead's face in a warning. Rockhead withdrew and looked to the ground at his feet.

In front of them a great wall of boxes was stacked neatly all the way to the ceiling. The group stopped in front of it. The blonde woman looked to the right and left, mainly out of habit. She pulled on a red box with the faded photo of two children playing and laughing on it. It was decorated with big balloon-like letters. When she pulled the box, several boxes moved in tandem revealing an empty space with only a metal platform and a series of controls lining the wall. They stood on the platform and waited for the last girl to finish her sweeping. As she closed the door, she reached out of it with the broom and swept the area right in front of the door. Then she hung the broom on a peg near the entrance to the empty space. She skipped over to the platform and stood next to Rockhead.

The platform groaned downwards and before darkness overtook them, Isaac spied the sweeping girl whispering something to Rockhead in his ear. While she talked, the smile grew on Rockhead's face. As mere dusk faded to blackness, the blonde woman shouted an order, "Hold hands, everyone!"

Isaac begrudgingly gave his injured hand to the same girl responsible for biting his finger. He could not see her take his hand, but she gripped him at the wrist when he winced. Together, they stepped into the darkness.

From the freight elevator to the She-Wolf's lair, they walked through darkness as black as any hole covered with earth. The girl tugged at his sleeve pulling him along in the blackness. Isaac put one clumsy foot in front of another, fearful that he might fall into a deep hole. The ground became squishy and Isaac smelled a horrible sulfurous stench. After many footsteps of walking in what felt like the muddy forest floor after a hard rain, the surface became solid again and the smell disappeared. The train procession stopped. With a pop and flash that illuminated the women's faces, there was light.

The blonde woman stood in front of a red door with a metal doorknob. On the door was a poster of a statue of a female wolf suckling two young boys who groped upwards for elongated teats. Isaac wondered to himself if this scene happened somewhere out in the forest. There were four letters on the sign but Isaac could not make them out. Rockhead laughed at something the girl next to him whispered to him, but no one else could hear what she had said. The blonde woman pointed to the door with pomp and said, "Behind this door is She-Wolf."

"Pay your respects to her for she does not like strangers milling about. Your presence is already known to her, for she knows all who come and go."

"Then why did you have to treat us like prisoners?" Isaac asked.

"A test."

"A test of what?"

"Her tests are for her to know. You're still alive, so you both passed. Congratulations."

"Wow. What's our prize?" Rockhead said.

The woman glared at Rockhead and said, "Ugly has no prize." Then she smiled and pointed at Isaac, "But maybe we've got something for him."

Rockhead breathed deeply while he concentrated on something else to say. Isaac could see the gears spinning in his mind, but his mouth produced no sound.

"Be wary. She-Wolf speaks in riddles. Do not answer her until you have thought out your responses fully."

"Don't worry. Isaac here is smart," Rockhead quipped.

"Among other things," the blonde said, looking at Isaac like no woman had looked at him, not even his wife. Isaac wondered why she paid him this attention.

The blond opened the door. The first room was richly decorated. Tables and chairs, polished and glowing in the torchlight lined the walls. Pictures hung from the walls above the tables. Some showed families: a man and a woman and children walking on the beach holding hands and smiling. One showed a young girl with dark skin shoving a piece of split bread sandwiching a rubbery piece of pink meat into her mouth. Yellow and red sauce covered the meat and she smiled while she ate it. Another picture showed a boy holding a pink puffball, grasping at bits of the puffy stuff in his hand. His face beamed pure delight. Another photo showed a man dressed in floppy multicolored clothing wearing big shoes. The man had paint all over his face. The brightly colored man held another child who was laughing. There were pictures of very

156

nice beds that looked much nicer than anything Isaac ever slept in. There were photos of men without any other clothing besides a small, white piece of cloth that covered their genitals. They were muscular and good-looking and all sat around a fire. One of the men was drinking from a white cup. One of the other men must have said something very funny because all the men appeared to be laughing heartily. Maybe the men laughed because they were sitting around with just a little clothing on.

"What are these pictures of?" Isaac asked.

"Scenes of life from the past. We think they're at least five-hundred years old. We cut them out of our book."

"You have a holy book?" Isaac said with some excitement.

"No. It just reminds us that people were happy in the past and that we can be happy once again."

"There's some writing on the picture. What does it tell you?" Isaac asked.

"We don't know. We can't read it. We can only look at the pictures. We put our favorites up here. Like the one with the men here. We wonder about them. We wonder their names. We wonder if there are men like these sitting by fires out in the world today."

"All the men I've met are nasty," Rockhead said. "These men wouldn't survive in the world today, and definitely not in those clothes."

"We think that life was so easy then that all men had to wear were those little pieces of clothing covering up what they didn't want the other men to see. But some photos show them in fancier clothes. So we just don't know. Maybe that is all that they wore when they had meetings around the fire."

"They looked happy though," Isaac said.

"We think they were. We think that life then was wonderful. Much different than today," the blonde said.

"I have a holy book," Isaac said.

"What does it tell you?"

"Just a bunch of stories. It's not like this one that's all pictures. It doesn't have any pictures," Isaac said.

"Can you show it to me?"

"No, some people took it. But I'm getting it back."

"Did you read it?"

"No. I can't."

"Then how do know what it says?"

"My Grandmother used to read it to us."

"And how do you know she tells you the truth about it?"

"I don't think she would have lied to us, but she did lie, I guess, sometimes. But never about the holy book."

"When you get it back, you'll have to read it. You'll have to learn."

"Can we get on with this?" Rockhead asked. "I want to meet this She-Wolf."

"Oh yes. Sorry, I get distracted here, because I find these pictures so interesting. But come now, your friend is right; She-Wolf is waiting."

The two boys entered her chamber. It was barely lit with flickering mushworm shit torches. The smell of the room was a mixture of floral perfume and the rank scent of burning sulfur. The room was circular-shaped with metal control panels lining the walls.

The lights and dials were dead from centuries of disuse. At the center of the room sat the woman known as She-Wolf. The plain looking woman was surrounded by more of her troupe of female protectors. She wore a simple, dark blue almost black pair of pants with a matching color cloth shirt. A simple white string tied around her midsection kept her pants on her bony frame. Looking at her, Isaac could not fathom why her followers, who were all so rough and strong, put so much faith in this feckless woman.

"State your business here," She-Wolf said.

"We were wandering through the forest in search of something, and we sort of wandered in here," Isaac said.

"Wandering or seeking, whatever men please, did your little noses smell something on the breeze?"

"No. We thought there may be some things of use to us in here."

"Things of use? What is of better use to a man than a woman? You see twenty young women here, do you not want to use them, boy?"

"No. I was just looking for some tools, really. My brother and I were just scrounging around. We meant no harm, and really, we should be getting on our way," Isaac said at the same time backing up.

"You lie, boy!" She Wolf hissed.

Isaac went white with fright at the consequences they would have to face and repeated himself, this time stammering.

"No. No. Ma'am, we do not lie."

"No, you are lying. This boy isn't your brother. He's too ugly to be your brother. Why even if you don't have the same father, I don't see how this troll could come from the womb of your mother," she said pointing at Rockhead who frowned suddenly.

"What's your name, handsome?"

"Rockhead," Rockhead said.

"I'm not talking to you, twerp. If I call for ugly, you answer me. Got it, ugly?"

Rockhead looked at his feet and did not make another sound.

"Go on, handsome. Tell us your name?"

"Isaac."

"Oh well that's a right weird name there, Isaac. What happened to your finger?"

"One of your girls nearly bit it off," Rockhead said.

"Ugly twerp, shut up! You don't learn do you, ugly? Shut it!" She-Wolf hissed again to Rockhead and then made the hand gesture like she was going to order his head to be cut off if he continued speaking.

"Does it hurt, handsome?"

"It is starting to throb," Isaac said.

"And none of my companions treated you yet?"

"No. They brought us right to you."

"I shall have to chastise those girls later. That is no way to treat such a handsome guest," She-Wolf said.

"Where do you come from, Isaac?"

"Well I live in the Forest now," Isaac said.

"Oh, that's dreadful. Just dreadful."

"No, it isn't bad."

"Then what brings you up here?"

158

"Nothing in particular."

"You aren't with that horrid Institute are you?"

Isaac paused and answered, "No, what Institute?"

"Those dumb bastards that go flying all over the forest studying things and trying to get their hands on all the good loot that people have. They're led by a pure madman they are. Why, if that psychopath, Tanner, knew we were here he'd send a raid team to this place for sure. Take all of our rightfully gotten stuff we've got here. Probably kill us. Those Institute types don't have much use for a bunch of women. Bunch of weirdoes always studying things. No time for women. Do you have anytime for women there, Isaac?"

"Well, not right now. We had best be getting on with what we were doing."

"You mean you don't want to stay here with us for a little while? Are you sure, Isaac?"

"Yes, I'm sure. We really need to be going," Isaac said.

"Why you're breaking these ladies' hearts, Isaac. Look at them."

"I don't think there's anything wrong with us staying," Rockhead said. She-Wolf spun and looked at him with wild eyes, pointing her finger.

"You little fucking twerp, if you open your mouth one more time, I'm going to have you crushed in our elevator. Do you understand me?"

"Yes," Rockhead made to say to answer her.

"Ahhhh! Don't talk! Who knew someone as ugly as you could even form words!"

"Why are you so mean to my friend here?"

"Friend? Ahh, see, you did lie. I knew you couldn't have been brothers. I do apologize, but it's really part of my upbringing."

"Your parents taught you like that?" Isaac said.

"No. No. Where I'm from no one really knows their parents. You're just born in a great big nursery, and you grow up and go to school with your classmates, and no one worries about their parents. It doesn't matter."

"Where are you from?"

"I'm from the nicest place left on this unfortunate little rock. Moojtema, the last big city on Earth. I doubt you've heard of it."

"No, not really," Isaac said.

"It's lovely, Isaac. You really should go. It's all Beauty and Youth and lovely beautiful people doing lovely beautiful things with their time. Everything is provided to you, well provided you work for it. I mean, not everyone was afforded the station I had in life there. Some people had to work really, really hard there, but it was all out of my sight so I didn't care."

"Why'd you leave?"

"You're forced out really. I mean once you reach a certain age and you no longer have Youth or Beauty on your side anymore, and you just have to find somewhere else to go. But enough of that. Oh, you are a simpleton aren't you, but so handsome. Yes you'd do marvelous there."

"How'd you get here?"

"Oh, that's quite a story. I was escorting these girls when they were very young to the Outer Colonies. I had passed all my tests and was told that I'd be a perfect fit for

Governess for one of them. They just never told me which one I was going to. So, we boarded this ship, and shortly after we left it started shaking, and all the little girls started screaming. Oh, it was horrible. They started grabbing at my clothing and ripping it to shreds as we just plummeted to the ground. I did my best to keep myself calm, and in an instant there was nothing. Just a horrible crunching and then...no sound."

"How did you survive?" Isaac asked with a look of horror on his face.

"Well, my survival is a shame, really. I think some of the poor children broke my impact. They were quite smashed beyond repair when I came to. Oh, it was horrible...I layed in the wreckage for what seemed like days trying to will myself to move. I heard the cries of the little ones around me. All of my girls you see here today survived that wreck. When I saw them all around me, I knew I had to be strong for them. I wasn't going to be a Governess in the Outer Colonies anymore, but I would be the Governess of them. All my girls. Aren't they beautiful? All my children are survivors...."

Rockhead went to say something but stopped himself. Isaac could see the pain on his face, he wanted to say something so badly.

"All my beautiful children...it was our destiny to come to this place. It was up to me to save them, Isaac. First I had to save our beautiful girls from the crew of the ship. A few crewmembers survived and were moaning in their seats, but I took a heavy rock, I did, and I saved my children from the....I saved my children one by one. We came to this place. Delivered here by a miracle. This place was wild and overrun by weeds, but I battled the weeds. I hacked at them with anything I could find. I cleaned the knives before I hacked the weeds. I hacked and cleaned and ripped the weeds to shreds. All the while my babies were hungry--screaming and crying for food. I found them food...I rescued them from the nature all around them trying to destroy them. We found this hole in the ground, and we have been here ever since. We're hiding from the patrols that want to round us up. We're hiding from those horrid men at the Institute. And we're hiding from those that want to return my lovelies to Moojtema. Isaac. You must know something. We will never return!!"

Isaac looked at Rockhead, who had a smile on his face. Isaac figured that Rockhead thought she was insane and thought that relieved him of the burden of ugliness she labeled him with. Isaac looked back to the door signaling to Rockhead that they should try to make a hasty exit. Rockhead shook his head no.

"Tell me, boys. Don't you boys want to stay here with us? You two boys and all of us? Wouldn't that be fun, boys?"

"Really, ma'am, we have to be going," Isaac said and started to back up towards the door. Rockhead stood his ground.

"Why, Isaac? I know you want to stay here with us. Don't you think my girls are beautiful? Show him ladies."

The tall blond woman, the one with the menacing gun, pulled her top off to expose her breasts as easily as opening a door. Rockhead beamed with delight.

"No. We really have to go," Isaac said.

Rockhead pulled Isaac close and whispered in his ear, "You fool. Look at these girls. We can fuck them all and just sneak out." His voice carried in the small chamber.

"Who said anything about you, ugly?" She-Wolf screamed. "All your friend has to do is say the word, and you're dead. Then he can stay and fuck us all for all time! There's no way you're touching any of my girls."

Rockhead turned to her and screamed, "But, he's a fucking cripple!"

Isaac grabbed Rockhead and started to pull him towards the door towards the exit, back to the forest and their mission, and away from these insane lonely women.

The bare-breasted woman shot the gun in the air, racked another shell into the chamber, and bid them to halt.

"Be honest," she said. "Why do you not want us?"

"I am married," Isaac said. "I could never stay here with you. I have the one woman in the world I want. Even if I had all the women in the world and not her, I'd still be alone."

"So, you love this one?" She-Wolf said.

"Yes. Even though we just met, everything is right and beautiful."

"Where is she, dear? Don't spend your life in vain pursuits like a bumblebee buzzing from flower to flower for a speck of nectar. Don't burn up like a candle lighting the sunny afternoon. There is something here for you. Seize it! Seize us!"

"I will return to her."

"You've chosen your life. Your path is laid out for you. You must follow her now. To the very end."

They turned to leave. Rockhead's head was drooping downwards like a defeated dog.

"Wait!" She-Wolf cried. "Someone bandage our friend's finger!"

The blond woman bandaged his finger with the dexterity of an inept and cross-eyed surgeon. Rockhead and Isaac had only walked for a mile before the bandage fell off, landing in the dirt. They continued walking and the only thing that passed between them was an odd, uncomfortable silence.

The two boys trudged until nightfall. In the darkness they could no longer make their way through the woods without brushing against branches that snapped back into place violently about face high. Rockhead had been making the branches snap back and hit Isaac for most of the night. Just the thought of a great clutch of pine needles smashing Isaac's beautiful face was enough to keep him going forward. When it got so dark that Isaac could not see when the pine needles were loosed back towards him, he demanded they stop and rest for the evening. They made camp at the base of a walnut tree that was intertwined with a strangling vine. The strangler began its career as a small tendril at the base of the great tree rife with nuts. It grew, tracing itself on the surface like the cancer of pride and then burrowed into the tree's bark seeking its tender heartwood soul. The tree no longer produced walnuts. It towered like hulking death in the greenery. Rockhead looked to his friend, his brother on the mission, and envy crept into his heart. He gave life to it by staring at Isaac's face in the moonlight. Rockhead wanted to be him. Then he looked to Isaac's gnarled foot and brushed the thought aside, considering himself to be fortunate.

"Time to eat brother," Rockhead said holding some of the dried deer meat out to Isaac.

"I'm not feeling well enough to eat. I think my finger's going sour," Isaac said, holding his hand to his chest like his grandmother taught him.

"I would have showed that cunt a thing or two, had you let me brain bash her we never would have met that nutty woman back there," Rockhead said.

"I never want to go back there," Isaac told him.

"Why not, brother? That place could be a small paradise in this wretched place," Rockhead mused.

"My place is with my wife, no one else," Isaac said trying to beat back the pain from his throbbing finger.

"She's a beauty, all right," Rockhead said.

"Let's hurry and get this done tomorrow so I can get back to her," Isaac said.

Rockhead was silent but wondered to himself what he had to go back to. Still the desire for revenge burned itself like hot lava through his mind. He chewed the salty meat and washed it down with water from the water bladder made out the stomach of a deer.

"We should go back there after our mission is over, Isaac," Rockhead said.

"If you want to, go there alone," Isaac quipped.

"I don't think they liked me too much, but maybe if you aren't there they will," Rockhead said.

"Can you find your way back there, Rockhead?"

"Sure. We've walked precisely seven-thousand-five-hundred-sixty-four paces towards the setting sun. All I have to do is walk in the opposite direction from here. I'll remember it. I've got a good memory for the woods."

"What do you see in those women, Rockhead?"

"They needed men there. They were of the right age for that sort of thing," Rockhead said.

"They don't need anyone. They just need to get rid of that woman they worship." Isaac said thinking back to the Glorious Mother and her command of the Congregation.

"Any time you give up your own thoughts and let someone totally make your decisions for you, you're giving up yourself."

"You think the Institute's as bad as she made it out to be?"

"No. She's insane," Rockhead said.

"Then why do you want to go back there?"

"I liked that young girl. The one that did the sweeping."

"The one that paid attention to you?"

"Yes. She's the most beautiful girl I've ever seen. Besides my wife-to-be. But she's gone now."

"What happened to her?"

"She kept disappearing into the forest. One day she didn't come back. I guess she didn't love me enough to stay."

Isaac felt the Amulet around his neck. "What did she look like?"

"Black hair, beautiful. She just disappeared."

"I'm sure something bad happened to her, that she wouldn't just leave you, Rockhead," Isaac said. He didn't know if she was the girl that he saw with Jesse, but when the two went to sleep that night Isaac dug a small hole and buried the amulet in it so Rockhead would never see it. He didn't need anything else for Rockhead to be mad with him about if they were to complete with their mission, if anything, so that he could back to his beautiful wife.

162

The least of what men call nature, the system of balancing needs and the struggle for survival all begins with the sun. It crosses its threshold and burns the grasses of dew. The sun is the source of life, but it is fixed. The sun does not shine for the satisfaction of men or to warm the brow of smiling babes. The men once thought it a powerful god crossing the sky on a great chariot, and some of them paid it blood sacrifices so it would not burn out, but it burned on in spite of them.

The sun burned Isaac's face. Birds sang in the trees that formed a circle in a green meadow flecked with orange wildflowers. In his dream, the warmth was caused by his wife's caresses. He looked into his wife's green eyes and saw himself in her black pupils. He lost himself in her kiss and then realized the songbirds no longer sang. He looked into the sky and saw the outline of a great hawk. It circled above them with its head darting, keen eyes fixed for any change of the scene below. Suddenly, it swept downwards on powerful wing-beats and pierced a brown hare. It stared at the lovers and brought its cruel beak downwards onto the rabbit's head. It hopped and flew to a tree right above them. The hare kicked its legs twice in a vain remembrance of life and then lay still. The hawk stripped little bits of flesh from its supper and the blood flowed from the hare's body. It began as a trickle but then became a fountain spraying onto the lovers as they reclined in the soft grasses.

"You are the hare," the hawk said to them with a voice that was an octave above sanity. The hare stared at the lovers with dead, black eyes.

Deer began to laugh. Without saying a word to Isaac, she jumped to her feet and bounded across the grassy plain towards the gaping forest. As she entered it, it closed around her. Trees and briars blocked his path and grew thicker with each encroachment. When he grabbed for a branch, it disintegrated into his hand, and the wound grew tendrils into his flesh tearing into his tenderness like worms. The tree seized his shoulder blades and hurled Isaac to the earth. While he lay there, he heard what sounded like bark being ripped from the oak tree with an axe. Isaac opened his eyes.

He was face to face with Rockhead, who shook him.

"Get up, you fool, we've really overslept! The sun is nearly at its peak. We have to get going!" Rockhead yelled only and inch or two from Isaac's face. Isaac rose and dusted himself of the sticks and mossy bits that covered his clothing.

Rockhead counted out two-thousand-five-hundred and fifty-seven paces in a vicious monotone before they came to the great oak tree that had fallen. Squirrels clung to its dying branches out of desperation. They ran up and down the length of the tree, chattering to each other and digging into its bark with tiny claws. Two of the squirrels stopped and stood on their haunches to look at Rockhead and Isaac. They shouted a warning to the other squirrels, and they responded by darting into their nests on the branches. The root system pulled up the mossy forest floor when the tree collapsed. Ferns on the rug-like moss arched themselves to the sun because they could not walk away from the disaster. Many now hung dried and dead in the air. Soil formed muddy beads on a necklace, created by the individual tendrils driven down deep in thirst.

"The main root is what did this one in," Rockhead said.

He put his hand on the bright white husk that split in the middle and picked a fat grub out of it about as long as his thumb. The grub writhed blindly from side to side.

"These little bastards brought down this huge tree!" Rockhead proclaimed.

"What is that?" Isaac asked looking at the translucent grub. He could see a mud colored tube inside of it and some other liquids swirling around.

"Look at this fat little bastard," Rockhead said as he squeezed the grub between his thumb and forefinger. The white root flesh seeped out of its backside and the grub writhed in agony at being squished. "One thousand years or more this tree has been here. One thousand years from being an acorn to a huge tree, only to be eaten by these little worms." He scooped his hand into the mush root and pulled out about twenty of the grubs. He pinched their heads as he dropped them into Isaac's backpack. He fished around in the root and pulled out many more.

"What are you doing that for?" Isaac asked.

"I'm saving them for later," Rockhead said with a smile.

"Why?" Isaac asked with a look of disgust on his face as he dreaded the answer.

"We're low on the dried meat. These things are just as good as meat. Well, I mean, in what they have in them, not in how they taste."

"That's disgusting!" Isaac said.

"No, what's disgusting is when we run out of food and your stomach is eating itself. Starving to death is disgusting."

"Whatever you say; you're the expert around here," Isaac said shaking his head. He really hoped they could find the Congregation before they ran out of the dried deer meat because there wasn't enough water in the world to wash those grubs down.

"You don't have to enjoy it; you just have to eat to live," Rockhead said.

A scream shot from the distance. At first it sounded like an animal. The boys looked at each other with puzzled looks on their faces. The discord shot from the forest harmony again. It was no animal. Rockhead ran in the direction of the caterwaul.

They ran. Isaac struggled to keep up with Rockhead who reached the vantage point first. Rockhead dropped to the ground like he was hiding. The screams sounded like a dying animal. Rockhead motioned for Isaac to get down and he quickly dropped into the leaves to mimic his friend. Through the thicket, they spied two naked men holding down a woman with a fire red shock of flowing hair that spurted through the brute's bloody hands. A third man mounted the woman. Rather, he was half of a man: shorter than even Isaac or Rockhead and proportioned like a dwarf. The dwarf heaved himself in and out of her as he grunted like an animal. She screamed with each of his thrusts. She managed to get a hand free and punched the dwarf in the side of his head. He turned his head and snarled, revealing to Isaac a horrifying scar. The little man continued his work but screamed to his assistants, "Damn you! Hold her, idiot!"

"Yes, Sambus," the youngish looking man with brown hair and skinny arms said.

Three red cloaks were strewn haphazardly on the branches at least ten strides from the rutting pigs. Rockhead nudged Isaac and pointed to their weapons. The fools lay them on near their cloaks. Two long knives, still in their scabbards, and a spear, long and deadly sharp in the sunlight, invited them over. Rockhead stared at the red cloaks and a tear formed in the very corner of his eye that rolled down his face and rested on his chin. He put his finger to his lips in order to tell Isaac to be quiet. He bade Isaac to remain in place, but started crawling towards the weapons.

The woman screamed and groaned. The dwarf shook in a spasm and squealed high pitched like a pig. He lay still for a moment, catching his breath before he got to his knees. The dwarf slapped the other man on the shoulder and yelled, "Got her all ready for you! Get at it!"

The man took his position and thrust inside her. She screamed this time like her guts were being torn from her body. The only time that Isaac heard a woman scream like that was when the women came boiling out of the nursery yelling that one of their sisters was giving birth. Since no boys were allowed in the nursery, he listened to the screams and struggle from a distance. The memory surfaced in him each time the fire-headed woman wailed. He remembered that these pigs were his people. He wanted nothing at all except to watch them die.

After a minute of the tall, skinny man thrusting in her with all the same vigor and enthusiasm as the dwarf Sambus had, the woman stopped her screaming. The man thrust a few more times and then arched his back so his head was nearly perpendicular to the ground. He cocked his head to the side and Isaac could see that an expression of stupid glee coated his face. There was no need to hold her.

The third man, short and stocky, screamed at his comrade, "You fucking killed her! Where am I going to get my turn? You fucking murdered her!"

"What of it, brother?" Sambus said with a laugh.

"I didn't get my turn!"

"So? We'll go find another! Don't cry over her," Sambus said as he stretched.

165

The thin man wiped off his bloody midsection with a piece of cloth. The stocky man caught him unaware from the backside, tackling the thin one into the underbrush. They fought like dogs over a piece of garbage.

"Break it up, break it up you two," Sambus said half-heartedly, still very drunk from the excess. He grabbed the dead woman's red hair and turned her face from side to side as if he was admiring her features. "It's a shame. So pretty," Sambus said.

The men rolled on the ground each trying to get the other on his back and deliver a deadly blow. They were not playing. The man who had been slighted got his hands around the other's neck screaming, "I'll fucking kill you!"

His rage broiled through the forest and birds exploded from trees flapping their wings away from the center of mass of the sounds of destruction.

"Now, now, children," Sambus chuckled. He would have to break them up soon before someone got dead. Now it was too entertaining to interrupt.

A yellow butterfly flapped through the clearing and came to rest on a tall orange flower. The butterfly lingered for a moment before the men rolled on top of the plant in their combat. The butterfly sprang away and flapped its wings lazily stirring the air in the hot sun as if nothing happened.

The combatants rolled close to their weapons and back a few feet towards the scene of the crime. Rockhead emerged calmly from his hiding place and grabbed the spear from the ground. Sambus still looked into the dead woman's blue eyes. He could almost see the treetops reflected on their mirrored surface. The two men locked in a death grip, with the man who killed the woman on top of the man who was left with nothing. Rockhead walked, holding the spear just as his ancestors taught him, without a sound. He didn't make a sound when he raised the sharp shaft over his head. The only sound came from the thwack of a spear against flesh and whistling air that escaped perforated lungs. A disciplined Congregation raider kept his spear razor sharp at all times. The spear ran through the thin man like a hot knife through bear fat cooked on a spit over a fire. The top man tried to raise himself off his comrade. He pushed about half a foot up the spear before his muscles gave out and he joined the heart-stabbed comrade below him in death. Rockhead grabbed the knives from the tree and yelled to Isaac to help him take the dwarf.

Sambus sprang to his feet like a tiger and charged straight for Rockhead. He lowered down to tackle Rockhead's legs, but the boy of the forest's reflexes proved to quick for the drunken dwarf. Rockhead sidestepped and sent the dwarf careening into the underbrush flat on his face. Rockhead remembered the little bastard from the raid on his village. He kicked the vicious dwarf in the side of his demented, half snarling half smiling face until he stopped struggling. Rockhead put his knife to the dwarf's unconscious neck and breathed deeply. Rockhead would enjoy the dwarf's blood shooting from his neck like a geyser when he decapitated him. He barely made a scratch when Isaac yelled, "Stop!"

"What do you mean? This little freak was there when my village was destroyed!"

"He can lead us right to the hive of them, don't you see?"

"So can you, Isaac," Rockhead said.

"No, I can't, not without meandering all over the place like a lost snake. He can get us right there."

"I want to kill him," Rockhead lamented.

"Bind him. Once he leads us there we'll put the little one out of his misery."

Rockhead conceded and gathered a length of bristly twine from his knapsack. He bound the dwarf's hands tightly and used a stick to achieve maximum tension on his wrists. Rockhead wanted to make the dwarf suffer before he killed him. The dwarf started stirring. Rockhead did everything he could to prevent kicking him until he was just a bag of pulp.

"Walk, you bastard. Walk in the direction of the Congregation," Isaac said with the most gravelly tough-guy voice he could muster. Sambus laughed at Isaac.

"Aren't you the little runt the women beat up at that Joining Ceremony? How's life in the woods been treating you? I guess you want to go back already?"

"Don't you worry," Isaac said.

Sambus got to his feet. He looked Isaac up and down. Isaac stood nearly a foot taller than the dwarf.

"I see you ain't found a cure for that peg leg of yours."

"Has life found a cure for your face?" Rockhead said and slapped the dwarf hard across his mouth.

"Damn you. When I'm untied, I'll show you something," Sambus said glaring at Rockhead. "I'll have you know that I was quite good looking before I won this mark fair and square in battle. It was my choice to enter that battle. The Father marked you both from birth, you with your peg leg and you with that ugly face of yours."

"You're hideous," Rockhead said to the dwarf.

"Look who's talking, your face looks like the ass of a boar after its hair has been roasted off of it," Sambus said.

Isaac chuckled at Sambus' humor, but then shut his mouth when he saw how red in the face Rockhead became.

"Just how did you end up so squat? Maybe your Father also marked you from birth," Rockhead said.

"Aye. I was marked from birth. When I was just a child, all the other children made fun of me. I took it though. I held my tongue against them. I swallowed it down," Sambus said proudly.

"Why didn't you do anything about it? You were a coward, right?" Rockhead asked him mockingly.

"I am no coward. I held their taunts inside. It kind of burned whenever the insults were tossed. They stung like little acorns thrown by children for a minute or two, but when I buried these seeds of hate, they grew into massive oak trees within me. I could have cursed what the Father gave me in life, but I didn't. I took what He gave me, and I made it grand."

Isaac looked at his foot. The dwarf picked up on this. "What did you do with your rage, son?"

"Nothing," Isaac said, as he backed away from the dwarf's hidden accusations.

"You had to have done something with it. It would destroy you otherwise. I know you have rage within yourself," Sambus said smiling.

"I don't."

"I know you do. I know everything about you."

"Shut up, stumpy, just keep walking!" Rockhead shouted.

"Your friend here is a little spy, ugly," Sambus said to Rockhead.

"No, I'm not!" Isaac shouted.

Sambus broke into a peal of laughter that could wake a corpse from its dusty death sleep. "This little one wasn't allowed to participate in anything, so he conspired with an old woman to have his own brother killed."

"I was tricked!" Isaac said.

"No, you were not. You knew exactly what you were doing. You took that anger from your brother's insults, and you used it against him. You told your grandmother that your brother had been sneaking off into the woods to fuck a local woman, which was also something that you could never do. You did it because you were jealous, pure and simple. You were a jealous little boy, who behaved like jealous little boys do. They tattle. They run and tell someone," Sambus said laughing.

"I didn't tattle. She tricked me."

"That old hag wasn't capable of tricking anyone. Maybe you're just too stupid to realize that," Sambus said and walked ahead of the two. Rockhead kept pace with him to make sure that he wouldn't run away.

Isaac fumed. Then he ran forward screaming, "Damn you, you fucking dwarf!" Isaac put his shoulder into the dwarf's back and knocked Sambus forward. The dwarf thrust his legs wildly to try and regain his balance but failed and fell sprawling onto his face.

Sambus lay on the ground for a full half minute before he began laughing wildly. He turned onto his back and said, "Come now boy, that's no way to treat your father!"

Isaac looked at Sambus with rage in his eyes. "What did you say?"

"I said that is no way to treat your father, son," Sambus said. The part of his face that could smile crept ever upwards as it formed a hideous half crescent.

"Not possible," Isaac said.

"Oh, but it is, my son, and it is true."

Rockhead looked at the dwarf and then to Isaac. He looked at the dwarf's bright blue eyes and then looked at Isaac. The eyes seemed to have the same shape. Sambus' face was too scarred to be able to distinguish any other features.

"If it's true, you must have had a gorgeous mother," Rockhead said.

"How old are you, Isaac?" Sambus asked.

"I'm fourteen."

"Remember what your brother did at the Joining Ceremony? How he joined all those women to the Congregation?"

"Those women he fucked – three of them are with child now. So you see how women join to the Congregation? They are bred in. They bear our children."

"I don't see what you are getting at," Isaac said.

"Oh, Father, this son of mine is impossibly slow. How can you be my own flesh and blood?"

"Maybe I'm not," Isaac said, hoping his words were true and his father was some unnamed man.

"Oh, no, you are," Sambus said. "I was the champion fourteen seasons ago. Envision me in the Sanctuary laying waste to all those gorgeous captives. I filled them all up, believe you me, I did."

"How many children did you have, sickfuck?" Rockhead asked.

"Only one. He had a horribly deformed foot. His mother died squeezing the little monster out. We were going to immolate him but some old windbag interceded on his behalf. She said she saw something in the baby, some sort of future greatness. Everyone in the room laughed. You know at the time, I couldn't even stand to look at you. If they would have given me the Father's Crucible I would have made myself a diamond!" Sambus laughed and rolled on the ground. Isaac grabbed the spear from Rockhead and thrust it next to Sambus' head, where it stuck from the ground.

"Father damn you for ever bring me into the world!"

Sambus laughed and sucked air through his scarred nose. It sounded like a pig oinking.

"Sometimes the truth is ugly, son. Sometimes the truth is obscene. But you can't damn your own existence. You had no choice in the matter. You can only choose what you do with it."

Rockhead put his arm on Isaac's shoulder and tried to calm his friend who was on the verge of tears. "He's just trying to get to you. Don't let him. You aren't your father," Rockhead calmly.

"I'm not? Maybe it is true, only a freak like this could produce a freak like me!"

Sambus laughed, "Oh now you're just being mean!"

"No, it's the truth!" Isaac screamed to the nasty, little dwarf on the ground.

"The only truth, my son, is what you do, whatever you think in that mind of yours is shrouded in the mists, certain, but hidden, like the death waiting for us all. That's it. You and I and this ugly one next to you will meet it all the same. You can take this knowledge I gave you and build on it. Or, you can take this knowledge and let it destroy you. I don't care. It's your choice."

Isaac yanked the spear out of the ground and tossed it to Rockhead.

"Get up! Take us to the Congregation!" Isaac ordered the dwarf.

"Oh, if you insist, my master!" Sambus mocked him.

"I insist," Isaac said.

Rockhead kept the spear ready aimed at the dwarf's back. He tapped Sambus from time to time to remind him to keep walking. Every time Rockhead tapped Sambus, the dwarf looked back and glared. Their surroundings slowly became more familiar to Isaac. He started to remember some of the features that stretched in front of them.

"I assume you've both got business with the Congregation then? You've come to beg your way back in, and you've brought your friend to see if they're accepting ugly people as guards? You just better know what you're doing," Sambus said.

"We know what we're doing. You just better hope your people are ready," Rockhead said to Sambus.

"We're ready for anything," Sambus said.

"Then how were we able to take you so easily?" Rockhead said.

"Well that was a little distraction. That lady strayed to close to our forward observation post there and wouldn't give it up willingly," Sambus murmured.

"It looks like a cripple and an ugly boy just destroyed your forward scouting element then," Rockhead said laughing.

Sambus turned red with rage. He hated to let people know how he felt because they could use his feelings against him. He buried them deep in his gut where they darted around like a piece of onion in a black iron skillet glowing red hot over a mushworm shit fire. Sambus took a deep breath to calm his boiling rage. He had to act soon because they were getting close to the Congregation. He couldn't be accused of leading these two morons there, no matter what short work the Congregation Guards made of them.

Rockhead brought up the fire haired woman again, hoping it would stoke some rage in Sambus, "That woman back there, tiny. Is that how you treat all your guests?"

"Yes. But on a really good day, there's more of us," Sambus chuckled. Rockhead thought back to his village. He could barely contain his boiling rage for the little dwarf.

"I'm going to like the way your head looks on the top of this spear."

Then Isaac said the magic words. He said the words that the two mortal enemies had been waiting for. It was like the referee in their death match told them to fight. "I know where we are now," Isaac said without realizing that he had opened the floodgates.

"You won't live it!" Sambus screamed, and at the same time he had spun and kicked the spear from Rockhead's grasp. Rockhead recoiled and Sambus charged, jumping and wrapping his legs around Rockhead's midsection. The two fell to the ground and Sambus was on Rockhead, squeezing him like a python. Rockhead swung and connected with Sambus' face, but his punches lost their bite after he threw a few.

Isaac grabbed the spear from the ground. He ran to help his friend. He waited until Rockhead's head was clear and watched as the dwarf struggled for air with his mouth open. The scar was about to open up. Sambus made one final push with his legs to squeeze the life out of Rockhead. Just as he opened his mouth to draw a breath, Isaac thrust the spear downwards and didn't stop pushing until he felt the crunch of the back of Sambus' head. Sambus kicked wildly twice and then became still. Rockhead freed himself.

"Damn, I didn't think you had that in you," Rockhead said. He breathed deeply trying to fill his lungs with the oxygen of which they were deprived.

"You will be surprised at what I have in me," Isaac said.

"You sure you know where you're going?"

"Yes. It's only a few hours walk from here. Let's get going."

# #

The boys made their way to the edge of the forest as it butted up against the jagged outline of the silver protrusion. Rockhead could not see it because his eyes were untrained. When Isaac showed him where the Congregation Sanctuary rose slightly above the trees in an oblong protrusion covered with slightly brown vegetation, it looked reminiscent of a turd plugged up in the bloated ass end of the earth.

"The building itself is mostly underground. Our people say the Father for them made it in Heaven. It's a really magical place," Isaac said.

Rockhead was incredulous. "You mean like it flies or something?"

"No, it's full of secret passageways and the walls move on their own without sound. In some of the places it's as light as day, but there is no fire to make a glow."

"Who built it?"

"The Father built it to protect us from the world," Isaac said.

"Whatever. Where is the device?"

"It's still in my backpack."

"Where we gonna put it?" Rockhead said.

"I know the perfect place," Isaac said with a smile on his face. The exit door from the Sanctuary that he left the Congregation forever from was obscured enough from the rest of the buildings that they could place the device and get away. They could avoid any of the stone buildings because perhaps some of the women were looking out windows, longing for their freedom, or reminiscing about chance encounters in the woods with untamed men. Isaac hoped that the Institute people would arrive to being their negotiations very soon after he activated the device. Every moment they were near the Congregation buildings was a moment where the Congregation men could discover them and bring their lives to a sudden and painful end. If they recognized him, like Sambus did, they would most certainly torture him before they brought his days to an end.

They walked towards the door that spilled into the valley. Rockhead picked up a light jog when they crossed into the plain and Isaac did his best to keep up. Rockhead seemed to glide on air when he jogged: the complete opposite of Isaac's manic discombobulated shuffle.

"I want to be done with this. I really don't feel well around this place. This place drips death. I feel it in my bones. Let's hurry and plant the device and leave," Rockhead said with a face as devoid of color as a corpse drained dry by leeches. "You don't feel that?"

"Feel what?"

"The entire ground is vibrating under my feet."

"I don't"

"Can you hear that?" Rockhead asked, growing more agitated the closer they got to the door.

"I don't hear anything. What do you hear?"

"Things whispering."

"I can't. Maybe your time in the forest made you more sensitive. I swear I don't feel anything," Isaac said.

"It sounds like a thousand insects screaming at the same time under a thick cover of mud. They are screaming as they struggle for air, each of them writhing and chewing through his fellow insect for a chance to breath. Each of them shouting his own importance…," Rockhead said in a daze.

"I can't hear anything," Isaac said.

"I can't take it!" Rockhead said.

"Be quiet, damn you!" Isaac said under his breath. "If they hear us we're dead!"

"You go ahead and plant it. I have to get out of here!"

"Where is the device?"

"Right in your backpack," Rockhead said.

Isaac fumbled through the contents. The grubs had been crushed and their guts coated the plastic bag. It smelled putrid.

"Uggh, your snack didn't make it," Isaac said choking back the urge to vomit.

"Here's the damn device. What was I supposed to the with it?"
Rockhead started running back to the wood line and called, "They showed you what to do Isaac! Don't tell me you forgot!"

Isaac did not watch Rockhead run off. He approached the door and pulled the device from the magic bag. He thought about how Cornelius taught him to activate it. When he twisted it open the device began to vibrate. He tried to remember if he did it right. It vibrated with four distinct pulses and continued in this fashion as Isaac held it in his hand. *What now?* Isaac thought. A voice shot from his interior. *Run!*

Isaac's finger throbbed as he started scuttling towards the wood line. He kept shuffling after he reached the trees and zipped past the forlorn branches as fast as his legs would allow. Rockhead called to him from the cusp of a hill, bare of trees, where it seemed that a giant meteor had skidded across the earth and ripped the trees from their moorings, bouncing randomly like a flat pebble across the surface of a pond. The trees on the perimeter of the Congregation towered over the boys. They waited. Nothing was happening.

Rockhead tapped Isaac on the shoulder to break his concentration and pointed, "Look up in the sky!"

In the distance, towering in the skies above the Congregation, was a silver object, which appeared to be the size of a fly from Isaac's vantage point. It was moving very fast. It dove downwards and quickly up again into the sky. They heard a roar like thousands of pieces of paper ripping at the same instant as the bright silver bird ripped through the sky above them. Then a blinding flash of light and a fireball that billowed upwards. Two seconds later came an explosion.

"Oh, my Father, what have I done!" Isaac yelled to Rockhead. Rockhead's face was covered with surprise and a mordant glee. The metallic bird dipped again and rose into the heavens. A second explosion, more massive than the first, illuminated their faces. In the distance Isaac could see lumbering shapes on the horizon moving slowly. They looked like flying green shoes and their sound was that of a rapidly beating drum.

"What are those?" Isaac screamed.

The flying shoes circled the Congregation and descended. What looked like tiny strings flipped out the side and men that looked the size of ants jumped down the tiny strings. The whirlybirds hovered above Isaac's former home, and thick, black smoke topped the fires that raged underneath them. Their propellers whipped the smoke and dispersed it so that the smell reached the Rockhead's nostrils as he ran to the scene. Isaac was not far behind him.

Men dressed in black with shiny metal armor ran in groups of five throughout the Congregation. They sprayed fire onto the place from black sticks that popped loudly. Their faces radiated rage on all around them. They ran from building to building and the tiny explosions that sounded like the insect larvae popping to death in a worm eaten log bursted from within. Isaac watched and vomited. His finger throbbed fire. Rockhead ran off to join the melee but was accosted by two massive sentries. Isaac could not make their eyes out underneath black visors. They carried Rockhead, kicking and screaming, away from the action. Isaac approached them to aid his friend, and they drew their weapons on him, shouting, "Hands up! Don't try anything! We'll kill you where you stand, boy!"

I'm Isaac. I'm responsible for this!"

"You're the source then! You two will have to wait out of harm's way why we mop this place up."

"Where is Cornelius?"

"Who?" the men said looking at each other with their shoulder's shrugged. Isaac realized they were only soldiers and probably didn't know anything.

"What are your orders here?" Isaac implored them.

"We are to liquidate the inhabitants. We are to secure the Termiculum sources and any alien technology for our exploitation teams. The Liquidation has already begun and is nearing completion. We've radioed ahead for the exploitation teams. They are enroute to our location. ETA: ten minutes."

"I've seen enough," Isaac said and the bile rose in his throat. He could not hold back the waterfall of vomit that shot from his gut. All that he came from was in the process of being destroyed and it was his doing. Just as he had destroyed his brother and his grandmother, he was the death sentence of his people. What revenge had he paid his them and what was its worth? He understood fully when the first screams pierced his ears with their pathetic tremolo. They were going to the Father. They should have been overjoyed.

Two guards marched a group of male prisoners wearing tattered crimson capes past Rockhead. The worn souls scrapped any thought of resistance, and their weapons lay broken at the heels of their vanquisher. Rockhead looked to one of the men who walked more slowly than the rest with blackened hands bound behind him in cruel handcuffs. His visage, worn and dour under the obscuring haze of black smoke looked vaguely familiar. He was the man who savagely chucked the spear at him as he was trying to escape.

Rockhead asked the sentry that was guarding him, "How does your weapon work?"

The sentry looked to his partner puzzled and held the rifle at port arms for Rockhead as if he were a senior officer prepared to do an inspection.

"My gas operated, magazine fed, Tanner Industries X-11 A5 automatic rifle fires 5.7mm magnetic projectiles at the rate of 4000 rounds per second. The principle of operation is that I the soldier, in this case, pull the trigger here while pointing at a legitimate target."

"Let me see your weapon, soldier," Rockhead said in a voice that bespake authority.

"A good soldier of the Tanner Institute never surrenders his weapon, sir!" the soldier said in slightly sheepish voice that was the best he could muster.

"What's your name, soldier?" Rockhead said.

"Novice Second Class Valerian, sir!"

"Damn you, Valerian. You know why you're here? You're only here because this gentleman, and I led you here. So give me your damn weapon. I want to see it."

"Sir!"

"Give me your god damn weapon before I beat you with it!" Rockhead screamed.

The other sentry nodded, "You better let him see it. They're the sources of this operation."

"Sir, please don't tell my superiors."

"I wouldn't think of it," Rockhead said. Valerian handed Rockhead the weapon like he was handing over his first-born son.

"How do I fire this thing?"

"There isn't a safety. It's just your finger and your mind. Just point it and pull the trigger."

Rockhead's eyes glazed over. He breathed deeply with the automatic rifle in his hands. His lips formed a cruel smile. In an instant he darted from Valerian's side. He ran up on the prisoners and stood next to the man that tried to spear him.

"Hey! You there! You remember me?"

The man's head was fixed on the feet of the prisoner ahead of him.

"Look at me, damn you!" Rockhead shouted at him.

The man looked at Rockhead. He had the mark of a vicious, rifle butt stroke across his face.

"No, I don't," the prisoner answered meekly.

"Let me help you remember, good sir. You know the place Rimbleton Valley, right?"

The man smiled and laughed. "You're the quick one that got away, right?"

Rockhead's face went red. He shouted to the guard, a bulky man who swayed from side to side as he walked. "Where are you taking these prisoners?"

"To the waiting helicopters. They will be processed into the Institute after that."

"What? Let go? They're to be released?"

"Sure. I guess, we're just here to remove their ability to resist," the guard said.

"Stand back," Rockhead ordered the guard.

"What?"

Rockhead raised the weapon and pointed it at the dilapidated red wall in front of him. Some of the prisoners tried to run, but they were chained together. They bumped into each other and yelled. Some screamed like little girls to Rockhead's ears.

Rockhead pulled the trigger gently. The tiny whooshes sounded like gentle rain on the surface of an animal skin tent or cooings of newborn babes dressed in furs suckling from their mothers' loaded breasts. He did not let off the trigger until the thousand round magazine was spent. The sound reminded him of his childhood with his family sitting in tents listening to wise old men tell stories of the past. He did not know if it was his tears or the burning in his eyes from the acrid smoke that belched from the weapon. All he knew was that he felt better.

The bodies of the dead were piled up, much like those piled outside the gates of Sodom and Gomorrah before the towns were razed to the ground for the evils they had perpetuated on the Earth. All was ordered according to plan. When the torches were set to them, they burned with the same pop, hiss, and crackle that the Sodomites burned with. Greasy ash covered the bright blue sky and fell like black snowflakes on the desert. The soldiers whistled, joked, and asked each other what they planned to do on liberty, much like those soldiers of Judah did as they piled the bloody mangled corpses on top of each other. In the end, they huddled by their radios and awaited the voice of the Father, or their higher command, to give them their marching orders.

As the smoke began to settle, Isaac watched the Institute Technology Exploitation Teams comb the intact remnants of the Congregation buildings as they searched for anything of scientific value.

Isaac followed the men dressed in their white suits and hard black helmets as they investigated every square inch of the enormous, light, metal cylinder that was partially above ground and mostly below. He listened to them speak in terms that he did not understand, and he only understood that they were often lost. He led them towards the Sanctuary, through the pathway that his Grandmother showed him. They marveled at the hallway that lit up as you walked through it. He heard them furiously scribbling in notebooks as they walked through the corridor, each scientist speculated how the metal was made with the capacity of producing light. One of the scientists, a short pudgy man who introduced himself as Gimbal and wheezed while he talked, said to the others as they walked, "All of this technology is at least one million years more advanced than any technology we have discovered on Earth."

Isaac could not contain himself and said, "That is because it is not of this Earth; it was made in Heaven."

The scientists exploded into peals of laughter that dripped around Isaac's head like molten bits of lava projected from a volcano. Gimbal's rank of Senior Science Officer Second Class (SSOSC) was stenciled on the back of his white lab coat. All of his movements were jerky and it looked to Isaac as if he was nervous just to be breathing. Gimbal looked at Isaac closely and pulled his black-rimmed spectacles onto the tip of his long thin nose. He looked from side to side and said in a low voice, "You are correct, my boy. This is not of this Earth. But it is not from the place you call Heaven. It comes from a civilization as old as our sun."

Gimbal's words sent a shiver through Isaac's spine. What the scientist said was not possible. Isaac had always been taught that the Father made the Sanctuary for Isaac's now destroyed people. It had been taught to him and was the truth. Isaac said a key phrase to Gimbal, which struck the scientist dumb and totally ended any future discussion. As they stopped at the door leading into the Sanctuary, Isaac said, "I don't believe anything you say."

"Then don't, son. There is no sense in arguing with you. I mean you did grow up here, right? Your beliefs are immaterial to our mission now, but please lead on, we've a job to do."

176

When Isaac opened the door by placing his hand in the one area that was cool to the touch, Gimbal yelled, "I know it! I know the answer!" The metal itself is an alloy that responds to electrical impulses in the hand." The other scientists nodded in agreement with the exception of one of them who slouched over studying the wall while he made notes seemingly at random in a notebook. The man, tall and thin, with a scraggly beard, reached his hand to touch the wall. Isaac saw this and screamed a warning to him not to touch, but it was too late. When the scientist's fingers made contact with the wall, he yelled in pain as if he had dipped his hand into a scorching beaker of high molar concentration acid. His fingertips glowed white-hot, and the searing brightness continued down to where his wrist met his hand. The hand dissipated with a sudden sizzle into gas and nothingness. The scientist held his missing hand at face level, screaming out of shock.

Gimbal yelled, "My God, Assistant Glompus! What did you do?"

"I touched the wall! That's all I did!" Glompus yelled.

"Most interesting reaction. It appears the wall has caused your hand to be cauterized off. Tell me, what did it feel like?"

Gimbal stood ready with his notebook, jotting down notes.

"Well it doesn't feel like much of anything now. But it got hot like I dipped it into lava, then for a split second it felt like it was on fire, and now nothing."

"So your nerves were completely burned away. Very interesting, Glompus. Thank you for your observation. Don't worry about your hand; we shall have it fixed as soon as we get back to Tanner HQ. You will be compensated for that hand, and you have given the Institute a valuable opportunity to experiment with prosthetics."

Isaac though to himself, *If they can fix a missing hand, they can surely fix a foot.* He tried and failed to divert his attention away from himself for a moment. His bitten finger throbbed, and each time his heart beat it felt like a white-hot flame was shooting from it.

"Assistant Kleebus, make note of Glompus's infirmity!"

"Yes, Sir!" Kleebus shouted and scribbled furiously in his notebook. He was shorter than the rest, standing just a few inches taller than Isaac.

The assembled scientists walked into the Sanctuary. They were silent, as if the eerie immensity of the place had cast aside their ability to speak.

"This is the story of the last battle among men on Earth," Isaac said pointing to the mural.

"It looks like the Paraclete," Gimbal said, pointing to the Angel with the giant yellow eyes. "It's eyes! They're marvelous!" The yellow eyes simmered and glowed in the darkness as if the giant gemstones were passed through the rays of the sun.

"Gentlemen!" Gimbal exclaimed. "We've found what we're looking for. All other scientific research here is now secondary to the Termiculum."

Isaac stared at him dumbfounded. "You came for the Angel's eyes?"

"Yes. That was our primary goal."

"This was all over these rocks? All of this death and destruction...over some rocks?"

"They are more than mere rocks, Isaac. These are the future."

"What future?"

"Your future, son. You have aided the Tanner Institute immensely today. I'm sure your reward from the Paraclete will be great. In fact, I'm very jealous of you," Gimbal said with a smile, and he leafed through his notebook to scribble and scrawl a few notes.

"Don't you want to see through the eyes? Don't you want to see what this place looks like?" Isaac asked.

"I've seen crashed Mashgool Cruisers before, Isaac. If you've seen one, you've seen them all. Unfortunately, I forgot to tell our friend Glompus not to touch anything, but you live you learn, right?"

"What do you mean *Mashgool Cruiser*?" Isaac said dumbfounded.

"Isaac, come now, son, you don't actually think this place was created by some disembodied Father just for your people to live in it and do your strange rituals do you?" Gimbal said with a laugh. "Let me tell you about the first two principles of the Tanner Institute. Principle one: nothing comes from nothing. Meaning, if you see something in the world, it must have come from something else."

Gimbal paused to see if Isaac understood what he was talking about. It made sense to Isaac so he just nodded his head. "Principle two, Isaac, was first formulated about one thousand years ago by a monk by the name of William of Ockham. He said *entia non sunt mulitplicanda praeter necessitatem*. Which means, in your and my tongue, entities must not be multiplied beyond necessity. Which means, ever more simply for you to understand, if you have two competing explanations for an event, you should choose the simplest explanation. So, Isaac, tell me, do you think the better explanation is that this Sanctuary here as you call it, which really is a Space Cruiser of an extremely intelligent and developed civilization from a home planet approximately 4750 light years from our planet Earth, is in fact created by some disembodied Father in some disembodied Heaven and suddenly cast into reality and tossed to the earth just so some gang of strange ritual performing freaks could find it? I don't think so. What do you think, Isaac?"

"I really don't know what you're talking about," Isaac said looking around at the sudden strangeness of the place.

"Don't worry, my boy. All will be explained."

"If you say so," Isaac quipped.

"Isaac. Your people were living amongst the ruins of this ship. This ship crashed during a great war on this planet. This war was fought between the forces of good, that being the Paraclete Robert Tanner, and the forces of annihilation and what we could call *evil*, that being the Moojtema Twelve and the Mashgool, their alien masters. I'm sure none of what I'm saying to you makes sense right now, but I swear all will be explained. You lived here on this crashed ship, and somehow it was taught to you that the ship was made for you. In the past, the people that you descended from found this ship, crashed here and buried into the Earth, much like how rats find and occupy abandoned buildings.

"While your people were in here performing your strange rituals, all the while the ship was performing calculations, maintaining lighting and life support systems, and conducting tests in ignorant bliss that it had crashed centuries ago. You see, Isaac, this ship is just one giant computer, really, and the Termiculum, that substance, which makes up the Angel's Eyes in that strange mural your people, created, is the power source behind the entire ship. Termiculum is a wonderful substance really. It is a verifiable river of energy behind a great dam. It's capable of powering a machine indefinitely, provided the machine has been engineered to run on this substance. I must tell you though, Isaac, the people who designed this ship, the Mashgool, they have their hands wrapped around the universe."

"I don't believe you!" Isaac screamed at Gimbal.

"There, there, we often react with violence at beliefs which do not coincide with our own very well. Do you need to see this in a book or hear it in a story to believe me? Isaac, you will come to believe. I know you will. It all seems fantastic to you right now, but it will all begin to make sense in time. Just know that you were once a castaway Isaac, and now you are part of the Institute."

Before Isaac could respond his finger sent a jolt of pain up through his hand that traveled past his elbow and ended in his armpit. Gimbal took a look at it. "Goodness, son, this finger is horribly infected. We'll have to get it treated."

He shouted orders at the rest of the scientists to wake them up from the entranced state the scenery in the Sanctuary had lulled them into. "Call the Salvage Team in to extract the Termiculum and continue scouting the area for anything of interest."

Assistant Glompus dialed the radio frequency for the Salvage Team with his remaining hand and informed them that there was work to do. The scientists nosed around the Sanctuary for a few more minutes before they decided there was nothing more to be found. One of the scientists asked Gimbal if they should remove the diamonds from the wall to which Gimbal replied that they weren't scummy traders and they had no use for the diamonds. This reminded Isaac that his brother's diamond was somewhere on the ground. Isaac disregarded the pain in his finger and knelt underneath the center podium. He felt along a seam that ran beneath it all the way to the far wall. As he reached into the crevice his hand came to rest on a smooth, hard, glassy surface. He grasped his hand around it and freed the diamond, holding it into the light for a brief moment as his heart leapt with joy. He put it in his knapsack for safekeeping.

The remainder of the day was like a bad dream as Isaac watched the bodies of men and women being carted past him for the bonfires that raged in open plain. Each child that perished was branded into his soul. If anyone had survived he would have gone down in infamy among his people as a horrible sinner, just like the men he hated and despised in the stories his Grandmother told him as she read from *The Gideons*. When the Salvage Teams removed the Termiculum from its metal anchors and pulled the eyes from the head of the Angel, the lighting in the Congregation's Sanctuary flickered briefly and died.

Isaac walked like a haggard ghost to join the rest of the armored soldiers on the Whirlybird. He mentioned to Rockhead that he needed to get back to the Forest People and his wife. Rockhead looked into his face and told him that he did not look well. Isaac stared at his finger and there were red streaks extending from the vicious tear at the knuckle, up his forearm, and past the elbow. The hand shook uncontrollably.

"Where are we going?" Isaac yelled to a bearded soldier trying to scream over the constant chop of the beating props.

"Back to Tanner HQ," the soldier said blinking his blue eyes repeatedly.

"I can't go there. You have to drop me off."

"We can't do that. This is a one way trip, son. We've got captives to deal with."

"Forget those captives. They're my people. Throw them off the damn whirlybird."

"We can't do that. Just sit tight. You look like you need medical attention."

Isaac yelled to the men, "I need my wife, damn you! I don't need medicine! Take me to my wife! I'll tear this whirlybird apart!" Isaac grabbed onto a bundle wires like he was going to rip them from the wall. He couldn't form strong enough a grip on them. The soldiers laughed.

Rockhead said something about getting Cornelius on the radio. That would reassure Isaac enough to allow him medical treatment, and then he could go back to the Forest People and live out the remainder of his days with his wife. Rockhead's words passed in and out of Isaac's consciousness, and he couldn't quite grasp what was being said. One of the black clad soldiers turned up the volume on a green metal squakbox that filled the whirlybird with sonorous voices.

"Forward Recon Scout Cornelius, this is Raid Operation Leader Bumpous. Over."

Bumpous repeated, talking gruffly into the handset the whole time looking at Isaac. On the fourth or fifth call, Cornelius responded. Bumpous relayed the information to Cornelius, and there was a long pause.

Cornelius's voice came over the radio like a poison dart into Isaac's heart, "There is a problem."

Isaac shrieked like a madman. He bolted forward and grabbed the handset. "What problem? What problem, Cornelius!" Isaac heaved, sweating pure lava on the ground and swaying back and forth loosely.

"Isaac. Now do take your time to get better, but unfortunately…."

"Say it Cornelius! What happened?"

"The Chief is dead. He was murdered in his sleep by one of his whores. Crow and his men departed for Moojtema with Deer and the rest of the girls. She did not go willingly, Isaac."

"Why didn't you do anything, Cornelius? You coward…."

"I am only an advisor, Isaac. I couldn't do anything. They overwhelmed us with the suddenness of their attack. I'm sorry…."

"Why are you still living?" Isaac screamed into the handset. Empathy for Cornelius formed a bridge in his being, but spanned a crevasse rage that grew so deep, so suddenly, whatever understanding he had for the old man's failures crumbled away.

Isaac clutched his hand as the rage bubbled up inside him so fiercely that it felt like something cracked in his brain. He looked to Rockhead and fell on his face, landing at the door gunner's feet.

The whirlybird flew with Isaac unconscious. Rockhead took delight in looking at the weary, staring faces of the Institute soldiers and asked them how he could join. They told him it was easy, but he would have to pass the rigors of the selection process and get through all the training, which could take upwards of four years. It was good that he was young, they told him. Rockhead looked to Isaac. The boy had paid his people the ultimate vengeance. He didn't think that Isaac would last the trip back to the Headquarters, but he also did not know the distance they had to travel.

Isaac did not feel the ancient whirlybird as it pitched and yawed through canyons and chasms into the barren rocky crags. He did not feel it as the whirlybird touched down on the landing pad that lay amongst the brutal metal spires the jutted like wolf's teeth in a rocky jawbone. Isaac's head lolled as the men carried him on a stretcher past the spare parts and scavenged military grade equipment that littered the hangar into an elevator that descended into the Institute's bowels. Like the Congregation, it was mostly underground, buried into a mountain of granite. Unlike the Congregation, it did not fall whole from Heaven; it was built with the blood and sweat of men.

Isaac did not come to when the soldiers dumped the contents of canteens into his face. The elevator whirred and groaned downwards into the depths. Isaac coughed and burned with fever. He was near death when the soldiers delivered him into the Institute Infirmary. He heard the yells of men and women and felt the sudden jabs of needles, and then came the blackness.

Suspension in black nothingness. His eyes…does he have eyes? No photon is presented to them. He breathed. It was possible to breathe in the blackness, yet there was no cooling on the nostrils of his nose. A pinprick of light in the folds of the blackness appeared. Did it appear to him, or did he will its appearance? He looked for his body. There was none. Nothing but empty space. His only means of perceiving the empty space was in relation to the pinprick, which was growing. Or was he getting closer to it? Was he travelling to it or it to him? In an instant he was in the center of the pinprick but it had become a giant ring of light. He was positioned at the exact center of this ring, disembodied. His existence a mere point.

He could make out a tail and a mouth in the great glowing worm. The tail was the end, and the mouth a beginning, but only by virtue of the process they engaged in. The rest of the light was indistinguishable and the same on the giant worm being. The teeth of the head cleaved the tail, one segment at a time for each time period elapsed. For each segment cleaved, Isaac could see the energy in the worm's body being digested and dissipating. Each time a segment was cleaved, a new segment grew at the base of the worm's glowing head, and it appeared at the exact time that the mouth bit the tail. A portion was destroyed and a portion created at the same moment.

Isaac, at a pinpoint, felt the need to ask the question, "What are you?"

The great worm being did not cease in its endeavor. It vibrated, and the vibrations formed words. "I am what I am. Nothing more, and nothing less. I am the beginning in myself and the end in myself. I am annihilation and creation. I am ceaseless activity. I am the essential activity. I am without point and need no reason. Do not question me."

"You are the Father? Am I dead?"

"I know not what you speak. Silence! Your life is your own. That is your miracle. I am only the greatest slave of existence. All is built upon me. Wake."

His fever broke. The doctors rejoiced and celebrated their triumph over nature with a five-hundred year old bottle of cognac they foraged from the archives. The 2004 Hennessey VSOP was well preserved and had hints of cinnamon and chocolate. The doctors did not drink too much for fear of their patient suffering a relapse.

When Isaac came to, he demanded to be let out of his oxygen tent. He cursed the doctors in their white lab coats and plastic, triangular helmets. The doctors told Isaac that he could possibly be contagious and had to remain in the tent for upwards of a week. He thought about Deer out there in the woods, and he had to rip himself free from his bindings. He thought about Crow's disgusting hands all over his wife. He thought about her screams piercing the twilight conifers. He tried to rip the plastic, but his hands slipped off. One of the doctors, a man of medium build whose head was shaved bald on the sides underneath his plastic helmet, ordered the nurse to put a sedative into his IV. The orange liquid coursed through the plastic tubing and into his vein. Isaac tried to pinch the plastic tubing off, but it had already reached his brain by the time the thought occurred to him, and he fell backwards onto the bed deep in sleep.

Over the next week, he was kept under constant sedation as the doctors monitored his blood bacteria levels and determined that he was no longer contagious. When he woke, Rockhead stood with one of the doctors. He was no longer wearing his forest leathers; instead, he dressed in a simple grey uniform, and he had a smart looking hat on his head.

"Rockhead," Isaac called.

"That's no longer my name there, friend. Since I came here they have been doing memory recall therapy with me, and I've been able to reconstruct much of what I blocked out due to my traumatic experience. You know they can also blank your memories out. I'd suggest you do that and move on with your life."

"I have to find my wife, Rockhead."

"She's long gone, Isaac. And my name isn't Rockhead. It's Nathanael Hardoak."

"I need to speak with Cornelius. I need to go out into the forest and track her down."

"They've got three weeks head start on you. But I wouldn't worry about her. She can handle herself."

"Not with that sicko, Crow, around."

"It's not like my people to rape forest women. Unlike your people, Isaac. Well that's an aside. I've been asking around. Cornelius stopped by here for his monthly debrief and said that Crow was headed to Moojtema with her. He told me that the women will be let inside the gates, but he and his hunters will probably be turned away at the front door."

"So I can go to Moojtema and find her?"

"Ideally. But how will you get in? I'm afraid you don't quite have the entrance fee."

"What's the entrance fee?"

"More than you've got I'm afraid. I don't really know."

"I want to speak to Cornelius!"

"He's of no consequence around here, Isaac."

"If you're smart, you'll join the Institute like I did."

"Take me to the person in charge then!"

"I have no access to Paraclete Tanner. Then again, I'd guess that he's not in charge of the day to day operations of this place."

"Who is?"

"That would be Commander Jacobus."

"Who's he, that bearded guy on the whirly bird?"

"No. That man is of no consequence here either. He's a minor Raid Team Leader."

"Let me speak to Jacobus then!"

"I guess you could put in a request. He's very busy though, we're planning a major operation."

"Like what we did with my people wasn't a major operation."

"Frankly, Isaac, it wasn't."

"I don't like you much, Nathanael. Why don't you bring Rockhead back?"

"Rockhead died in the raid, Isaac. I've been born anew since I came to the Institute. I've been waiting for you to wake up to show you the wonders of this place. Unfortunately, I've got training now that's very intense, so I won't be able to show you around. If you were smart you'd join up to."

"I can't."

"Sure you can. Anyone can. You just have to pass the selection, Isaac."

"What is it?"

"They sit down and interview you and make you do all sorts of physical exercises after that. Not too bad."

"Rockhead, err, I mean Nathanael, I can't you know…my foot."

"Oh, they've got cures for that foot of yours I'm sure."

Isaac perked up and sat up high in his bed, "What do you mean?"

"Ask the doctor. They've got cures for everything here."

"Is it true?" Isaac shouted to the doctor who stood nearby spinning dials and looking into a black apparatus that glowed green on his face.

"You're interrupting my calculations," he said with a cross look. His face contorted, and he remembered his bedside manner his instructors told him about once. "Well, son, if we can cure you of your sepsis, we can cure you of that foot of yours. It's really not that bad. Nothing a few billion nanobots couldn't fix. Of course, you'll have to get the operation approved."

"Who can approve it?" Isaac asked.

"Commander Jacobus or Paraclete Tanner. That's the only two I know of. You'll have more luck talking to Jacobus."

"I want to see him then!" Isaac demanded.

"I'll see what I can do, Isaac. Making demands will get you nowhere. What happened to that innocent, sweet Isaac I met in the menagerie?"

"I led a hostile army to my people's home. That should count for something."

"No, you helped rid the world of some nasties that killed my entire family. And for that I thank you, Isaac."

"We still in this together, Rockhead?"

"Call me Rockhead one more time and I'll disown you," Nathanael said with a laugh.

"Sorry. I've gotten used to it."

"How much longer does he have in here?" Nathanael asked the doctor.

"We have to finish his final treatments, so I'd say he has to stay here for another three days."

"Isaac, don't worry. I'll get you an appointment with Jacobus by then, but think about what you want to tell him, because he's a very very busy man."

Hardoak snapped to a position of attention and raised his right hand in a crisp salute. Isaac laughed because he thought his friend looked absurd. Hardoak did not drop the steeliness of his gaze or his salute, but performed an about face, turning towards the door in a crisp movement. Isaac reclined back in his bed and watched Hardoak walk purposefully out the door. In only three weeks, his friend had become impossibly strange.

Isaac lay in bed for three days but did not have the slightest notion about what he would discuss with Commander Jacobus. He first thought that he would demand that Jacobus aid him in finding his wife, that they launch whirlybird patrols around the clock looking for her. Then he thought to just demand his copy of *The Gideons* and leave the Institute. He would find her on his own. The thought of being alone in the woods again frightened him; he would probably sooner be eaten than ever find his beloved.

Hardoak entered his room with two doctor scientists. They released Isaac from his clear plastic cage, and the doctors removed his IVs.

"Good news," Hardoak said, "I've spoken with my first line supervisor, who spoke with his supervisor, who talked with the Intelligence Officer, who spoke with the Operations Officer, who spoke with Commander Jacobus over dinner, and the Commander has agreed to meet with you privately."

"I guess that's good," Isaac said.

"Why so down? Don't you know what you're going to request?"

"Not really. I'm sure everything will be figured out."

"Just make sure you do what's best for you. These gentlemen will show you the way to Commander Jacobus' office."

"Follow us, young man," the elder of the two scientists said. The group departed the medical wing and Hardoak peeled off to go to his training. Isaac imagined in his mind that he was undergoing the same training as his friend. He wanted to find his wife, but secretly he yearned to be part of something. It had been denied him ever since he could remember. The people around him treated him differently, like he didn't belong. He doubted the Institute could cure him. He doubted anyone could cure him. He lay in his bed at night and prayed to the Father to cure him, but nothing ever happened with his foot. He woke up in the morning, and it was still there, smiling its twisted smile at sunrise.

The Tanner Institute Military Wing was just another activity that he would not be able to participate in, Isaac thought. Instead, his new benefactors would probably give him the job of cleaning the nooks and crannies of the grime and filth that accumulated over the weeks. When Isaac doubted himself because of his foot, he was playing over and over in his mind the impossible dream of what might have been if he was born a whole person. He knew that life would have been sweet. The fantasy played itself out in his mind. He would have joined his brother among the men a few years after and been surprised by his own joining ceremony. He would have been a hero, instead of a traitor and penny Judas. Isaac, he thought to himself, Isaac was the cheap sellout of the people that raised him up. He knew what he would say to Jacobus. He would demand everything of Jacobus: help with finding his wife and *The Gideons* back. Finally, he would have his foot fixed and be on his way. Isaac did not understand that these were mutually exclusive propositions. He thought that he could just walk into Jacobus' office and make demands. He did not know that Jacobus and Paraclete Tanner were already thinking about their special little guest and discussing ways of putting him to good use.

The group rounded the corner. Nothing seemed amiss, and only the sounds of whirring and machinery came from the small rooms they passed as they travelled down the corridor. Isaac had his head down, staring at his foot as it sloughed forward.

"Watch it!" one of the scientists screamed. A bolt of plasma hurled through the air in front of Isaac and incinerated a target, blowing it into thousands of glowing little stars that settled as cinders on the ground.

"Damn you! Make sure your warning signs are in place before you test those energy weapons!"

"Sir, we didn't think it would fire!"

"Well congratulations on your successful test run, but you could have killed our guest."

The other scientist bowed to the weapons testers and said, "We expect a full report by the morning."

As the group passed towards the end of the test area, another bolt of plasma illuminated the corridor with the brief blue corona of a sun. The target exploded, and the testers clapped with glee. As he passed through the mechanical door that whooshed open gently, Isaac heard the furious scribbling of pens in notebooks.

The group descended down a revolving staircase for what seemed like twenty levels. The stairs also went from having about a foot of space between them to being entirely flat. The scientists mentioned that the staircase was built on a geometrical theorem that the amount of work performed in climbing the stairs was the least amount of work possible. While they descended the stairs, one of the scientists described this theorem as elegantly as he could. It was very boring, and Isaac didn't understand the first thing the scientist said. He might as well have been barking like a dog.

Isaac asked, "Why didn't they just install an elevator?" The other scientist laughed hard and it echoed down the staircase. In the light, Isaac could see that he made the theorem explicator turn red with either embarrassment or anger. As they descended, the staircase grew wider and wider and the space between the stairs less and less, until they reached the bottom station, which was their destination.

The scientists stopped at a double door that opened into a foyer lined with marble. There were hundreds of hanging plants, each bursting with color.

"This is as far as we go," the scientist who laughed at his colleague said.

"Sure," Isaac quipped.

"You make sure that you're polite to the Commander," the red faced scientist said.

As he walked forward into the immaculate foyer, he heard the scientist he insulted say what a disagreeable fellow Isaac was. He said it in a condescending tone and that made Isaac chuckle. Soft music, unlike any that Isaac ever heard before, was being piped into the room. It sounded like the music was being played in another part of the massive Institute catacombs, and traveled through the vents to Jacobus' office. The room smelled sweet like good smells of the forest concentrated.

Isaac started tapping his feet to the music. The music died down and was replaced by a voice.

"State your name," the voice said.

"Isaac."

"State your business."

"I have an appointment with Commander Jacobus," Isaac said, trying to put some timbre into his voice.

"What is the square root of one over two pi?"

"What?" Isaac said.

The doors whooshed open. Standing in front of him was an impressive man with a shock of white hair. His left hand was a cruel black gauntlet. He had the same armor as Cornelius, only more ornate. In his right hand he carried a sword. Isaac slunk into the room, afraid to look at the man. The man turned to his left and began making thrusts at a torso, deftly stabbing and retreating with his sword. Its razor point got stuck a few times in the goopy target, and the man lunged forward and kicked his leg and black boot up to retrieve it.

"I apologize for the security computer, it has quite a sense of humor."

"I didn't really think it was funny."

Jacobus' office was the exact opposite of the foyer. There was plenty of space for practicing fencing. A large wooden desk stood off to the side of the room. A seal depicting an eagle holding a branch of a tree in one talon and in the other talon, arrows glimmered on the front of the desk. Behind the desk, an overstuffed leather chair that looked centuries old kept vigil over the room. Several maps and opened books covered the desktop. An notebook lay open and Isaac could make out the figure of a city with arrows pointing out the plan for an extended siege. A painting of an old gentleman, wearing a black suit and a high frilly collar that his shot out of like a cannon ball decorated the back office. Isaac stared at the painting and stepped back slightly in revulsion. It looked just like the paintings of the ancients in the Congregation, but this one was better composed.

"Galileo," Commander Jacobus said.

"Who?"

"A scientist from the past," Jacobus said.

"Never heard of him," Isaac quipped.

"I wouldn't expect you to. You're Isaac, right? Let's have a look at you."

Commander Jacobus strode around Isaac like a man sizing up a prize horse he was about to bid on.

"Kind of small, aren't you? How old are you?"

"Fourteen."

"Fourteen. You're of the right age. Sorry, I have the tendency to talk out loud sometimes." Commander Jacobus' voice sounded domineering, slightly harsh, like metal scraping against metal. "So, what do you want from the Institute?"

"I'd like *The Gideons* back."

"The book that Cornelius delivered to us? He didn't say it was yours."

"It is mine. It's the holy book of my people."

"The people you led us to?"

"Yes. I'd like it back. It's special to me."

"Well, we understand it's special to you, but it's more important to us. We'd like to preserve it here. We're fairly certain that it is a very rare book. We can't just give it back to you."

"It's mine though."

"No, sorry, Isaac. It's more important than for sentimental reasons to a boy. We're going to put it to use. It holds much value for the future of humanity."

"Whatever you say."

"Cornelius told us in his report that you may want our help with locating your wife. I personally think its quite strange that a boy as young as you should have already taken a wife, but I guess that is your forest people's way of life, and I can't judge it," Commander Jacobus said.

"Yes. I need your help. I'd like you to start scouting the forest for her."

"Again impossible."

"Why is it impossible, sir?"

"They're on their way to Moojtema, right?"

"Right. At least that's what Cornelius said."

"He's not one to fabricate reports. If they're going to Moojtema, it will bode well in our favor and yours."

"Why?"

"She'll be safe there. Cornelius said in one of his earlier reports that she is quite beautiful. Is this correct?"

"Yes. You said your man never writes a false report."

"Then the girl will be fine. She'll be admitted, and you can find her later," Commander Jacobus said matter of factly.

"When?"

"When you're ready to go. They'll never let you in with that foot of yours."

"I heard you can cure it."

"We have gained the ability to cure several maladies over the years, Isaac. The question is, do you want the cure? Do you want to have two perfectly functioning feet?"

"I do."

"I knew you did," Jacobus said. "I knew you did before you opened your mouth, it was written all over your face. You won't have to worry. You'll be taught how to disguise your true emotions better."

"My people didn't allow me to show any emotion, really," Isaac said.

"Ahh yes, your people. They were quite a strange bunch. I'm really sorry that things had to be this way. They couldn't be reconciled. You see, our beliefs are diametrically opposed."

"What?"

"Mutually conflicting. Butting heads. At each other's throats."

"Because we believed in the Father and *The Gideons*. What do you people believe in?"

"We believe in the primacy of science and that all good things come from hard work. Nothing falls pre-fabricated from the sky, my man. Science is a method. A tool. It is a tool to discover the world around us and ourselves. Needless to say, your people wouldn't have listened."

"They wanted to do things in their own way," Isaac said.

"Too bad that way involved kidnapping and killing. But I suppose they thought it holy."

"I don't know about any of that. I wasn't allowed to participate."

188

"Would you have?"

Isaac couldn't answer. He hoped that Jacobus would change the subject but the man just stood and stared at him with dark eyes. Isaac fumbled for something to say and ended up tossing out a declaration that sounded like an accusation.

"I know you just needed me to lead you to the yellow crystals."

Jacobus broke his gaze for a moment and returned his eyes to staring at Isaac. "You're a very inquisitive and bright young man, Isaac. Those are the most beautiful specimens we've ever seen. The Paraclete is very pleased with you. His fortune may smile upon you, and if fortune smiles on anyone, it is Paraclete Tanner. But it was a chance discovery."

"Cornelius lied to me. He said you would just talk to my people."

"Cornelius always writes the truth, but what he speaks what is expedient."

"I don't understand you," Isaac said.

"There are forces at work in this world which you cannot fathom, Isaac. We only know that you have the ability to play an important role in them. You could say that your role has been thrust upon you. However, we know that you are not ready for this role yet. You require training. You will require a new foot. The time is not right now, but our founder will wish to speak to you. That is a great honor, boy. He wants to see you in person. Not many people get that honor."

"How much training? I can't stay here forever! My wife is out there!"

"You're as good as dead if you leave here. If you allow us to train you, you'll be able to go get her. But let's not go putting the cart before the horse. You can't do anything until you let us take care of that foot of yours. I know you want that, don't you?"

"I'll do anything which allows me to see my wife again."

"In order to see your wife again you must meet Paraclete Tanner."

"Why? He's got her?"

"No. Don't be silly. He merely has the key to her."

"When can I see him? I want to get this underway."

"You are mighty proud of yourself, aren't you? Why I think your pride rivals the Paraclete's pride. Are all great men proud?"

"You don't know me."

"You'll see him soon enough. Consider yourself fortunate. Also consider yourself fortunate that you're getting that foot taken care of."

"When?"

"When do you want it to be done?"

"As soon as possible."

"Done. Go up to the medical wing. Your orders will be waiting for you."

Isaac smiled and thanked the Commander. He turned to leave. Jacobus called him to attention with a sounding, "Recruit, Stand at Attention until you are dismissed!"

Isaac stopped and looked over his shoulder.

"You have a lot to learn," Jacobus muttered.

Isaac apologized and did his best to look soldierly. Jacobus smiled at him and said, "Dismissed. Go and get your new foot."

Isaac turned and started walking up the stairs as fast as his legs would carry him, imagining the whole time what it would be like to walk with two functioning feet. He nearly skipped back to the medical wing.

Jacobus feinted and stabbed at the ballistic gelatin torso, opening a gash in its face. A grandfatherly voice piped over the loudspeaker in his room. "Jacobus," the voice said, "I would appreciate you being nice to him next time you meet."

Jacobus stood to attention like the voice of God had spoken to him and said, "Yes, sir."

When Isaac was called into the Surgical Chamber he did not expect to see only one person sitting down at a chair in an all white room. Isaac expected to see a team of doctors, a few of whom he expected would hold him down while one pulled out a hacksaw and started cutting. That was at least how the women in his home performed an operation, and that was after all the prayers ceased to work and the smelly infection spread to the point that there was no other option besides death or amputation. Jacobus promised him a new foot; a normal foot that would work! He called him a recruit. It made Isaac beam with pride. He would finally be part of something fully.

The man sitting at the white chair was dressed from head to toe in a white plastic suit. He even had a white mask over his face and white colored spectacles. He sat in front of a machine with translucent tubes that ran the entire length of the machine from its tripod legs to its bulky midsection. The tubes were bundled into cables that coalesced into a single tube at the end of which Isaac saw a large needle. He shuddered when he looked at it. The needle was at least the thickness of the nail bed of his pinky finger. The technician typed something into the machine from an externally mounted keypad. He looked through a viewfinder and pulled his head away from it. Isaac saw the reflection in the man's glasses, and it looked there were hundreds of lines of text flowing past his eyes like a river at a rapid rate.

"What are you doing, doctor?"

The man either didn't hear him or didn't care enough to answer.

"Pardon me, what are you doing?"

The man looked up from the machine and said rather crossly, "I'm not a doctor. I'm a genetic technician."

"Sorry," Isaac said, "I didn't know. You act like I called you an idiot."

"Doctors are idiots. Doesn't take too much smarts to give people pills," he said and went back to gazing through his viewfinder. "Basically I'm determining if the abnormality of your foot is caused by a genetic problem or just a defect of fetal development."

"What do you mean?" Isaac asked.

"Oh dear, I can see you don't know what I'm talking about."

"I don't."

"It's an elusive science requiring years of study. But I've been able to determine that the problem isn't in your genes. This appears to be a something that just happened when you were forming in your mother's womb. You're lucky. We can move forward with the procedure."

Isaac stared at the huge needle again. He wanted nothing to do with it. "Are you going to shove that needle in my foot?" Isaac asked.

"What needle?"

"That huge thick needle there."

"No, don't worry, that's just an attachment point," the man chuckled. "Everybody always asks that. I'm going to give you something that will take away any pain that you would have experienced in the process, and it will make you go to sleep until all the procedures are over."

"Then my foot will be good?"

"As good as gold," the man said.

"What are you going to do?"

"I'm going to inject billions of tiny building robots into your body that will follow the blueprint stored in this machine to break down the bones in your foot and rebuild them in a perfect form. I can't really get into the principle behind it because it's far too advanced for you now. Just know that it will work."

"Have faith?"

"Absolutely not. Trust in the equipment and the science. It has all been verified thousands of times over. You are not an experimental subject here. I've rebuilt thousands and thousands of limbs that our soldiers had hacked or blown off in battle."

A nurse, a plain looking man with the same white spectacles as the technician, entered the room and scooted across the floor without a sound. He handed Isaac a small yellow pill and then gave him some water to take it. Isaac hesitated for a moment.

"Can't I just do the procedure without being asleep?"

"No. You'd probably die from the pain."

"I believe the Father would protect me."

"Nonsense. I've heard of those reports coming from your people's interrogations. Talking about some force that protects them in the world. Did it protect them from us? Let me ask you. If your Father was so all knowing, why did he not tell your people that you were coming? Also, why doesn't an all knowing God share all of his knowledge of the inner workings of nature with men? Why did he just give us moral codes on how to live?"

"I don't know, maybe that's all He cares about," Isaac said.

"It doesn't make any sense."

"You can read about the Father in *The Gideons* that Cornelius brought in. That book is from me."

"I don't care to. I'm a busy man."

"The book has some truth in it."

"I don't consider that it contains any truth I'm after."

"What is that?"

"Scientific truth. Truth that has been verified independently by experiment."

"And there is none of that in *The Gideons*?"

"I've never read it, so I can't know."

"There is. It tells stories of people that lived a long time ago and all their trials and tribulations. It tells about how they overcame them. It tells about the rise and fall of peoples. I guess you could say that it is a story of the human experiment."

"Does that human experiment require God, son?"

"The Father created us."

"There is much you have to learn. Now, be good and take the pill so I can get started."

192

Isaac stared at the man and said, "I'll think of something to convince you to read *The Gideons*."

"Have you read it?"

"No, it has been read to me. Maybe I can learn to read here, and I will read it. I have a question for you though. Can you explain why we are here?"

"What do you mean?"

"I mean can you tell me why you and I are both here?"

"Do you mean in this room, or are you asking for the meaning of human life?"

"The latter," Isaac said.

"A meaning comes from the heart of each individual man. It is our own choice whether to live a life of meaning or fritter away our time. That is our free will. We choose our path in life. We choose what we do with our time between birth and death, and that is what means everything to our fellow man. Our life is our own, but in a sense, it is also lived for others."

The words rang hollow off Isaac's eardrums because he was thinking about his beautiful wife lying naked in the sun underneath an apple tree overloaded with the ripe, red fruit. The branches bowed nearly to the ground and they laughed and smiled at each other as the apples dropped around them like rain.

"Please take the pill, and let's get on with this."

"It won't kill me?"

"No, I promise it won't kill you."

"Okay, I trust you," Isaac said and swallowed the pill in one gulp. He paused for a moment, gathering his thoughts. "Doctor," Isaac said starting to feel drowsy as the pill dissolved in his stomach lining.

"I'm not a doctor."

"Okay, sorry, but I think the meaning...," Isaac said, breathing deeply, feeling waves of sleepiness break and wash over his body, pulling him to a bright and calm blue sea.

"I think the meaning is...," Isaac slurred. And he was asleep.

The technician moved quickly. He stuck the needle into Isaac's arm and billions of tiny ringed nanoworms began swimming against the current in his vein towards the afflicted foot. In twelve hours the foot would be completely repaired. The technician left to use the restroom, and when he returned there were three individuals in the room. One was an implant technician that he recognized from his medical training but had since disappeared to work with the military wing. The two gruff men told him to get lost when he opened the door, and that they were on official business of Paraclete Tanner and Commander Jacobus. The technician knew not to ask questions. He did not say a word and walked swiftly back to his sleeping quarters.

Isaac was asleep for a full twenty hours, thirty-seven minutes, and fifteen seconds before he was given an injection to bring him out of the chemical sleep. The chemical was a powerful sedative that induced hallucinogenic dreams, trapping the patient in a lucid dream state for the entirety of the operation. Many patients reported that when they woke up they only wanted another pill to go back to their dreams. In his dreams he was a warlord living in the middle of the forest surrounded by beautiful, savage women. He didn't know the slightest about the world and didn't care to know anything. He was happy, making love to his women soldiers, commanding other men to bring him food, and bouncing his many children on his knees. The dream focus shifted, and he was on a distant human slave colony, where the humans were working in mines for monsters. He organized a slave revolt against the taskmasters. It was long and bloody but the men proved adept at killing the monsters when they lost their fear of them. In his dream, he heard the other men calling him Moses and he led them into safety and organized them into a society. He awarded the best and brightest people around him with jobs, and the society fell apart when the dumbest demanded their fair share. The next society he organized he gave all the most leisurely positions to his friends and family members and they made up stories to keep the others entertained and working hard. Society ran well until some people stopped believing in the stories that came down from his mind and made up new ones. There was no easy way to keep the people from coming up with their own stories and they did like an unstoppable force. He kept coming up with stories he thought were the answer to everything, and the people kept telling him no. Wars were fought in his mind. Cannon shots bounded over bright green pastures and killed man and cow alike. Smoke lingered on the horizon and the smell of rotting flesh pickled his mind. His visions disintegrated and grew worse and more terrifying. When he was shoving some of his fellow men feet first into a furnace like Meshach, Shadrach, and Abednego and slamming a heavy iron door on them, he woke up in a cold sweat, and a scream lingered in his throat but didn't come out. The alarm rang in the room like a silver sounding bulled through all the corridors of the hospital section. The nanoworms had just been extracted out of his toenail where they congregated after the procedure, forming a metal slab the size of a dime. Isaac looked down to his foot and his heart leapt from his chest with joy.

"What a great gift the Father has given me today!" Isaac exclaimed.

The technician, a dour man, with his mask pulled to the side revealing at least a three days growth of beard said, "We gave you this gift, now learn to walk on it."

"Wake up!"

The slap came across his face and welted his cheek. Isaac's eyes tore open through the curtain of sleep, and he saw his friend.

"Rockhead!"

"That's not my name, you trainee puke."

"Nathanael, sorry!"

"That's not my name either. It's Trainee Hardoak."

"Okay," Isaac said smugly.

"Damnit, Trainee, that's no way to speak to a senior trainee. Now get up and follow me. You're to report to Trainee Substation Five Alpha for your initial inprocessing."

"How long is the training?"

"Four years."

"Four years! I can't stay here for four years! My wife is out there!"

"You got the foot operation! They get your time!"

"I didn't agree to this!"

"Sure you did, Isaac."

"I didn't."

"You told that to Commander Jacobus. You told him you wanted your foot fixed and look, it's right as rain. You want your wife back, well – they're going to send you Moojtema you lucky bastard! They're sending you in. Of course, you've got to get trained first. We can't go sending a greenhorn into that place; you'd get smoked for sure."

"We're training together?"

"Nah, kid, I'm just a nug. I'll be training to be a Raid and Technology Acquisition Leader. They got big plans for you though. That's what I heard at least."

"Damn. I was hoping I could get out of here in a few weeks."

"You really don't know what you're dealing with, do you?"

Isaac looked to the side at the wall. He didn't know what he was dealing with. It seemed these people were full of tricks disguised as his best interest.

"Why can't they just send me to this Moojtema and let me find my wife and be on my way?"

"They need you to do something for them. I don't know what it is exactly, but I tell you they think you're the key to something. They have big plans for you."

"And I have to get through this training? What if I refuse it?"

"Listen. We're both part of this Institute now whether you like it or not. Hell, I'm a hero around here, and I haven't even been through the training yet. They're expecting big things from me, too. Look at your foot, man! You're cured! You can do anything now! The best course of action you can take now is to just take the training from them. Even if you don't stay after you go to Moojtema and find your wife, I'm sure the training will benefit you in whatever you do."

"I guess I don't have a choice."

"Well you have a choice, but this is the wisest choice. Don't bring anything. Just follow me."

Isaac rose to his feet and looked to his friend. Rockhead's muscles seemed to be taking on the look of pure rock like his brother's once were. Isaac reached into his pocket and stroked the diamond there as if he were asking it for strength. The pair walked innumerate corridors, and soon Isaac realized that he would be inextricably lost if he did not have his friend with him. He was being led to the training, but he would be unable to escape. Nathanael walked naturally as if he were being pulled to his destination.

"How do you know where we're going, Rockhead?"

"Can it with the Rockhead, damnit!"

"Sorry. I can't just give you that nickname?"

"No. That's a period in my life I'm trying to forget."

"Well, when I get out of here and go start to find my wife, I'm going to teach that Crow a lesson," Isaac said puffing himself up to seem bigger.

Hardoak's uniform seemed to be made of wool that would be fine to the touch, much finer than the bristly wool that Isaac's people had made to survive the harsh winters. Isaac reached out to touch Hardoak's uniform, but withdrew his hand. Given Hardoak's violent disposition, the amount of suffering he endured, and the recent increase in the size of his musculature, Isaac believed that Nathanael could possibly rip his head off his shoulders if provoked. As the pair walked, Isaac looked at his own skinny arm compared to Hardoak's and was suddenly ashamed. It looked like a spindly twig straining for sunlight in the midst of sunlight obliterating shade oaks.

The two entered an elevator. Nathanael remained silent and pressed a button next to which there was a long phrase in the language that Isaac still did not understand.

"What does it say?"

"It says our next stop, the Tanner Institute Military Wing Academy, Authorized Personnel Only."

"I'm authorized?"

"Sure. You're reporting for training. You're authorized. If anybody asks, you're with me."

"Hold on. It's a long way down there."

The elevator creaked as it descended the long shaft. Isaac felt a shudder as the elevator strained against the metal track as it sought its way to their destination. The elevator was pitch black now except for the glowing red and yellow buttons that signified which destinations they had passed.

Before he entered training, Rockhead was a pretty jovial fellow, but now Isaac felt like he had to initiate all of their conversations and Rockhead only answered in short terse sentences.

"What can I expect at the training?"

"Don't ask me. It's tailored differently for everyone."

"What do you do everyday?"

"I'm in the process of banishing any hint of fear from my mind. I am taught that fear is a primal reptilian emotion and the emotion of cattle and swine. It is the least developed of all the emotions that human beings possess. Even less developed than anger."

"What is the highest emotion then? Love?"

"I'm a soldier trainee of the Tanner Institute. I have no place for love in my existence. I am taught that it is the conjunction of at least three weaker emotions, all of which we will master in our four years at the Academy."

"What emotions?"

"Hope, comfort, and safety."

"You're forgetting about happiness."

"No, I'm not. Love has nothing to do with happiness. Happiness is separate. Doesn't the feeling of love come bundled with the feeling of anguish at being separated at the source of your love?"

"No, it comes at different times. Unless you're always separated like I am. Then you feel nothing but anguish."

"If you want my opinion, it is best to not love at all. If you have love you have the comfort and safety of today, but shrouded over all this is the inescapable fact that love, like life, must come to an end."

"I think it is best to live in the moment with your love than an eternity without your love."

"No. You'll be taught that it is best to live for an eternity."

"It's not possible."

Hardoak smiled and said, "There is much about the world you do not know, Isaac. But you will learn."

The elevator doors opened without a sound. Hardoak used the sudden change in lighting to grab Isaac by his shoulders and hurl him in a cold heap into the middle of an empty white room. Isaac looked to his friend's face for any sign of compassion, but it was completely absent of emotion as he stepped back into the darkness. A door opposite Isaac opened, and a man in gray uniform with a floppy purple hat on his head and a waxed moustache from hell ran into the room screaming at the top of his lungs.

"Get up! Get your worthless ass up, puke!"

Isaac had the wind knocked out of him by his sudden fall, and he looked towards the door to see if Rockhead was still there to help him. Nothing remained but closed doors. Isaac wheezed and tried to pick himself up. He fell back down on his face.

"Get up! I won't tell you again, boy. I'll commence to start kicking the shit out of you!"

Isaac struggled and fell again. He breathed enough through his spasming lungs to say in a weak voice, "I can't."

The man screamed like a blood vessel burst in his brain, "God damn you! God damn you! If you ever say those two words together like that again I will end you! Get up!"

Isaac struggled again to sit on his ass.

"Answer me, you fucking bacterium! If you ever say you can't do something again, I will fucking murder you! No one will know you're gone. I will murder you and drag your still warm carcass to the incinerator. You be will be ashes come morning! You got it? No more saying I can't."

Isaac nodded his head.

"Answer me like a man, not a damn head-bobbing bird, retard!"

"Yes."

"Louder!" the madman said.

"Yes!"

"Louder!"

"YES!"

"Louder! Sound off like you're a man, not a maggot!"

"Yaaaaaaaaaaaaaaaaaaaaaaaaaaaaaasssssssssss!!!!!" Isaac roared. The yawp felt exhilarating, like he'd been waiting to do it his entire life.

"Excellent! Now get your puny ass into the shower! We want to make sure you're not carrying any of the disgusting forest parasites with you into my glorious institution."

Isaac ran through the door and the madman followed right behind him. Isaac came to two doors, each marked with a word in the language that he could not read.

"Get your ass in the shower!"

"Which door is it?

"First test! Failure!" the madman shouted. He rang his hands in mock despair and said, "Why the hell can't you read, dumbass?!"

"No one ever taught me!"

"First things first. You will address me as Senior Instructor Aristo. Now, don't make excuses. Why the hell can't you read?"

"No one ever taught me, Senior Instructor Aristo."

"There you go again making excuses. I want you to repeat what I say after me. I can't read because I never asked anyone to teach me to read. I can't read because I was lazy in the past. I can't read because my people were morons that didn't value education."

Isaac repeated him with a look of shame on his face.

"Okay. You've admitted your failures. We will teach you to read. First lesson! The sign pointing to the right says S-H-O-W-E-R-S show-ers and the sign to the left says I-N-C-I-N-E-R-A-T-O-R incin-er-ator. The steely way that the word incinerator slithered off Aristo's tongue sent a chill up Isaac's spine. He had heard the word before. It was like a fireplace, but meant for burning things to get rid of them, not for heat.

"Every day that you pass your training you go to right. The day you fail you go to the left, because that means you're dead! The incinerator is how we get rid of the bodies of a worthless little bacterium like you. Wait! I'm giving you too much credit! At least a bacterium knows how to survive in this world. You're worse than a bacterium. You're nothing!"

Isaac stood frozen, waiting to be told what to do. He was frozen, staring at the heaving, sweating face of Senior Instructor Aristo. Aristo's eye twitched.

"Get your ass to the shower!"

Isaac ran in the door to the right and entered the industrial aluminum shower. It was cold, sterile. Benches for clothing ran along one wall. He came face to face with about twenty other boys around his age. All were naked, standing along the wall underneath a spigot.

"We're waiting for the green light," one of the boys said. A darkened green orb hung from the ceiling. The boy pointed it out and said, "When it comes on, the showers come on. We only have one minute." Isaac sheepishly took his clothing off in front of the other children.

He recognized some of them as the children of his people. He hoped they did not recognize him. The Tanner Institute had spared some of the children. The boys cowered along the walls grasping each other, their eyes wide and lips white with terror. All of their eyes plastered him. Isaac felt awkward. He was the one responsible for their present situation. He took his place up against the wall underneath a dripping spigot. All of the children looked at him.

One child shouted, "It is you! The brother of Jesse! The one that sold him to his doom! The one that sold our people their doom!"

"I don't know what you're talking about!" Isaac said looking to the exit, but it was closed.

"I know you, damn you! I know you!" the child screamed at him. He pointed Isaac out to the other children, "See, that's him! That's the gimpy-legged bastard there!"

Isaac held his foot up in his defense, "See my foot's perfectly fine!"

"He sold us all! Look at his foot! It's fine! He sold us all in exchange for a new foot!"

The five children joined in the mocking rage, mimicking the boy that first started it all, "May the Father damn you to your tenth generation, you bastard!"

"I don't know any of you!"

"It's enough that we know you!"

They began to claw and scratch at him. One slipped on the wet floor and began grabbing at Isaac's legs trying to pull him to the ground. They were like a gang of crabs picking the flesh from a corpse washed up on a beach. Isaac balled his fist and punched the kid clawing at his legs. He then kicked at the boy's head and missed. The larger children tackled Isaac to the cold aluminum floor. Their fists stung like pelts of rocks from an angry mob.

"You little bastards!" Isaac screamed.

"You'll have to kill us," the largest of the boys said.

Isaac grabbed the original mocker by the throat and squeezed. The boy gagged and his face started going purple. Isaac screamed, "Get away from me, or I'll crush his throat!"

The punches stopped. The little snares withdrew themselves to the corner of the room where they huddled like tiny mice, their black eyes burning through Isaac as he slowly released the biggest of the boys from his death grip. The boy gasped and crawled back to the corner. "I swear you are cursed," the boy said clutching his injured throat.

"You're the destroyer of a people," the little mice said.

"No! We are all that people. So we aren't destroyed! I saved you from them. Did you all want to be the Glorious Mother's slaves?"

"We would have served Her until the end!" the mice said.

Isaac reached inside his pocket and pulled out the diamond that was his brother. "You see this? This diamond? That's how you all would have ended up! This is my brother. All that remains of him after they killed him. The Glorious Mother killed him in front of my eyes. His only crime was loving another woman other than Her!"

"She never would have found out if you didn't inform on him! You're scum! When you don't get your way with our people as a spy, you turned spy for someone else! You're the worst sort of person. You get someone's trust in order to do them in! Who are you spying for now, spy?"

"I've never been a spy. I've never had a choice. I had no choice at the Congregation. I had no choice to be in the forest. And I certainly would rather be somewhere else than sharing this shower with you."

"Our mothers told us you were devoured by a mushworm. They told us to be good or we'd get expelled and get eaten by a mushworm, too. You got your recognition, spy. You were infamous before you led the army to our home. But, oh! You didn't have a choice! You're the same whiny Isaac that got picked on all the time. It's just that now you've got a foot because you betrayed us."

"No. You all betrayed me when you sent me off into the woods to die alone. I guess you all underestimated me. What could a poor gimp possibly do to us, right?" Isaac said coldly.

The boys that were in the shower who were not a party to either side of the argument looked at Isaac with respect. Their parents had sent them, from their small forest villages to the Institute in hopes that they would have a better life than living hand to mouth in the forest could provide. The Red Death had also terrorized their tribes. To them, what the man Isaac had done had taken a lot of courage.

The green light shone in the darkness. The pipes groaned and steamy water and a soapy emulsion shot from the head high spigots. Some of the children looked to the faucets when the green light turned on and had soapy water shot into their eyes. They wailed while the others laughed at them and played in the hot water. It would be the last time that the boys would know the joys of innocent play because their games were about to become deadly serious. The military trainers enjoyed the fight via hidden camera. When the water turned on, the scientists began scribbling in notebooks in shorthand decipherable only by them.

After the shower, the screaming recommenced. He was told to move everywhere at a high rate of speed. If he lagged, he received a slap. He was given uniforms that were to be in a neat and presentable fashion at all times. A fat, cackling woman with sweaty armpits gave him three uniforms and two hats from a small pass through. She tossed two pairs of boots through the porthole right after and they crumpled on the floor. Isaac could barely hold everything, but his savior came in the form of a sack to hold it all in, which he slung over his shoulder mimicking the rest of the harried recruits. They told him to make sure that he didn't crumple one of the hats so he put it on his head. One hat was to be on display in his room wall locker at all times. When the Senior Instructor saw Isaac with a hat on his head indoors, he lost his mind and slapped the hat off his head. It fell into the dust and looked ruined. Isaac was made to pick it up and dust it off until only black remained. He was given his room. He would only sleep in the room. It was four feet by five feet: about the size of a prison cell. It had a bed and a wall locker. His clothing went in the wall locker. His bed had two white sheets and a gray wool blanket of very coarse fiber. The bed was to be made at all times, unless he was sleeping. He was warned by his Senior Instructor that if he was caught sleeping on top of the bed so he could avoid making it in the morning he would be given a small tent and made to sleep outside. When the lights came on the morning, Isaac was told that he had fifteen minutes to make his bed, put his uniforms on, and make ready for inspection.

Recruit Trainee Isaac was given a test that would measure his abilities and that way his Senior Instructor could focus on those. The Institute did not want to make well-rounded men that were mediocre at everything they did. They wanted to make men whose natural excellence was sharpened to a razor fine point through superior training.

The test was given orally because Isaac couldn't read. It was a series of questions about what he would do in certain combat situations. It asked him what weaponry he would use to produce a certain explosion. Isaac did not have the slightest idea about anything the computer asked him and he answered the questions by guessing.

The next set of questions had to do with sneaking around. They were questions about meeting in secret, storing documents and transferring them in secret, and killing persons in secret. Isaac felt that he had to do a good deal of sneaking around when he grew up in the Congregation so he felt more confident about this section. When the computer asked him the best place in the human anatomy to stab a sentry, killing them, without alerting anyone - he thought that if you stabbed them in the throat from behind, cutting downwards between their collarbones they would be unable to scream out for help. He didn't know if it was correct or not because he had never done it himself, but in his mind he imagined that it would work. He found it slightly disturbing that he could imagine these things.

Other sections involved flying whirlybirds, jets, dealing with explosives, performing minor surgeries, and general questions of science. As the test wore on, Isaac became more and more frustrated at not knowing anything. He guessed randomly at answers composed of words he hadn't the slightest idea of their meaning. When he got the results he found out that he fared well in Espionage, about 45 percent correct, far surpassing the average performance of 10 percent. He got about 5 percent in combat, 10 in medicine, and by far his lowest performing category was Jet Flight Operations, where he scored a goose egg.

For show, Senior Instructor Aristo burst in the booth to chide him for his poor performance. He then relented and asked Isaac, "Are you frustrated with yourself?"

"Yes. Greatly," Isaac said.

"Good. That means you want to improve."

Isaac was not issued a schedule until he learned how to read. He was given specialized reading modules and he sat in the library all day long listening to the sounds of letters and forming words. His reading progressed, and Aristo was pleased with the progress reports.

"At this rate, you'll be entering the class far ahead of the other students," he said. Aristo went from being the thorn in Isaac's side to being a mentor, but he never dropped the separation between trainee and instructor. Aristo's primary function at the Institute was to mentor a student and indoctrinate him into the way of life of the Institute. One day after Isaac completed his readings, Aristo had him read a document called "The Way of the Tanner Institute."

"The way of men has been strife and conflict and bloodshed. Those who would eschew this are seeking their own destruction. The Tanner Institute does not start wars. The Tanner Institute finishes wars through superior tactics, strategy, and equipment. The

Tanner Institute takes science as the ultimate and final practice of human inquiry. Science has the final say, we say. All of our operations are geared towards our scientific endeavors. As the Paraclete, Robert Shay Tanner, who discovered the fundamental particles of the universe, lives, so we live. His wisdom is the fount of our hopes. His vision is our vision. We are united, one body, under the governing principles of the universe.

"Do you understand it?" Aristo asked Isaac in a corner of the library. The library did not contain any books like *The Gideons*, only hundreds of terminals that lay flat against the tables. The walls were decorated with paintings and pieces of marble that depicted scholarly endeavor throughout the ages. Isaac did not recognize any of the names underneath the friezes, but he assumed that he would in time. All the books were stored on a central computer. Isaac couldn't wait to search it and see if *The Gideons* had been put on the computer.

"I do understand it," Isaac told his Senior Instructor.

"Tell me why you are here, then," the Senior Instructor said.

Isaac thought about his wife and going to Moojtema and being reunited with her, but he knew better than tell Aristo that.

"I'm here to be a man," he said.

Aristo nodded and said, "And how do you think you'll do that?"

"When I join the other men here, when I'm done with my training."

"Being trained doesn't make you a man. Your will makes you a man. What you intend to do, and if you do it, that's what makes you a man."

"I've been being a man for a long time, then," Isaac said.

"You're ready for your schedule," Aristo told him. "I'm proud of you. During your time here, I will be your advisor."

"I'm eager to start," Isaac said.

He received a small computer that was no thicker than his finger. His schedule was open. It stared at him in black and white.

TANNER INSTITUTE MILITARY WING SCHEDULE OF COURSES
NAME: ISAAC
RANK: STUDENT TRAINEE 1st CLASS
CAREER FIELD SPECIALITY: EAIO (Espionage, Assassinations, Information Operations)

YEAR ONE:
BASIC MILITARY ACHIEVEMENT PROGRAM (BMAP) DESIGNED FOR THE MILITARY MINDED JUVENILE AGED TWELVE TO FIFTEEN. APTITUDE IN READING AND WRITING THE ENGLISH LANGUAGE IS PREREQUISITE FOR ENROLLMENT INTO THE PROGRAM.

PROGRAM OF INSTRUCTION:
MSCI 333: MILITARY STRATEGY FROM THE BEGINNING TO THE PELOPONESIAN WAR.
SCI 222: SCIENTIFIC ENDEAVOR: THE ANCIENTS TO SIR ROGER BACON
E12: BASIC TRADECRAFT IN HUMAN INTELLIGENCE OPERATIONS

MSCI 123: SMALL LETHAL WEAPONS AND EMPLOYMENT IN COMBAT
OPERATIONS
MATH1: ARITHMETIC THROUGH ADVANCED MULTIVARIABLE
DIFFERENTIAL EQUATIONS

YEAR TWO:
INTERMEDIATE MILITARY ACHIEVEMENT PROGRAM (IMAP) DESIGNED
FOR THE MILITARY MINDED YOUNG MAN AGED THIRTEEN TO SIXTEEN.
APTITUDE IN READING AND WRITING THE ENGLISH LANGUAGE AND
SUCCESSFUL COMPLETION OF THE BMAP ARE PREREQUISITES FOR
ENROLLMENT INTO THE IMAP.

PROGRAM OF INSTRUCTION:
MSCI 444: MILITARY STRATEGY FROM ALEXANDER THE GREAT TO
NAPOLEON. SUBTOPIC: ALEXANDER AND HIS MILITARY
SUCCESSORS, WITH SPECIAL EMPHASIS PLACED ON ROMAN
MILITARY CAMPAIGNS DURING THE REPUBLIC AND IMPERIAL
ERAS.

SCI 333: SCIENTIFIC ENDEAVOR: RENE DESCARTES THROUGH ALBERT
EINSTEIN WITH SPECIAL EMPHASIS ON THEORY DEVELOPMENT
AND SCIENTIFIC EXPERIMENTATION.

E34: EMPLOYMENT OF TECHNOLOGY IN CLANDESTINE OPERATIONS

MSCI 456: SMALL ENERGY WEAPONS AND THEIR EMPLOYMENT IN
COMBAT OPERATIONS

MATH 2: ADVANCED GEOMETRY AND PROBLEMS IN TOPOLOGY

YEAR THREE:
ADVANCED MILITARY ACHEIVEMENT PROGRAM (AMAP) DESIGNED FOR
THE MILITARY MINDED YOUNG MAN AGED FOURTEEN TO SEVENTEEN.
APTITUDE IN READING AND WRITING THE ENGLISH LANGUAGE AND
SUCCESSFUL COMPLETION OF THE IMAP ARE PREREQUISITES FOR
ENROLLMENT INTO THE AMAP.

PROGRAM OF INSTRUCTION:
MSCI 555-666: MILITARY STRATEGY FROM NAPOLEON TO WORLD WAR II.
SPECIAL TOPICS INCLUDE GENOCIDE AS STATE POLICY AND
ATOMIC WEAPONRY. MILITARY STRATEGY FROM THE AGE
OF TERRORISM UNTIL THE GLORIOUS RESISTANCE.

SCI 444: ADVANCED PHYSICS, EINSTEINIAN PHYSICS, THE STUDY OF
THE LIFE AND SCIENTIFIC ENDEAVORS OF S. TANNER.

E45:   WHEN ALL ELSE FAILS (WAEF): ADVANCED ASSASSINATION OPERATIONS IN SPECIAL INSTITUTE MILITARY OPERATIONS (SIMO)

MSCI 789:   EMPLOYMENT OF MASHGOOL TECHNOLOGY IN INTER-HUMAN WARFARE.

MATH 3:   ANALYSIS OF THE TANNER QUANTUM REDUCTION PROBABILITY EQUATION.

YEAR FOUR:
INDIVIDUALIZED TRAINING PHASE (ITP) FOLLOWING COMPLETION OF THREE PHASES OF MILITARY ACHEIVEMENT PROGRAM (MAP) THE ITP PROGRAM IS COMPOSED OF HALF A YEAR, APPROXIMATELY SIX MONTHS OF INSTRUCTION, IN THE CAREER FIELD SPECIALITY (CFS): EAIO ESPIONAGE, ASSASSINATIONS, INFORMATION OPERATIONS.

WHEN ALL ELSE FAILS (WAEF) PHASE 1: TARGET INTERDICTION (WHO IS A VALID TARGET)

WAEF PHASE 2: MDK OPERATIONS CYCLE (ESPIONAGE, ASSASSINATIONS, INFORMATION OPERATIONS)

WAEF PHASE 3: TARGET INTERDICTION METHODOLOGY (IN CLOSE OR AT A DISTANCE?)
AT LEAST TWO HOURS PER DAY WILL BE SPENT IN PHYSICAL CONDITIONING DURING ALL PHASES OF MAP AND ITP.

*

      Isaac was taught during his training that war was the worst endeavor of men. It was a catastrophe, plain and simple, and nothing good ever came out of it but more war. He was constantly reminded, as he went through the modules on computer in the Tanner Institute Library that the knowledge he learned was only to be used for good. What good was exactly, was up in the air, because he did not study ethics. He only learned the most expedient ways to kill, ways to blend in with his surroundings, how to kill silently, and how to kill spectacularly. At the end, he learned how to write well so that he could make people believe that it was in their best interests that the target was killed and make them love and respect and also fear the Tanner Institute.

      He learned to fight well so that the fight could be brought to an end as soon as possible. He learned and studied the horrors of the past: when the first tribes, then cities, then city states, then kingdoms, then empires, then alliances, then economic blocs of trading partners and energy producing commonwealths made the poor shoot hot lead, drop bombs and rain fire on each other's cities. The poor among them were trained to use the weapons of war which were built with large factories that knew no real masters, but only servants, servants such as the men who shoveled white phosphorous and chemicals into the system, that when combined, exploded. War formed the middle, with its requisite piles of dead. Money poured out out the other end. The monies went straight to the accounts of the owners who never touched the weapons they made. They sold promises of security and hope in the form of superior armament. The politicians climbed into bed with them, and they awarded successful weapons tests lucrative contracts. The whole system was a big sucking mouth and shitting anus much like the mushworm. In his explorations of the Tanner Archdatabase of Human Knowledge, known affectionately as the TADHUK, Isaac discovered:

......TANNER DATABASE OF HUMAN KNOWLEDGE

Login: Cadet016587
Passcode: !!2@socrates@348

ENTRY: MUSHWORM.........mushworms are an invasive species on the planet Earth, originally indigenous to the planet Terra X where they are approximately one centimeter long. Following the first meeting of Human and Mashgool in 2045, it is speculated that some of the mushworms that had stowed themselves on the Mashgool ship escaped onto the surface of the earth where they thrived in the high oxygen content atmosphere. There are no natural predators for the Mushworm on the planet Earth because the flesh contains a highly potent neurotoxin. A full grown Mushworm can measure up to a mile in length and consume approximately 10,000 KG of biomass in one day. Its waste material from cellular respiration is high sulfur content unrefined petro carbon, which is highly flammable.

......................//END ENTRY//......................
Is there anything you wish to add/change/delete?

Do you desire another search?

It made more sense to Isaac than the story his grandmother told him about the Father creating such a vile species to clean up the battlefields of men. He read in the TADHUK about some ancient battles where men slaughtered each other with metal swords and sharp spears in great formations directed by generals in golden armor from hills surrounding the valleys. Upwards of 100,000 men were butchered in the heat. The victors stripped the dead naked of their armor and weapons. With no mushworm left to clean up after them, the dead men were left to rot in the sun. After the carnage, the men went onto the cities of the men they slaughtered and crashed down their walls and entered the women and after their penalty was paid, the women who were not taken captive--the old and the ugly--would steal out amongst the stench and sound of flies buzzing and search the bloated dead for husbands or lovers only to have their lamentations drowned out by snarling packs of wild dogs.

The more Isaac learned of warfare, the more he hated it. The more he learned, the more he learned to be a genius in its application. Warfare was to be avoided at all costs until it was necessary. The Institute taught him that if War could not be avoided, the enemies that made it upon the Institute should be obliterated. They should be ripped up by the roots and cast aside like thorny weeds from a lush garden. Overwhelming force was the only answer.

After Isaac learned to read he searched the TADHUK for a copy of *The Gideons*. He wanted to read it for himself. After several seconds of searching, the TADHUK flashed NO RESULTS in stark black and white on the screen. He rose from his chair in the library infuriated and demanded from Aristo, who sat relaxing in a plush chair, where to find it.

"I've never heard of it," Aristo said. His eyes indicated a sudden aversion to his pupil.

"My grandmother used to read it to me."

"If it's not on the Tanner Database of Human Knowledge, it doesn't exist," Aristo said plainly.

"Sure it exists! I've held it in my hands!" Isaac said.

"Watch your tone, trainee," Aristo said gravely.

"Yes, sir," Isaac said. Secretly he would not forget to demand of Jacobus where the book was after he graduated.

*

During his third year, the course of study got so strenuous that Isaac felt his brains were coming out of his ears, and his eyes burned each time he looked at the glowing computer screen of his small tablet. His only release was in the massive Tanner Gymnasium where he worked his muscles and let his mind rest. Isaac had exchanged his uniform no less than five times because he grew so much during the past three years. When he raised his hands over his head, his biceps bulged and stretched his uniform to capacity. He received an unsatisfactory plus in his final Mathematics class because he could not quite wrap his head around the famous Tanner Equation.

In his fourth year he learned that the best way to kill a sentry silently was in fact to sneak up behind him and stab him in the throat in a downwards motion, finally having your knife blade come to rest when the hilt touched the place on his chest where the clavicles came together. He learned about explosives and all the tools available in his arsenal of secrets. His favorite was a miniature robotic mosquito that could inject a fatal dose of Mushworm toxin and was controllable by remote. He practiced dispatching them into the forest where he flew them through the trees using their tiny camera eyes and delivered fatal doses to deer and birds before he announced that he had the hang of it and didn't need to kill anymore until it was time to use it for real.

On his last day of instruction in his fourth year at the Tanner Institute, Isaac took his thirty second shower in nearly scalding water in the small, stainless steel cylinder that looked more like a coffin than an amblution chamber. Water and soapy emulsion sprayed him from nine separate high-pressure nozzles. He covered his face with his hands and held the position until the spigots stopped delivering their magic. When the water and soap stopped flowing, high velocity blowers dried him. The warm rushing air licked his bald head and sent a shiver down his spine.

He walked into his undecorated, small, white room. He attended his classes like every other day for the past four years. During the last hour, he allowed himself to think about his wife. He suppressed the thought when he was alone and took his want to escape out in the gym. He kept his eyes focused on the ground in front of him as he heaved and grunted against the heavy cannonballs attached to rope that he slung. He did not make a sound. The exercise made him feel disembodied, and he imagined his soul flying across the open plains like a bird, flying towards her. He flung the cannonball to the ground, and the sweat ran into his eyes, robbing him of the vision. He had counted down the days when he could seize his wife from behind and go inside her like Solomon did Sheba. He was taught that his urges were natural, but he had to divert their raging waters through the dam of his intellect, routing lust to his budding talents so they could achieve fruition.

During his four years, Isaac became little more than a machine, taking in food and turning it into muscle. His mind took in words, and he passed the tests and was called knowledgeable. Isaac spent much of the time alone. He benefitted from the isolation. His body raged against his mind's control of its urge to fuck something. Some of the recruits trained themselves to achieve orgasm during the thirty-second shower. The chamber was small and the flying soap suds obscured the camera. Some of the recruits turned to their fellow recruits. In the shower, Isaac kept his hands over his face and the pressure built.

Isaac achieved the highest marks possible in his classes, with the exception of the math class that introduced the Tanner Equation. He fared better than the rest of his peer group and graduated at the top of his class. He also stood like a colossus over many of the other men. He remained taciturn, nodding vaguely when spoken to and opening his mouth to dispense wisdom that chopped through the hoary brambles that crept from the mouths of his classmates. Back in first year, some of the trainees told him with red faces and giggles that there was a level of the Tanner Institute that studied Human Sexuality, and when they graduated and were full members of the military wing, they would get to take part in experiments.

There was no graduation ceremony. Personal victories were savored personally and there was no need to show off in front of others. If there was a graduation ceremony, Isaac would have spent it alone in his room thinking about his wife.

Aristo congratulated him on his way out of the library and told him that he looked forward to serving with him. "You were the best damn trainee I've ever supervised," the bull of a man said.

"You were the only Recruit Instructor that I've ever had," Isaac said and they both started laughing. Some of his fellow graduates grabbed him as he was heading up to his room to be alone with his thoughts. He followed them to the Tanner Institute Sexology Center. It was buried in the mountain's heart and served more to relax the troops than study the human sex instinct.

The room was white with a wrap around vinyl couch. Mirrors lined the walls. The lights were low. Isaac glanced at himself in the mirror. One glance and he thought he was looking at a stranger. He was the doppelganger of his older brother. Strong. Handsome. Powerful. One of the mirrored panels opened and a naked woman with dark hair and soft white curves scattered giddy tidings into the room. Some of the graduates walked away from her in fear. They slunk to the corners like ooze in a tilted room. She walked up to Isaac like she owned him. She grabbed him by his waist belt and pulled him along, ignoring his protests. His classmates clapped and cheered him from their wallflower garden.

Her features, from the back, seemed chiseled from the marble in mimicry of the ancient statues. She was perhaps Venus foamed from the penis of Zeus. At least, she was Diana with her bow string taut. The woman guided him to dark room. She groped him in the darkness, and his protests increased.

"I am your prize," she said, speaking with a voice soft, like a dream.

"I don't want you," Isaac said, pushing her hands away. "I can't."

"You have to want me. Everyone wants me. It's part of a study."

"I don't want you."

"You've been stealing kisses like sweets in the dark corners of this place?"

"No." Isaac said plainly.

"Calm down, dear."

"I'm calm."

"Why don't you want me? Everyone wants me."

"You just said that. I don't care."

"Come here and touch me," she said shattering the darkness.

Isaac hesitated. Then he thought, what would be the harm? After all, it was an important study for the Institute. His mind and body flipped on and off, each overriding the other.

She reached her hand inside his pants and tickled the tip of his penis like she was flicking the petals from moist spring flowers. He tried to pull away. Then she grabbed his hardening penis and squeezed.

He pulled her hand off and slapped it out of his pants.

"Damn you!" she exclaimed. "Are you some kind of weakling?"

In the darkness she put his hand between her legs, and he felt the wet warmth. His lust bubbled up inside him. She brought her lips to his.

"What is the matter, dear?"

He broke into a sweat. Her voice was familiar. He couldn't place it. "Be a good boy and come on the bed and have me."

"I don't want to."

"Aww, you've just been cooped up, love. That's all. You can have me all night long. It's just you and me. No one will know. I don't care if you burst like a rocket in a couple of seconds. I'll make a man out of you."

"I won't be able to live with myself."

"Why? You're a young guy. And I'm a beautiful woman. What's the problem? I don't care if you explode right when you get in. I'm used to guys doing that."

"No."

She reached inside his pants again and stroked the head of his penis. She whispered into his ear and guided his hand between her legs to where her body parted ways. She thrust her breasts in his face.

"Please don't deny me. I was a queen in this world. Now I'm just a dirty whore. Don't deny me. You'll break my heart."

"You were a queen?"

"I was precious. The queen of an entire people! But then soldiers stormed my Congregation...."

Isaac leapt up. His reaction came uncontrollably.

"I must be going now!" he said, his skin crawling like soldier ants sprang from the mattress and invaded his genitals.

At that instant, one of the other trainees burst into the room and turned the lights on. He had a small camera in his hands and took a picture, hoping to catch Isaac in the act.

"Awww, no fun!" he said. He was much smaller than Isaac with black hair that stuck from his head like bulrushes. His eyebrows came together like a hedgerow set over ocean blue eyes.

Isaac looked at the woman over his shoulder as he bounded from the room. She was as radiant as he remembered and the past four years stresses had only slightly worn on her face. She looked at the other trainee and spread her legs slightly so he could see. He blushed.

"You want some sugar, stud? This guy was worthless," she said pinching the trainee's cheek.

In his room that evening, he laid in the darkness and regretted that he had not taken every inch of rage out on her. Then, he felt sorry for her.

He fell into a dreamless sleep that lasted until Commander Jacobus himself roused Isaac out of bed. He was dressed in a black robe with a hood pulled neatly over his face.

"Follow me, Isaac," Commander Jacobus said with a finger over his mouth to indicate to Isaac to be quiet.

"No one must hear of what we are about to discuss," Jacobus said to him.

"Okay. I take it I'm going operational."

"Quiet. You'll find out directly from the Paraclete."

The pair wound their way through the metal catacombs to Commander Jacobus' office. Jacobus pressed a button on the great mahogany desk and the portrait of Galileo cleaved in two, sucking back into the darkness of a passageway. Jacobus led the way into the blackness. The end of the tunnel was only a pinprick of light, and it reminded Isaac much of his unforgettable comatose dream where he met the giant light worm.

"We walk through the darkness, so that we appreciate the light, my son," Jacobus said eerily. "But do not be afraid, it is only a temporary transit to the light."

When they stepped into the light, Isaac stood in a rotunda with four halls. Isaac could see that portraits and busts of men stood next to a machine or device or famous theoretical paper they had published. He pointed down a hallway. "These are the halls of gods among men, and one hall for men among the gods." Jacobus announced.

"Gods among men?"

"All of these men advanced human knowledge the most during their lifetimes. You see, here is Socrates. Plato. Aristotle. All the famous philosophers who taught us how to interpret what we see in the world." He pointed down another hall and said, "The Hall of Science, Kepler. Newton. Einstein. Those fellows. With all relevant subsections, of course. The other hall is devoted to Religion to remind us of where we came from and where we can never go back. You can see all of this later though, we have business to attend to."

"What's the last hall?" Isaac asked.

"That son, is where we're going, the Domain of the Paraclete, Robert S. Tanner."

"Good I can ask him about the Tanner Equation then; I could never wrap my head around it," Isaac said as the two walked down the hallway.

"I saw your grades," Jacobus chuckled. "All will be made clear to you, Paraclete Tanner will tell you what really happened to the world and everything in it."

"How does he know? Did he read it all in the TADHUK?"

"No, my son, he was there."

The two turned a corner and entered an all white room.

Isaac, ever curious and ever questioning inquired further, "How could he have been there, my Granny and the TADHUK said all of this happened over five-hundred years ago," Isaac looked up and saw Robert Tanner and only the sound of shock slipped from his lips.

A massive computer, lights blinking and tapping off a rhythm to final wanton snare crash of time, sat in a semicircle in a white domed room. A metal body sat in a black leather chair, arms splayed out to the sides resting on the armrests. The legs were together. The surface appeared translucent and Isaac could see the crystal from the Angel's eyes inside. It was the Termiculum: the universal power source for infinite possibilities. The body looked just like the Angel's body in the mural of Isaac's youth, only this one was without a head.

The human head of Robert S. Tanner was suspended above the body on a robotic arm. The arm moved downwards, slowly lowering the head to the body. The head's eyes were closed. There was no movement behind the eyelids. The head was completely bald; all that remained human was the face, which looked plastic. The rest was the same metal as the suit. A single data link, copper plug of intertwined double helixes wrapped around a red metal rod changed colors to glow nearly white hot as it approached the metal body's attachment point. The head dropped into place and the body received it with a tightening of bolts and wave of metal that peeled from the chest and shoulders to make up the neck. The veins in the face seemed to glow with a strange blue illumination, faintly visible through the skin.

The eyes moved opened. They appeared dead. Blue eyes yellowed at the periphery minus the spark. The lips formed an enigmatic Mona Lisa smile. It spoke in a metallic voice that was clear and faded away to static.

"You must be Isaac," Robert Tanner said. "I've heard so much about you." Isaac stared, silent.

"Please pardon the young man's silence, sir. You are quite a puzzle to some people who are ill prepared to meet you."

"I know, I know, five-hundred-fifty-plus years does not bode well for one's face," Tanner said with a metallic chuckle. "I heard you had trouble understanding the Tanner Equation of Quantum Reduction Probability."

"I did, sir," Isaac said sheepishly.

"It is quite alright. I'll tell you how I came to it. I thought of time and matter. If there was something at the beginning of time there wasn't a beginning, and if there was nothing there could be a beginning. But how can this something come from nothing and bring time into being? You are faced with two impossible poles. However, between the two, young man, possibility creeps."

"There is no time," Isaac said.

"There is no matter. We thought in the past that matter was just there. But we find at its most basic and infinitesimal level that it is both something and nothing at the same time. Particles, the smaller you get them, remain in existence for ever-smaller amounts of time. And how are the particles formed? The particles are formed by the interaction of an infinite number of multidirectional fields of varying frequencies. The Tanner Quantum Reduction Probability Equation describes the interactions of these fields and the solution predicts which particle is generated through their interaction. So, Isaac, you see something can come from nothing in that the fields are not matter; they are energy. However, there was not ever nothing. There was no beginning moment of time. Only a continuous buildup and breakdown of matter as the fields realign themselves."

Isaac stared blankly at the Paraclete.

"I don't understand. I am sorry, but I can't understand it," Isaac said frowning.

"That is okay. Not many people understand. I may be the only person *living* that understands all of the implications of my theory. You don't really have to understand it though. You're not on the science track here."

Jacobus butted in, "We've trained you to be a spy, Isaac."

"To go to Moojtema, right? You want me to go to Moojtema and do something."

"Not just anything, son."

"First, I want my copy of *The Gideons* back."

"I'm afraid that is impossible, son. That is a priceless, controlled item."

"But it's mine."

"It belongs to humanity now, what's left of it. We're storing it here to guard it from the elements. It is in a temperature and humidity stored vault," the Paraclete said.

"It is far too important to just be left out in the woods, son," Jacobus said.

"I was hoping to read it now that I can read," Isaac said.

"You didn't tell him Jacobus?"

"Not yet, sir."

"Tell me what?" Isaac said.

"During your foot surgery we took the liberty of putting some additional modifications into you. *The Gideons* is now very much a part of you, you could say."

"What do you mean?" Isaac said.

"*The Gideons* is written in a language. It is information we've taken *The Gideons* and encoded it into the language of DNA. We inserted it into a virus, which inserted the DNA encoding all the information of *The Gideons*, into the DNA contained in your finger. We're sorry we didn't tell you, of course, but we couldn't have you trying to read that nonsense book when you were supposed to be studying."

"I don't know why you'd do that?"

"The computers in Moojtema are organic entities that do their computations with DNA. Their entire system, including their Security and Life Support Systems, runs off of a system they call the GOD. The Graphical Object Database. Our Special Security Section has determined that if you are able to insert your DNA containing *The Gideons* into the system, then we are fairly certain to induce a system error."

"How?" Isaac said.

"Well, that's a good question. As our computer scientists explained to us, all of the information contained within the system is internally coherent and consistent. All the propositions stem from one another; they grow from one another. This is absolutely essential to the proper functioning of the GOD. Meaning, in layman's terms – like you are – the system continuously fact checks itself to make sure that the information in the GOD is dependent upon other information contained in the GOD. Inputting something like *The Gideons* into that system would be just like inserting an absolutely foreign object that the system would recognize as nonsense," Tanner stated matter of factly.

"Why?" Isaac asked.

"Oh, goodness! Jacobus, I thought you said this young man was the best we've got?"

"He is, sir. What about that Major Hardoak? We could use him," Commander Jacobus said.

"No. He's too valuable on the Tech Acquisition Teams. He'll have to lead the eventual assault on Moojtema." The Paraclete blinked his eyes several times and then looked to Jacobus, "Still I don't trust this blathering idiot here to be able to get himself to Moojtema."

Isaac tried hard to maintain his military discipline and said, "I'll get there, sir. It's all I've been thinking about for the past four years. The mission."

"I want Hardoak to accompany him as far as the Caravan City, Jacobus. Just in case we need some firepower out there."

"Yes, sir. I believe Major Hardoak is on an operation now, but he will be informed as soon as he returns," Commander Jacobus said.

"You still haven't told me why, sir, and I'm not stupid; I'm only trying to make sure I understand everything I'm going to be doing," Isaac said still chewing back the growing anger he had for the Paraclete.

"What's the fundamental proposition of *The Gideons*, Isaac?"

"I don't know. I haven't read it."

"That's right, we taught you to read. Well if you read it, you'll see the fundamental proposition from which all the other logical propositions grow is *God Exists*. We believe that this proposition is either not contained in the Graphical Object Database, or is not in that formulation. Frankly, we don't know what those Mashgool believe."

"I still don't understand," Isaac said.

"Okay, Isaac. It seems I have to spell it out easily for you. Say, for your whole life, you had played with red balls. You had bounced them off the walls and played catch with them and had red balls of various sizes as your playthings. That is all that was all that was given to you to play with. Just red balls. You had been taught by everyone around you, all the adults, that the only types of balls in existence were red balls. You had come to accept this and internalized it. How would you react to another child who told you that he played with a blue ball? What would you think?"

"I suppose I would call him a liar initially."

"You probably would. You had been taught and conditioned to believe that the only variety of ball was red. It's not your fault; that is what you were taught. Now, say that, for your whole life, you had been taught that *God exists*. You had heard descriptions of God. You had heard that God was merciful, just, righteous, upright, well meaning, and a Creator. You had been taught to pray to God. Your whole life had revolved around the proposition that *God exists*. Now say that someone came and told you that there in fact was no God and that the proposition that you had been operating under your entire life was false. In fact, the correct true proposition was *God Does Not Exist*."

"There would be conflict between us," Isaac said. "We would probably have problems communicating."

"That is what we are trying to introduce into the GOD. *The Gideons* has the fundamental proposition God exists and various other propositions outlining the attributes of God. Such as God exists and is merciful and is powerful and is omniscient and is righteous and is a creator and…so on and so on. We are betting that the Mashgool's system either does not contain reference to God, or contains reference to a God with a entirely different set of attributes, or makes the explicit statement *God Does Not Exist*. Any of those three arrangements, and we introduce a contradiction into the system."

"But what if the Mashgool conception is the same as our conception?"

"I highly, highly doubt that, knowing them."

"What do you mean that you know them, sir?" Isaac asked.

"There is much you do not know about the world, Isaac."

"You're probably wondering just what the hell I am."

"It did cross my mind, sir."

"Then by all means, ask, son."

"Why are you just a head?"

The Paraclete laughed. It sounded like an engine starting in the cold with a hint of raspy static bringing up the tail. Jacobus joined in. They laughed for what seemed like minutes while Isaac's face burned.

"What did your people teach you about the world, son? Those were those people of yours living in the Mashgool Cruiser?"

"Yes. They taught me what was recorded in our holy book, *The Gideons*. They taught that all of the good people of the Earth were raptured up to live for all eternity with the Father. They told me that we were all waiting for the Father's return."

"First things first, Isaac. That book is not called *The Gideons*. It is called the Holy Bible. An organization called *The Gideons International* used to distribute copies of the Bible to hotel and motel rooms; those were rooms that people used to rent to sleep in when they were away from home on business or vacation. I figure at the time before the Great Darkness, there were about eight to ten billion Bibles in the world. That is more than one Bible per person. They were translated into nearly every language. I really thought that the Mashgool did their best to destroy all the copies along with the other distinctly human holy books and works of literature. I guess a few made it through the flames."

"Why did they destroy the Bible? Why get rid of books?"

"Are you familiar with the First Emperor of China?"

"No."

"Of course not. Here's the story. Pay attention. The first Emperor of China not only built the Great Wall of China, which still stands in some fashion to this day, but he also ordered all of the manuscripts written before his reign to be destroyed so that all philosophy and literature could begin with him. When the history of China was traced back through the documents, it could be seen to have begun with the First Emperor."

"Ahh," Isaac said with wide-open eyes, "The Mashgool destroyed the works of men so they could own his history."

"Yes. You will see, Isaac. You will see these bitter effects when you go to Moojtema. You will see how utterly dependent these people are on the Mashgool. It's sickening."

"That's why you want to attack Moojtema? You want to liberate them."

The Paraclete smiled and nodded his head. "Well, son, I'm really the one that is responsible for the Mashgool arriving here. I mean, inadvertently. And really, this will answer your first question as well. The question of why I'm just a head."

"Sir, should we tell him everything? I mean he can read it on the TADHUK later."

"Quiet now, Commander. He should find out from someone who was there. Better to have him sure about things than keep on guessing for himself. This young man is very important to us."

The Paraclete's body whirred and metallic clicks came from his head. The lights in the room went down, seemingly on their own. The Paraclete's eyes flickered with light. Vents in the room spritzed a gas, which seemed to hang in the air in front of his eyes like a white cloud. A moving picture began to play in the cloud, projected by the Paraclete's eyes. Sound poured from his voice box.

A gray haired man with a beard and small beady eyes made an announcement. "You have it here first on CNN, October 20, 2025 physicists working at CERN LAB II have discovered a new type of fundamental particle which they are calling the "God Particle." From what the physicists are reporting this particle has some amazing properties. I'm going to ask the research team leader from the Quantum Particle Physics Research Group at the Massachusetts Institute of Technology, Dr. Robert S. Tanner, just what he and his team have discovered and why it is so riveting. Dr. Tanner, can you describe in layman's terms just what this God Particle is, really just what it is you have discovered?"

"Luke, I really think it is fully impossible to describe in layman's terms because quantum physics is best described in the language of mathematics, but I'll try my best. The particle in itself is a paradox; basically, it lies at the halfway point between being and nothingness, oscillating between the two states. Its net average probability state was predicted by the formula my team and I came up with at MIT and we just needed the CERN II to be able to isolate it. The particle only durates for nano fractions of a second but it may serve as some proof, however subtle that *it is possible that something can come from nothing*. The particle's decay and subsequent self reassembly releases unprecedented amounts of energy. The reason this is so huge a discovery, and I'm not an engineer, but I'm thinking this will enable the world to move beyond merely burning plants like we have since the beginning as humans and will give us an energy source that is indefinitely sustainable and safe. This is the same energy that holds the universe together."

Isaac flashed back to the dream of the worm eating itself.

"I don't understand any of this," Isaac said to Jacobus.

"Don't worry, Isaac, most of us don't. We're dealing with the most pre-eminent genius of the twenty first century, son," Commander Jacobus said blushing.

"More like the biggest moron the world has ever known," the Paraclete said.

The Paraclete's eyes flickered again and the lights went down again in the room.

"CNN…April 15, 2045…on an otherwise clear Sunday Morning…our innocence lost forever. The President of the United States and other world leaders addressed their frightened nations as strange craft appeared over major cities throughout the world. The President addressed the nation in a special press conference from the Oval Office…My fellow Americans, as of 0600 this morning, many of you are well aware of the visitors that made contact with the peoples of Earth…we do not know exactly where they are from but they appear to have peaceful intentions toward us and have agreed to an open exchange of science and technology, having counted us, as they say, among the learned peoples of the universe. They have invited our top scientists, as well as scientists from around the world to an open panel to be conducted at a location of our choosing. I have been asked along with leaders from the European Union, the Confederation of Energy Producing Nations, China, Russia, the South American Commonwealth and League of African Nations to name a list of scientists to attend this meeting. This is the first day in what we hope will be a beneficial partnership between our two peoples." The lights flickered on the scene as the President, a man who appeared calm but shaken, folded his hands over his knees and turned to his wife who accompanied him on the stage. Static crackled, the scene went black, and Paraclete Tanner spoke to Isaac.

"My experiments are what brought them. They told us during the meeting that their sensors that had been in place for millions of our years started detecting high energy fluctuations in our sector…energy fluctuations that could only mean that an intelligent life form was doing experiments at the quantum level and had made a significant finding. They wanted to meet the person responsible. If the president would have chosen a wiser person, maybe we wouldn't be in all of this trouble. I was intelligent, but intelligence should never be confused with wisdom. The meeting was a damn test. We fell for it. We went into the meeting like children in a candy store."

"What happened, sir?" Isaac said.

"The Termiculum happened."

"The crystals?"

"Yes. The Termiculum is the stable fuel form of these particles fashioned into a lattice array by Mashgool engineering. It is a fuel supply without end. It would have taken us millennia from the discovery of the God Particle to be able to fashion anything like it. The applications were endless. We saw all of their technology, space travel to distant galaxies. And the reason why I'm only a head, it's this damn curse they gave us: Immortality."

"What?"

"A cure for death, Isaac."

"How?"

"It was always a given: death. Always lurking around the corner to take you. Always ready to dash the most well planned plans. No matter who you were in life, it was a fact that you had to die. The Mashgool's technology changed all of that. They made me the man I am today. The suit. It is their design. It is powered on the Termiculum crystals. It keeps what is left of my organic brain alive. It has kept me alive for these five hundred years."

"How was it a test?"

"After we accepted the Termiculum, they told us that it was a test. It was a test to see if we had overcome ourselves or we were just a big gang of individuals. They had tempted other civilizations before with this curse. They knew what would happen. Anyone out there would choose immortality. Wouldn't you, Isaac? Anyone would choose what they offered. They had the experience. They knew the outcome of our choice and they offered us no council. They must have watched our eyes light up and had known. They had us."

"They offered to coach us with their scientists. They offered to exchange our scientists and teach us the hard earned secrets of the universe."

"What happened instead?" Isaac said.

"In the end, we chose the outcome. We chose the product without even caring about how it came about. They said we were greedy little children. And they sent us back to the surface as these freaks, more machine than man. Naturally everyone else wasn't pleased."

The lights flickered in the Paraclete's eyes again. The gas cloud filled with an eerie green. Robert Tanner stood in his metal suit at a podium in the Vatican. Eleven others just like him sat in chairs behind him. The aged white haired pope shuffled past him without even recognizing his presence and sat in a plain white high-backed chair. A younger cardinal stood at another podium and spoke into a microphone that boomed off the high marbled walls and grim reaping statuary. Politicians formed the crowd of onlookers. Photographers clicked photos like strobe lights that blossomed in slight explosions off Tanner's waxy face.

"We are urging you twelve to destroy yourselves. You are all an abomination."

"Why are you even speaking, Cardinal? Doesn't this prove that you are the abomination? We know the Mashgool are real. They came here to share science with us. They do not care about your petty religion. I'm sorry they didn't care enough to speak with you. You are irrelevant to the future progress of humanity."

"You are not even human so you cannot even make any sort of value judgment. You gave up your humanity when you sided with those creatures."

"They are not creatures, Cardinal. They are the most accomplished scientists in the universe that we know of. If anything, you are only upset because their discoveries only further make your religion unfounded and obsolete."

"We are speaking for humanity and humans, Mr. Tanner. Creations of God. the Father, who live bounded by conception and death. You twelve have revealed that you cannot die. You are no longer human. You can no longer speak for us. We don't know who or what you are you speaking for. You are all abominations. You must destroy yourselves for the good of humanity. You must destroy yourselves...."

"We will not destroy ourselves. Since we returned from our meeting with the Mashgool, we have been discussing many future plans. Humanity is no longer bound to old superstitions and ways of doing things. Religion is an utter falsehood that we no longer need. We have the answers within our grasp! Do you see these men here? This old man here? This Pope? What answers does he have? Nothing! Humanity is stronger than any of you. We have the answers in our grasp!"

A man leapt from the crowd, screaming. "Die! Lucifer! Die! Antichrist!" Six gunshots sounded off the marbled walls, emitting small puffs of smoke in the streaming lights. Robert Tanner stood and laughed into the microphone. The Vatican guards fought with the deranged man as he tried to reload.

"What happened?" Isaac asked.

"The thoughts of men had been growing in two separate directions since the advent of science. One aimed at expanding ways of seeing the world. It aimed at verifiability. It aimed at inclusion. It aimed at leaping off of this rock into the great beyond. The other thought of men aimed at buttressing dead arguments that were really crumbling castles of sand built when men knew nothing. It aimed at holding onto thoughts that were conceived when men thought that they were the *CENTER OF THE UNIVERSE*. It pulled quotes from a book written when men thought they were the *CENTER OF THE UNIVERSE*. We started to discover that we were a small place, like a speck of dust in an immense infinity. When the Mashgool came, we knew. We knew we were nothing much at all. We are not a beautiful creation of an all good, all loving, all protecting God. We are, just like the Mashgool, just something that happened."

"Yes. But what happened, sir? You haven't told me what happened!"

"Patience, my son. Please give the Paraclete some time to think," Commander Jacobus cautioned Isaac.

"There was a final war among men. We were accused of trying to be Gods ourselves. We were accused of aiding the Mashgool. We were accused of secret deals. I wrote the treatise that would become the founding document of this Institution. I gained adherents. Our arguments were more vociferous. Our arguments made more sense. Of course, they were angry. They were being selected against. They couldn't fight and struggle against the truth anymore. What we knew grew up and around them and choked their belief from the sunlight. Oh…they claimed it came from within and was based on faith, but it made absolutely no sense after the Mashgool came. They wanted everything to return back to when we were the center of the universe. Back when everything made sense. When they brought down a Mashgool Cruiser, we knew it was time. The Mashgool wanted to bombard the surface and destroy everything but we told them that we could handle the problem. All we needed was their help. They helped us. And they destroyed nearly all the past works of men in the process. Those bastards knew what they were doing. They found our fault lines, the divisions in humanity, and exploited them to the utmost. And we didn't even know what was happening until it was too late."

"And what happened!"

"The inevitable final war among men. Men aligned themselves and polarized into groups that fought to determine the future. Men fought it out, and of course, we won. But not after civilization was destroyed and there was near mass extinction. Moojtema was established for the survivors. They were corralled there like cattle driven over the land. At first, it was ruled over by the thirteen of us in an enlightened despotism. Those twelve are still sitting there in their throne room ruling over that putrid fucking city."

"Did they kick you out?"

"No, I left willingly. I wanted no part of it. I will not serve the Mashgool. I would rather live free out here than accept their largess. I would rather make discoveries on my own than get them handed to me like Christmas. So I left. I took with me a cohort of my companions; others who thought similarly, and I established my Institute out here. They can have Moojtema. They can have their sick little heaven. I want the world. The Institute provides the best possible avenue to cooperate with the Mashgool and still have a vibrant future for humans."

"Why do you want me to go to Moojtema?"

"We told you. It has to be destroyed. Those people must be liberated. You need an entrance fee though; you cannot get in if you're empty handed. They won't even make you a slave. If you're born there, you're good. If you're a beautiful woman, you're good. A male outsider doesn't have a chance. But we've thought of that."

Jacobus butted in, "You are to take one of the crystals of Termiculum there. It is pure and will be priceless to them."

"It is priceless to them because the bastards didn't negotiate with their alien taskmasters very well and didn't realize that the Termiculum they were getting to keep themselves alive was low grade bullshit that petered out every ten years. They kept needing a resupply. The Mashgool strung them along like clients, delivering them all sorts of goods and keeping them pampered up in their metal city. Sickness. I'll be damned if humanity is remembered for just being slaves to those fucking jellyfish.

We've got more in us than that. The Mashgool may think of us as children, but we're not."

"Isaac, you must accomplish your mission. You must insert *The Gideons* into the GOD and disrupt their systems."

"I will not fail you."

"Major Hardoak will accompany you as far as the perimeter, and then you will be on your own."

"I understand," Isaac said, thinking about his wife. He tried to trace the contours of her body in the Paraclete's face and failed.

Isaac was dismissed. His mind was reeling as he walked past all the Institute scientists laboring at their tasks designing weapons systems and elucidating the unknown secrets of the universe. What was completely unknown was the future, and Isaac was being hurtled towards its uncertainty at the speed of light. He went back into his room and used a TI-43XC DNA Reading Device that he borrowed from Glompus to analyze the DNA sequence embedded in his finger, for the text of *The Gideons*.

THE RELIGION STAIN
By Academy Graduate 1A Isaac

Truth being told, we do not know when the beginning was. Based on the duration of the God Particle in the universe, Paraclete Tanner claims that we can up with an approximate value for the age of the Universe through the use of his calculation of Quantum Reduction. I am still unclear how he came to this conclusion, but all my reading indicates that it is possible. Scientific evidence places the beginning of the species *Homo sapiens sapiens* at least over two-hundred-thousand years ago in the continent formerly known as Africa. We do not know what the denizens of Africa call it now or whether there are any men living there. It could have gone back to the wild like much of the continent of North America following the Great Resistance. I do not know why they called it the Great Resistance; who were they resisting? Certainly not the Mashgool, they seem to have won.

In accordance with the books that men grew to revere as Holy Books, *The Gideons*, say that in the very beginning man was born into a great garden. The garden was the planet itself, the planet Earth. The men did not know it at the time; but the planet was only one tiny planet in a great swirling dust cloud known as the Milky Way Galaxy. This galaxy was only one small galaxy among infinite galaxies.

The Holy Book, *The Gideons,* tells us that the Garden had everything that the men needed, but they had to toil for their food, just like the animals. They slept on the rocks, trying to hide from the vicious animals that gave them fits at night by carrying their children off into the trees to eat. One of the men, or maybe a woman, came up with the idea of living in caves. The idea was good, and it spread amongst the people. The idea was not written in *The Gideons* because *The Gideons* was actually written down thousands and thousands of years after men and women had forgotten that they lived in caves.

The men ventured out to hunt animals for meat. They were often successful. Sometimes they were not. They were forced to follow the big herds of animals, and it spread them all over the planet. The men did not know they were on a planet. The men knew that they were hungry and needed to follow the animals to eat. They lived in houses that they could take apart easily. All of these houses were made out of the animals they ate. While the men hunted, the women searched throughout the big garden for vegetables to eat and learned ways to get the most out of the vegetables by beating them against rocks and grinding them to a pulp.

A woman discovered that part of the plant they gathered would grow into another plant. Being naturally lazy, the women began to have small patches of plants that they maintained. It was a garden within a garden. At the same time the men realized that some of the animals were slower and weaker and more stupid than the rest. Like the lions and jackals, the men had formerly chosen these weak animals to kill. The men, being lazy, realized that they could capture the stupid slow animals and force them into pens. They realized the animals would breed and have offspring and eventually the animals were so dumb they just stood around and ate and happily waited for their slaughter. Watching the animals, the men discovered the secrets of sex. They enjoyed watching the animals procreate, but then became fearful because they realized that they too procreated in the same way. The men looked about their homes and at the women that surrounded them. The men looked to the women's swollen bellies and wondered if the result, the screaming babies that steamed up the night air were theirs. They saw the attentions that their wives paid the younger, stronger, more handsome men. The men wondered what happened in the night while they were sleeping. Nature, operating only on laws of attraction, conspired to force the young attractive ones into each other's arms. The old men thought. *What had these young men built? What did they possess? What did they have other than non-existent flocks and farms made from the dust of imagination?*

One man with the uncanny ability to assign animals as breeding partners gathered around himself the largest flock of animals known to man at that time. He required vast amounts of water for his flock and vast amounts of the grain that his fellow farmer reaped. He enlisted the help of others and they came because he had food to give them. They were hungry and they outstretched their hands to him. He filled them up. They lived hand-to-mouth and did his dirty work. He took the best among their daughters and raised them up. The others, those not fortunate enough to be born beautiful, were left in the dirt to couple with the shepherds. As long as there was expansion in the food supply, there was plenty, and it was good. The moment the hand-to-mouths overwhelmed the food supply, rot set in the land. The fat and comfortable men sat with their fat wives and rotund sons and suggest to the hand-to-mouths who begged them for a pregnant cow to get their own start, "You should seek your fortune elsewhere."

The hand-to-mouths started raiding. The stole flocks and the women of other fat and happy people. They butchered the men like they would cattle and left them to rot in the sun. Was it wrong? And where did the wrongness come from? Every person that was born into the world came with his or her own set of needs and met with the demands of other people.

At the very beginning the needs were the same. The needs have always been the same. Wants multiply like flowers in a field. The seed of want floats happily on the air and blossoms into blood-red flowers on fields of avarice. The needs for the men:

1. I demand a woman. If there is not one for me, I will take one of yours.
2. I demand a space to sustain my life. If you take all the space, I will take some of your space.
3. I demand productive work. I want to make something. I do not want to remain a hand-to-mouth animal for my entire existence. I want to be a man!
4. I demand to know that there is more to life than just this. I look around myself and I ask, is this it? Is this it?

The beauty and disgrace of religion lie in bed together. The beauty speaks, "I am descended from God. I am whole and complete. I am the regulator and ruler of you life. Lie in awe of me. Worship."

The disgrace answers, "But you cannot be whole and complete because you do not satisfy me. I will always want more. I will always rip the apple from the branch just to taste its sweet flesh. Even though it is forbidden, I do not care. I was forbidden to go against you, but as soon as I experienced you, I wanted to lie with your sister."

The beauty says, "How dare you!"

The detriment says, "How dare you!"

In place of mutually antagonistic demands between peoples and between peoples within a single people, it is best to posit an arbitrator that has the authority to settle disputes.

"On whose basis?"

"On the basis of God. It is God's basis."

"That is something that cannot be argued with."

That women went from being persons of veneration and the guardians of mankind through its infancy in caves to becoming mere property like cows and donkeys when men in fits of rage swaggered in front of columns against stone walls and reduced the cities by half; the only reminder of their existence was the stench that brought buzzards for a few short weeks while the ladies were carted off to Jerusalem.

That the Israelites made a ritual of every human activity under the sun is not surprising, considering they chose themselves for the role. Did it bring meaning to their lives or was their meaning their unity? For every civilizing impulse and rationale of man, there is an infinity of contraries. There are an infinite number of ways to live. Why this one? What made this way of life so important? Someone answer me!

That God is an entity is to me patently false. I formerly believed. I did not know any better. It was what my people taught me from the time I was a child. I was thrown aside by my people like a piece of garbage. I ventured out into the world an outcast like Cain. I have no skill with farming. I am sure if I place a seed into the ground it will grow. It is within the seed to grow, my say means nothing in the matter. I am sure that when Cain, throughout his wanderings, realized that his sacrifice of grain and his brother's sacrifice of animal were both equally meaningless, he would have much rather had his brother back.

My Grandmother told me a story from the Holy Book of our people, which we had taken to calling *The Gideons*. I since learned that this book is actually called *The Holy Bible* and it existed all over the planet. There was a time when the one book held sway over power. It was supposed to be the source of power and its guiding hand. Babies were taught to regard it as important. Much like if babies were taught to regard this document I have written, as important, they would. They don't know any better. What sickens me is that my people kept me from learning anything of any importance whatsoever.

I learned that it wasn't even written at the same time. It did not fall from Heaven like Grandmother told us. It was written over hundreds of years. *The Holy Bible* was written, telling stories about men who claimed to be following the voice of God, however I do not think this is possible. Are prophets chosen people? Can a people be a chosen people? Are people of a great destiny because they are chosen or because they have ambition? Were they told to reduce cities to ashes because they could or because they were told to? Does everyone commit mass murder with a divine purpose?

What is the worst thing that one life can do to another life? Extinguish it? Were they not ordered to do this by the Lord, God? Perhaps it is not the worst life can do to other life. The Lord, God, ordered them to rip the other evil peoples up by the roots because He could not in good conscience order them to confine them to pens, breed them, and eat them. Why not? This is not a prohibition of any of the divine commandments. It is a much much older unwritten law. It was possible to bind another human being to an altar and cut out their heart as a sacrifice to an infernal God, which did not exist. But don't dare eat them after you cut out their heart and immolate them. That would be vile.

In my conclusion, before I make my way to Moojtema, religion has a basis in the practices of men. Its foundation in otherworldly beings is patently false. We are reminded to think before we bring our ideas to birth, for once ideas are put into action – whether they be ideas in agriculture, religion, warfare, mass murder, death camps--they are impossible to stop without the weight of powerful minds allied against them. Accepting that everyone in the world has his or her own individual needs and providing for these needs is the only way to achieve any lasting peace on this doomed little rock of a planet.

I must think of a principle. I must tell the people about it so they will discard all of the rubbish that is piled up to the rafters. There is one way to discover truth. The rest of it is flaky, dead, fat particles puked from the minds of madmen. That way is science. It is not a way of life. It is a tool of free men.

Respectfully submitted to the Head Scientific Council of the Tanner Institute,

Operator 57-2A Isaac

He typed the document out after he had read *The Gideons* from cover to cover. It was as nonsense now as it was when he was a child because he did not accept its fundamental premise. But were all the copies better off destroyed? Was it the most unique expression of the human experience?

The flesh of Robert Tanner's cheeks appeared more vital and less like the ashen dust around the lips of a volcano forever silenced by the primeval eruptions of a misspent youth. He was like a walking god, a scientist rock star, founder of Tanner Industries who's market cap in the first half of the 22nd Century outweighed the collective Gross Domestic Product of the League of Developing Nations. Not many places in the world were undeveloped. When Robert Tanner looked in the mirror he saw the future: a future that he would bring about. He wiped the lipstick from whatever supermodel accompanied him from the collar of his French, high thread count, tailored shirt.

Robert Tanner's teachers at the University Satellite High School told him that his natural abilities would take him far but his work ethic and love of play would take him straight to the poor house. His second grade science teacher told him that he would amount to nothing after he kept interrupting the class to say that he didn't believe a word of what the teacher told him. The teacher, an oldish man with an off color beverage in his hand and hair that went from kinky yellow to wiry white said, "Oh yeah? Why don't you discover something?"

His classmates laughed at him. His path was set. He was the head of the National High Energy Physics Laboratory at the age of 35. The day-to-day operations of his multibillion-dollar corporation were managed by businessmen who knew nothing of the science but everything about the projected sales revenue. The final coal fired power plants succumbed to his Tanner Reactors and the old-science nuclear power plants were replaced shortly thereafter. Some people moaned about a monopoly but the new reactors were just too efficient with almost zero waste.

Robert Tanner owned seventy five percent of Tanner Industries (TID) and never searched the interWeb for the value of his stake. His advisors pestered him to expand his conglomerate. All their talk about this property, that building, expanding into defense contracting, building space shuttles, even the design of the corporate logo were mere trifles to him. He would turn his Personal Communication Device off and just travel. He didn't ever remember the names of the beautiful women on his arm. None of them really mattered. The girl last week was plucked out of a remote Greek fishing village by a Ford Modeling Agency Talent Scout on vacation with his family. This one was a phenomenal actress in her native language but was struggling in Hollywood because she couldn't compete with the digitized actresses who looked dynamite but couldn't quite pull off being fully human because they were too perfect.

Newspapers followed him everywhere. It got to be that he didn't want to go out in public anymore. He sat in the world's tallest building, near the very top that wasn't taken up by radio towers or whirlybird pads and looked at his collection of priceless artifacts that an art dealer picked out for him after scouring galleries around the world for a year. The man asked him in a high-pitched voice what sort of things he wanted and suggested that Old Norse artifacts would allow him to connect with his inner warrior spirit. Tanner told him just to find some things that were colorful and that money was no object.

The desert sands blew against the glass surface of the building and sounded like the fingers of tiny children tapping ever so gently. When he got bored he would stare at the treasures behind the glass and wish that he could touch them but the clauses in his insurance contracts stipulated that they had to remain in their state of perpetual regulated humidity and air conditioning, lest they decline in value and leave the insurance contract null and void. Tanner imagined that a wing of a museum or perhaps an entire museum would be named after him at his eventual demise, but that would not come for several years. Still, when he looked at his reflection in the glass he saw crow's feet and lines and gray hairs.

His latest girlfriend called his personal assistant and would arrive at his whirlybird pad within the hour. He took a shower and the fine mist that sprayed from the aircraft titanium shower heads was designed to exfoliate his skin without being overbearing. It wasn't working. After the shower, he gazed into the mirror and the crow's feet still remained. He took a shit in a heated toilet made of recessed obsidian. He looked into the mirror again. He was not vain enough for plastic surgery. At the parties he attended, he saw women who were octogenarians that looked like they were still thirty-eight. Their skin was firmed with treatments that cost them millions of dollars. They weren't fooling anyone. There was no stopping the oxidation of your internal organs. No matter how good you looked on the outside, you were still going to die after which you would know nothing and the maintenance of whatever you built would be up to the businessmen and lawyers that you hired and retained in life. What did they care about your dreams and hopes? They cared about the number of zeroes at the end of their paycheck and an annual bonus. This was all up to corporate board members and governance committees. If someone was willing to give your employees more money, they would depart your company in the space between two heartbeats. They reminded you of this fact every chance they got. Tanner knew that he was the genius that came up with the theory that went into their vast catalogue of products. He was the one that took the risk to found Parabolic Industries, and then change the name to Tanner Industries to be his tombstone. He met with the venture capitalists and saw the gleam of gold and madness in their eyes when he explained what he wanted to do. He didn't need a fancy presentation. They signed on the dotted line and the three-hundred-million dollars of seed money was his. That bought him a single reactor factory. In ten year's time he turned that three-hundred-million into well over a trillion dollars of profits. How many people did he make as rich as Midas? They glistened in the sun for a moment until they dried up and fell to the earth with their fortunes. He nicked himself and the blood beaded for a moment on his face before it dropped into the mirrored sink and spattered randomly. He heard the approach of a helicopter. It was not the Brazilian girl with whom he tore down the curtains as he carried her around the room on his phallus, thrusting as he tried to break her into two. She was long dead. Dust.

The whirlybird popped his memories like a bubble grown too large. It landed on the pad just outside the operations room. The Paraclete looked out the blast reinforced glass and watched as Major Nathanael Hardoak ran purposefully up to the iron doors separating the mountain chill from the temperature controlled Institute. He looked back to Commander Jacobus, who greeted his young prodigy.

"All phases of the operation were a success, Commander Jacobus," Hardoak said as he saluted.

Isaac snapped to attention and saluted his old friend who appeared to have grown more than two feet and gained a hundred pounds of steel cord muscle. The operations room as a former skiing lodge that Robert Tanner, the man, threw lavish parties in. All the comforts of home were replaced with a Spartan nothingness and refusal of luxury, like a former dictator's palace overrun by his fastidious conquerors.

"No need for that, Isaac," Hardoak said with a smile. His face bore more scars: the results of fights and military operations. Over his right eye he wore a patch. The Institute offered to replace his damaged eye, but Major Hardoak told them that he wanted the wound to serve as a reminder for his failure. He did not fail in his mission, he just failed to plan for all the possible contingencies.

That Hardoak was being groomed to take over for Commander Jacobus in the future was no secret. It was openly discussed in the cafeteria over impervious biscuits and pre-fabricated gravy. He had proven himself invaluable mission after mission. Hardoak took to his profession with relish. Protecting the weak and serving the defenseless in the world appealed to him. It came out of there being no one to protect him that day when he was a boy.

He dealt death to the enemies of peace, the enemies of the Institute. The Institute sought to impose the rule that humans would not make their way through the world murdering each other for trifles. Moojtema was no trifle. Sacking it had been his preoccupation since he graduated the Tanner Institute Advanced Combat Assault Track early and at the top of his class.

"We've been planning to insert you into Moojtema for years now, Isaac," Hardoak said.

"Longer than that, young man," Commander Jacobus said.

"You have all the qualities we look for in our undercover agents," the Paraclete said in his metallic gravel tone.

"You're smart, resourceful, and most importantly, you stick to the mission and see it through to the very end."

"But there have been others before you who have gone into Moojtema."

"What happened to them?"

"A good agent doesn't ask questions of his handlers, but in this case we'll have to tell you. Moojtema can be very distracting. They also have some of the best spy catchers. These are men who were sent and then switched sides. You'll have to watch out for them. They can spot Tanner Institute mannerisms a mile away."

"You're going into the lion's den, son. So you had better trust us. Ultimately, Hardoak will accompany you to no more than five kilometers away from the Moojtema Gray Dead Zone. That's the area surrounding the massive complex where nothing really grows. It sort of just wilts and dies like the ground is poisoned. Before that, however, you have to travel to Caravan City and pay the piper. Solomon Trading Company. Everything going west of Caravan city is prone to attack by his merciless hordes unless you pay them their damn protection money. That will be comp'd, of course. Hardoak will have the credits on his person. You are by no means authorized to discuss what you have in your satchel, Isaac. Termiculum is priceless, and there will be no end to the people trying to take it from you."

"I understand," Isaac said adjusting the backpack so that it fit snugly. "How will I contact you if I need anything?"

"You're going to be on your own once you enter the Gray Dead Zone. We're sorry our comms can't penetrate Moojtema's jamming devices. You could probably send a message out, but we can't send one in to you. However, if you send one out, you're running the risk of it being intercepted. You know your mission. Now you can go and accomplish it."

My mission is love, Isaac thought to himself.

"I understand gentlemen," Isaac said.

"Ready, Isaac?" Hardoak said, adjusting his civilian model cap. "We have to be smart on this one."

The young men saluted Commander Jacobus and the Paraclete Robert Tanner swiftly and ran to their awaiting gray whirlybird that functioned well but looked like it had seen better days centuries ago.

Commander Jacobus and Paraclete Tanner watched the whirlybird depart, kicking up a cloud dust that formed mini tornadoes and spun up into the air before it settled randomly on the cold smooth granite.

"I will kill myself after we liberate Moojtema, Jacobus. If I am too much of a coward to do it, you must do it for me," the Paraclete said.

"Why? You have more work to do!" Jacobus said flustered.

"Immortality is a bitch," Tanner said sitting in his high backed black leather chair. "Immortality is a bitch...." His words trailed off like the whirlybird chop that echoed into the distance from the high canyon walls and marked the petty pace of the mission at hand.

The whirlybird exited the canyon and skimmed the surface kicking up dust devils that died as soon as given birth. Dull and gray, the bas relief on the roof showed Apollo subduing Dionysus in a wrestling match, with the world at their center. Apollo's gold leaf crown, either had been looted in a heartbeat or weather stripped by the ages, no one knew. Migratory birds built nests in their hollow mouths and eyes and nestled in the spaces made by flowing intricately carved hair. From the whirlybird's gun port, Isaac could barely make out the glowing face of the Paraclete watching them through the blast glass, his metal arms folded in front of him like he was a child impatiently waiting for a visitor.

In the past, Tanner often looked out the glass to the glow of the city of Denver, which now looked like a massive black stone quarry carved out of the mountains to build a monument to God knows what somewhere. Tanner looked at the massive hall behind them. It was one single room bare of furnishings. Times were different now. It used to be full of life and full of plush reclining furniture modern in its appearance and fully programmable for variable intensities of massage and lumbar back support. The furniture cushioned some of the most well-proportioned posteriors in the fashion world and stored the farts of many famous Hollywood directors, tooted at parties, which often degenerated into massive orgies that would make Nero blush with shame. Tanner started the Bacchanalian frenzies with a flick of his wrist and a drop of the robe he wore. All the eyes were on him. Asian midgets bore golden bowlfuls of experimental, diamond-shaped, orange cock raisers and brown pussy ticklers. The pharmaceutical division of Tanner Industries kept him well-supplied with drugs and gorgeous young pharmaceutical representatives who were more than willing to let their lord and master do his experiments on them. As Tanner reclined like a Caesar, he looked up and down the hall and spied a gorgeous woman who looked like she hailed from some Scandinavian country or perhaps a Denver trailer park. The entire palace erupted with laughter and cheers when he chased her down, running with a hard on the size and thickness of a small French baguette. She screamed, but it was all a ploy, and everybody laughed and urged him to fuck her brains out. He caught her in the entrance to the kitchen and dragged her across the marble floor. She begged him. The crowd went wild as he wedded their bodies together at the hips. He left her on the floor bleeding and inseminated and wiped his brow with a 1000 thread count, Egyptian cotton towel and tossed it to her.

The next day, he awoke in a bed big enough for ten grown men surrounded by sleeping women and a two snoring dogs. He thought about the blonde briefly and went back to sleep. The guests filed out and were given nondisclosure agreements by the butler at the front door.

The space of five-hundred-twenty-nine years, three months and fifteen days had elapsed since he raped the buxom Scandinavian and watched her tits smack off her face. The scene and the people that participated were as good as buried in the dust of pastimes but it brought a smile to his dead, gray lips when the memory trickled through his metal brain.

*

The whirlybird picked up speed as it skirted the mountain peaks and aimed at the valley below. Isaac watched the tops of trees ripping upwards, so small that they looked like the moss on rocks blanketed with a haze of dew. The chopper blades *whop whop* rhythm lulled Isaac into a state of relaxation that was interrupted only by the pilot's rapid descent and ascent in elevation. These maneuvers appeared to have no motivation other than the pilot's lack of skill. Hardoak and Isaac's heads bobbed up and down each time he swerved up or down. What seemed like hours passed by them with the same dull regularity. The cold wind from the outside seeped through the doors and ran through crevices formed by his pant pleats and coarse leg hairs where the pants drifted over his boots. Hardoak slapped Isaac on the shoulder and woke him. They could not speak in the noise so Hardoak gave him thumbs up to make sure he was doing well. Isaac returned it and nodded. The whirlybird descended, tilting slightly, and Isaac was able to see out of the window a patchwork quilt of charred buildings and greasy blotted out automobiles that had not known drivers since they were stopped dead hundreds of years ago. The char crept on like a poltergeist in every direction, spread like a black mold on the surface. Rubble. Unnatural conglomerations of rocks and rusted rebar smashed to bits decorated the mold like ashy accoutrement. The place looked like it had taken hundreds of years to build up and a few short seconds to destroy. It was quiet below, like the destroyer erupted onto the surface of the planet in a day, demolished wholesale under the charms of a broiling sun, and retreated to subterranean caverns to sleep. Isaac saw movement below. A few pinhead-sized dust mites scampered from one little hiding spot in the rock to another. They probably returned to the city's black wreckage to forage little bits of metal, coming out in daylight to avoid the ones that came out during the night. It was a war of all against all down there. The forgers at Caravan City fueled the war with the prices they paid for scrap and sold it back in the form of bullets and hackneyed weaponry. In the utter black waste of time, humans did what they did best throughout the golden ages: fight each other over the last scraps of a civilization. Each time they turned over a rock and found a gleaming hunk of metal, they discovered truth.

The whirlybird beat the air over their heads, and the scavengers scratched their smelly bodies with blackened fingers, looked to each other, and shrugged. They assumed it, whatever it was, had to be carrying someone or something important. Everyone else walked with two legs if they had anywhere to go. Their lives only knew wretched freedom, and their time passed with work.

Isaac looked at Major Hardoak who was busy sketching something in a notebook.

"What are you drawing?" Isaac shouted.

"What!?"

"What are you drawing!?" Isaac shouted again, pointing to the sketchpad and making like he was drawing the air.

"I can't hear you! I'm by the turbine!"

Hardoak moved and sat next to Isaac. "I'm notating how we need to organize some patrols and investigate some of those buildings down there!"

"There weren't any buildings down there! Everything's destroyed!"

"No…you could see the people down there! The place is teeming with them!" Hardoak exclaimed.

"Yes!"

"Chances are they've found all the hidden nooks and crannies of the entire city. Remember this, if there are people there, they've found their way into everything!"

"Just like rats in a pantry!" Isaac said.

"What!"

"I said, *just like rats in a pantry*! They sample everything with a nibble before they eat your oats!"

"Just like rats doing dances?" Hardoak asked.

Major Nathanael Hardoak shook his head back and forth and his face was red like a beet. They descended in altitude, and are now skimming the treetops. The whirlybird roaned forward into the uncertain future, whizzing over destroyed little hamlets and boroughs and melancholy one-horse towns of the open plains. One-hundred feet over the ground they fly. Occasionally they pass a road, a dash of yellowed grasses in the otherwise green plain as if the decaying asphalt poisoned the plants in their development. They passed a road on top of a road hanging by strands of metal like muscle fibers groaning downwards with all of its might to topple the two immense columns: the only source of support for this monument to progress.

They flew past rivers, overflowing and clear. The bottom was nearly visible with just a slight twinge of muck clouding the surface. Isaac could see fish from the whirlybird – schools of them hanging just below the shimmering surface of the water. When the whirlybird whipped the surface to a boil, the fish darted for the safety of the weeds. In the distance to the west, black smoke coated the horizon like an oil slick. The whirlybird turned toward the smoke as it followed the river, which peeled off behind them like a snakeskin. Was it more beautiful when the buildings stood and the people had their lives, or is it more beautiful now? The smoke called the whirlybird like a siren. In the distance, to the southwest, Isaac could barely make out the apex of a tall spire that looked as if it sought to punch a hole into Heaven.

The whirlybird descended further and rolled and pitched. Isaac's stomach felt like there was a knot of curdled milk in it. Hardoak snored soundly next to him and even rolled his head onto Isaac's shoulder, totally unconcerned. He was already heavily decorated and had been on hundreds of combat missions. Isaac made for the window and Hardoak fell onto the canvas seat. The contents of Isaac's stomach shot from his mouth like a volcanic eruption. It hit the wind and sprayed back into the cabin, coating the door gunner. He screamed and wiped the spit up from his visored helmet. He pointed a gloved hand at Isaac and screamed, "Go sit down! Puke on the floor!" Isaac slinked back to the canvas seat and sat near Hardoak's head. Hardoak sat up to stretch and yawned widely like a male lion sated from the blood of an antelope.

The whirlybird he was riding in now began to slow down and descend.

The pilot called over the intercom, "Gentlemen, Caravan City, FIVE MINUTES!!!"

The gunner racked a round into his machine gun and looked intently at the ground beneath him. Isaac looked out the plastic bubble window through flecks of his own dried vomit. The steel bird descended into a valley of fine sand that kicked up and circled through a vortex until it settled. Small shacks lined blood-red thoroughfares. As the bird whipped over them, children ran out of their cardboard scavenged homes and pointed upwards to the loud, gray object. As the whirlybird continued onwards towards the center of the city where Cornelius waited for them, the homes became more and more ornate in concentric circles. Skeletal buildings had ripped sideways, dragged down by gravity's effects on weak concrete. As the bird passed, the gaping holes of their foundations looked like the empty tooth sockets in an animal's dried jawbone. Every building over three stories was a skeleton. Only one building was unscathed. One building had flesh on its bones. Gray flesh and pink paint. A sign dominated the entire front façade, and even the daylight was outshone as it throbbed on and off to life. Over and over it pulsed: SOLOMON TRADING CORPORATION. Why the building needed a sign was beyond Isaac. All around it were the piles of fishbone girders flung haphazardly by the giants who played with the Earth. The smell of the place was a disguised electrical fire that seeped into the whirlybird in slow bucketfuls. The smell seemed disguised with a plastic floral arrangement smell that did not mask the underlying calamity.

The whirlybird circled the building and landed on a large whirlybird pad. The whirlybird bounced twice and jostled Hardoak and Isaac who felt the shock in their hips and intestines. The pilot killed the whirlybird and after the engines stopped their shrieking whines the men exited. All Isaac heard was what seemed to be one vast collective groan from the men and animals that toiled throughout the remnants of the city. Isaac walked to the edge of the roof and looked to the ground. From the entrance there was a line that stretched and snaked as far as the limits of his vision. The line oscillated back and forth at a frequency determined by the travelers' fatigue and the excitability of the beasts of burden they drove forward.

Caravan City was the collection point for all trade wagons heading west to Moojtema, and all of the trade wagons flowed through the Solomon Trading Corporation. After the caravan made it to the farthest point of civilization west, the Solomon Corporation would take care of the rest and provide convoy security, quality control, and ensure against unfortunate incidents. If the convoy decided to go it alone they were marked, and the vicious gangs under the employ of the Solomon Trading Corporation were notified of the route the convoy was following to Moojtema. Sometimes the convoys were marked with transmitters that made it possible for the raiders to find them. You either paid for protection or you met your doom in the outskirts of Caravan City. It wasn't fair, but nothing was fair once justice went the way of civilization. Fairness and propriety now stemmed from the barrel of a gun. All of justice's luxurious garments of tradition and process fell away to reveal a stark, skeletal hag.

Cornelius exited an elevator and bade the two enter with motioned by a flick of his wrist. Hardoak and Isaac trotted from the launch pad to the fancy marble-floored elevator with expensive wood paneling and golden buttons. The elevator doors closed, and Isaac noticed a drastic decrease in temperature. Whereas the outside world was a blast furnace, the inside was cool and licked the sweat from his brow.

"Welcome to the Solomon Trading Corporation: the last stop between the Great Wilderness and Moojtema. You'll remain here for a few days before you depart for Moojtema disguised as ordinary traders. I've arranged for you to accompany one of the Solomon scrap metal convoys, so you shouldn't run into any problems."

"Nice to see you again, Cornelius. You wear out your welcome with those forest people?" Isaac asked.

"No. I got recalled to the Institute and then assigned here. I'm making sure that no Institute mission critical military equipment makes it here. If it does I find out where the traders obtained it. It think my intelligence aided you in a mission you did, right, Major?"

"Why didn't the whirlybird just drop us in the woods and let us hump in?" Hardoak asked unconcerned about Cornelius's parries for recognition.

"Well…uh…the woods are full of savages, thicker than the woods you're used to sir."

"Not like I haven't dealt with savages before, where can a guy get a weapon around here?" Hardoak said folding his arms viciously in front of his chest.

"There's an arms market out in the city bazaar. Most of its junk, held together with glue. Why didn't you bring a weapon from the Institute?"

"I was told it wouldn't be necessary and I could get one on the economy."

"That's strange."

"They don't want us looking like we're from the Institute," Isaac said.

"Right," Cornelius answered raising his eyebrow. "You've got the package, then?"

"Of course. I'm not supposed to discuss it."

"Right. Make sure it's on you at all times. I've heard that Mr. Solomon wants to get his hands on some."

"Whatever offer he makes me, I'll refuse it."

"He doesn't know you're carrying it," Hardoak said.

"Oh, no. He knows. He knows everything that comes and goes through to Moojteama."

"How did he find out?"

"I didn't tell him!" Cornelius said.

"Why are you being so defensive, Scout?" Hardoak asked staring at Cornelius intently.

"He just knew. When I got here he asked where the boy with the Termiculum was and said he was looking forward to meeting him."

"Damn. Then our cover's already blown? Blown wide open."

"No. We'll make him realize it's in his best interest not to tell anyone."

"He won't try and steal it from us will he?"

"Mr. Solomon is a businessman. Pure and simple. He'll try to make you an offer you can't refuse."

"There is no offer he can possibly make that I'll accept," Isaac said. He cradled the backpack like a newborn baby and could feel slight warmth through the black cloth. He could not touch the Termiculum with his bare hands, or it would excite the particles that composed his fingertips turning them into gas. This would in turn excite the particles adjacent to those particles until he was nothing but vapor. The process could take hours to complete. Excruciating hours.

Hardoak stared at Isaac and put his hands ungraciously on his hips as the elevator door opened. He wanted a weapon badly. He felt naked without one. His hands and feet would have to do for now. As the group left the elevator, he was looking for avenues of escape and possible attackers.

Isaac had his mind on what he thought about in his restful moments like when he first woke up in the morning and the last thought like a ghost ship on the horizon of his dimming consciousness before sleep took him. Under the glowing moon, the thought was of his wife's eyes, her lips, her voice, the voice he had forgotten the sound of and struggled to reconstruct. He felt closer to her than ever now and felt her presence all around him. The excitement tickled his stomach like a witch's brew and trickled downward ending up in his testicles. It rimmed his epididymus and lingered there like a cat about to pounce on unsuspecting prey. It did not abate with deep breaths. Deer danced across his body like a dream. A smile came to his lips.

They stood in a massive foyer. Isaac could barely see the end of it in the darkness and could not tell if the size was just mirrors playing tricks on him. Beyond the steep marble stairs, in the dimness of light with spotlights from the ceiling, he witnessed treasures displayed as far as his eyes could see. It was not piles of diamonds or rubies and sacks of gold. That was too simple. There were chests and furniture. All were ornately carved and more luxurious than anything he had ever seen. The group began walking down central stairs past concentric circles, which formed levels in the massive gallery. All the levels were on top of each other each, adjoined by stairs that formed a labyrinth up to the top. As far as he could see, there were paintings, huge murals, and statues on each level. They became more and more colorful the closer and tighter the concentric circular levels pitched towards the ceiling. Isaac stared at the ceiling of the sphere. It was a painting of a massive human eye, with galaxies at its center that seemed to swirl around an axis.

On second look, it was almost too real. He swore if he would have stared at the eye any longer, it may have blinked. As Isaac reached the bottom of the stairs, he looked at the furniture. As the group walked past each piece it lit up from a spotlight projected from the central eye at the top of the sphere. Isaac now knew the eye's purpose. The eye illuminated each piece of artwork with a spotlight and projected a detailed description next to it as the group passed. They walked past furniture that depicted scenes from the past: women fat in all the right places running naked through wooded areas running from pan flute playing creatures, half men half goats, gleefully laughing in the bright sunshine. They walked past hutches of children clutching fistfuls of grapes with cherubic grins on their faces. One stood over the rest in that section. It was a white marble statue of a muscular young man. Underneath the large white marble statue Isaac saw that the projected light sign read: DAVID. The statue reminded Isaac of his brother Jesse. He walked up to it and saw the fine print under the title: *Michelangelo.* They passed Greek and Roman statues in marble and bronze of the human form, the muscles of the men gleamed as the spotlight bathed them in splendor that seemed to come from Heaven.

Cornelius appeared out of the darkness to Isaac's right. "Here is the really interesting thing," Cornelius said. "Call out a name of a work of art."

"I don't know any off hand," Isaac said.

"What? All that time at the Tanner Institute Academy and you never learned to appreciate art?"

"No. We learned about science, and I studied religion on my own. I never delved into art."

234

"Yes. I guess it all sort of ended up here: the art, which wasn't destroyed in the fires. The Tanner Institute teaches you all about science and technology-- all the practical things of the modern, destroyed world, but doesn't teach you about anything that gives the world meaning. You learned how to destroy the world over and over, but you learned to create nothing."

Major Hardoak chimed in with a phrase that he had memorized, or rather was forced to memorize, during his academy days. Isaac memorized it as well but apparently did not take it to heart the way that Hardoak did. "Technology is that which gives life meaning and it comes from the womb of science. Through technology we ripped ourselves from the level of the animals and climbed to the level of men. Through science we come to understand ourselves. Science is an infinite process: the best tool of mankind. Science drives technology. Technology never drives science. That was the folly of the former dark ages: the age of the last men. They thronged for technology to make their lives better but forgot the hard labor of science beneath the technology. Science is our only savior. Science shows us that like the universe, mankind can be infinite. Our place is among the stars if we only choose science for science's sake."

"No!" Cornelius said emphatically. "This is what makes us men. Other things, disgusting, degenerate things in the universe like the Mashgool have science that has far outstripped and outpaced our own, and they are not men! Art is error. Art is folly. Art is life coming to recognize itself. It contains error because error is in life. It teaches humans to see beauty because beauty lives in men. Science makes no room for error. It explains error away. The universe becomes a perfect crystal with many facets."

"Whatever," Hardoak said.

"Just look. Look at this painting I am about to show you," Cornelius said. He called out, "The Last Supper. Da Vinci!"

The massive eye whirred. The ambient lights came down. A single concentrated spotlight illuminated the specific work: a large painting of men at a dinner table. It rested on the wall, three-fourths of the way up in a concentric circle from the center of the sphere. The floor underneath their feet lighted up, marking a pathway detailing the shortest path possible to the work of art.

"Splendid!" Isaac exclaimed.

"Reload," Cornelius said.

The ambient lights went up and the large eye stopped its whirring.

"This is Solomon's hall of masterpieces. Only they made the cut."

"Who decides what counts as a masterpiece?"

"He does. He collects many things, many exquisite works. You may find them much more stimulating than these works of art. Let's go meet the man. I warn you, however, to be on your guard."

They walked through double doors at least thirty feet tall and the scene in the next chamber was nothing they could have prepared for.

Women. Naked women. Groups of women in various states of undress lounging on pithy, multicolored couches. Black and white and yellow and caramel and all shades in-between skin. Breasts like apricots. Breasts like cantaloupes ripe from the vine. Hundreds of women dripping with jewels. Most carried the same expression of utter boredom. Some spoke to each other in hushed tones when the men entered. Some stretched into the distance. Isaac squinted to see the end of them. He looked for one woman in particular: his wife. Each time he saw a woman he hoped it was her.

Mirrors lined the walls making the room seem more massive than it was. Strobes pulsated on the ceilings. The room was like a conic section of a pyramid. The massive pyramid hollowed out. A mobius strip hung from the ceiling pulsating lights--greens and reds and purples – which painted the women in hues of brilliance. They made their way through the women careful not to step on a leg or kick a rump.

The women did not notice them or even bat an eyelash in their direction. A few yawned. Isaac searched the field of breasts and curly hair for a hint of Deer. He almost called her name but felt it would be inappropriate. At the center, a woman about six-feet tall with breasts like juvenile watermelons, white skin and red hair lounged with two smaller women using her breasts as pillows. She yawned and blinked her bright, blue eyes once and then twice.

Hardoak stared at her. He stared between her legs at the blond-red bush that looked like the bush Moses saw when he was in the desert hallucinating with thirst. This one did not speak. When she saw the man staring, she moved and covered herself. The small women at her chest groaned and readjusted with her. She glared at Major Hardoak and, sensing her power, licked her lips. Hardoak turned red: a reaction totally unbecoming an officer of the Tanner Institute. Cornelius chuckled.

A booming voice shot from every corner, "Cornelius! Get those two back to see me and stop gawking at the pussy!"

"Let's go men," Cornelius said. He laughed again at Major Hardoak who couldn't speak but only wiped a bit of saliva from the corner of his mouth and smiled like an idiot.

Isaac had been searching the women for his wife and found no comparison to her. Some were taller and some had fuller breasts. Some had hairier midsections some had fuller lips. Some had eyes that stared through your soul if you allowed them entrance. Some had darker skin, some had pearlier smiles, some had poutier cheeks, some had fuller asses, some had curly black hair that shimmered in the artificial light and set off their almond eyes like a dream that you did not want to wake up from no matter the hell you dreamt. Some could enslave your soul with a mere glance and drive it in bondage to her salesman. Isaac did not see Deer. He breathed a sigh of relief and averted his gaze from them lest he be tempted more.

The mahogany door opened like a door to a crypt. The women clamored to get a look inside the room. It seemed they all spun around like cats when the door opened. A short, fat man with a shock of all too black hair bade them to enter. He was dressed in a purple one-piece suit interspersed with gold thread. He smiled to them and motioned his arms for them to come in with haste. When he turned to walk to his desk Isaac saw that the back of his suit read SOLOMON TRADING CORPORATION. The little man had to advertise even to himself. He sat at his desk and motioned for them to sit down in the overstuffed leather chairs arranged in a semicircle in front of his massive desk that made him look even more miniature.

"Welcome to my humble abode," he said smiling.

"Thank you," the men said in unison. It came off as being awkward.

"What's with you?" the man asked Hardoak. "You see a ghost?"

"No, a redhead," Hardoak said with a chuckle.

"You've been eyeing my property?" the man said with a smile on his face that was not friendly but more aimed at intimidating someone. It was laughable that he would try to intimidate Hardoak who seemed double his size.

"It's impossible not to. You should hide them somewhere," Hardoak said gravely.

"I don't hide. My father's father's father's father's father started this little trading institution. Then, it was in a fucking tool shed! He married the most beautiful woman in town. There were still rules back then. Now, I make the rules. I want seven-hundred women all to myself? I have them. Who's gonna stop me? The thing is, everyday, more just keep showing up."

"You're quite the man here then," Hardoak said smiling, trying to intimidate Mr. Solomon as much as Mr. Solomon tried laughably to intimidate him.

"I am the man here. Who the fuck are you?"

Hardoak smiled, "I'm Maj –."

"Shut the fuck up! If you talk one more time while we're here I'll have my guards cut your fucking tongue out, you annoying bastard!" He pointed his small finger in Hardoak's face. Isaac watched Nathanael's nostrils flare in rage for a moment while his brain, wired for combat, weighed possible courses of action and outcomes. He could avenge the insult and probably face certain death. Maybe ridding the world of Mr. Solomon was worth it.

"Cornelius, where the fuck did you find this guy?" Solomon asked.

"Somewhere out in the woods. He's a good enough guy."

"That's your problem over there at the Institute. You're always coming up with *just good enough*. It's because you don't pay that well. I mean, you give castaways a place to live and give them training but in order to get the best you need to pay 'em."

Cornelius laughed, "Our men are principled."

"Bullshit. Those principles fly out the window given the right price."

"Perhaps yours do. But ours don't."

"My principle is the right price. Where'd you find this other guy? The quiet one?"

"Somewhere in the woods, too. And let me tell you something about him. As much stuff as you have around you, he has inside of him."

"Where'd you get this treasure at, then?"

"He just showed up one day."

"Another treasure from the woods. How quaint. I suppose he has what I want."

"I don't have anything for you," Isaac said.

"Sure you do. What's in your backpack?"

"Nothing you'd want," Isaac said.

"I'm the one that decides what I want. I want what's in your backpack."

"It isn't for sale. Sorry. How'd you find out about it?"

"Someone told me. It's not important how I find things out. What's important is what I have to offer you."

"You don't have anything to offer me."

"I have much to offer. That's what separates men like me from men like you or those pathetic little traders outside. I built everything here with my bare hands. I've got an abundance to offer you."

"You said you inherited your wealth," Isaac said aptly.

"Yes. Touché. But I've kept it instead of frittering it away, and I've increased it ten-thousand fold."

"But you've really got nothing, because you can't have what's in my bag."

"Aren't you the fucking philosopher? Tell me what I want in life!"

"You don't want any of this to end. It will end. All things in life come to an end. The things you love you don't accept that they will end; but you know they will. You just end up devoting your life to them. If you love nothing, like you do, you merely accumulate. That's what you do. You accumulate and think it will bring you happiness but it won't."

Solomon stood up and paced the marble floor back and forth like an emperor.

"What do you love," the little red faced Nero said.

"One person. That's it."

"Awww. How quaint. I know you're going to buy your way into Moojtema with what you've got in that sack. It isn't worth it."

"Sure it is. You don't know what's in Moojtema."

"You can get everything right here that you can get in Moojtema, and you can watch the sunrise."

"No I can't."

"What's in Moojtema that you can't get here?"

"My wife. And my mission."

"Which one first?"

"My desire lies with my wife. My duty with my mission."

"Whatever you say, philosopher. I know your wife."

"Sure you do."

"She's from the forest, too, right?"

Isaac was silent.

"Come on philosopher. Share with me. I'll share with you what I know about her."

"Yeah, right."

"I know where she went."

"So do I. She ended up in Moojtema."

"How do you know that she made it there? She got captured did she not?"

"Yes."

"Maybe she escaped them."

"Could have."

"She's a smart one, isn't she?"

"Yes."

"How do you know she isn't out there in Caravan City? Or in the forest? Or lying dead in some ditch somewhere?"

"I know I will see her again."

"How do you know?"

"I just believe that I will."

"Keep the faith, right?"

"Yes."

"What if I told you that your wife is nothing but the biggest whore of Babylon? A regular Theodora, a circus performer capable of riding dozens of dongs a night? If she's at Moojtema she's no doubt fucked her way to the very top by now. If she's not there, she's probably in some little forest whorehouse shack fucking her way to retirement. You should have seen the short work she made of the caravan traders, bar keeps, pimps, and scavengers. Why, she let anyone mount up that paid her a diamond, no matter how big or how small, but she preferred them big, let me tell you. She left with sackfuls! I'm a betting man there, philosopher. I'd bet she's totally forgotten about you."

"I don't believe you."

"You don't have to believe me. Just believe whatever you have in your heart. But I've a proposition for you. You can save yourself a lifetime's worth of embarrassment by staying away from Moojtema. You see everything in my museum? You see all those hot bitches out there? It's all yours. You can have it all if you just hand over the sack."

"I can't do that."

"What's more important to you? Your whore of a wife or the future I'm offering you?"

"My wife is no whore!"

"You don't care about your mission. You only care about that little whore. She ain't worth it!"

"You call her a whore once more and I'll take your fucking head off," Isaac threatened. Something inside of him was beginning to break. Solomon seemed to be pushing all of his pressure points at the same time.

Hardoak rocked back and forth on his chair with rage. The room seemed full of the steam that poured from his seams. Solomon looked at the Major and smiled. He said very plainly, "I'll extend my offer to anyone who brings me the contents of that sack."

An eerie silence fell over the three men and they looked at each other and back to the tiny man dressed in purple and gold. Beads of sweat dropped from Solomon's face. His eyes stared at the book bag. He started to weep.

"Okay. I give up. Your wife's not a whore. She passed through here three or so years ago. I was on the roof staring at the minions in line when I saw her pass by with a party of hunters. They looked torn and ragged, but she was the most beautiful creature I'd ever seen. I leapt up and ran down to catch her. I offered her everything she could ever desire, but she told me that she had made someone else a promise. How I longed to be him at that moment. I offered her three times thinking she would change her mind, but she did not. She told me that even if she was an old woman in danger of being blown to the dusts that her heart would always be with Isaac. She made me promise to tell you that. I promised her and because she was so beautiful, I could not say no. The last I saw her she was leading her companions to Moojtema."

Hope jumped from Isaac's heart and forced a smile in him. Mr. Solomon changed his demeanor and started his sales pitch again, "I still want what is in the sack. My offer still stands."

"You've got everything you want Mr. Solomon," Cornelius said.

"Don't be dumb, Connie. We all know that substance's power. Right now I'm forty years old. My father died when he was fifty. My father's father died at fifty five. His father died at forty. Longevity is not in my family. You could call it our curse. No matter what we do to prolong our life, we die young. A doctor told me that he heard regular sexual intercourse could reduce stress levels and prolong life. It isn't working. I know the one thing which will prolong my life indefinitely. I'll give up everything I've built. It is all yours. Just give me what you have in the sack."

"So what if you are going to die? You may go to Heaven," Isaac said smiling.

"Nonsense. I've lived in a Heaven of my own design for forty years. It seems like Hell more and more everyday. Their Heaven would be a deprivation. I've seen it in my artwork. It looks boring. The only Heaven I want is to be surrounded by choruses of naked, nymphomaniac angels and all the pills I can pop. I really doubt it would be like that. It's more just like the lights will go out. But only I won't know they went out. Everybody else knew they went out for me. I can't bear that."

"Neither could the Paraclete, and he's miserable," Hardoak said.

"Shut up you," Solomon said.

"It's true. He is," Cornelius said. "I mean, I've never seen him, but I've heard."

"You want to be immortal yourself, Isaac," Solomon said pointing his tiny finger at Isaac's face.

"No, I don't," Isaac responded shaking his head.

"Yes, you do. There is no way that you cannot. All humans desire immortality. Everything you do is traced with this desire's stain."

"No, I don't. I have envisioned my death, and it is nothing. It is most beautiful that it is nothing. My old wife is by my side. She shuffles her feet on our cold cement floor because she has a hard time walking. Her withered hands, marked by the struggle of her days, dab my forehead with a cool cloth. I look into her eyes. In the brown depth I see the hopes of all my future generations. I know my time is through. My time has winnowed away to nothing, and my hopes have expanded to fill the void. I have no regrets for the time I walked in the sunshine. I wasted not one moment in her pursuit. I caused and intended to cause no misery. The misery that I caused unintentionally has been repaired through my works.

"My sons and daughters file past my bed with their families. They touch my hand. They kiss my forehead. I see sadness in their eyes, and I tell them not to lament. My sons calm me with their joy and bring their children in close to gaze at my wrinkles. I reach out to feel the soft skin of their cheeks and listen to them coo the words they are just learning. I struggle with my last words. Before the wave crashes and I slip from life I say to them, 'Do Better.' I feel a sudden sadness as the wave builds and the completion of my life gains its momentum, but as it crashes onto the shore of my highest hopes, I trust they will carry on my wishes. It crashes, and joy floods my soul. I slip from the world knowing nothing more than I knew when I was born. All becomes unknown and a mystery. I have envisioned my death, and it is nothing."

"You still have time."

"No, I do not. I have pared down what I care about. That is all. I live in a world. I am walking towards my future, which I will not overcome. I am marching towards my end. I go willingly. You are in flight from yourself. You are running faster and faster to stay in the same place. You flee your inevitable death. You kick and scream and think you are shaking the foundations of the universe, but it will only answer you with silence.

"Give me the Termiculum, God damn you!"

"No," Isaac said.

Solomon turned bright red. He began to shake uncontrollably. A few tears broke from his eyelids, but they were for nothing but himself. A high-pitched squeal, either that of a baby or a pig, formed in his throat and broke through his lips' defenses. He cocked back his head and howled like a dog at the moon. A deep cry of pain broke from his body that he trapped to end with a pathetic whimper. He took a deep breath.

"I reiterate my promise. I will give all my worldly possessions to the man who brings me the Termiculum! Evvvvvveeerrrrrrreeeeeyyyyythiiiing!"

Isaac and Cornelius turned with haste to leave. They exited the mahogany double doors and looked back. Hardoak lingered in his chair. Solomon shot him a wink. It melted on his red cheeks. He paused and rocked up and down on his heels.

"Don't forget our agreement, Nathanael," Mr. Solomon said.

Hardoak nodded and joined the man who he called his brother and who had pledged unending fidelity to him in the gallery of women.

The women slept. Heads lay in laps. A few snores of varying pitch and length broke the silence. Cornelius and Isaac had just crossed the threshold to the museum when they heard Hardoak behind them tripping and kicking women who complained out loud at his boorish brutality. Hardoak reached down and shook one of the women awake.

"What's your deal, asshole?" she said.

"You see those two bastards over there?" Hardoak said pointing at Isaac and Cornelius.

"You're being rude, you maniac!" the woman said.

"Those two bastards have something that belongs to me in that sack, I need you to help me."

Cornelius looked to Isaac with his eyes wide with fear and whispered, "Get the hell out of here, Isaac."

Isaac stood still.

Other women woke and started shouting obscenities at Hardoak for disturbing their peaceful sleep.

"Who among you is going to help me get a crystal of pure Termiculum from that bastard?"

A few of the women shot up on their feet and said, "What did you say?"

"The man who thinks he can just walk out of here without sharing any of this one-hundred percent pure high grade low weight straight-from-the-fucking-Mashgool themselves Termiculum!"

"You moron! You complete and utter moron!" Cornelius shouted.

"Pack that talk up your ass, you old idiot! I've had it with you. I've had it with Isaac. I'm sick of listening to him whine about his wife. I'm sick of hearing him get the world offered to him and never take it. Well, the world was just offered to me and I'm going to take it."

Cornelius pulled Isaac in close, "Get to the helicopter, Isaac. I'll hold them off for as long as I can. Radio the Institute and tell them that Hardoak's lost it. They'll think of something. Just get out of here. You're on your own now. Run!"

Isaac ran into the museum. Behind him he heard the building frenzy. The voice that shrilly smashed down all the female screams was Hardoak as he screamed, "Murder him!"

Isaac ran past the ancient statues. He heard Cornelius wail like he was being torn to pieces. Isaac ran into the lower level of the gallery. He stopped only to push two large statues from the Roman era off their pedestals and onto the ground to slow down the mob that pursued him like packs of wolves. The statues smashed onto the floor like a forgotten dream.

The double doors ripped from their hinges and gunshots penetrated the gallery. Isaac could not reach the elevator without being in their line of sight, so he changed his course and ran up the side of the gallery towards the paintings. Rifle slugs pockmarked the walls and hit paintings, sending ancient oil paint particles careening into the temperature-controlled atmosphere. Each shot sounded like a sledgehammer hitting a side of beef.

The overhead loudspeaker boomed, "You fools! This isn't authorized!"

The mob kept firing at Isaac. Vases smashed as bullets ripped through their airy guts. Faces of statues dug up in Pompeii shattered as bullets struck them. Isaac crawled between the wall and podiums to avoid being shot. He got to his feet and ran again. He looked over his shoulder. The gang of nuts gained ground while he had taken cover. Bullets whizzed past him and impacted frescos and mosaics, sending colored chips flinging through dead space.

Statues crumbled to the ground when their legs were shot out from under them. They women sprayed and prayed like stampeding elephants tiptoeing through an eggshell church. If Isaac could not get to the central platform, they would have him surrounded. He ran as his lungs burned fire and blood.

The loudspeaker boomed, "You fools, stop!"

The mob pressed on rifles at the ready.

Isaac climbed the height of the gallery and started back down the opposite side of the central staircase. The women foolishly followed him to the heights, and they sucked oxygen hard into their lungs. Their life of lounging had not prepared them well for this. Isaac started to descend again, running randomly towards the central elevator shaft. He hit the gallery floor and stopped to throw a vase in the face of a woman who dared catch up to him. She was unarmed; there was no rifle to slow her down. Isaac flung the priceless Grecian funeral urn and it smashed on her head and sent her flailing to the ground. Isaac climbed the two-hundred steep stairs toward the elevator shaft. Shots careened off the marble. An alarm sounded that filled the gallery. The loudspeakers boomed again, "Emergency procedures enacted to protect gallery content. Firing a weapon in the gallery will result in immediate destruction."

Isaac pressed the elevator button, to the roof and the doors did not close. Did emergency measures include locking the elevator down? If so, he was as good as dead. He turned and looked to the stairs. Hardoak ran up them with murder in his eyes and his hands gripping an antiquated rifle. He ran at the lead of hundreds of naked women, their breasts bouncing up and down with each step upwards. If they didn't intend to rip him in pieces they would have been a sight to behold. He jammed the button again. Hardoak leveled the weapon at Isaac.

"Father damn you!" Isaac screamed. At the same time as Hardoak fired, Isaac turned his back. The bullet's velocity pushed him forwards, face first into the corner of the elevator. It struck the Termiculum and dropped harmlessly into the backpack. Simultaneously, the computer triangulated the blast and fired countermeasures. The intense burst of directed microwave radiation ripped through Hardoak's body. Before Isaac turned around, he heard a pop and sizzle like a worm eaten log thrown into a fire. Isaac sat in the corner of the elevator. Hardoak's boots and clothing were all that remained of him. A scorch mark on the marble served as his memorial. Hot viscera covered the bodies of the women in the front rank and dripped from their noses like tears. They stumbled backwards.

The loudspeaker boomed, "Leave this man be. He is above the business of business. If you touch this prophet, you will meet the same fate as the other two…."

The elevator doors began to close. *Fucking Rockhead.* The last thing Isaac saw was his smoking shoes and the women who had blank stares on their faces. Too blank for comfort, a mix between boredom and death. *Fucking Rockhead. Why weren't they just dropped in by the helicopter? Why send them here?*

In the elevator, it seemed an eternity from the underground gallery to the rooftop. When the elevator doors opened, Isaac stumbled out into the sunshine in a daze. The whirlybird was not there. He sat in the corner in frustration at first and then stood up to see if he could find an exit to the ground. The sides of the building were smooth. He thought for a brief second about jumping, but there was no way he would survive. He looked to the heavens. Venus, the morning star, came off slightly larger than the other stars that were beginning to appear in the dusky sky. It shined brighter because it was closer to the Earth than the other stars, which contained a leap of infinity between them. On those planets around those stars, there was a similar scene in the nighttime sky – if there was anyone on those planets to comprehend the grandeur. Life had happened in the dusts of galaxies. It had happened once. It should have happened again and again. Once their sensors got fine tuned enough, once they could distinguish between the background noise and what they were looking for, they came. *But why come? What was the point of it? What did the Mashgool have to gain?*

Isaac looked to the heavens again. In each star he saw his wife dancing. She dipped and pirouetted, spinning like a top on its axis, like a planet around a hot alien sun. He sat in his corner again and closed his eyes until he dreamed nothing.

He was awakened by the sounds of clanking: metal against metal that ended in a high-pitched, annoying scraping. Something was coming up the side of the building. It sounded like a puppet yanked upwards by a giant. Sinister.

Isaac sprang to his feet and looked downwards but it was too dark to see what was coming for him. As the metal beast crossed over the SOLOMON TRADING CORPORATION sign, it came into view.

It shambled over the sign clicking its metallic legs over the red glowing letters. It stopped. It flexed up and down on its haunches a few times to get a better grip. The beast sounded like a diesel generator short a few quarts of lubricating oil. Perturbed pistons grinded against their crankcases and shot fire into the night air. When the arachnid came to the edge of the building, bright spotlights shot from its face. Eight metal legs crested over the building edge. Its great bright ass sat on the corner, ready to pounce and focused its spotlight on Isaac. He covered his face with his hand in an attempt to beat back the brightness. The spider coughed a few times, hiccupped, and made what sounded like a low, guttural fart before its gears ground to a halt. A few hisses escaped from its joints as they relaxed. The lights did not die.

A booming metallic voice came from a loudspeaker, buried in its stringy wire guts.

"Isaac! Is that you?"

"Who are you?" Isaac asked.

"I was told you answer questions with questions. Of course it's you!"

"Who is asking me?"

"I'm from the Institute."

"Where the hell are you?"

244

"This thing is fly by wire. I'm back at the Institute. I'm piloting this vehicle remotely."

"Why didn't you just send a helicopter?"

"Sorry all the pilots are otherwise occupied."

"Whatever. You know that Major Hardoak is dead and so is Cornelius."

"Yes. We were informed of that."

"Who told you?"

"The Paraclete informed Commander Jacobus of the news. Commander Jacobus is quite saddened by the loss of his prodigy."

"How the hell did Tanner find out?"

"Beats me? I'm supposed to take you within five miles of Moojtema and let you off."

"Why the hell didn't we do this from the beginning?"

"I don't make the plans. I just drive this Land Hopper. We've got to go. Time is wasting."

Isaac climbed into the contraption and sat in the seat. He fastened the safety belt until it was very snug against his body. The spider roared to life. It coughed, and a great glob of viscous oil shot from its insides and splatted on the building. The spider leapt up, and gravity took hold. Isaac screamed like a shark attack victim at the suddenness of it all. The driver laughed over the loudspeaker, waking citizens of Caravan City from their beds who kicked their nighttime lovers thinking there was a giant robot madman sent to ravage the city. The spider's legs tensed and shock absorbers cushioned the fall when it hit the ground. Isaac did not feel a thing except his stomach sinking.

"Damn you! Warn me next time you do something like that."

"I'm sorry, sir. I figured you'd get used to it quicker if I just did it. Like ripping a piece of tape from your skin."

"Oh, okay."

"Are you ready? This thing moves very fast."

"Sure go ahea –."

The shock absorbers disengaged with a whirring that terminated in a click. The legs started moving up and down, but the body remained in place. Then the spider leaped into the air at a forty-five degree angle covering at least two-hundred feet. Isaac vomited as the Hopper made its descent and barely missed getting splashed when it rebounded.

Robert Tanner received the idea for the Tanner Industries Mark IV L332 Personnel Transport Vehicle (PTV) by seemingly divine revelation when he was at one of his vacation homes in New Zealand. While eating his breakfast which consisted of his usual poached eggs with white wine lemon hollandaise sauce, beluga caviar, and white flour kosher sea salt crackers, washed down with a champagne spritzer, a spider no bigger than his thumbnail leapt onto his plate. His lover screamed and forced her spoon into the sauce to smash it. The spider leapt away at the last instant, and the Italian beauty from Milano, ended up with sticky yellow hollandaise all over her Piaget watch that Tanner purchased for her as a combination birthday present and apology for being seen at the National Science Foundation annual dinner with another woman – this time a tall, buxom Norwegian.

The idea hit him like a bolt of lightning from above, not so much a light bulb. The newly formed Armaments and Weapons Systems Division of Tanner Industries had been contracted to produce Armored Personnel Carriers capable of evading Chinese Anti-Armor missiles, given that the powers that be in the United States Department of Defense believed land conflict with China was inevitable. Lockheed Martin proposed a strange wheeled contraption that had a jet turbine for propulsion. It moved fast, but so did the missiles. The prototypes were left smoking hulks on the testing field. He called his design teams with his idea. He ordered them to Google the spider and look for photographs. He paid entomologists from the University of Auckland thousands of dollars for their time in capturing live specimens to be slow motion time captured. He called all of his engineers into a room and said that if they wanted inspiration they should look at the ultimate of all engineers, Mother Nature, for design concepts. Thousands of spiders were dissected and the arrangements of their leg muscles were studied to see what gave them such spectacular leaping ability.

At the annual Board of Directors meeting of Tanner Industries, right between the announcement of the dividend of $5.00 per share and the vote on a stock split, Robert Tanner announced that the priority of Tanner Industries would be to search out Mother Nature in all her infinite wonder and put their knowledge of advanced mathematics and physics into copying her wondrous works. He announced that Beauty did not drop from Heaven, but rather came from the ground up, piece by laborious piece. Two years after the annual meeting Tanner Industries fielded the prototype in Pentagon trials. The Chinese missiles that seemed slow and clunky in comparison did not damage a single spider bot. There was no troop compartment on the unit that Isaac rode. Otherwise it could hold thirty personnel in a flexible compartment modeled after the spider's abdomen. The abdomen attachment slowed the troop transport down slightly. Otherwise, the spider was gut wrenching to ride on – as Isaac was learning. The Institute soldier that controlled the spider bot talked in soothing tones to Isaac to keep him conscious.

"When I get back, I want to meet you. I'm going to look at your certification. Did you fail this block of instruction?"

"Nope. Things could be worse. Verenus could be driving you. The last guy ended up with a broken pelvis."

"Who the hell taught you how to drive this thing?"

"The Tanner Industries Operator's Manual 16-A, sir."

"Can't you go slower? You're riiiiping my guts up."

"No. The slower we go, the more shock that goes through your body. I have my orders that you're to arrive in one piece."

Isaac did not think he would need to be rescued like this at the very beginning of his mission, but he had come to expect the unexpected. He thought he would do better if he just let his will evaporate and started letting things happen to him. Resistance was no way to deal with the fundamental randomness and insanity of the world. The friend he slugged through the woods with was dead. He deserved his death, but it all came so suddenly. He felt like wretching again. Nothing escaped him but a dry heave.

"Damnit, ease up on this thing!"

"We'll be there shortly, sir."

"Why the hell did the whirlybird leave? What is this damn thing?"

"Shock and awe, sir. Shock and awe."

"What the hell does that mean?"

"Imagine a thousand of these things coming at you. Not only are they hard as hell to hit, they're damn scary in a massed formation."

"They're probably useless against planes."

"Oh, no, they aren't. That's their advantage. In a combat situation this little bot would come with anti--aircraft countermeasures."

"Excellent. We're not in combat."

"Nope. This one has been stripped to its bare essentials."

"Great. I want a damn whirlybird to pick me up."

"I think you're on your own with that one."

"I'll just walk out of there with my wife."

"What, sir?"

"If you see that sickfuck, Tanner, back there, tell him to fuck himself."

"Sir? The Paraclete?"

"Yes, him. Tell him to fuck himself."

"I can't do that, sir."

"Why can't you?"

"It's just insane to say that, sir. We owe the Paraclete everything."

"He's no savior."

"I came to the Institute when I was just a child. I can't bear to think what would have become of me if he hadn't taken me in."

"You'd probably be happy and not wearing that cheesy uniform they have you in."

"I'd be one of the lost ones. The Paraclete led me to the truth."

"You are one of the lost ones. You're a fool."

"You're a fool to go against him if that's what you're planning."

"There's only one truth my man and it's written in you. Its got several faces depending on which crowd you're around. The truth wears a mask. Its mask is your face. Just remember the truth isn't something out there. It's what you do."

The spider bot pitched violently like it was avoiding a missile. It righted itself. It landed and didn't rebounce.

"Damn, watch it!" Isaac shouted, angry with the invisible man on the other end of the controls.

"Sir, there's a problem."

"What? What could possibly be the matter with this modern marvel of engineering dreamed up by those Institute geniuses?"

"One of the legs has seized. Let me try a remote reboot of the system."

"Get me a helicopter, damn you."

"We're too close now."

"Don't talk about *we're too close*, like you're actually here. I'm the one out here. You get to go back to your comfy room after your shift."

"Rebooting. If this doesn't work, you're on your own."

Isaac waited patiently. The sound of nocturnal animals and trees surrounded him. Insects gyrated violently, adding to the symphony.

"Sir, it's not going to reboot. You have to exit the vehicle and stand at least one-hundred meters away while I initiate the self destruct sequence."

"Try it again."

"I'm sorry I have my orders."

"From whom?"

"Please stand away."

A beam of light flashed from the spider bot into the darkness. It hit a thicket of trees and illuminated some night creature's eyes.

"Walk in that direction. You'll run into Moojtema."

"Shine the light in the darkness again, please," Isaac said.

"I'm sorry. No time."

"I guess I have no choice," Isaac said as he jumped down from the bot onto the soft ground. He started walking into the darkness. He did not even look back when the spider bot exploded and the fireball set the surrounding trees' upper leaves on fire.

Isaac stumbled through the dense woods in darkness. What made his way more difficult was navigating the hilly terrain while despair clawed at his heart, trying to scratch out a hole. Despair desired to plant a barbed seed that would sprout weeds of all encompassing doubt. Logical doubt was possible but when you start to doubt with emotion, as Isaac was starting to doubt after his best friend betrayed him, and in fundamental goodness of the people in the world, you make yourself capable of anything. If you believe the world is fundamentally rotten to the core, you open yourself up to being rotten. It is the way of the world, so why go against it? Isaac thought about the people in his life while he walked forward into the darkness. Their faces swirled at him in the darkness, and many just looked deformed and hideous. His wife was the only whole and good person to appear in front of him. His whole life, he thought, people were using him for their own purposes. They picked him up and sharpened him like a tool and used him and tossed him to the side to rust. What would he do though? Give up? He kept trudging forward.

Riotous peals of laughter ripped from the forest to the side of him. He turned in that direction. The laughter did not come again. He stood still. He listened intently. The laughter did not come.

He read about people losing their minds. Like Moses, they saw and heard things that were not there and used external things to give their inner voice credence. A natural order is in human societies, and it stems from the will of individual human beings. If humans will freedom and act in accordance with this will, they are free. Free will is a tautology. To call the will free is to make a completely empty statement. Humans are born free. Their mothers must feed them from their breasts. When these babies age, they must fend for themselves. Humans work and struggle and earn their freedom day by day. When they are merely provided for, they slip into the most ignoble of slaves. Whatever Isaac read about a world spirit or a harmonious arrangement of parts of society constituting a greater whole than the sum of its parts, or the state having authority over the individual were all falsehoods. All were abstractions to give purpose to purposeless nature. No meaning could be imparted onto Isaac externally. Isaac had trudged though hell and he knew that he would continue to trudge through hell until he found his wife. For him, the universe was quickly becoming a cold and ugly and a never-ending nightmare, but he chose to keep walking forward. He could have sat down and died many times. He kept putting one foot in front of the other. Isaac was a champion. Everyone around him was dead. He was still alive.

A faint glow rose from the depression in front of him. Another peal of laughter shot from the behind the birch trees that ringed the bowl. Isaac thought, *Will I meet death down there*? He paused at the edge. Two women danced in firelight with their bare breasts shining. Men laughed and clapped. Isaac walked down into the middle of them.

"I need your help," he said.

The women gasped and covered themselves.

A burly bearded man, shorter than Isaac, leapt to his feet and puffed his chest out screaming, "Just who are you, boy? Are you lost!"

"I'm not lost," Isaac said gravely. He ran his hands through his hair to show the man he was of no consequence.

"Who are you?" the man demanded, eyes wide open in the firelight.

"I know my direction," Isaac said with a smile.

"Just answer me, who the hell are you?"

"Just a lonely traveler. I heard your laughter and some women's voices and I wanted to see what was happening."

"So you came for the girls, eh? Now all you did was make our girls uncomfortable. Why don't you tell us your name so we can all be friends," the man said with his white teeth showing through his bristles.

"I'm Isaac."

"The girls are Rosy and Sabrina. They're dancing for us. Maybe later we dance for them. Right, girls?"

The pair nodded submissively. They looked like forest women. The older was probably between eighteen to nineteen years old. They younger looked a clone of her sister but probably four years younger. In the darkness Isaac could see they were beautiful, though not as beautiful as his Deer. Still they would have been many men's dreams.

"We're taking them to Moojtema. They pay top price for young ladies like these. Where are you going?"

"You didn't tell me your name."

"Sorry. How rude of me. I am a businessman; I should know better. But my clients usually aren't into me, if you know what I mean," the bearded man said smiling. He extended his hand and Isaac took it forcefully. "I'm Flynn," the man said. "This other man is just a business associate of mine, of no consequence. A bodyguard. The woods are full of brigands trying to take people's hard earned property. Are you a brigand? You trying to take my property?"

"No, Flynn, I'm going to Moojtema, too."

"Say, you want to take these girls off my hands for the right price?"

"I already have a woman."

"Well all you have to do is just escort them there, and you'll probably get double what you paid for them."

"What is it that you do?" Isaac asked with a cross look on his face that was obscured by shadows.

"I deliver these girls to the city where they'll be safe. These woods are no place for a woman to be alone. I find lovelies who need help, and I help them."

"How much do the women get you at Moojtema?"

"Forty or fifty diamonds a piece. The little ones though. That's just enough to pay for my protection here and put a little into savings to buy my way into that place."

"How's business for you?"

"Good."

"You own these two women here?"

"I bought the right to take them to Moojtema fair and square. Also, the right to do with them what I wanted on the way, right girls?"

250

The pair looked to the ground, and did not answer.

"My pretties don't talk much."

"Who sold them to you?"

"I don't remember. Who was it again, girls?"

They spoke in unison, "Father."

Flynn laughed and smiled. "Oh, yes. He couldn't find them suitable mates, so he traded them for forty skins. Can you believe it? Forty skins for these two beauties! What a bargain!"

Flynn stroked his beard and laughed. Isaac turned redder and redder by the minute standing with this man. The bodyguard lounged by the fire dozing off now that the show had ended.

Isaac pulled the diamond that was his brother Jesse out of his pocket. He held it up to the fire. "That's about ten or twenty diamonds, right?"

Flynn gasped when he looked at the rock, "Dear God, where did you get that?"

"Long story," Isaac said.

"For that diamond I'd let you have one of them, though I'm kind of taking a liking to the younger one."

"We stay together!" the older one said.

"See?! Too feisty! She doesn't submit willingly, do ya, girl?" Flynn said, laughing as he stepped close to her to give her a grope. She pulled back and pulled her younger sister back with her.

"I couldn't do it. I can't part with this diamond."

"Well, suit yourself, but this Rosy's a gem. I'd be willing to let you wear her out so she'll sleep tonight for free. I guarantee you'll be giving me that diamond."

"No, I won't. This diamond is all I have left of my brother, Jesse."

"He gave it to you before he left home?" Flynn asked.

"No, you know there's a weapon that turns a person into a diamond? You shoot someone with it, and they burn up and all that's left of them is this," Isaac said holding it up.

"I wish I could get my hands on this weapon," Flynn said gleefully. "I'd be making diamonds all day long."

"I know you would, Flynn, would you turn these girls and me into diamonds?"

"No. I can get fifty each for them. I could probably get one-hundred for the young one. She's a little talent. You know these forest girls start up when they're nine, don't ya? Plenty of years of practice! Look at her," Flynn said squeezing the girl's cheeks. She pulled away from him.

"These girls don't want to be here, do they?" Isaac said.

"No. I don't think so. You should have heard the way they screamed and cried when their father sold them to me."

"Your man here, he doesn't talk much, does he?"

"No. He's paid to shut up and keep the girlies in line and other men's mitts off my property. Unless they pay the price, then they can touch, but I decide when they stop. You ask a lot of questions, don't you?"

"Maybe I like your line of work. How long you been doing it?"

"As long as I remember."

"You deal in all Forest women?"

"Mainly. They're easy. Off traipsing in the woods alone gathering blackberries and such. You can just sneak right up on 'em."

"My wife is a Forest woman," Isaac said.

"Oh? Where's she now? You better watch her," Flynn said laughing.

"Some person like you stole her from me," Isaac said with a smile.

"It wasn't me!" Flynn said emphatically. The bodyguard didn't budge, his head was drooped down between his legs.

"I know. I know who did it. She's in Moojtema now."

"That's why you're going there? To get her back?"

"How are you going to get into the City?"

"I know people. I'll get in."

"Can you get me in?"

"I can't promise you anything, but if you let me accompany you, I'll ask them for you."

"Thanks. I've been saving forever and can't seem to meet their asking price," Flynn said shaking his head. He tugged his beard again. Isaac noticed that when Flynn talked about something that made him uncomfortable, he tugged his beard.

"You want a go with the girls?" Flynn asked.

"No, I need to sleep. Plus, these girls look tired."

Isaac stretched and sat by the fire. Rosy and Sabrina sat on the opposite side of the fire and held each other. Isaac closed his eyes and then opened them when he felt their eyes on him. He stared at Rosy and she did not drop her eyes from looking at him. She smiled slightly. He shifted his focus to Sabrina, and she smiled and whispered something to Rosy. They kept staring through the fire at him while Flynn and his bodyguard snored. Finally the younger sister motioned him over to them. Isaac did not feel like getting up from his comfortable position but stood and walked over to them. He sat down between the two. He felt the warmth radiating from their bodies. The racket from Flynn and his bodyguard was enough to attract packs of wolves.

Sabrina spoke to him so close that he could feel the moisture from her breath on his cheek. "Isaac, tell me, do you love your wife?"

"I do," he said.

"How do you know?"

"I don't know how, really, but if I could die knowing that she would be safe and nothing bad would ever happen to her, I would willingly do this every day of my life," he said.

"What does your wife look like, Isaac?" Sabrina asked innocently.

"She has black hair and eyes like emeralds. She's the most beautiful woman in the world to me."

Rosy sighed. "Ohhh...you are sweet, and your wife is lucky to have you."

The young girl spoke, "My sister had a lover before. A secret man she loved. He was not an important man, and worse, he was not from our people. Our father would never have accepted him. Roxanne told me everything about him. She had me lie to our father about where she was going when she went alone into the woods. I tried my best, but he never really believed me. One day he told me that he was going to find out for himself where she went. So he followed her and discovered her with her lover. He flew into a rage. He killed her lover with his bare hands while she watched. He sold us both

252

to the wretched man to punish us. I don't understand. It was only love. It was only two young people in love."

"My brother died for love, too," Isaac said.

"It doesn't make any sense that old people who have already had their chance interfere with the young people in love," Sabrina said.

"My father said that only he can choose for me. We both disagreed. He chose for us, and now we're here."

"You'll both be safe once you get to the City."

"Isaac, have you killed men before?" Rosy asked.

"Yes. I have had to," Isaac said.

"The sleeping men, would you smash their heads with a rock?"

"No, I can't."

"Why not? They're horrible men. My sister and I will be all yours if you do."

Rosy scooted over so she could be closer to Isaac. Her sister Sabrina did the same.

"If I kill them, you'll just end up in the City. I won't leave you out here alone."

"But you'll be saving us from them. Their sick touches! We don't know the City. We know the woods. You know the woods. Kill them and be with us."

"I can't. He hasn't wronged me."

"He wronged us. Do you know what it's like to be with a disgusting old man?" Sabrina said.

"I can't imagine," Isaac said wincing.

"He can't make it hard, so he just has me lick him all over his body," Sabrina said crying.

The vision of the young woman with the old man made Isaac sick to his stomach. The rock seemed like a good proposition.

"I can't kill someone while they sleep. There is no honor in it. It's cowardly."

"There is no honor in the world, Isaac. Look around you."

"Of course there isn't. But I'm honorable. I won't do it."

"You're just a weakling. My sister and I need a hero. We need some one to save us, and we met a coward."

"You have no idea who I am," Isaac said with a hint of anger.

"We just know that you won't help us."

"Maybe he can't get his hard," Sabrina said.

"Why don't you do it yourselves?"

"No, we couldn't kill them both at the same time. I don't think we could hit them hard enough to kill them. Just piss them off. Then we'd really get it."

"Please help us."

"I can't. Why don't you just convince his guard to turn on him?"

"That idiot? He doesn't know his way around the woods or a woman. We want you to help us," Rosy said. She brushed her hand on top of Isaac's and let it linger there. Isaac did not sweep it away. It felt nice and warm like spring sunshine.

"I'm sure you can use your charms to convince that guard to separate himself from that gun he has," Isaac said.

"No, we want to go wherever you're going, and we don't want them along," Rosy said.

"I'm going to Moojtema, and there's no stopping or sidetracking me."

"We'll follow you then. We trust you know what you're doing."

"Why don't we leave now?"

"I'm tired," Sabrina said.

"Let's rest and leave tomorrow," Rosy said.

"We'll sneak away from them," Isaac said, not really sure the plan would work. He was scared that the two sisters would be able to convince him to abandon his mission or at least delay him. The both lay nearly on top of him for warmth as the fire died down. He fell into a deep sleep as he felt their breasts and warm breath on his neck. Before things went dark, he felt the girls kissing him gently on the side of his neck, and he wanted to reciprocate. He stared up at the stars and thought of his wife. Twilight batted at the margins of his mind like a kitten at play where sleep unwound like a ball of yarn. He only woke when he felt the weird absence of the little women.

He opened his eyes. The guard stood over him with the barrel of his antique rifle pointed at Isaac's head. His gnarled hands were taped in places as if his skin wore off and were wrapped around the splintered stock. All the way up the stock the guard had scratched when he delivered someone from this world to the next with a gun blast.

"Should I do it, boss?" the gunman asked.

"He got a fuck in without paying for it. Plus he convinced those two sluts to run off. Take that diamond of his for payment. Hand over your knapsack, too."

"Where are Sabrina and Rosy?" Isaac asked.

"You aren't in the position to be askin' questions. You hand that damn diamond over."

"I didn't touch them."

"Why'd I wake up several times in the night and hear them moaning and carryin' on if you didn't touch them?"

"I can lay down on the ground with a woman and not make love to her, maybe you can't, but I can."

"Pay up, son. Your diamond and knapsack or your life."

"I'm not going to pay you anything. I didn't touch them."

Flynn stroked his beard. In the sunlight it was more salt and pepper than black, and his face was full of wrinkles that Isaac couldn't discern last night. The guard's gun looked even more ancient than Flynn though. The guard twitched like he was nervous and did not look a day over seventeen years old. His face had a baby like innocence. Isaac speculated that this was his first trip out, given that he had been sleeping when he should have been guarding last night.

"Let me tell you something, my boy," Flynn said, still running his fingers through the tangled mess of a beard. "You should have done what I did in life. It's the only way to succeed on this little mess of a world we've got. It's the reason I'm gonna leave this little situation we've got alive and why your carcass is gonna get picked clean by the coyotes and wolves and your bones will bleach in the sun. You have to steal as much as you can. That's the way of this world, boy. Avoid other people unless you're gonna steal from them. That's old Flynn's way. That's the world's way. You should of done gone around us last night. Not even come by. But, my granny taught me a lesson. Curiosity killed the cat."

"I don't think so," Isaac said. His stomach was doing cartwheels. The barrel was right at his face. He imagined the blast would hurt at first and then peace would come over him. The guard tensed up as if waiting for Flynn's signal.

"Wait!" Isaac said.

"The diamond. It's yours. But what I got in my knapsack, you can't have it."

"Oh really? You're in the position to negotiate?"

"You better hand that knapsack over," the guard said trying to act tough. He thrust the weapon forward threateningly. His voice squeaked at the tail end of his words like a tuft on the tail feathers of a bird.

"Just the diamond. Then I get moving on my way."

"No. We'll be taking that knapsack," Flynn said with a smile.

"Give him the damn knapsack!" the pipsqueak said.

"Fine, but I'm warning you. The men who own that knapsack will not be happy. They're going to come looking for you to get the contents of it back."

"I don't care. I'll be long gone."

"Hand it over," the guard said.

"Fine. Take it."

Isaac tossed it to Flynn and smiled widely.

"Wait," Flynn said, "How do I know you're not tricking me. This could be full of your dirty underwear. It's too light to be gold."

"Check it," Isaac said.

"Yeah, check it," the guard said looking at Flynn, taking his eyes off of Isaac for a second.

Flynn opened the knapsack up and the brightness of the sun shone in his eyes.

"Dear God, it's beautiful," Flynn said.

He grabbed the Termiculum crystal with his bare hands. That was all the touching it took. Flynn screamed like Hell had come open and demons were fire torturing his testicles. The guard looked to his employer shocked. Isaac grabbed the barrel and pulled it away from his head. The gun yanked from the guard's hands. Isaac made his legs into a scissor and swept the guard's legs. The boy landed in a heap on the ground. Isaac grabbed the gun and sat up on top of the bodyguard who struggled to get his bearings. Isaac pulled the trigger without hesitation. The gunshot pierced the morning like a ribald nightmare. The guard tensed and went silent.

Flynn rolled on the ground trying to stop the slow disintegration of his hands. Isaac stood over him with the weapon leveled at him.

"It isn't going to stop, Flynn," Isaac said. "I can shoot you or just leave you die slowly and painfully."

"Damn you," Flynn said.

"I guess curiosity killed the cat, right, Flynn? I'm giving you a choice. The choice you didn't give me. Do you want me to shoot you or leave you here to suffer?"

"That isn't a choice," Flynn said.

"Sure it is. You feel that burn? That's spreading. Imagine what it will be like when it burns past your shoulders. You better hope it burns up towards your head and not down towards your heart and guts and balls, Flynn."

"Fuck you. I'm not going to give you the pleasure of killing me, you son of a bitch," Flynn said.

"I'm going to walk away and leave you to your fate, Flynn," Isaac said. He started to walk away.

"Wait! God it burns! Just fucking wait! You liked those two sluts, didn't you? You really liked them, right?"

"I felt sorry for them, that's it," Isaac said.

"You didn't hear them this morning, did you? You didn't hear my guard and I take them out into the woods and kill them, did you? You know why, lover boy? It's because we strangled them nice and quick. We wouldn't let two sluts get away from us. That's what I do to sluts that don't listen. Your wife, was she with a group of forest men, oh, 'bout four years ago?"

"That's who kidnapped her, why?" Isaac said glaring at Flynn.

"Oh God, it burns! Can't you make it stop?"

"Why Flynn? Why? Did you see a woman with a group of forest men?"

"I did. They were run ragged. Sorriest group I've ever seen. I offered to buy her off them. They said no, of course. Fucking fools. I asked her if she wanted to come with me to Moojtema, because I had more food with me. This was the dead of winter. They got all upset. So we stole her away. My guards and I followed them and killed the men she was with and stole her. Haha!"

"What did you do with her?"

"What do I do with sluts that won't listen?"

"You bastard!" Isaac screamed.

"You idiot! You think that was your wife? You know how many forest women get sold through here everyday? It must be thousands!"

"What men was she with?"

"I don't remember them. They were nasty dirty creatures. Black stringy hair, unwashed, filthy," Flynn said, whimpering from the pain he was in.

"What did she look like?"

"Black hair, green eyes like emeralds, my God her beauty shone through all that filth. When I fucked her it was like Heaven wrapped around my cock," Flynn chuckled for a second, then when back to muttering.

"You're lying."

"I'm not," Flynn said.

"You heard me talk to the girls last night," Isaac said.

"Still I fucked her well and left my little swimmers in her breadbasket. Your wife's cunt is like a hand. But I bet you know that. She milked me dry, boy. 'You're so much bigger than my husband' she said. Ahhh, what a lovely."

"You're pathetic, Flynn. You're going to burn to death slowly. I won't give you the pleasure of dying with a gunshot."

"I'll just lay here and think about your wife's round ass and how she gave it up to everyone we met, 'til I got sick of her and sold her to the trading post. Aye. I'm telling you where to find your wife. She didn't make it to Moojtema. She's sucking and fucking for a living right now. If you hurry you can get one off too with her. Maybe she'll remember you. Of course, you'll have to be daddy to her five bastards. Say hello to my son for me."

"You sick liar," Isaac said.

"No, Isaac. I'm one of the happy ones. The ones that never knew, never tried to know, never even cared to try. I'm one of those ignorantly blissful clowns, the ones that fuck and forget and love life without thinking anything higher or lower. I'm blessed. I'm on the level of beetles and worms while you're trying to soar with the eagles. I'm a happy one, the grease of history, and the lubrication for the machine. Without men like me, humans would have perished from this planet by their own hands eons ago. You begin and end in a woman. That's the life for me! The wise men say the meek shall inherit the Earth. So one last time I'll go and be meek! Lets drink and fuck and prop me on my nose when my arms burn off! Or prop me on my back and let them file in. You said it's a slow burn. I'll get up! First one in your wife's well laid pussy is the winner!"

Flynn sat up on his ass with a smile on his face. He struggled to get to his feet without using his arms. They burned past the elbow. He looked to Isaac with wide eyes.

Isaac shot him in the head, and Flynn's body flopped to the ground. Isaac pulled the bolt back to reload but the magazine was empty. He placed the rifle near the guard's body. Flynn's corpse still popped and cracked while Isaac walked into the distance.

Two old whores, one tall and thin with a narrow face and the other short and squat with a face like a bulldog sat outside a yellow, packed mud building. Whitish gray smoke leaked from their mouths slowly and trickled into their noses. They smoked in tandem, passing a small pipe between themselves. The women were dressed in rough woolen blankets draped over their shoulders and nothing else. When he approached, one of the women opened her blanket to reveal her advertisement: a pair of large dangling breasts that went unappreciated for at least twenty years. Perhaps the women were not old for the establishment and there were grandmothers inside with their skirts hiked up.

"You have any young women in here?" Isaac asked the taller of the two women.

"Sure, love. Sure you don't want a go with some experience? Lubby here could accommodate you," she said with a hoarse voice.

"Sure could, stud," Lubby said.

"No. I'm looking for someone. Someone special," Isaac said.

"What you have in mind, sugar?" the tall one asked.

"You have a woman named Deer that works here?"

"Nope. No Deer here. That's a strange name. Where's she from?"

"The Woods."

"We're all from the woods, dear. We're in the woods. Where's she from specifically."

"I don't know. These places have names?"

"Sure thing, lover boy. Looks like you're not from here. Are you lost?"

"No. Just looking for a woman."

"Plenty of women go in and out of these parts. Plenty of men go in and out of the women," the tall one said laughing.

Lubby interjected, "Can't you see the young man is upset, Saffie?"

"Aww, sorry, dear, she close to you?"

"Just doing a favor for a friend," Isaac said.

"Your friend did right by sending a big, strong man like you our way," Lubby said, snorting as she laughed.

"What does she look like, deary?"

"Black hair, shorter than me, green eyes."

"Oooh sounds lovely," Lubby said.

Saffie shushed her and said, "Oh, I remember that one. A plain bitch she was."

"What do you mean?"

"She wouldn't work. She just sat there in the corner sulking."

Isaac smiled. His heart leapt at how strong his wife was. "Where is she now?" he asked eagerly.

"The Mashgool Priest came and paid for her. He said he was going to take her to Moojtema."

"When did they leave?"

"Well, honey, that had to have been about four years ago now. Only reason I remember her is because she drove away so much business crushing men's berries like she did."

Isaac laughed.

"You think that's funny? You want your berries crushed? Lubby here will crush 'em good and flat for you."

"What did the Mashgool priest want with her?"

"What does any man want with a woman?"

Isaac's heart started to sink. He could only hope that she crushed his berries, too.

"That queer just wanted to take her off to Moojtema. Women make babies. You can't do it without them. Milking a man is easy. A woman's gotta be coaxed over years."

"You sure?" Isaac asked harshly.

"We don't know for certain. We've never been there. Why else would you take such a pretty lady to the City? She's probably just a pillow slave or sweet treat for the eyes. That's the lot of a woman in this world."

"Don't this pretty owe us something for our help?"

"I think he does."

"What you got to offer us?"

"I'm sorry, nothing," Isaac said.

"What's in the bag?" Lubby asked.

"Just provisions."

"Give us some," Saffie demanded.

"No, I need it to last me."

"We'll call the guards. Tell him you're trying to rape us for free. They'll kill you."

"Maybe you've got a sausage in those pants for us," Lubby said, pulling at Isaac's waistband.

"Come on now, me first, then her," Saffie said.

"No."

"You've got to give us something," Lubby said pulling his waistband out so she could look down his pants.

"Very nice, Saffie!"

"Let me see," Saffie yelled.

"Get off me, you two!"

"Come now come out here in the woods. It's on us."

"No."

"We'll scream. In five second's we'll scream for the guards."

Isaac looked at them. They were hideous. He thought about giving them the diamond in his pocket. He couldn't bear to part with it.

"Whatcha got for us man?"

"Something big, Saffie. I saw it."

"Just a kiss, then you can be on your way."

"Give it here," Saffie said and grabbed for his hand.

He pulled away, then grabbed Lubby by the back of her head and closed his eyes and kissed her rotten lips. He stepped back. Lubby smiled with bewilderment.

"I saw him first, Lubby!"

"Well he kissed me!"

"You're the ugly one, Lubby!"

"I'm not ugly! You're the old one Saffie!"

The women ripped at each other's blankets. Lubby wrapped her fat arms around Saffie and started to squeeze. Isaac snuck away around the trading post building. As he walked into the woods, he could hear the sounds of struggle but did not know if it was the death match he started or the business being attended to inside the building.

Isaac walked through the forest in the way that the betrayer, Rockhead, taught him. He walked for days eating nothing but berries and the meager provisions he packed. Soon the only foodstuffs in his backpack were crumbs. He licked his fingers and smashed them into the crevices to get all the hard tack out. It dissolved on his tongue and left his mouth pasty. His stomach contracted and rumbled even more when the gastric juice flour slime trickled inside.

On the fifth day Isaac heard a voice. It came when he stepped from the tall trees into a lush plain that descended towards the coast. First he heard something whooshing and thought it was the waves. He strained his eyes, but could not even see whitecaps. Then he thought it came from the wind rushing between the trees. He turned and the leaves were not blowing. The whooshing descended upon him again.

Isaac began running.

Weak from hunger, he fell to his knees and he hit his head on the ground. It was a minor bump, but he felt his brain rattle inside his head.

The whooshing pounded into his brain like a scream.

SSSSSSSHHHHHH…location!

"Is that you Father?" Isaac screamed towards the sky.

SSSSSSSSSSSSSSSHHHHSSSHHSSHHHHHSHSHHHSHHSHSHS your location!

"Where are you?" Isaac screamed in terror spinning around to find the source of the noise.

SSHHSHSHSHSHHSHSHS Commander Jacobus at the Institute. What is your status? You have not made a single report back to us.

Isaac fell to his knees. "Get out of my head!"

Isaac. Isaac. Listen to me. This is Commander Jacobus. I am speaking to you through an implant. You are not going crazy. You are not hearing the voice of the Father. We need you to head towards the sea. We are tracking a large congregation of people moving towards Moojtema. We need you to link up with them. They should have food to give you. If you hurry you can find them. Turn towards the sea, son. Walk towards it. Hurry.

Isaac screamed, "Yes, Father! I had given up believing in you. You have given me a sign, and I will follow!"

I am not the Father. This is Commander Jacobus, Isaac. I need you to comply with my orders.

"Father, I am walking towards the sea! Just like you have ordered me."

This is Commander Jacobus. I am not the Father. I am not the Son. I am not the Holy Spirit. Do you remember me, Isaac?

"I…yes…I think I do."

Snap out of it. You need to keep your wits about you. No matter what, keep walking towards the sea, Isaac. Do you understand?

"Yes Father. I understand!"

Goodness the man's lost it.

Isaac heard a sound in his head that sounded like metallic scratching.

Isaac fell to his knees again as the feedback made his legs weak. "Get out of my head, damn you!"

He started running again. He ran towards the ocean. It looked like a blue scarf cast into the distant wind by a forlorn lover. A deep blue tear streaked across the horizon.

Isaac! That's it. Keep running towards the ocean.

"Yes Father, I hear your call!"

The metallic scratching echoed again across the heavens. *This is Robert Tanner, Isaac. I need to know that everything is on the up and up with you. First, let me tell you that I apologize for what happened earlier at the Solomon Trading Corporation. Mr. Solomon sent a dispatch and told us that you had made it out alive. I guess all his women turned on him. I told him they would, but he just wouldn't listen to me. I'm sorry I put you through that test, Isaac. I just had to be able to trust you. You will face far greater temptation in Moojtema, son. We cannot have you deviating from the path. I knew that scoundrel Hardoak would turn on you. I did not trust him from the moment I saw him. Jacobus loved him like a son. I see that his sentiment sometimes gets in the way of his ability to do business.*

That is not true, sir. I disagreed with sending them on your little test but you insisted.

Commander Jacobus, that is quite enough. Another word of disrespect and I'll have you brought up on charges.

Sir, I apologize, but you can't keep butting into operations.

Jacobus, I am the Institute. I'll butt into anything that I want to.

Isaac tried to tune out the war of words that was brewing in his head. He could not. Their voices seemed to fill up the heavens.

"Can you both just leave me alone?" Isaac said.

Can you just let us be, sir?

Jacobus...your trust of that idiot, Hardoak, leads me to doubt everything on this mission. You handpicked Isaac as well. He could already be compromised. This mission is too important to get fucked up.

Sir, can you please just let us run our military operation here? We respect you as a scientist. I don't tell you what theories to go theorizing or hypotheses to hypothesize. Please sir, for the love of God, leave the operative alone when he's operational.

Jacobus. If you fuck this up you're going to regret it.

Sir, don't worry. Please...it is under control. Isaac do you have anything to say before the Paraclete signs off?

"Tell him to fuck himself," Isaac said.

I won't hold that against you, Isaac. I understand your frustration with me. The things I did were things that needed to be done.

"Sir, with all due respect to you, I know you think you do, but you don't know everything."

Isaac, carry on with your mission. The Paraclete will not bother you again.

*Isaac, you had better not mess this up. I swear if you mess this up...*Isaac heard the sound of metallic clanking and the voices disappeared.

Isaac, I trust in your abilities. Do the job well. Never forget that you are a champion.

"Sir, please do not get inside my head again."

Only if it is imperative, Isaac! Only then will I contact you. If the Paraclete makes contact again, do your best to block him out. He's been a bit, well, perturbed recently. Just concentrate on your mission.

"I shall," Isaac said.

The static that coated his synapses faded and he felt like his thoughts were his own again. He breathed deeply. The hunger in his stomach subsided as the ocean gave up its facile blue for the chaotic chop of whitecaps. Gulls screeched overhead lodging protests against the wind. A lonely, broken road pummeled the earth ahead of him. As he got closer, he saw the weeds growing through cracks in the hard surface. Anywhere a plant could take root, it did. Neglect and nature's leveling hard hand did away with the work of men in a bitter year's time. The plants did not ask questions. Their roots penetrated the soil in a lust for moisture. Their flowers mindlessly machined olfactory shackles for millions of honeybees. The discarded plastic monuments to the last great civilization of men not covered in messes of tangled briars and dense trees got picked up when they surfaced and made use of. What metal was not oxidized or oxidizable was made into sharp implements to stab through the flesh of marauding bands of people doing their best to survive. What concrete was not smashed to particles like the quartz sand littering desolate beaches, stood like great gray ghosts with thick, rusty rebar hair. What people were not forced into hiding in holes in bombed out cities like rodents afraid of the dawn took to the forests.

As he walked towards what the human beings of the past called a modern superhighway, he thought of the Institute. Operations like the Tanner Institute sought to marshal human beings behind ideas, like the idea that governed it: that the preservation and furtherance of science for no other end than the preservation and furtherance of science was the ultimate goal of mankind. In Isaac's thought, the Institute built something instead of leaving mankind to destroy each other savagely at the level of animals. He had not seen Moojtema yet. Was it built around a central principle, too? Would he be able to survive its rigors? Were there any rigors to survive? He knew that many people wanted to go there. They said life was easy in the confines of its walls. Perhaps when he found his wife they would settle down and have a small family amongst the corridors and markets, grow old, and die. He would be happy as long as he was with her.

Isaac walked south. His stomach stopped hurting him. He walked towards what looked like a great needle thrust through the eye of Heaven. Moojtema.

The road lay between a mess of tall pine trees and the cold ocean. The ocean sounded out its immortal call. Boom...hiss, beating like the heart of the planet.

Gangs of rival gulls circled each other at high tide. Isaac watched them from a group of lonely rocks at the edge of a cliff. Down the cliff were doom and the beating of the surf. Their fights intensified when the waves receded and one spotted washed up food -- be it crabs, clams, or anything else the ocean coughed up. Gulls dive bombed, squawked, pecked bodies with beaks, and drew blood. Enemies fell to the sandy beach. Waves carried its body into the churning surf and drove it underwater. The white corpse surfaced briefly and was dive bombed again. The victors flew to the rocks with tufts of feathers and gristly cannibal meats held in their sharp beaks like communion wafers.

At night blackness like none he had ever experienced overtook his eyes. He was nothing than another morsel to be bumped into and consumed in the wilderness. At night he hurried his pace; by day he slept underneath pine trees in the soft wiry needles.

He managed to kill a hare with a rock. In his weakness, the chances of hitting it were nearly nil, but it struck the hare's head. Isaac thanked his skill and picked up the floppy carcass. He beat back tears as he ate the rabbit raw, first stripping its guts from its body and flinging the filth into the forest. He slept soundly for the first time in a week; he dreamt he lived in a small cottage by the sea, and all day he listened to the waves crash against the shore. Soon this became commonplace to him and he ignored it. He sat at a plain empty table. Anticipation clawed its nails into his soul. He had no idea what he was waiting for. In his dream this went on for years.

One day there was a heavy knock at his door. It was summer; Isaac could tell by the green of the grasses on the hills leading to the sea. It was the most beautiful day he ever saw there. A man entered the sun spilled room. It was midday. Even though the sun shone brightly, the man's face was obscured by shadow. He spoke of coming trials that were long and difficult and that many men in the past failed.

Isaac laughed. "I have been waiting my whole life here, only boredom has been my companion," he said.

"Are you ready for anything?" the man asked. He pulled off his hood. It was Jesse. "Even ready to die? If you do not succeed, know that you, too, have killed me."

Isaac pushed the ghoul from the room and slammed the door. He went back to his table. He stared at the wall, and the ocean's humdrum smashing filled his hopes and dreams with their salty despair.

When he woke, the earth was about to be warmed on its face by the sun. With the dawn of a new day, his belly took on the gastric rip of the starved man he knew well. He looked from the hill down the long road he traveled. He looked to his future. It snaked off into the horizon where it dipped between two hills and disappeared. Through the fog that slowly burned away as the sun rose, he could see torch lights. People carried fire into the distance and were swallowed whole by the fog. From his vantage point, it looked like a long fiery snake. They poured into the opening the road made in the hills. He approached them feeling nothing.

When he got close he heard they were chanting something.

"Guardians of life unto you we walk, our travails mighty you lay them low. Our lives now to you we owe. Blessed among mere mortal men, a purpose for our lives in the bitter end. Blessed by our lords and masters, the Mashgool. The universe designed by the Father, God, for them to rule. We are an atomic fragment in the masterwork. Blessed are the Mashgool, the true masters of this universe. Blessed are they in the eyes of the Lord ,God, who created them first among the species...."

Isaac was walking near the assembled group when a man called to him, "What are you doing over there? Have you decided to save yourself and join us?" The man was tall and thin and had a beak-like nose and bald head. If his nose was any longer it would have served as an equator line that divided his face into eastern and western hemispheres. His head was shaved. He was bald by choice. As the man approached, Isaac could see that his head was shaved violently. There were long cuts in it; some of them still looked fresh.

"You, there. Who are you?"

"I'm Isaac."

"No. I did not ask your name. I asked who are you?"

"I'm a man."

"What are you doing out here all alone?"

"I came to join in, and I'm very hungry."

The man called out, "Someone bring our brother some food."

Two other bald men ran up and handed Isaac a loaf of bread. They smiled and bowed to him. He ate it greedily.

"Now that your belly is full, please answer my question. Who are you?"

"I'm Isaac. I'm a man."

"You told me your name already. Your name is not you. Tell me who you are."

"I've introduced myself."

"That you did. But you did not tell me who you are."

"Who are you?"

"Only an acolyte. I hope to be Mashgool Priest by my twentieth birthday."

"Where I'm from we introduce ourselves by our name our parents gave us," Isaac said.

"But it doesn't answer the question of who you are," the acolyte said.

"In one way, it does, just as your answer only describes you in one way. I don't know all about you."

"You know as much as you need to know, because I only just met you. So, who are you?"

"In the woods I was a hunter. I came to hear and join."

"Do you know what it is you'll be joining?"

"Not really."

"But you really must know. You can't just expect a free ride to Moojtema. Come speak with my Mashgool Elder."

"What is his name?"

"Hildebrand."

"That's odd."

"They all have strange names. They say strange things. It's all very beautiful."

"I will go if you lead the way," Isaac said.

The two walked past innumerable people, people with infirmities, people with babies clutching at them, eyes wide open with torch tallow burning in dripping, smoldering, smoking offshoots. They looked at him with suspicious glances perhaps in wonder as to why the Mashgool acolyte paid so much attention to the newcomer. *Once he's accepted he'll be just like us*, they may have been thinking. There were beautiful women among them. There were men with shirts off, rippling forest forged muscles, hair like wild straw interspersed with suckling vines. He kept his eye on the crowd for his wife.

"We will help you find your way in this life, Isaac. We are all going to the same place, and you will join us in our travels. You know, strength in numbers? I wouldn't want you getting killed on this lonely, cold road and never make it to your destination. You have to tell Hildebrand that I convinced you to join. Please, you must."

"Why do you want me to do that?"

"I have to bring people. I must. It's the only way they'll let me be a priest."

"If that's what you want, I'll do it."

The pair hurried past the men and women chanting in unison with their eyes on each other's backs like a great cattle train heading to the city. They had been some time without food, and they drank water sparsely during their pilgrimage to Moojtema. They fasted by choice. It was not necessary, nor recommended. They had heard somewhere that fasting would bring you closer to sanctity. Many pilgrims wore loose white robes with nothing underneath. Isaac could see the women's breasts as they walked. He tried not to disrupt their sanctity by staring. He knew that even perceived violations of sanctity were often answered with violence. Only violence would return the rites to their proper holiness. One man called out, "Hey, you two, why are you cutting in the line?"

"There is no line," the acolyte called to him.

"These people told me this was a line," the man said angrily.

"Sorry. They told you wrong."

"Damn! You mean this whole time I've been marching ahead slowly when I could be up near the front?"

"Walk however fast you want to walk; no one is stopping you," the acolyte said.

The man started running ahead with a smile on his face.

Isaac assumed the procession was holy because people were doing holy-looking things as they walked forward. Some muttered to themselves. Some bowed their heads in unison. Others chanted. Isaac did not mimic them. He did not understand the significance of the event that these people were commemorating or if they were even commemorating an event at all. Some of the people may have just seen a group of people and decided to participate. Maybe they were bored. Maybe others were on a secret mission like Isaac. He heard that the Institute dispatched spies in the past, and they just disappeared in the mists.

Many of the participants had looks of utter boredom on their faces. If the procession turned towards the cliff, Isaac thought that they would follow without even a glimmer of excitement painting their face. Sandwiched between the meek and the bored were the restless. The acolyte was one of them. At the slightest lull he filled the air with words, strange words, not beautiful words.

"Your life is nothing, Isaac," the acolyte said.

"I don't think so."

"No. It is nothing. You came from nothing, and to nothing you will go."

"Right now, I know I'm alive. I mean, I'm talking with you," Isaac said wondering at the strange turn the acolyte's conversation had taken.

"These are the parameters of our experience and the parameters of our religion. It is all nothing. Once you accept that your life is nothing, you will be truly wise. The wisdom of life lies between birth and death. Once death was despised. Now it is glorified."

Isaac could not follow his convolutions but did not tell the acolyte. He nodded and looked interested. The acolyte continued, telling Isaac what his Master had told him just the other night at a campfire.

"Once a man is born, he lives. He lives at first with the aid of his mother. Then, he lives by his own accord. When he dies, nothing becomes of him. It is not a cause to be celebrated nor mourned. If he lived well he ought to be emulated. All told, the man lived according to his means. If he lived stupidly his errors should be noted and avoided. What is important is that he lived and underwent his trial. All reduces to zero. All becomes nothing."

Isaac smiled and nodded. The acolyte stopped walking and smiled.

"You know, Isaac, you are a smart man."

"Sure thing," Isaac said.

"You know that the religions of man that came to dominate the planet among the ancients were religions based on an all-knowing, all-powerful God. This God was written about, thought about, and gave the ancients messages through special men they called prophets. The messages were delivered piecemeal: revealed they, called it. No, discovered. I always wondered, did men think that they were important before or after this God told them they were?"

"Before. Long before," Isaac said. "They had been seeking meaning for themselves long before this God was dreamt up."

"And they made this God the end-all be-all of meaning."

"Well, they thought they did. They thought they dreamt a thought that could not be surpassed."

"The Mashgool have surpassed it."

"How is that?"

"Their tenets. They postulate this life only--nothing beyond it and nothing behind it. It is this one and only life. Their tenets carried them across the universe. They have documented every species that came to be, and they continue ever onwards into the unknown. They say that the unknown will come to be known, by them."

"Can you tell me these tenets?"

"I have no knowledge of the Mashgool language, so I have not read them yet. Priest Hildebrand is instructing me, but his instruction is thorough and slow. I have seen the book that Hildebrand carries. He showed me the language. It looks like queer stacks of concentric circles that each represents a single sound and meaning for them. Hildebrand is well studied in it. He will tell you."

A man ahead of them lay at the side of the road screaming. His feet were bloodied and his eyes were far off and distant.

"Brother, why do you scream?" the acolyte called to him.

The man looked up and beckoned the acolyte over. Isaac followed, eager to hear what the man had to say.

"I scream at my past. It fills my nightmares, which now creep into my days like spiders abandoning webs of night. My father was a horror, a terror to our family. He was given a fortune, but he gambled and drank and fucked all of his wealth away. To finance his lust for whores, dice, and booze, my brother and I were sold into bondage in a nearby village. I toiled all my life at a wheel breaking grain into flour. All day long we walked in a circle listening to the crunch of the wheel against grain. Stone against stone, the individual grains popped and cracked under our labor. My brother did not last; he was small and weak. The pace I kept was too much for him to bear. The next slave I did in as well, and the next one as well. I could not bear hearing the popping and crushing of the grain, knowing the one who bested me would mean my end. I walked in a circle my entire life until I was sold to another man. My back is broken. My feet are bloodied. Now all I hear is the popping and cracking of grain under the millstone. Even in my dreams I am yoked. I still feel the burden on my neck and the stone's weight in my arms."

"Celebrate, man. Celebrate that you are walking a straight line now. You are heading to a destination. You are no longer driving a hole into the earth. You are climbing into the heavens," the acolyte said to the man.

"No. I fear to move from this spot. I am still at the millstone, as are all of you."

"We are walking forward, brother. You should join us," the acolyte said. He did not say another word to the old, former slave.

They came upon an old woman sitting by the side of the road, rocking and weeping.

"Sister, why do you weep?" the acolyte said.

"I cry because of my past. All the men who told me they loved me and wanted to be with me forever disappeared. They left me only with the burden of their children. My children once needed me. They clawed and sucked at my full breasts greedily. Now even my children have abandoned me for the wider world. My breasts are desiccated. No child will issue forth from my loins. My hair is matted and stinking. I was once beautiful, I swear! Men found me lovely. What became of them? What became of my children's many fathers? When I became old and drooped, they abandoned me for greener pastures. They ran to young women, needy and neglected. I am needy and neglected. The only thing those women had was youth and that is everything I have come to learn. The women bore my men daughters and sons who will repeat this cycle until the last stink of this rotten world wafts over yonder sea. But there will be no end to it. I weep. I cannot see an end. I cannot see a purpose."

The acolyte spoke to her in a soothing monotone while Isaac stood over her but looked beyond. "You followed the path of nature, mother. You paid and were paid back in full. Consider yourself fortunate that the men loved you in your youth. Nothing is worse than an old woman who laments her past decisions and casts judgment on the future. Your actions were keeping with life. What would you have done? Shut yourself up in a cave? Do not cry, woman, for your lot was chosen for you when you showed the world your terrible beauty. Your sons and daughters are beautiful too, and so on and so on. Each person carries his or her past like a screaming newborn into their future. Is it not time we let the child grow?"

An order came up the ranks from the rear of the procession. Each man and woman tapped the person in front and said, "Stop!"

Priest Hildebrand shouted it, and it carried like tidal wave up the ranks. Hildebrand shifted the direction the line was traveling off the highway and onto a beach with light-colored sand, almost white but flecked with gray. As Isaac walked closer to the water's edge, he could see the particulate matter increased in size to the point where whole seashells careened onto the beach, propelled by the waves and smashed to smaller bits. Farther up the beach the sun beat down and bleached their vain hopes. The procession filed ominously down the beach and up a side of a cliff. They rested at the top. Hildebrand only spoke in locations at the margin of serenity and violent upheaval. He felt it added weight to his words, and if delivered in an all white room to an uninitiated ear, it would not have made much sense. In the bosom of nature, spoken with passion, his words sounded like creatures doing battle, engaged in strife with sharp claws. Hildebrand stood at the center of a throng. Two women attended to another woman who was screaming. Her belly swollen, her face blistering sweat in the sun, the woman dabbed saltwater onto her naked pregnant torso that they had dipped onto their white smocks from the breaking waves.

Hildebrand spoke over her anguish. "Our dear sister is going through the holy pains of childbirth. I see this as a fitting backdrop to make our recitations of the Holy One to Crown Prophet of Mashgool, Glibbet Globbet Gloob. GGG was the first mouthpiece of the Mashgool in the time when the first swirling dusts coalesced into planets. His name means, well…is best translated into our human language as this. He held a small, obsidian square up to his mouth and spoke the words "Glibbet Globbet Gloob."

The square purred, "He who is most high among the mouthpieces of Mashgool, the receptacle of the highest wisdom, First King of all Kings."

The people murmured among themselves. It broke as quick as it began.

"Glibbet Globbet Gloob impelled the Mashgool to cease their ways of strife and spread their civilization and religion across the stars. He is the King of all Kings. The Lord of Hosts. The Transfinite Precursor to Infinity. He has never died and returned. He was not born. He cannot die."

"It sounds like rubbish to me," a man said.

A few men, burly and foreboding, true believers, shouted at the man with raised arms, "Don't you know where the hell you're going? Get the hell out of 'ere if you don't want to be saved!"

Hildebrand, quick thinking, maintained order. He said, "Anyone who does not wish to hear a message as old as the stars delivered unto Glibbet Globbet Gloob will be missing a message as old as time and as meaningful to your existence as the very sun which warms our skins."

A few people trickled off. The man who voiced disapproval convinced a few people around him to leave. The pregnant woman continued her wailing. The women serving as midwives did their best to quiet her and stuck a salty sea stick into her mouth. They implored her to clamp down. The woman complained that the stick was sandy and spit out the grains. A plastic water bottle that a child found on the shore was substituted. It crinkled and collapsed as she bit down. The midwife parted the woman's sweaty black hair and encouraged her with soothing words.

Hildebrand reiterated his call for any apostates or phonies to leave now. "I tell you," he said, "you will not pass the test to enter Moojtema as an acolyte. The penalties are severe for failures. There are no second chances. Leave now if you only want a free ticket inside because none are to be had!"

A couple trailed off, walking down the beach hand in hand. An old man walked off alone, muttering to himself about how hot the sun was and how much nonsense the priest spewed with every breath. "I'd rather die alone on the beach," he called back to the crowd from a distance. "You made me come all the way out here, and you still didn't tell me the reason!"

Hildebrand laughed. It was a laugh unlike any Isaac ever heard come from the lungs of a self-proclaimed holy man. It began with a slight cackle, like the call of a crow to its compatriots: dinner bell from a rotting tasty corpse, rising up several octaves to the shrill scream of a woman penetrated by an overly adequate phallus; it crashed into the sound of stone grating against metal before Hildebrand went silent.

Hildebrand looked to the crowd with bright, gray eyes the color of death that became nearly white when in the sunlight. Maybe they are made of mirrors, Isaac thought. Alien technology, nothing the Institute possesses. They were unnatural, much like the sounds about to come from Hildebrand's mouth. The message exuded from his mouth as a devilish mixture of gastric noises and farts. He made the speech with his throat and tongue clapping and slapping off his palate. He held the small, obsidian-looking square near the emanations. A man in the crowd laughed. It escaped from him like the whinny of a horse. Hildebrand disregarded it at first. Like a fire in the forest, the laughter spread in the crowd. The source of the laughter was now on the ground, rolling over the small grasses that dotted the cliff top. Hildebrand stopped. He scowled at the man who interrupted what he thought to be the most beautiful poem ever composed.

Hildebrand looked at the muscular men who silenced the doubters and debaters previously. He smiled at them and shouted, "Would you kindly toss him in the ocean!"

The man sat up. He put struggled to get up before the brutes reached him.

"What it's funny! It sounds funny!" the man yelled as they grabbed him by his arms and legs.

The men heave hoed him in a one two three swinging motion over the cliff. He screamed until he cleared the cliffside and could no longer be heard.

The people in the crowd looked at each other in shock, but no one made a peep. Some of the women's faces that were previously full of joyous exultation now took on the stone worry of a tomb. Still no one walked away.

Hildebrand continued with his Psalter, or whatever it was. Isaac thought the noises sounded strange but was eager to hear what came out of the little black voice box when Hildebrand finished farting with his mouth.

The waves crashed and withdrew at least twenty times. Isaac found it a pleasant excursion for his sense of hearing from the strange, inhuman sounds Hildebrand made.

Finally the priest stopped and smiled at the crowd. Some of the women in the crowd smiled back. Everyone craned to hear.

The pregnant woman, who had been gagged for Hildebrand's speech now screamed out loud again. The baby's head was crowning. The midwife encouraged her but still the mother-to-be continued her screaming and panting. The midwife said gently, "Just think, dearie, your child will be born on the beautiful beach in the glorious sunshine."

Hildebrand brought the obsidian device over his head and pulled the sleeve of his black woolen habit down. He sweated heavily in the coarse wool. Isaac wondered why the priest kept the heavy woolens on. Some of the women were overcome by the heat and let their white robes open. The cool sea breeze tickled their firm breasts, licking the sweat in the sunshine. Isaac stared this time. He found even the older women's breasts worthy of praise.

The obsidian square delivered the message of hope eternal and greetings to the crowd. The voice was deep and foreboding. Isaac wished the voice was that of a woman, but it was a man's voice and slightly metallic at the end. It sounded to Isaac like the Paraclete Tanner's voice.

"In praise of the time of our violence, the weak tribes were ripped from the universe's infernal womb, never to return. Wiped from the slate and erased. You have prepared the way for the coming of the universe to its full fruition. You are the fruition of the universe. You have been designed by the Holy One, the Lord, to be busy. You gather up the masses with no direction and convert their energies to your own. You have dominion over all you meet. Your purposes are the Holy One's purpose. Questions of meaning are imponderable. Your very improbable existence is meaning enough. You will rise from your simple asteroid. Your descendants will be as numerous as the dusts of the universe. The races you meet are not in my favor. Any intelligence is beneath yours. Offer the races of the universe the gifts I bestow upon you; bend them to your glorious will. Mashgool. You, too, will go astray. Every billion years I send unto you a corrector in your course to infinity. You will know I have not forgotten my children in the empty gases. You shall know the corrector. He shall come bearing my infinite wisdom. Listen. Listen. Listen."

Past the whitecaps on the farthest stretch of ocean, Isaac could see only the margin of the sky's blue. It was not nearly as far as this strange message traveled. Five waves crashed onto the shore in the space of time that Hildebrand announced the basic principles of the Mashgool. The belches and farts came with greater staccato and ended with a quarter note high-pitched fart noise that Hildebrand formed by sticking the tiniest triangle tip of his tongue through his lips and squeezing the accumulated air from his cheeks past it.

"These principles are for eating. Take them and make them a part of you. Make their energy your energy. Make them part of your body like the star heat that radiates life. These principles are not binding. You may choose as you will. But you must choose principles in this life. Otherwise you are a slave.

"ONE! Your energy can be expended for work or stored. You must design your own system to put your energies into; otherwise, you are a slave being used for another's purposes. Seek to perfect your system even though perfection is impossible."

"TWO! Choose your partners in this life well. Make certain they will not harm you. Do no harm to them. Accept only the strongest mates and seek to be the strongest. The future will be rewarded."

"THREE! Generations proceed from the corruption and decay of previous generations. In our total conquest of Alerzion, twenty-thousand Mashgool generations passed into nothingness before we contained them to their home planet and they devoted their lives to us. Never think you are the end-all-be-all of existence. You are nothing but a waypoint to the future."

"FOUR! Accept your death as you accept your life. You did not choose to be born. You cannot choose not to die. We discovered technology to enable immortality. Several among have chosen immortality for themselves. It caused a civil war that nearly destroyed our civilization. The quest for personal immortality is the bane of life in the universe. Immortality comes when the old and tired die after having paved the way for the youth. This is species without end."

Isaac looked into the crowd. Many dozed off into sleep, snoring softly in the sand. The woman in the midst of her birthing pangs stopped her screaming. She followed the midwife's advice and started breathing in short rhythmic pulses. The midwife patted her head down and held her hand. The woman sent a young man running to the sea to fill the water bottle up. He returned panting with cold water. The midwife poured it over the pregnant woman's thighs, washing away the blood that trickled into the now pink sand.

The head appeared and then an arm. One leg. And then, nothing else, only a small unformed nub for the other arm and leg. One half was perfect, the other half left out. The midwife screamed. The pregnant woman fainted. Onlookers thronged around. Women shouted. Their men held them back. The baby writhed with the normal half; its umbilical cord still connected it to its mother. It screamed like one of the innumerable gulls that ripped and tore at the washed up seashells. The midwife clutched the child to her breast. The mother did not move.

"Where is the rest of you, dearie?" she said to the infant. The young man returned and gasped as he handed her the cold seawater. She poured over the infant and washed it clean.

Hildebrand looked at the babe with wild eyes, "A test of our principles brothers and sisters! It is an omen!"

"Of what?" some women said.

"Our belief in the principles!"

"What do the principles tell us, priest?" the midwife said.

"Toss the child to the sea!" Hildebrand screamed.

"Toss the child to the sea!" the burly men echoed.

"She can make another! But this time, choose a more suitable lover!" Hildebrand yelled, then broke into a laugh.

"She is dead!" The midwife wailed, clutching the culprit to her chest.

"The child will never survive this world. Moojtema will never accept it. It longs for perfection. Remember the principles!"

One of the women from the back yelled, "Damn you and your principles, priest! What does the child's mother say?"

"She's dead! Bled out all over the sand!" the midwife screamed.

The woman stepped forward, "Then I will take the child with me and depart you crowd of fools. Priest, your principles will only create a Hell on this earth."

"The principles are not from this earth; they are from far beyond anything you can imagine. Do what you will though. I predict that you and the baby will be devoured by sunrise. The woods are lonely, old mother. There is not a man in sight who will help you."

"Listen, priest. I don't know what you believe in, but I cannot stand by and let this child be tossed into the ocean. I will love it like it was my own and my breasts will respond to my intentions."

Hildebrand laughed at them. The others stood around sheepishly wondering what would happen.

Isaac wanted desperately to tell the woman to take the child to the Institute. He had to remember his present company and keep his mouth silent. He raged inside. The child could be saved! He wanted to toss Hildebrand into the ocean. He could not. He was on a mission.

A man came forward, "I will go with this woman. I cannot stand to see an innocent child destroyed."

"Suit yourselves!" Hildebrand mocked with disapproval in his voice. He became very quiet and spoke to himself. Isaac heard him. "Giving up paradise for a helpless freak better dashed upon the rocks," he said.

The man cut the umbilical cord and wrapped the child in his mother's robe, leaving her naked body with black, dead eyes fixed towards the sky. Hildebrand reached down and closed them. He belched a few words over her toward the burly gang of men.

"Toss her to the sea."

The men grabbed the dead mother up and followed the order of the young priest with silver eyes. No one spoke of what had happened. As the pilgrimage procession approached the outer gates of Moojtema, Isaac walked near the priest and attempted to engage him in conversation. Hildebrand's eyes were focused in the distance, and Isaac's words seemed to just melt through his ears and not stick. Isaac trailed behind him and watched the priest as he slithered from one acolyte to the next, nodding, laughing and smiling at them with a mouth that disguised razors.

The needle that scraped space came closer and closer with each step the giant caterpillar took. Thin like a line on the horizon, it gained depth and width the closer the procession crept. As they neared, some of the tired pilgrims began to cheer, whooping into the heavens like the cranes that speared frogs in the canals and marshlands and paid no attention to the silliness of men.

Hildebrand walked confidently among his flock that he shepherded to the gates of Moojtema. How many of them would fail? He cared not. He did not care if any of them made it into Moojtema. His orders were to bring them to the gates for their test. By doing that, he had saved them. Isaac cornered him after his last sermon before they descended into the valley. Like all the holy fools he had known in his life, his departed Grandmother included, Isaac found Hildebrand to be a man of few words of his own.

"Just what is that space needle there?" Isaac asked to Hildebrand on the off chance that the priest would talk to him.

"I'm not sure, son. Why do you ask?"

"It's all I've seen for the past week. You can see it from hundreds of miles away. I figured you would know because you're from Moojtema."

"I'm not. I'm from the outside, just like you, son. I've never been inside. So I have no idea."

"If you've never been inside, how did you learn that poetry, you know, the strange tongue you speak in."

"That was taught to me by my master, his excellence, Tugg Powell. He worked his way into the city just as we all hope to."

"Why do you want to go there so badly?"

"It is Heaven. Or, so I've heard," Hildebrand said.

"How did Powell earn his way inside?" Isaac asked.

"He brought one-hundred-thousand to the gates."

"That's it? Then they let him in?"

"He shepherded them well, recruited them from their villages, and convinced them through the power of his words," Hildebrand said with a smile.

"How many have you brought Hildebrand?"

"I've been doing this for fifteen years of my life. I do about thirty pilgrimages a year, back and forth. Some are a trickle some are a deluge of souls. It all depends. If the times on the outside's good people don't want to go in, they pick up during the winter."

"So judging from the hundreds here," Isaac began.

Hildebrand interrupted him, "There are one-thousand two-hundred and forty-four, wait thirty-eight now. A few disbelievers walked away. Plus there was that unfortunate birth," Hildebrand said.

Isaac bit his tongue, not wanting to go down the path of confrontation. "Maybe you've escorted near one-hundred-thousand?"

"Tens of thousands, but I don't keep track. They do. They have the tally. They keep the ledger in the Book of Life."

"You convince them with the principles?"

"No, most are here for the benefits only. They'll study the principles so they can talk the talk and walk the walk, but when it comes down to it they don't give a damn about the principles. If I said that one of the principles was that they had to savagely kill the man next to them and make love to their sister, many would gladly do it."

"That woman back there wouldn't throw that poor child into the sea," Isaac said.

"I know. I was hoping she would walk away. Still, I was trying to save that child the misery of its existence," Hildebrand said proudly, folding his arms against his chest as he walked.

"I was born deformed, Priest. I was cured," Isaac said, unable to hold his anger back.

"You look normal enough to me. Was it a miraculous cure, then?"

"I fell in with some scientists," Isaac said.

Isaac heard metallic scratching worm its way through his head. *Make no mention of the Institute to this man, Isaac!*

Isaac grimaced, barely able to contain the need to answer Commander Jacobus.

"What's wrong, man?" Hildebrand said.

"Ahh, my affliction. I hear voices sometimes. The bastards cured me, but they left me with some side effects," Isaac said wincing.

"Ahh, yes. The so-called miracles of science. They cure your ailments and introduce ten others," Hildebrand said laughing. "It's all too hard for me. I don't have the mind for that. I've got a memory for the Mashgool language and their poetry. I can recite stanzas and principles, but ask me to think of something original, and I'm lost."

"Me neither, no mind for science. I really envy those that have it."

"I don't. They can have all their tables and their secret knowledge. They can keep it all for themselves. I just want its benefits."

"Right," Isaac said.

"Do you know that the Mashgool worked exactly in converse to what happened on this planet? In their infancy as a civilization they were a barbaric people. They constantly fought amongst themselves. Each family fought every other family for supremacy. They did not question whether all the warring or fighting was proper or ethical. They just did it because that was all they knew. They had to make weapons in order to survive. They needed technology to dominate their opponents who were all around them. That was their way of life. It is all there in the Vast Canticle of Mashgool. All the millions of years," Hildebrand said.

He produced a thick volume from the front of his black wool cassock and showed Isaac page after page of tightly stacked concentric circles.

"When I get inside Moojtema, I'll teach you," Hildebrand said.

Dogs barked and howled in the distance. Hildebrand piqued like a cat hearing a mouse rustling in the tall grasses. He called the procession to a halt.

"Where there are dogs there are usually people," he said to Isaac. "Especially the whimpering sissy dogs we just heard."

He called the thugs to his side, and the bald men were drooling with anticipation. Isaac did not like their look,; their eyes seemed to lack any life, like they had seen too much in their youth and gone away feeling dead inside from it. For some reason, Hildebrand bade Isaac to follow him and the men. They cut through the dunes and saw a walled compound at the edge of the forest. Hildebrand demanded a pair of looking glasses. A bald thug with a face like a piece of meat, strained and visceral, produced them from his off gray cassock. Isaac could see that it was white at one time, but age and coatings of grease had made it dull gray. Underneath the cassock the man had a bright pink bag that strapped around his waist. As his cassock was splayed to the side, Isaac could see the contents of the bag that zippered closed; inside the thug had a shiny silver pistol.

"See anything, boss?" one thug, a blockheaded man with head that looked shaved with acid, said. He wore his robe like a cape and had a small leather for his genitals.

"Shut it. I'm looking."

"There's a fire. People live there," Hildebrand said.

"When we going, boss?"

"What's this I see? Is that a woman?"

A smile came across his face even as the binoculars were still on his face.

"A nice blondie. Look at her! What a site to behold."

"Top dollar in Moojtema," the thug said. "She look better than the biddies in the procession?"

"Exquisite. She's drawing a bath. Her breasts are like full moons."

"Think she wants to come with us, boys?" Hildebrand said.

One of the thugs whooped like an idiot. The blockheaded thug slapped him. They started to argue.

"Shut it ree-rees," Hildebrand said. "We'll go."

Isaac said, "Maybe we should leave them alone. You never know where there's women there are men, maybe armed better than you."

"Nonsense. We just want to go and talk to them. You know, missionary style," Hildebrand said laughing. His laugh sounded more sinister now, like a crow cawing with a hole whistling in its throat.

One of the thugs who had not spoken previously and only stood back and blinked copiously while the planning went on, grabbed Isaac by his shoulder and flecked spit through his rake-like teeth when he talked, "You ain't talking us out of this one, boy. Why don't you just stay put here."

"I'm just thinking of the consequences," Isaac said.

"Get lost. Go back and babysit the others. You don't believe strongly enough," the rake tooth said.

"Just sit this one out," Hildebrand said.

"You better be here when we return," the blockhead menaced.

Isaac walked back to the crowd. The people were tired and clung to the small amounts of shade they found under windblown trees, small and salt poisoned. Some of the old men looked to be near the edge of the precipice between life and an abyss.

"Get these men some water," Isaac yelled at two women who chatted with a group of adoring men. The men were all smiles and fawning attention. The girls played with their hair and ordered one of the men, a small guy with eyes too widely spaced for his narrow face to find water. He complied with their orders like a servile helper monkey. Isaac sat next to the women who spoke and prattled off nonsense. One smiled innocently at Isaac and the corner of her pink lips barely crossed the threshold at the base of her nose. Isaac did not reciprocate, so her smile turned drooping to a frown. She adjusted her hair and looked off to the distance and then back at her sycophantic posse.

"What's with you?" the older of the two girls, who looked like she had been driftwood her whole life, said with a smile that revealed bright teeth and a gappy space between the two front ones.

"I am looking forward to getting to the City," Isaac said.

"Us too. We're going shopping first thing," the woman said.

"Great. What are you going to buy?" Isaac asked.

"Whatever they have. We don't care. It's all lovely."

The younger girl smiled again and nodded in agreement. She had turned her attention away from the fawns when Isaac began talking to her friend.

"Yep. Whatever a girl wants, it's there."

Isaac listened in the distance. but he heard nothing. He breathed a sigh of relief for a moment and then heard a few muffled shots in the distance. Only he could tell what they were because only he was listening. No one else reacted. A few more waves crashed. A few more shots popped in the distance.

The girls kept babbling about what they wanted to buy. They had no idea what was for sale. They had no idea they were for sale. They wanted it all.

"Couches in the shape of hearts," one giggled.

"T-shirts."

"Jewelry!" they said in unison and laughed.

The older girl screamed.

Hildebrand staggered over the dune. A bright splash of crimson blood coated the front of his tunic like a military sash. His thugs dragged the blonde by her hair over the dune crest.

Hildebrand called to the lazing, tired people, "Whoever wants to try and tame this wild woman can."

The thugs dragged her over the dune, and her ass left a double streak in the shifting sand. A few of the fawning young men followed the thugs over the dune.

One of the tired old men called to Hildebrand, "Just what the hell kind of pilgrimage are you running here?"

Hildebrand shot him a gaze from Hell and said, "The Mashgool have shown us a religion of strength, something you know nothing of, grandfather."

After this incident a few more pilgrims trickled away. Some of the old people walked to the compound, now emptied of life, and busied themselves making it their own. A room with a view by the beach was not a bad place to spend one's golden years.

As one old woman left with the geriatrics, she yelled to Hildebrand, "You're a pied piper if I've ever seen one!"

"The old and useless have departed us, you brave, young children!" Hildebrand announced.

The thugs took their time with the blonde. She trailed behind them with a cruel yoke around her neck fashioned from branches stripped from scrub trees. Hildebrand laughed and force-marched the youth forward to Moojtema. Days passed and Isaac marched on like a drone staring at the luscious round bottom of one of the faithful women. The needle swelled in the distance; Isaac suppressed his excitement.

From the standoff distance, where the pilgrimage train crested and began its descent into the valley, beyond the pearly gate Moojtema loomed like a wart on the skin of a baby. The gate was not really pearl, but composed of a plastic stronger than steel, white in color, and so slippery to the touch so that no human no matter how nimble could amble themselves over it. Behind the pearly gate that opened for them automatically, Moojtema projected huge and bulbous from the earth's surface with no warning. Unlike most earthen cities, surrounded by shanties and lean-tos, Moojtema assaulted the surface with silver walls, gleaming in the sun, violent walls that echoed the sun's rays toward heaven. They were sloped like a Guggenheim and over one-thousand feet tall. The great gash assaulted the earth's surface as far as the eye could see.

The inner wall had a coefficient of friction less than that of ice on ice. Behind them metal tubes hundreds of feet in diameter lie coiled like great chromosomes. The circumference of Moojtema took up an entire valley, in the past known as the San Bernardino Valley, the location of Moojtema was described in the TADHUK as having been built over the ruins of a city of ancients best known for producing entertainment. According to the TADHUK, The city was the first to be wiped from the face of the earth by the Mashgool. In previous human conflicts the city turned its lust for money into making propaganda films that aided the war effort. The Mashgool could not have this happening again, and according to the TADHUK the city of Los Angeles was liquidated and reduced to ashes in a day.

Moojtema's surface was anticlimactic for Isaac. He dreamed that it would have more lights. In photographs he saw on the TADHUK, cities all had lights that blazed in the darkness of night and made eternal day for their inhabitants. There were no widows on the surface of Moojtema. Isaac speculated the inhabitants had little to no eyesight, like rats living in caves that supplanted their vision with an outrageously developed sense of smell.

On the whole, it looked like an alien appendage grafted onto a human body. Moojtema jumped out like a circus freak, particularly the needle that Isaac first witnessed from hundreds of miles away. The entirety of Moojtema concentrated in that needle like a giant phallus aimed to pierce the wet folds of the sky. There were no lights on the needle, for there were no airplanes to avoid collisions with it. Isaac traced its path and looked for an apex but could not see one. It just faded into the blueness of the sky.

The pilgrims formed a line and Isaac fell in with them. A narrow passageway formed in the shiny metal surface; it peeled backwards, chunky Riemann sums underneath the integral, just as Isaac had seen in the Mashgool Cruiser Sanctuary. This wondrous sight, confirmed to many of the faithful, that their time was not going to be wasted. A round man who's head seemed to pop out of his body with no neck, bugged out blue eyes, and teeth long and white interspersed with gaps so his mouth looked like keys on a piano, exited the folds of Moojtema and smiled widely, lingering with his mouth open, so that one wished Etudes of Bach would spring from the player piano mouth.

Women snickered.

"What's the count, Hildebrand?"

"Lost a few on the way this time, Smythe."

"Don't you always?"

Hildebrand and the thugs received their bag of diamonds and walked back towards the pearly gate without turning to say goodbye. As he passed Isaac he smiled widely and brought his index finger across his throat like he was chopping his head clean from his shoulders. Isaac stared at the strange priest puzzled.

Smythe asked the line, "People to be screened, does anyone want to leave? This is your last chance!"

Isaac sinched his backpack down so that it was tight against him. There was no turning back after he went inside. A few last holdouts trickled away and tried to catch up with Hildebrand and his men; they were the boys that walked over the dune to have their way with the blonde woman.

"Does anyone wish to leave?"

Gunshots perforated the peace across the plain. Hildebrand's thugs shot the hangers-on and left them to lay the sun. One tried to run, but the thug took aim and dropped him before he could get back in line. His space was not saved. The faithful shuffled forward. When they looked back and saw the bodies, they were reminded that the world they came from was dangerous and full of horror. They stood wild-eyed with fear, but no one moved.

Isaac made to move out of the line. Smythe approached him, laughing heartily. "Don't even want to try? Shame on you!"

"I've something to sell," Isaac said.

"Why didn't you just take a caravan from Caravan City?"

"I tried, it didn't work out," Isaac replied taken aback by the man's jolly nature.

"Not much does in that cesspool. Please, take the test anyway. You score well, you get preferential treatment," Smythe said.

"Sure. What happens to people that fail?" Isaac asked. Anything that came from Hildebrand's lips and brain was fraught with falsity, so Isaac had to separate Hildebrand's fiction from any real happenings.

Smythe saw this as an opportunity to address the pilgrims. He walked to the center of the line and said, "There is no room in Moojtema for those who are phony, spurious, fake, charlatans, proselytizers for dead Gods, hypocrites, apostates, snake oil salesmen, witch doctors, fools, hooligans, spies, or assassins be they of character or person! There is no room for idolaters. No room for philosophers. There is only room for true believers. Think about it! Do you believe in the principles? If you do not, turn around and go back to your home and your strange ways. Don't let us discover that you only wanted to come into our illustrious city because you desire clean air, clean water, and good food for the rest of your days."

Smythe's face looked at the crowd with a gaze as serious a doctor informing a cancer patient about his slim prospects for recovery.

A few raised their hands and said they desired to leave. The blonde woman was among them. She was still in shock and some men convinced her that she should try to start a life with them.

"Okay, then!" Smythe bellowed. "Enter Moojtema behind me, no pushing, no shoving, no talking, no running, only walking, no kissing, no hugging, and no loving. Absolutely no public displays of affection are authorized. At this point forward if you desire to leave, you will require a thorough debriefing by Moojtema Security Personnel, and waiting for those bozos could take a lifetime."

The packed line of people now stood along the cold walls. All were now inside. The door closed behind them like a wave, shutting out the light.

Holy fools were often excellent actors, and Smythe was no exception. He bowed at the waist to the pilgrims and introduced himself. "My humblest apologies," he began, "I am test administrator Smythe Mapplethorpe. I'm sorry I've been so rude. You see, I'm only the lowest rung on the echelon. I live right around the corner, right when you walk into Moojtema. I'm not the Illustrious Potentate. I'm not the Sultan. I had dreams much like many of you. I'm making my dreams reality everyday in Moojtema."

His speech trailed off, he was a magnificent actor.

"Anyone want to leave?" Symthe Mapplethorpe said grinning.

"Never!" a middle-aged woman hissed.

"Oh, you're a feisty one! Come see me when you get done," Smythe said licking his lips.

"Give us the test!" she yelled.

"Extra credit for you, dear," Smythe laughed.

"Come on, stop the delaying. We're hungry!"

"Okay, I hope you're ready," Smythe Mapplethorpe said looking at the ground. "I hope you're ready."

They were led to individual rooms the size of a closet with bare metal walls. There was a camera in each corner. Isaac could see the tiny, wide-angle lens. He waved to it jokingly, wondering who was watching him. A single flat screen punctuated the otherwise bleak wall. A robotic voice bade him to stand at the intersection of two laser beams. He could see an "X" on the floor in dazzling red light. When he stood at the "X" the voice told him to remain very still. The female voice sounded tempting, but old fashioned.

"Initiating. Baseline brain scan."

Blue Lasers traced the curves of his head and were followed by a whirring in the walls like a distant avalanche of static.

"Initiating. Body scan."

This time a green laser mapped the contours of his body. I went right through his clothing.

"Initiating. Mashgool Aptitude and Reasoning Test."

"Question 1. Who are the Mashgool?"

"Uh…," Isaac said unsure of how to answer.

"Repeat Question 1. Who are the Mashgool?"

"I think," Isaac began.

"Question 1. Skipped. Question 2. Where do human beings, the species *Homo sapiens*, fit in the overriding scheme of the universe?"

280

Isaac answered, "Don't know, really."

"Question 3. How is true happiness defined by the Mashgool?"

Isaac answered, "I don't know."

"Question 4. Should a mortal being desire immortality?"

"No," Isaac answered, "There is only this life. The desire for immortality caused a civil war that nearly destroyed the Mashgool."

"Question 5. What is most desirable in the universe, according to the Mashgool?"

Isaac thought about the word that Hildebrand callously employed to justify their rape of the blonde woman.

"Strength," Isaac said.

The walls began whirring again. The static avalanche subsided into a gentle pinging, which culminated in a bell ringing.

The sexy robot voice, soft and welcoming, explained the results.

"You answered one question correctly out of five. Your brain scan indicates a general lack of emotional concurrence with the words you speak. This is not indicative of a genuine religious experience. You either do not sufficiently believe in the principles of the Mashgool, or you have not studied hard enough to warrant your acceptance into the Holy City. If you feel this is an error, please contact your test administrator. Please wait for your debriefing by the Security Personnel. We wish you a safe and pleasant journey back to your point of origin. Have a nice day."

"Total bullshit!" Isaac yelled. His own voice echoed back to him in the small chamber.

The door opened behind him. Others were still in their testing booths.

"I have something to sell!" he shouted as he ran into the hallway.

"You failed. You must leave," Smythe declared.

"But I told you I have something to sell!"

"You had better have a diamond as big as your head."

"I've something better," Isaac said.

"Go to the customs point then, but it better be good. We don't tolerate hucksters here."

"Where is it?"

"I don't know. I just work here at the place for true believers. It's not like I bought my way in here."

"Can you take me? I'll make it worth your while."

"I'm only a red badge. I'm only allowed to go to my place of duty and home. I can't go with you," Smythe said.

"Listen, can you get someone to take me to the Customs area? I've something important to sell."

"You don't have a haul with you, what could you possibly have of importance to sell to us?"

Isaac opened his bag. The Termiculum lighted up the passageway. Smythe gasped, "Where did you get that?"

"I'm good at getting things. Now you have someone take me," Isaac said.

"Is it pure?"

"Yes."

"Where did you get it?" Smythe asked again.

"Doesn't matter. All that matters is I have it. Get me somewhere I can sell it. I'll report any further delays to your superiors," Isaac said with authority.

Mapplethorpe dashed to his quarters. Isaac followed but stood outside because there was no room. It was a bed and a toilet and nothing else, for sleeping and shitting, like prison. Mapplethorpe clicked away on his computer, typing like a madman composing a novel in a dreary hotel room. Not less than a minute later two security personnel dressed in all black with faces like bricks, flat and uninspired containing no hint of emotion behind their cold eyes, entered the corridor.

"This way, sir," the shorter brick said.

"We will take you to customs right away," the taller brick said with his arms to flat to his side like a somber gravedigger exhausted at his battles with the earth.

The office was packed with people waiting in a line that stretched at least a mile, snaking around itself in a well-established grid, roped off painstakingly from interference and attempts at cutting. Isaac was sped to the head of the line. To his right there was a snack bar lit up in neon and staffed by a bored young lady. Her face was a mixture of frustration and loneliness that teetered on the fencepost of despair. She looked gorgeous with that long drawn face and black hair pulled tight against her temples in two balls. Blue eyes sliced through the center of her face like moonbeams. She moved mechanically like a robot as she made orders for customers. They dashed out of their place in line and told her to hurry before the space filled. Some of the sellers had waited for days. To their dismay, the security personnel put Isaac right at the head. The man behind him lodged a complaint.

The short brick turned to him and said, "If you had something valuable maybe you'd get to the head of the line, too?"

"Tin's valuable," the man said.

"Not as valuable as what he's got," the tall brick said.

"What's that?"

"Mind your own business," the short brick said and pointed a finger in the man's face.

Behind a bulletproof, bombproof, energy weapon-proof, and flame-proof, translucent blast shield, sat a strange little man that Isaac thought looked faintly like a lazy turtle. His nose came to a point in the middle of his face and his forehead and jaw line gently sloped towards it. He wore black body armor, which made up the turtle shell. He spoke with a nasally voice that annoyed Isaac. As soon as Isaac spoke to the turtle, he wanted to run away and cover his ears. Isaac noticed an amber chip hanging around his neck next to an identification card. The thin plastic wafer had a picture of him that looked more hideous than the gentleman did in person. The turtle launched into his pre-recorded greeting. It was almost like talking to a computer, but the turtle could blink.

"Hello, good sir, I understand you have something special for us?"

"Perhaps."

"And, yes, good sir, are we expecting you?"

"No. I don't think so."

"I've not been informed of any manifest bearing the load you have."

"I guess you aren't expecting me then," Isaac said and smiled.

"I've been instructed to take the substance off your hands, sir."

"What do I get in return?"

"Do you know the approximate value of what you have?"

"Of course I do. Why do you think I came straight here?"

"How did you find the substance? I'm told it is quite rare."

"I'm an adventurer. Don't ask me any more questions."

"Right, sir, I only have one more for you. Please be honest with me."

"What?"

"How much do you think the Life is worth?"

"My life?"

"No. The substance you have, the Life? How much do you think it is worth?"

"It's priceless I'm told."

"I just need the value for the customs form," the Turtle said, and typed viciously into the computer sunken into the desk in front of him.

"It is worth whatever you're willing to pay. What are you willing to pay?"

The voice of God, or rather Robert Tanner, rang out in his head. *Don't settle for anything but an all access pass and plenty of credits. That way you don't have to worry about having a dumb job or place of duty. You have time to concentrate on your mission.* Isaac grimaced. "I'm not a moron!" Isaac snapped.

"Excuse me, sir?"

"Sorry. Hey where do the women come from the outside?"

"What do you mean, sir?"

"The women, the beautiful women from the outside that you allow admission to. Where do they go?"

"Ahh, yes, those women. They go for a physical and if they pass, then they go inside. I don't know, sir. I'm not a beautiful woman."

"You're impossible. What's your name?"

"Clerk, sir."

"Clark?"

"Clerk, sir. We don't have names here. That is considered extraneous nonsense. We have functions, pure and simple."

"Your name, sir? I need it for the customs form."

"Isaac."

Turtle the Clerk tapped out the remainder of the form slipping his tongue in and out of his mouth as he concentrated.

"I've your quote, sir."

"One point six five seven eight pounds of pure Life, comes to five point five seven eight three repeating billion credits."

"Is that good?"

"That's excellent, sir," Turtle said flabbergasted.

"Throw in an all access pass. You have those, right?"

"I cannot just give you that, sir," Turtle said

"Why can't you?"

"No one has all access. It can't be done."

"Let me speak to your manager, then," Isaac said coldly.

"I am the manager here, sir," Turtle said unfazed by Isaac's rudeness.

"Let me speak to someone who knows something, then. I need a pass anywhere and everywhere in Moojtema."

"The best I can offer you is Level X Diamond Pass. That offers the most luxurious housing accommodations and access to the finest stores. He winked at Isaac and said, "It also gives you access to something else, champ." Turtle winked again. It was creepy.

"What are you getting at?"

"You get access to the best women in Moojtema, too. Moojtema's finest."

"How so?"

"They all want a level X'er. They have a saying. The best sex with a level X."

Isaac grinned. "We'll see."

"Okay, so we have a deal? Five point five seven eight three repeating billion credits in exchange for your one point six five seven eight pounds of pure Life."

"Yes, do it."

Turtle's screen flashed red. It highlighted his lips giving him the appearance of wearing lipstick.

"Sorry. I'm only authorized to deposit twenty percent of the total into your account. The remainder will be deposited when the Life is tested at 99.9 percent pure. Of course, you'll get your Level X Pass right now."

"I don't have an account."

"With your permission I'll create one for you right now. You'll just have to sign the Life over to me."

"Create the account first. Then I will sign the Termiculum over to you."

"Okay…Wait! What did you call it?"

"The Life. I said the Life."

"I could have sworn you said something else," Turtle said looking suspiciously through his glass cage. "I will create your account now."

"Divide by ten carry the twenty round out the prime factorial of pi subdivided by the nth digit of the infinite Fibonacci series…blah blah blah…and your total comes to, one billion point one one five six six Moojtema credits."

"Sure thing," Isaac said.

The counter in front of Isaac lit up and displayed:

XXXXXXXXXXXXXXXXXXXXXXXXXXXXXXXXXXXXXXXXXXXXXXXXXXX

Account: XXXXXXXXX7097536el3-cf-93-2231488

Account Owner: Isaac

Account Balance: 1,115,660,000 MC

Deposits: 1,115,660,000 MC

Withdrawals: 0.00 MC

XXXXXXXXXXXXXXXXXXXXXXXXXXXXXXXXXXXXXXXXXXXXXXXXXXX

"Is that a lot?" Isaac asked.

"You're one of the richest men in Moojtema. Maybe Random Robbie has more money than you, who knows. I only get paid four-hundred credits a year to sit at this desk," Turtle said sighing.

"Jesus Christ," Isaac said.

"You're rich."

Isaac turned to leave with the possibilities for the huge sum of money already burrowing through his brain like mind worms.

"Wait, sir!"

"What is it, man? Aren't you ever done?"

"You haven't received your level ten pass or identification card yet."

"Oh, yes," Isaac said. He had more money than time now. His patience with Turtle was wearing to a shred.

"Sir, do you see the small box to your right? Please look into it."

Isaac looked over at the indentation in the wall.

"Here?!" he asked.

A flash popped and temporarily blinded him.

"Jesus!"

"Sorry, I had to take your photo for your identification card. It's printing now."

Turtle slid the still warm card to Isaac through the shallow receiving slot. The photograph was hideous. Isaac only had one eye open. His lips were pursed like he was about to blow someone a kiss. One of his eyebrows was raised like he was scolding a child for misbehaving. Worse, he saw there were a few unsightly pimples on his forehead. He raised his hands to them to gauge their weight.

"Can I have a redo?"

"Not possible, sir. I've already attached the photograph to your file and your Person Page. It can't be undone right now. As for the identification card, don't bend it, don't submerge it, don't wear it in the shower, don't expose it to temperatures in excess of three-hundred degrees Fahrenheit."

"Damn! Why don't you tell people that there is a photograph so they are spared a horrible fate like mine?"

"Sorry, sir, I will try to do that in the future. Please step to your double doors to the right. That is the medical portion of your inprocessing."

Isaac placed the hideous identification card and access badge around his neck and proceeded through the double doors careful that the envious stares of the people waiting in line did not burn up his newfound riches.

The Turtle smiled when he looked at the picture. There was no way that any woman would want the rich man when she looked at his Person Page and stared at freak show. Horrible initial photographs were just one way that Clerk got back at the people he could never be. He stared at the photograph and laughed again.

Isaac was greeted by a figure with a slim waist in an all white smock with a white mask that obscured facial recognition. This was similar to what he saw the doctors wearing in the Institute, but was far cleaner. Nothing looked frayed or out of place. He assumed the person under the white was a woman because of the hips and snow-capped mountaintops underneath the smock. She spoke in a high-pitched metallic voice.

"Undress, please."

"Everything?" Isaac asked incredulously.

"Yes. Everything. Anything of origin from the outside will be burned. Remember to remove everything from your pockets. For Mashgool's sake, don't leave your identification card in your pocket. That's your life from here on out. Give it to me; I have to encode it with all your data."

He handed her the identification card. She looked at his photo and laughed.

"This photo doesn't do your looks justice," she said.

"The man who took it wouldn't let me have a redo."

"You let that amber idiot tell you what to do?"

Isaac swallowed hard. There was much he had to learn.

"You're X level, baby. You can do whatever you want around here. Get those clothes off," she demanded.

He palmed the diamond studded X badge and tossed his clothing to the side.

"You're a big boy," she said.

"I was always thought I was too skinny," Isaac said laughing nervously.

"I'm talking about that missile you've got."

"What are you, a doctor? Where did you study?" Isaac said changing the subject. He sounded like a moron.

"No. No doctors here. I'm just here to take your samples."

"What samples?"

"Blood. Saliva. Fat Cells. Semen."

"What for?"

"Identification purposes. Also if you're suitable, you'll be enrolled into the Gene Flow Extension Program."

"What?"

"Our breeding program. Everybody that is anybody is enrolled into it. From the looks of you, you'll do just fine. You can never tell though; sometimes even the most handsome looking strong men like yourself have nasty little surprises in their woodpile. Maybe some naughty little genetic disease waiting to crop up when you least expect it."

She produced an elongated silver prod. She pressed a button on the silver body and the device made a sound like a flock of birds chirping in the distance.

"Stick this in your mouth."

Isaac complied with her wishes. He put the metal on his tongue and his mouth was instantly dry. He coughed as she removed the probe from his mouth.

"Dis suck all my spit aveigh," he mumbled.

"Sorry. Get some water from that fountain there."

Isaac walked to the wall and bent over to drink from a fountain of water in a nook that continuously bubbled from the center of a basin. It looked decorative, and he hated to disturb its beautiful flow. The water was clean and he drank heartily. He felt a sharp pinch on his buttocks like a bee sting. He rose up and hit his head hard on the ceiling of the nook.

"Damn it!" he shouted rubbing the tender area.

"Fat sample's done," the woman said with delight. "Believe me it's best to surprise you with that one."

Isaac stared ahead at her trying to see through her white coveralls.

"Hold your arm out. Time to draw some blood, stud."

"Can you just take it from my finger?" Isaac said, remembering his mission in the flurry of money and compliments.

The white figure seemed puzzled. "We usually take it from a vein."

"That will probably hurt," Isaac said.

"No it doesn't. The device numbs the area before it extracts the sample."

"Please, from the finger. Please, do it for me?" Isaac said in his best tender voice.

The white figure laughed. "Are you that big of a coward?"

"I am. I can't stand pain. Only pleasure."

"Okay, hold it out."

Isaac held his finger up to her proudly. The same finger that had formerly been bitten off and was now loaded with cells with containing the Gideons encoded into his very DNA.

"What happened to it?" she said.

"Accident in the forest."

"That's a dangerous place, right?"

"It is."

"You must be really strong to have survived that place," she said. Gripping his finger tightly in her gloved hands. She pulled him in close and his manhood glanced off her midsection. She moaned slightly under her mask. She pressed the device to his finger and pushed the button. Fire shot through his finger into his hand and up to his elbow.

"Damn, that hurts!" Isaac said.

"Sorry. You're the baby that wanted the sample from your finger."

"When will that go into the database?" Isaac asked.

"Could take a while. We're sort of backlogged around here," she said. "Now comes the fun part."

She put a special attachment on the tip of the probe. It looked like a pair of lips, soft and squishy, molded from rubber.

"Put this over the glans of that missile you've got there," she said lustily.

Isaac felt nervous. "Will it hurt?" he asked.

"No. Actually, it will be quite the opposite. Does it fit tight?"

"Yes."

"It's the right size."

"What is?"

"The probe tip. And you," she said.

She pressed the button. The gummy tip heated up to 98.6 degrees. Isaac's penis swelled immediately to its full size. He thrust his legs together uncontrollably. The feeling bubbled from his testes and he orgasmed into the collector. It took about three seconds.

"Nice, right?" she said.

"What the hell is that thing?"

"It isn't for sale anymore, that's for sure," she said laughing. "It was offered on the market a few years back but none of the men came out of their homes anymore."

"I can see why. Am I done?"

She didn't respond. She plugged the tip of the probe into the wall and pressed a button. The samples each rotated around the central axis and the computer shot beams of light into them. The slot that held his identification card pulsated with light and he could hear the vibrations.

"All done here. All encoded. Listen, I'd love to spend more time with you later."

Isaac looked at the floor.

"I understand, I'm just a yellow disker anyways. You'd never like me if you saw those level ten chicks."

He stepped into a chamber labeled "FOREIGN PARTICLE SCAN." Isaac gritted his teeth while the laser beams searched his body. He was afraid they would find the hidden communication implant. Tanner learned from his mistakes. The implants were biological, crafted from the DNA and cellular material of the recipient. When the door opened and the implants were not discovered, Isaac breathed a sigh of relief. Another woman dressed in white gave him a standard gray uniform to wear. It was one-piece with aluminum thread interwoven throughout. The lady in white told him it was bacteriostatic and flame retardant. Isaac nodded. She tugged hard at his waist straps in order to insure that he wouldn't get out of the uniform quickly if he had to piss. It had an elastic waistband. She gave him a pair of boots that fastened with Velcro. They were warm and comfortable like moccasins, and were a welcome departure from the Tanner Industries Combat Boot Mark IX boots that were rugged and dependable on missions but not comfortable for leisure activities. The boots went into the incinerator along with his clothing, clanging along the duct as they dropped hundreds of miles into the ground. Had the lady in white been more observant, she would have noted the manufacturer's label and reported Isaac as a spy. She was too taken by his blue eyes that reminded her of mountain lakes that she saw in the GOD as a child during her lessons -- Lake Mead or something like that. It was now dried up, she assumed. Like the rest of the outside world, it was all a never-ending horror. Isaac, coming from the outside world, intrigued her. She heard that all the men out there were roughshod rapists. He seemed nice, almost gentle. His charm put her off guard long enough for him to get what he wanted from her: her assistance in completing his mission.

As he walked through the threshold underneath a sign that read "NO EXIT" he saw a great glowing sign that read "WELCOME TO MOOJTEMA, A CITY OF WONDER AND LIGHT."

Ahead of him, he saw his wife. She stood three-hundred feet tall, draped down the center of an atrium that ran the entire length of a chromosomal tubule. The poster began at her feet, clad in stilettos, legs extended to the place where the giant sky should have started if it was visible. Her breasts dripped down the banner like a tear from a giant, and form fitting clothing accentuated curves that Isaac had never seen but wanted desperately, her black hair cascaded like a waterfall past her shoulders and ended a tousled screeching halt at her waist, her green penetrating eyes fixed on some far distant object. Her hand extended pointing at something, perhaps approaching, perhaps leaving. Her face was expressionless. Beneath her feet, the words BEAUTY printed in gold.

Isaac stood and stared with his mouth open, ignoring the flow of traffic around him. He could not breath. He felt the immensity of the place crushing him like a tiny flea trapped in an engine.

"Get out of the way *Level Effer*!" one lady screamed. She moved past him as soon as her words made contact with his eardrums. He did not break his stare at the poster. His wife was so close to him.

"Move it! Go with the flow *Effer*!"

Isaac struggled to remain in place. No one parted ways for him. He bumped into a man, tall and thin with a long nose and small blue eyes. The man's head, like all the others, was down on the floor as if he wanted to avoid falling in a hole. The man glared at Isaac and screamed, "Fancypants!"

"Where is that woman?" Isaac asked him.

"What woman?" the man yelled over the cacophony of bips and bongs, drum beats and orchestral crescendos playing to the masses.

"That woman there!" he screamed pointing to his wife's poster.

"That's no woman! Its an advertisement," the man said.

"What?"

"An advertisement! She's selling that fragrance, BEAUTY. Smells like a mixture of apples and hog dung. Disgusting. Only whores like her wear it. They love it. Men swoon to them like drunken bees. Whatever…she isn't from here. Those gorgeous level effers never come down here. The men come down here looking to score with our women, but their women never come down. Pity. Seems like all you have to do to be a level effer woman is be gorgeous. As a man it's more difficult. You must've worked your ass off, fancypants. Now get out of my way. I'm late for a very important meeting, you lost fancypants twerp."

The man pushed back into his position in the flow. Isaac watched him walk away with his head down. Isaac struggled against limbs and torsos as people all tried to get where they were going as individuals. No one talked to each other. Everyone seemed in a hurry. He finally picked his way forward to the man. The man walked like one leg was longer than the other.

"Where are you going?" Isaac asked him.

"Down to the employment office. What's it to you?"

"You're looking for work?"

"Yes, I am. My last employer went on pilgrimage."

"Where?"

"Are you new here? You just bought your way in?"

"Yes, my name's Isaac."

"Awfully young to have bought your way into the big city," the man said. "What did you do out there?"

"Hunted. Adventured. I managed to save up enough to come here. Found something really valuable and sold it to them."

"You need a Butler?"

"I may, I don't even have a place."

"I tell you what, good sir, I'll help you get a place if you hire me."

"What's pilgrimage?"

"You are fresh in the door, aren't you?"

"Yes. I just got out of medical."

"Pilgrimage is when a person is so in love with the principles and religion of the Mashgool that they willingly volunteer to go on to the Mashgool's home planet to learn further precepts and eventually be counted among the saved. Then they go on to spread the news to other planets. Humans make wonderful ambassadors, I'm told."

"What's your name?" Isaac asked.

"You are new here," he said. "My job. That's all you'll know me as. Butler."

"Let's get me my place. Do you want to work for me?"

"You look nice enough. You think I'll get to see some of those Level Effer girls? Wait a blasted minute though. How long will you hire me for? You're not going to get all uppity and send me away because your guests complain about my looks and me staring at the girls are you? That's what the boss before the last boss went to the stars did. Right bastard he was."

"I don't care about that," Isaac said.

"Same as what they all say. Then the women get uppity and the men send me away. Say, you hungry?"

"What do we have around here to eat?" Isaac asked smelling the strange odors in the air.

"All your same mass produced, bio-engineered, preservative laden rubbish, healthy but without any taste. Who really cares about fine dining though? That's rot for level effers."

He ordered a couple cups of gray slop from a straw haired, big nosed kid who looked like he struggled intellectually to ladle the greasy substance into the cups.

"Drink up. It's packed with enough nutrients that you'll hardly need to eat again all day. Well, unless you want to be a big fatso. Drink enough of this stuff in a day and you'll get good and round."

The broth tasted salty and fat laden. Tiny chunks of gelatinous membranes floated in it. Isaac winced when he drank it down. It was worse than eating just strips of hard bread or even the raw fish from the stream. Butler laughed and chugged the slop in one hearty gulp.

"Of course, there's better fare to be had than that, but we've gotta get you a place."

Throngs of people would come to be commonplace to Isaac, but for now Moojtema seemed a crowded personal Hell. No one wanted to have anything to do with you; they walked with their heads down towards their destination. If you stopped to talk with them, they would act surprised like they had seen a monster tearing through the corridors.

They stopped under a wall monitor stretched across an opening in the plastic wall with arrow signs pointing out "Housing Office" and "Level D Housing". The bangs and booms of the background soundtrack faded out near the shimmering television like they were jammed by some foreign signal. A man with bright blonde hair and a cherry lipstick smeared, exaggerated smile skipped on a soundstage pulsing electric flowers and gyrating his hips. As he skipped from blackened monitor to monitor, a scene within a scene seemed poised to explode into real life. Behind him the soundstage flickered "Random Rotten Robbie Reality Showcase."

"Fucking Random Robbie," Butler said.

He skipped past the monitors and turned them on one by one with a touch of his finger. The monitors flickered to life, showing the interior of a small room. He touched the monitor again when the room was empty. The monitor tuned into a different room. Random Robbie exploded into peals of laughter when he caught someone on camera. He watched gleefully for a moment, smirking to the camera and hitting the screen until he caught something that piqued his attention, "Ohhhh, Saucy!" he squealed.

Next he played highlight clips, he called them captures from his most prolific snoopings. He sang a little song:

"Jumping from life to life,
one fucking a maid another fucking a wife.
HOW BOOOORRING!!!
Lets play hooky from work, Clerk.
You feign an illness but play Virtual DOME.
A finger in that e-babe's behind, she won't mind.
That's her program!"

He skipped to a monitor larger than the others.

He put his finger to his lips, mocking silence. He said, "Lets tune in on the upper levels to find out what's happening with Mr. Financier. Is he licking some cock in his black wool socks like last Sunday? Drinking a beer? Jerking off to pornography on the GOD? In bed with his whore playing two peas in a pod? Whatever, remember our fun its--free! Unpolluted, pure fun! His voice got deeper, and he looked straight into the camera. He bowed humbly. Remember people, at your monitors; it's all good entertainment. The Random Rotten Robbie Showcase is also performing a valuable community service. How many terrorists have we caught plotting our doom in the Hallways of Moojtema? Three! Remember, boredom is the number one enemy of the people and must be done away with at all costs. It is my duty to slay the enemy of boredom. Shall we see what is happening with our dear Financier?" He touched the large screen with his finger.

"Oh dear God, he isn't home! I wonder where he could be?

"Perhaps in an orgy steam room in Level G!

"Rimming asses for free?

"Giving rusty trombones to men who write poems in Café's on LEVEL A50?

"Wouldn't that be nifty?

"Is this bisexual queer attempting to leer at the babes working in the nursery?"

He bowed to the audience again. "Random Robbie does not disappoint. We will find our dear Financier. We will find him, and we will make him pay for running off to fuck his starlet. No just everyone gets to lay that Beauty Perfumes Whore. Where's she at? I'm starting this rumor people! Spread it amongst the corridors!"

He touched the screen again. Deer lay in a bathtub naked. Soaking in steaming water. She shook. The camera zoomed in, guided by Random Robbie's finger on the screen. Tears fell from her face.

Cut away to Random Rotten Robbie.

"What a vision of beauty boys and girls. Did you see that pair of titties! And to think she doesn't shave! Au natural for our bush. Let it grow, ladies, let it grow! He exploded into maniacal laughter. What I wouldn't give to slide my little Random Robbie in the valley between those peaks until I….well you know! He mimicked thrusting with his head flared back like a rooster and his lips curled into a tight snarl.

"If I see this guy, I'll kill him!" Isaac said to Butler.

Butler shook his head, "Sir, he's the most popular man in Moojtema. He's how we get know about all the happenings here."

"Nothing he showed us seemed important to me," Isaac said snarling. "Just a bunch of trash."

"The people, they sign up for it."

"They invite his cameras into their homes?"

"Yes. It's a chance to be known. Especially you level X'ers. He focuses on all the parties that no one else gets invited to."

"Sad," Isaac said.

Each step he took with Butler he was more and more confused. He was walking the same way as everyone else with his eyes forward. Unlike the others, only he had no idea where he was going.

The pair arrived at the housing office. The woman behind the counter was fat with a bouffant of bright orange hair the color of an electric tangerine. Her looks were only exacerbated by the lighting that also made the blue veins in her face stand out underneath her purple eye shadow smeared on, it seemed to Isaac, by her fingertips. Isaac grimaced when he saw her and noticed that he had a substantial revulsion to her. When she spoke her tea-kettle whistle voice came out in short syncopated bursts like an irregular heartbeat. Glasses draped over her longish wide nose and the lenses magnified her bloodshot eyes. Even though Butler entered the room first, she pushed him out of the way when she saw Isaac's diamond badge.

"Good sir, please come and have a seat. I'm Styler, what's your name?

"Isaac."

"Hello, Isaac. You must not be from around here. What is a nice Level Tenner gentleman like yourself looking for today? Looking to upgrade? Did you just receive your new status?"

"No, I just got here today."

"I should've been able to tell by your name. Where are you coming from?"

"The outside," Isaac said succinctly.

"Oh…the outside. I hear the outside is lovely these days. How's life out there? I'm sure not as good as we have it here," she said.

"It's cheap."

"Oh, great, it's not too expensive then."

"No. Life is cheap. Isn't worth a damn."

"Oh. Okay. Well it is good to have you here, Mr. Isaac. I'm guessing you want a room with a view, right? Women love rooms with a view. Not just any man has one of those. I mean, we all don't have to live in the basement like us one namers."

Butler looked to ground and was turning slightly red, either with anger or embarrassment.

"Please don't insult my friend again," Isaac said.

The woman recoiled as if she were shocked. She immediately changed the subject to what was her pre-recorded message.

"Sir. Let's just look at various models on the GOD."

She made a few keystrokes on the stone desk in front of her. A screen flickered in front of them in the air.

XXXXXXXXXXXXGRAPHICAL OPERATING DATABASEXXXXXXXXXXXXXX
XXXXXXXXXXXXXXXXXXXXXXXXXXXXXXXXXXXXXXXXXXXXXXXXXXX
XXXXXXXXXXXXXXXXXXXXXXXXHOMEXXXXXXXXXXXXXXXXXXXXXXXX

Login: STYLER
Password: 8)))))))))))))0 …;

From what Isaac could ascertain the screen was composed of the intersection of three separate laser beams emanating from three locations on the stone desk that formed a holographic image. The first apartment appeared. The woman pulled at the representation with pinched fingers it moved as if they were walking through it.

"Can I get a view outside?"

"Not possible, sir, I apologize."

"Can't I live in that onion?"

"What onion?"

"The Onion halfway up that tower."

"I'm sorry sir, that's private. Not for sale."

"Who owns it?"

Styler and Butler looked at each other, shocked at the ignorance of the Level Tenner.

"That's where the Circle of Twelve reside."

"Have you ever been up there to see them? What's it like?"

"You're asking a lot of questions, sir. Do you want me to continue on with the homes demonstration?"

"Sure. I want all wooden floors though."

"You can have faux wooden floors with any of the homes I'm about to show you, but installation will be an additional surcharge."

"Very good. She took her finger and tapped the image on the floor and selected a menu for several variants of wood. Cherry. Oak. Pine. Maple. Mahogany. Teak. Cedar. African Rosebush."

"Just pick the most expensive."

"Sure thing, sir. Do you want heated floors?"

"Of course I do."

"Then may I suggest you go with the ceramic composite tile? Or a cultured marble? Why does a nice wealthy man like you want wood anyway? We have a nice Imperial Caesar style that I think you would like. It comes replete with three bathing girls, a cook, and butler."

Butler nodded to Isaac and smiled. Isaac nodded back to him and gave him a thumbs-up sign. Butler had a puzzled look on his face until Isaac said the words, "Okay."

"Let me see the Imperial Caesar."

"She clapped her hands on the projection, and it disappeared. Another menu popped up. She touched the box letters ROMAN, IMPERIAL, and CAESAR. The price listed was 45 million credits for the base model with option to upgrade. She mentioned that this was a Level 10 Palace fit for a Roman Emperor.

"Those Roman Emperors had impeccable fashion sense. Do you want the climate controlled odor controlled orgy room?"

"Does it come with a guest list?"

The fat orange hair smiled, "I'm sure you can arrange anything you want."

"Sure. Put the best of everything in there."

"Very nice."

"Couches?"

"The very best."

"Compu-rest 5121, sorbate softened Fenile leather imported by the Mashgool to us?"

"That's the best?"

"Sure is. It's the softest leather in the universe."

"I'll take it."

She added couches and drapes and bathroom fixtures and neat cooking doodads and gizmos that Isaac made sure his future cook would be trained to use. She asked him if he wanted a starter wardrobe inside a walk in closet that was so large Isaac would be able to run up and down its length in the morning. Isaac felt they had been there long enough and told her he would go shopping on his own.

"The total is one-hundred-million, five-hundred-sixty-thousand, six-hundred-twenty credits and fifteen decimals."

"Cheap," Isaac said.

"You must be a very important man to have all those credits available to you. What exactly do you do?"

"I'm in the business of getting lucky," Isaac said smiling.

"Here we think people make their own luck," she said.

"Don't we ever," Butler said. His words echoed in the room like an invisible gas. Unheard.

"Can I see your pass? That's how you'll be paying."

She put his pass in a small slot in the stone. A blue light flashed at regular intervals.

"Do you want a twenty percent discount for participating in the Random Rotten Robbie Showcase?"

"No way."

"You're sure?"

"Hell no!"

"You don't have to get hostile."

"That freak sickens me. If I ever met him I'd choke the life out of him."

The lady recoiled and gasped like Isaac had slandered a holy man.

The blue light flashed green and she smiled. "Your transaction is processing. It looks like it will go through. Usually participating in the Random Robbie show is the only way people can afford those level X places."

"They throw the parties. He publicizes them," Butler said. Again his words fell on deaf ears.

"You must have a very lucky woman," the tangerine hair said, running her fingers along her ears.

"She's here already."

"Is the lucky girl off shopping?"

"No. She's at home."

"But you just bought your home!"

"She's at hers. She got here before I did."

His luxury apartment only took five hours for a team of men all named Builder to slide and bolt the prefabricated pieces together. They put the final touches on the marble floor, sliding interlocking pieces together and testing the floor heater. On the way to level X, Butler accompanied him to several stores pointing out devices that Isaac would need to make his lifetime stay complete.

He purchased the latest edition of the person-to-person two way holographic communications device. It was the only phone that could call all levels, except of course the sky onion. He dialed numbers at random from his Compu-rest 5121 with the setting on Shiatsu massage – small Asian woman fingers subsetting.

7762469983455 – biiiiiing biiiiing biiiiiing biiiiiing biiiiiiiing

Female voice: Hello?
Isaac: Oh thank God. Deer is that you?
Female Voice: No. This is Analyst. Wrong number.
Isaac: Do you know where I can find her?
Female: Who?
Isaac: The Beauty Perfume Girl?
Female: Are you insane?
CLICK

3224566497007 – biiiiiing biiiiiiing biiiiiiing biiiiing biii

Male voice: Hello?
Isaac: Do you know a woman by the name of Deer?
Male voice: No, I don't. What type of stupid name is that?
Isaac: Your sister has a stupid name.
Male voice: I don't have a sister, Fancypants fucko.
Isaac: What's your name?
Male Voice: Engineer.
Isaac: Let me guess you're an engineer.
Engineer: What do you do around here, Level Effer?
Isaac: Sit on my ass.
Engineer: Yeah some of us work around here, Level Effer.
Isaac: Your wife puts in work up here.
Engineer: Oh yeah, Fancypants fucko? Come down to level G and say that to
        me. The G Spot, you fancy fuck.
Isaac: I'll be there to fuck your wife. She says I'm past due.
Engineer: You are dead! You hear me! DEAD!!!

Isaac continued cold calling for two days. It was always the same answer.

Butler watched him for three or four hours on the second day of his prank calling and inquired what he was doing.

Isaac looked at Butler despondently and decided to reach out. "I need to find my wife," he said.

"Who is she?" Butler asked.

"The Beauty Perfumes Girl. When I married her in the forest her name was Deer."

"That's not possible, sir," Butler said plainly. "The Beauty Perfumes Girl, the most perfect woman ever, was created by our computer geneticists in Moojtema by matching compatible sperm with compatible egg."

"No. I married her in the forest. She was kidnapped and brought here. I have been looking for her for over four years now."

"Sir, are you feeling okay?"

"Butler, you have to believe me."

Butler looked at Isaac long and hard. The young man had a seriousness about him that he had never seen in the other men he had heard raving about women they saw in advertisements. He remembered when a friend of his, Circuitor, bragged about sleeping with one of the Level X'er models. He said she was an underwear model who liked to go down levels for thrills. Circuitor said it was like sleeping with a wooden plank with a hole cut in it. He later told Butler that he had told a lie and it was only some married woman of the same level he had been running around with. Level X'ers never mingled among the workers, especially not for sexual pleasure.

Butler decided to trust Isaac. He didn't know why. Perhaps it was that Isaac had trusted him to be a good Butler and hired him when he was in need. Like a good Butler, he reminded Isaac that there were over one billion inhabitants in Moojtema. It was best that Isaac activated his PERSON PAGE. Butler showed Isaac his PERSON PAGE. It was simple, unremarkable really. There were a few friends, all plain looking. It listed Butler's hobbies as knitting and Biochemistry. Clicking on the two opened pages in the GOD with everything you would ever want to know about the two subjects. Butler showed Isaac that he had published several articles in the GOD about his two favorite subjects. Butler had completed all of the Biochemistry Modules on the GOD and was waiting for his certificate, which he would proudly display on his PERSON PAGE. Butler showed Isaac how to link their PERSON PAGES and add an accounting line so Butler's miniscule salary could be paid every month, straight out of Isaac's banking account.

Everything was handled through the PERSON PAGE. Notices to appear came on the PERSON PAGE so that other people could see when you were summoned by the authorities and could remind you even if you didn't view your PERSON PAGE on that day. However, no one went more than a few hours without viewing their PERSON PAGE. Butler told Isaac that PERSON PAGES were the best way to meet women in Moojtema. After Isaac's PERSON PAGE was completely setup and Butler's account was linked with Isaac's own account and Isaac gave him ten times the amount he was previously paid by former employers, Butler navigated to the Beauty Perfume Girl's PERSON PAGE.

He showed Isaac how to send a message to her. He wrote with gushing eyes, his fingers barely able to type:

Deer,

I have made it to Moojtema. I am here to take you away with me. I am sorry it took me so long to get here but I had to figure out a way to get inside. Please, if you get this message, come to my house or contact me on my PTP, number 547569492221. Honey, I have been dreaming of the day we would meet for four bitter years. I love you with all my heart.

Isaac

PS. I saw your poster on my way into Moojtema and my heart nearly stopped. You are more gorgeous than ever, honey.

A week after Isaac moved into the new place he had not heard from his wife. Cook moved in, as did the three Attendants. Cook busied himself in the kitchen. He was a plain looking man with a face that had no peculiar features. His face was smooth and hairs did not grow from it. Cook's face was what a man's face would look like if it could be afflicted by perpetual boredom. Isaac discovered he didn't need all of the fancy culinary gadgets because all of the food was delivered in individual containers. Cook was adept at choosing which containers, when heated, would produce the most flavorful and nutritious combinations. Butler, Cook, and the three Attendants; females which were blonde triplets and beautiful looking, though not as beautiful as the Beauty Perfumes Girl, ate their sludgy soup in silence, never speaking to each other. The Attendants bathed Isaac every night but he could not bring himself to be aroused. His mind was on his wife.

Isaac kept a journal on his GOD Terminal. He did not upload it to the server, so he assumed that it was private.

0004 When I first arrived in Moojtema it seemed a strange paradise. I am certain that it is Hell. I cannot bear to be this alone. Everyone has a wall around them separating themselves from everyone else. We are all individuals but it seems that no one is able to make a real authentic connection. When I speak to people it only seems like a dumb business transaction. I have not purchased a video screen. I have enough money to purchase anything I want. I have seen it when I was out shopping. It only has that jackass Random Robbie on it and advertisements for Beauty Products. All of them star my wife. She seems happy in them. They take place on the beach or in a forest, but I know she cannot possibly be there.

Random Rotten Robbie profiles her everyday on his show. She is usually in her room, wherever that is, and looks upset. I think she is crying over me. I am going to start searching every level for her if she does not answer my message on PERSON PAGES.

I only want to take her and leave here. I want to grasp her and kiss her and let her know that everything is okay and we can go and return to the forest people together.

I hesitate to write anything else about what I am here to do. I will not discuss that until I know my wife is safe by my side.

0040 This marks my fortieth day in Moojtema. Today I got on the GOD and searched around. I am upset that I didn't activate my GOD account sooner. It seems that the GOD is just a one-stop place for anything I want to know about under the sun. Earlier I watched a video of two level G women engaged in a competition to see who could take on the most men in a row; the brunette won over the redhead after two-hundred and seventy men had mounted her. I cut and pasted the following article from the GOD for further research. It is evidence that everything on the GOD is a falsehood or at least partially in error. I do not know if the citizens of Moojtema created the GOD or if it is

300

dangled from above to the citizens of Moojtema like a carrot, leading them onwards and justifying their existence that is as far as I can tell, utterly devoid of meaning. I believe the GOD has been created by the Mashgool and the Circle of Twelve in order to control the populace of Moojtema, but to what purpose I cannot fathom.

"…the outside world is a never ending horror of depredation, where fear rules the psyche of men. Fear is not known inside Moojtema as it has been banished to the outer reaches and replaced with the comforting feeling of security. The Mashgool decided, in their infinite wisdom, to protect us against this harmful emotion. There is nothing of danger inside Moojtema. Criminals are dealt with harshly and quickly, often before they act. Nothing will harm you inside Moojtema. You will have a peaceful and carefree life as long as you follow the four principles of the Mashgool…"

I have begun learning the Mashgool language, using a primer known as the Enchiridion, located on the GOD. I find it easier than people make it out to be. Perhaps this is because they lack the willpower. The written language consists of concentric circles. There is the open circle, and stacks of up to five concentric circles. Each word has three sounds and is composed of a combination of stacks of concentric circles. Three open circles is the Mashgool word for God. It sounds like three puffs of the tongue. Its closest approximation in the English language means source of the universe and origin of divine universal guiding principles. The Mashgool do not have a personal god. Their God could rather be the basic physical principles of the universe. Robert Tanner showed that the universe did not need anything outside of itself for its creation. That is the meaning of the Tanner Equation. Reading the Mashgool texts, it has started to make sense to me.

What is different about the Mashgool is how they interpret their meaning to the universe. In the first Canto of the Mashgool as told to the First Prophet of Mashgool, Glibbet Globbet Gloop, "…and when said of the universe and the highest order of all creatures, all created for one, Mashgool, be fertile and multiply, fill the universe and subdue it, have dominion over all the planets of all the suns in all the solar systems, over all creatures in those vast expanses. I give unto you all the planets of the universe. All the creatures whether they fly, or walk on four, or two, or slither. Exercise wisdom and do what is right unto them. Have dominion over them as you exercise dominion over their planets."

I remember the passage in the Holy Bible by heart.

"…God blessed them saying, 'be fertile and multiply; fill the earth and subdue it. Have dominion over the fish of the sea, the birds of the air, and all the living things that move on the earth." God said, "See, I give you every seed bearing fruit on it to be your food; and to all the animals of the land, all the birds of the air, and all the living creatures that crawl on the ground, I give all the green plants for food." And so it happened. God looked at everything he had made and he found it very good. Evening came, and morning followed, the sixth day…

Besides the *Cantos of the Mashgool*, which I have been translating, everything else on the GOD is a patent falsehood. I cannot find a shred of truth in any of it. Nothing about the world outside is true. Nothing about the entirety of human history is true. Nothing is mentioned about Philosophy. There is no human art mentioned. There is no human science remaining on the GOD. All is Mashgool science discovered by Mashgool scientists. I do not know the reason for this, but it must be what Robert Tanner said about the First Emperor of China destroying all the previous literature so it would seem like History began with him.

0120   The GOD has revealed that the Mashgool built Moojtema to protect human beings from eradication. They found human beings to be an interesting species worthy of preservation. The GOD makes no mention of what the Mashgool are protecting the humans against.

0145   I went shopping for shoes today again. I do not need any more shoes. My marble shoe closet with platinum racks, highly polished to be non-scuffing is loaded with shoes from the floor to the ceiling. I went to the fancy shoe store located on Level X and felt each shoe for the strength of its manufacture. I flexed them left and I flexed them right. I was approached by a short man with a large forehead that looked as if the weight of his brain was compressing the rest of his face into his neck. I pitied this man. He looked miserable. I felt the leather on the shoes before I made my selection. Some of the leather was coarse, some of it was soft, some shiny, some dull matte finished. Some shoes were colorful like a rainbow on a field, like the sun reflecting through a diamond, but the shoes are neither of those. They are not as beautiful as my wife. I want desperately to look out a window and see the sun. I felt the shoes again. I worried that the sole would not hold up on the lower levels where the floor is rough and unpolished and made of brass with wild rivets sticking out. The lower levels are not pretty like the top. I often go down there looking for my wife. I am ready to ask her to come up to the upper levels with me and start our life. I go and I ask questions about her but no one seems to know. Some of them say that she was created in Moojtema and is now married to some high profile governor out amongst the stars. I searched the GOD today for my wife. I always ask about her like a man crazed. No one knows anything.

0180   The GOD has been experiencing difficulties recently. I wonder if this is because of my placing my DNA into the repository. I sincerely hope that the DNA I inserted is starting to have an effect.

0195   Butler has informed me that he is attending church services in preparation to make a pilgrimage. He told me that I will need the services of another Butler because he will be going far, far away and will not be coming back. He asked me to consider going on the pilgrimage with him because I was looking more and more depressed at not being able to find my wife.

  I told him that I am an atheist and could never believe in God so I could never go on a pilgrimage. I asked him if he had ever read the *Cantos of the Mashgool* and told him that I had translated it. Still I could find no solace in its words. He told me it was good to go out amongst people and that I could attend the church just for a sense of community. The people ate their meals in common and if I did not want to discuss religion, I would not have to. I asked Butler what kind of schooling he had as a child. He told me from a very young age he was given games to play. All of the games involved learning how to be a Butler, solving menial tasks. Answering the door. Being polite. Pouring wine. The other children in the class with him all seemed to be the same to him. The children were told over and over again, that none of them were special.

None were special. I told Butler that he was special because he taught himself Biochemistry and could knit a scarf in under thirty minutes. Butler told me that he felt he was special because the computer created him especially for a specific task. He told me that the number of Butlers declined with people going on Pilgrimage or dying and that Moojtema needed Butlers so the computer created a Butler, and that Butler was him.

Butler asked about my parents and I told him that my mother died giving birth to me. He told me that was a deplorable way to be born and that I was a random birth. He told me that a random sperm inseminated a random egg and that is how he was born. Random births were not allowed on Moojtema because everyone's sperm was collected and stored so that no random births could happen. I asked Butler who controlled the computer and he said that he did not know. Perhaps the computer controlled everything and we were its mere servants, or we controlled the computer and it was our perfect slave.

0198   The GOD is continuing to have its disturbances and there was an outage today for approximately thirty minutes. Something curious happened which confirmed the Gideons presence in the GOD. Butler purchased a book that he had been reading on his portable reader. There are no writers in Moojtema really, the GOD either has works stored on it that are available for download, or the GOD randomly generates a work based on the works already stored in the Database. Butler asked me if I had every heard of a book where the main character was a man named Adam. I played dumb as he told me the story. He said that this man, Adam, was created in a Garden. This Adam had a wife given to him by the Lord, God, and they were kicked out of the Garden because his wife was tempted and ate something prohibited to them. I told Butler that it was a queer story, and I had never heard it. This means I must double my efforts to find my wife because the GOD could fail at anytime, and the Institute forces will no doubt attack to free the miserable slaves in this place.

0200   While I was shopping today I noticed there were several men wearing black clothing following me and watching me as I perused the wares. No matter what store I went into, the men followed me. I am convinced they thought I was trying to steal from the stores I was going into. Why would I need to steal? I am the richest man in Moojtema. On the way out of one of the stores I asked one of them men I suspected of following me where I could find a certain restaurant; he looked surprised when I asked him and could barely answer me. They are following me for some reason. Perhaps I and my mission have been compromised.

0225   The one source of enjoyment in the otherwise miserable meaningless existence that I live in Moojtema comes in spending the credits. I spend them on anything that catches my fancy. I walk through the corridors where no one knows me. No one talks to me. I think strange thoughts. The other day, I desperately wanted someone to touch me. Hug me, kiss me, punch me, stab me, or fight me. I try to distinguish myself by the way I dress. I purchase any product that my wife advertises. I looked at her in the photographs in stores. She wears tight jeans and gold foil shoes. I purchased all the gold foil shoes. It didn't occur to me that they might only be for women and the sales clerk did not warn me. That was no matter, but a man wearing shoes made for a woman? That is a sight to behold. Maybe someone will approach me and tell me that I am wearing women's shoes. No one did, and I stopped wearing them after a couple of days. I smile after I purchase a new product for a moment, and it is like a little island of sunny hope pops out of a stormy black sea. Soon it is covered again by waves. All I do is think about my wife. Her picture is always around me. In a fake wooden setting in which she sold rugged shirts fit for a lumberjack, I imagined her out in the woods the very last time I saw her. I wish I had just stayed and never gotten talked into my foolish mission.

My mission! There was now evidence that the Gideons had made it onto the GOD. Where was the imminent shutdown that Robert Tanner told him would happen? It was all hypothesis! It was one of his sick theories! It wasn't going to actually happen. The men dressed in black follow me more and more, even to the lower levels. People slinked away from them like they had some sort of disease. I tried to lose them but they kept appearing. First one of them. Then two. Then there were three that now follow me everywhere I go.

I told Butler and Cook that people were following me. They consulted with the Attendants who informed me that I was probably feeling some stress at being separated from my wife and should talk to a doctor. Two of the Attendants have been studying psychology on the GOD in their spare time. I reluctantly agreed. Cook dialed the phone and called up Dr. Sickwell.

Dr. Sickwell, psychiatrist to the stars, specialist in the treatment of people with heads full of fictions, and balding reducer of egos, egregious inflater of id forces, claimed in his advertisements he could reach the reptilian under brain. Saint Sickwell, patron saint of the confused and lonely, prescriber of carnal delight for the undersexed, guaranteed to get you laid. Chronic masturbation captured on film by Random Rotten Robbie was cured at no extra expense. Here, take a pill. There, take a pill. Slurp them down. Your brain is all chemicals anyway. Here is a pill with the same effect as a compliment. There is a pill with same effect as a pristine blowjob, to take the place of a backrub, to take the place of a soothing cunt. Gulp. There is a pill to cure your feelings of ugliness and more for the shopaholic. For the overworked Butler, for the fat Cook, for the tubby waddler reluctant to exercise, there is a pill to benefit the intellect, a pill to get over the fear of death.

The short, plump man with a bulbous head filled full of psychological test data and good, costly advice, hair that looked like a sparse tidal wave of shit crashing on an alabaster Faberge egg, and general amorphousness to his blimpy man-torso waddled into the room. Butler reached out to shake Sickwell's hand to welcome him. Sickwell backed up like Butler had symptoms of the bubonic plague.

"Damn you! Don't touch me!" Sickwell screamed. "Do you know how many germs are on those hands of yours?"

"No, I had no idea," Butler said.

"You have over fifty different species of bacteria on your skin alone. Why you may even have some Streptococcus on those cow udders of yours. That doesn't even count the various types of little gram stain positive sickos you have growing under those yellow fingernails. Please excuse yourself and stay the hell away from me. What are you waiting for? Where's the patient?"

Butler nodded sheepishly and exited the room, closing the door behind him. Sickwell sat on the Shiatsu massage chair next to Isaac's couch and turned it on.

"Why did you want to kill yourself, eh let's see here, what's your name?"

"I don't want to kill myself. I'm seeing people following me."

"So you've no reason to live?"

"I love life. I just don't love it here," Isaac said.

"Who's following you?"

"Men dressed in black."

"What funny business have you been up to?"

"Nothing."

"You sure?"

"Yes."

"Then those people aren't following you. They could probably care less about you. Does that upset you?"

"No."

"You don't think you're important, then?" Sickwell asked, with his head buried, scribbling in a notebook.

"Well, I don't see why people would want to follow me."

"Maybe they want your autograph. You're the richest man in Moojtema."

"That doesn't mean anything," Isaac said.

"Sure it does. It means something to the people here. What's this about a wife you've lost? Did she divorce you? Leave you for another man?"

"No. She came here before I ever came to Moojtema. I'm trying to contact her to let her know I'm here, but I can't."

"Why? Doesn't' she want you? She find another man? Who is she?"

"The Beauty Perfumes Girl."

Sickwell dropped his pen and looked at Isaac with one eye closed behind his thick glasses. He appeared to be winking at first. He looked at Isaac for a full five minutes, just staring, before he began taking furious notes in his electronic notebook. Isaac thought it was the signs of intense concentration, rather than flirting.

"Obsession. Compulsion brought on by a low self-esteem. You know many of my patients are captivated by her. Many also say they are married to her. I have a patient who shall go unnamed, but you may have caught him on the Random Robbie show. He has a chronic compulsion to drop his pants and masturbate every time he sees her. He cannot leave his quarters."

"I am married to her!" Isaac exclaimed angrily.

"Obsessive Compulsive disorder exacerbated by chronic low self-esteem and anger issues," Sickwell said in his personal recorder.

"Where did you meet her, Mr. Isaac?"

"In the forest."

"In your file here it says you were born in Moojtema? How did you leave and come back?"

"My file is wrong then!"

"No, it isn't. It has your picture on it."

"That was taken when I arrived."

"No, you're an upper cruster if I've ever seen one. I can't believe someone so perfect was a random birth. I have your DNA profile in front of me, and you're off the charts. Tell me, have you been stabbing that meat of yours into any of our fine Moojtema women?"

"No. None."

"Couple previous diagnosis with lack of sexual activity," Sickwell said into his recorder. "Come now, son. I know your diagnosis, and I know your treatment. All you have to do is talk to them, son. Don't be afraid. It seems you've taken your lust and transferred it onto an impossible conquest. We all want to fuck the Beauty Perfumes Girl, Isaac. Hell, even I want to bend her over. Problem is, we can't. It's an impossible dream, so get her out of your head. Try smiling more, son! Did you know that if you force a smile for thirty seconds that you will actually start to feel happy? Try it, Isaac!"

"No," Isaac said.

"Damn it, son! Don't you want to get better? You have to be a willing participant in your own cure."

"Smile damn you!"

306

Isaac tried to force a smile. It was pathetic at best.

"Wider, damn you. Smile! Let me see those white choppers of yours."

Isaac smiled so wide that his face hurt. He tried to speak and smile at the same time and his voice came out slurred and high pitched, "Is that adequate, Doctor?"

"Hold it!" Sickwell said, glancing at his Electronic Personal Assistant for the time. "Hold that smile, damn you. I don't want to see the corners of your mouth droop in the slightest. Twenty-seven, twenty-eight, twenty-nine, thirty! And release!"

Isaac's face collapsed like a bridge in a fat man marathon. The strange thing was, he felt better.

"Now do that every hour on the hour for a few weeks. I call that the Sickwell Smile Therapy."

Isaac nodded.

"Are you still suicidal, Isaac? Are you thinking about hurting yourself?"

"I've never been suicidal here. I just need to find my wife."

"Damn, I see that idea is firmly entrenched in that great grape of yours. Do I have to recommend you get sent to a neurologist and have that brain of yours examined?"

"No," Isaac said.

"Also, go out and try to multiply. You can't because all the women are sterile, but it will be fun trying, no?"

"Whatever," Isaac said.

"Oh! Isaac, you aren't…you know…a man lover are you?"

"No. I just need to get out of this place."

"Isaac, come now. Humans are a hearty group. You can either be one of the blessed many, or the cursed few that walk through Hell for no reason. You want to join in the fun, Isaac, right? Blessed are those that fuck a plenty. Blessed are those that make love to virgins. Blessed are the meek and mild that live day to day. They will inherit the Earth," Sickwell said with a laugh. He laughed again and a third time to try and get a reaction out of his patient.

Isaac stared ahead bleakly.

"Get over yourself. That's where to begin, son. You're nothing. Nothing at all," Sickwell said.

"You're insane, Doctor."

"No, son, you are."

"I'm not," Isaac said. "This place is insane. It's a madhouse."

"Think what you want, Isaac. But it's our madhouse. You're the only one thinking that. Look out over them."

Sickwell guided Isaac to a wall that he made transparent with a clap of his hand. People like ants milled about the stores. They crisscrossed the chromosomal hallways with bags in hand and blank looks on faces.

"They're all content, Isaac. Your problem is that you look down on them like a God from your ornate palace. Why don't you do something nice for all of them? Throw a party perhaps? People love parties. Why, Mr. Isaac, I do declare, you'd be the toast of all Moojtema! You know what? The Beauty Perfumes Girl might deign to come. Though I somewhat doubt it."

Butler encoded the invitation to the richest man in Moojtema's party in fancy lettering. He sent it in the form of a text message to all of the Lorentz X530, Nokia Z110s, Apple Computer iPortals, and Samsung G5500s. The equation he programmed into the message distributor was as follows: "MessageALL: iff price (cellphone) is > or = 15000 MCR"

Cook told them they had to keep out the riff raff. Isaac had wanted to invite everyone but there was no way for them to make it through the security checkpoints. Butler suggested holding a party on each level and arranged for posters of Isaac dressed in his best finery that said, "PARTY of all PARTIES," brought to you by ISAAC along with the caveat, "IF YOU KNOW THE BEAUTY PERFUMES GIRL, PLEASE BRING HER." Cook said if Isaac was going to be spending his credits, it should be in winning friends and influencing people.

Phones beeped, vibrated, and played computer generated pop music greetings at the same time throughout the highest levels of Moojtema. The lower levels were given paper copies with the location of their parties. The invitations showered down the levels like confetti and ended up waist deep on the lowest level. No one believed that a nasty level effer would ever throw a party for them. It had to be a trick designed to get them to miss work. When Isaac's posters displayed over posters of the Beauty Perfumes Girl, everyone took notice. She had lubricated the fantasies of many men. Videoscreens were smashed in riots in the lower levels. Change to routine was greeted with brutality.

Isaac began to receive RSVPs from succulent biddies with breasts that looked like diamond cones, sharp enough to poke your eye out. Photographs were often attached. There were questions of: What should I wear? Do you want me to bring anything? Is this a black tie event, I would expect nothing less from the prince of Moojtema. Some asked, "Are you married?" One said, "Can I please invite my friend, Garbage Remover, I promise to shower him; he's an inspired artist. Would you be interested in purchasing any of his works of art to put in your magnificent home?" Attached were photographs of black trash bags smeared with mustard.

Butler assigned the names in a list of Yeses, Nos, and Maybes. Isaac paced the floor of his sauna naked as the Attendants watched with wide open eyes, waiting to see if Deer had gotten the message. Was she coming? Butler kept shaking his head no. There was no response yet. He went back to the sauna to sweat it out and torture the Attendants some more.

Sickwell began seeing Isaac in his home. It was much nicer than the Doctor's office. He began staying well past the end of their appointment times. He always leered at Butler and the fat Cook, who nodded to the short doctor and stayed out of his way, lest they be psychoanalyzed.

"You need religion, Isaac," Sickwell said. "You have no way of life. You have nothing to tie you here."

"I'm having my party so that my wife might come," Isaac said.

"Ahh, yes. Hedonism. You're still holding onto the Beauty Perfumes Girl?"

"Yes. She is my wife."

"I see you're not cured."

"I think I'm thinking clearly now."

"No more people are following you?"

"I haven't really left the house. We've been planning the party."

"There will be thousands of beautiful women here I'm sure. I saw the invite list. All of Moojtema royalty will be here. Women that will make your soul squeeze out in droplets as you gasp."

"I really doubt it."

"Don't doubt the miracles of genetic engineering, Isaac. You want arm candy? You've got it. Order one up. Her growth will be hyper accelerated, and she'll be delivered to your doorstep. Don't want her? Fuck her once and send her back. She'll be ground up to make raw material for another one. You can order a girl with a pussy as tight as your fist. Quiet as a mouse. You can't teach them to speak in a week. Keep her around for longer and she'll be saying yes to your every wish, my man."

"No thanks."

"What musical catalogue will you be playing, Isaac?"

"I'm not sure."

"Pop trash resurrected from the twenty-first century!" Butler yelled from the kitchen where he and cook were making mousse for dessert.

"He sure likes to eavesdrop doesn't he, Isaac?"

"He's harmless, doctor."

"You never know, he could be a plant."

"I hired him the first day I was here," Isaac said.

"Then perhaps he was recruited."

"By whom? He's harmless. Don't worry about it."

"Isaac, as your physician and friend, I advise you to kill him immediately. Toss his body down the incinerator. Frame Cook. That big, fat man has the glinty, untrustworthy eyes of a killer."

"I won't do it. That's nonsense."

"Its self preservation!"

"If you're my doctor, why are you inducing paranoid thoughts into me?"

"I'm merely trying to make you feel something. Have a reaction. Your detachment worries me."

"I'll be fine once I see my wife again."

"You know, Isaac, I hate to be the bearer of bad news, but I saw the Beauty Perfumes Girl the other day," Sickwell said with a snide smile.

Isaac stood up off the couch ready to run.

"Where! Did you tell her about me?"

"No, she was with her man."

"Who?" Isaac asked, nearly shaking the doctor.

"Random Rotten Robbie."

"That's impossible! She'd never be with him.

"Why not? You may have money, but he's got fame and talent."

"He doesn't have any talent! He's disgusting."

"Well, Isaac, there's the rub. People like him. They like him a lot. You're just a rich nobody."

"I'll send him an invitation then," Isaac said. "I'll tell him to bring a guest."

"When he comes though, Isaac, you should probably do yourself a favor and do him in. I can't have you chickening out and regretting it. That could do a number on your psyche."

Isaac smiled at the doctor. Sickwell smiled back.

Gold and platinum pounded and microscopic foil streamers hung delicately from the ceiling. Techno music pounded from the carbon nanotube speakers so concentrated it went through you, forcing you to dance. It was in tune with your heartbeat. Diamond encrusted disco balls shot bullets of light on the floor. There was a room in the back to come down from the high. There were rooms to take the woman of your dreams. There were holes in inner spaces. Everyone was smiling. There were thousands of gorgeous women, sweaty and dancing, some acting as wallflowers sipping elegant chalices of bubbly. They all gave him looks as he sat in the corner peering through the ambergris and driftwood that washed up in his place. Isaac looked for her. Where was Deer?

Random Rotten Robbie entered the room like a frenzied jackrabbit of activity. Slapping asses. How ya doin'! Winking. Licking his lips. A beard like Pan, hair golden orange: died the color of a golden lion tamarin. He was small, shaking and stammering like a psychic woodpecker pecking prognostications from a crystal ball. He grabbed breasts with two hands and laughed at the screams of the upper class ladies. They shouted, "We love you, Robbie!"

He answered, "Pleasure fucking you!"

She followed behind him: a sweet vision of life in the vicious, bloated doom.

Isaac split the room. In the space between the twitch of a vas deferens and erectile dysfunction, he was on her.

"My love! My love! My love!" he yelled as he grabbed her in his arms.

She staggered backwards, upset at his assault. She did not speak. He came forward again, thinking she was surprised and kissed her face. He pulled his face back to hers crying. Her mouth gaped with horror.

"Get your own Beauty Perfume Girl, bitch!" Random Robbie shouted.

Random Rotten Robbie smacked Isaac on the head from behind. It was a real bitch slap, it didn't hurt, more annoying than anything.

"I paid good credits for that slut!" Robbie yelled grabbing at Isaac's waist trying to take him to the ground. The partygoers shrieked. Breasts popped from low cut Vuitton Chanel hybrid throwback dresses. Fornicating revelers popped from corners to see the cause of the fiasco.

For his small stature, Random Rotten Robbie was incredibly strong. He brought his knee into Isaac's testicles hard. He did it again. Isaac loosened his grip. The sickness crept from his gonads into his throat.

"Death to your children, fucko!" Random Rotten Robbie screamed.

Isaac had enough. With one arm, he tossed the spaz against a group of women in peacock feather dresses and little black sequined hats. They had not deconflicted their outfits and ended up wearing the same thing. When Robbie pounded into them, they collapsed like church steeples.

"I need my wife! My wife!" Isaac screamed.

Random Rotten Robbie picked his head up weakly and planted his hand on one of the peacock girl's tits for leverage.

"She's my clone. I ordered her a week ago at the advice of my doctor. She's not your wife."

"Doctor Sickwell?" Isaac said.

Rotten Robbie nodded grimly.

The clone stared blankly ahead, taking in all the wild shapes and colors. She was not a blank slate, but had the intellect of a newborn baby. The world was full of beauty. Everything was interesting to her. She smiled like an idiot and waved at the handsome man who now lay on the floor shaking in the fetal position.

"Wake up, Isaac."

He was in an all white room. There was a man dressed in all white with standing in the center of the room. Two men in black flanked him on either side. They were the men who had been following him all over Moojtema.

The man in white spoke, "I am Ridley. I believe Dr. Tanner told you about us."

"No. I don't know what you're talking about."

"Cut the shit, young man. We know all about you."

"I'm innocent. I'm sorry I attacked Random Robbie."

"Who cares about Random Robbie? You were told how there were Institute agents inside here who disappeared, right, Isaac?"

"I don't know what you're talking about!" Isaac exclaimed.

"You don't think we can't recognize one of our own? In Moojtema, where everything is accessible, we have to be good at recognizing patterns. You don't think we picked up on you immediately?"

"What are you talking about?"

"Come on I know the When All Else Fails course teaches you better interrogation resistance tactics than that. Did you sleep through it?"

Isaac did not say a word.

"We were all agents of Robert Tanner, Isaac. All members of the Institute sent in here. They gave you some Termiculum to get in here right? That's how you got your money."

"I found that."

"Isaac drop it. We know all about you. Tell us Isaac, what kind of scientist are you? Did you do any research on Robert Tanner's background besides what you heard from his mouth? We think you're a pretty poor one. We were all poor scientists too. We only believed one source of information. We believed the words straight out of that psychopath's mouth."

"Who is that?"

"Robert Tanner. Don't tell me you didn't look him up on the GOD? We know you didn't. We've been monitoring your activities since you got here. You checked on many things. Why didn't you check on him?"

"I was afraid that I was being monitored. Why would I check on him? I figured no one in here knew about him," Isaac said reluctantly.

"Yes. Everyone checks on him though. They live in mortal fear of him here. For you not to check on him in the GOD means that you were in league with him. If you had checked on him, you'd find out the truth."

"Everything on the GOD is just phony."

"Yes. Most of it is, but the story of Robert Shay Tanner is the truth."

"Do you have your Portable Display Module, Jenkins?"

One of the men in black produced one from a pocket. He touched the screen and handed it to Isaac.

Isaac read from the GOD entry on Dr. Robert S. Tanner.

XXXXXXXXXXXXXXGRAPHICALXXOPERATINGXXXDATABASEXXXXXXXXX
XXXXXXXXXXXXXXXXXXXXXXXXXXXXXXXXXXXXXXXXXXXXXXXXXXXXXXX

DR. ROBERT TANNER

Dr. Robert Tanner headed the Research Partnership at CERN LAB II responsible for the isolation of the Down Boson, otherwise known in popular literature as the God Particle. He is the first scientist to accurately predict the existence of this particle based on his Tanner Equation. He was, in all accounts, a brilliant physicist and mathematician.

The energy fluctuations produced by the isolation of this particle alerted an alien life form to the presence of intelligent life on the planet Earth. Approximately twenty years after Dr. Robert Tanner isolated the God Particle, the Mashgool made first contact.

Dr. Robert Tanner went from being a scientist to a multibillionaire industrialist after founding Tanner Industries, first built around his Down Boson Reactor and expanding into military contracts, aviation, and all facets of industry. As his wealth increased and he grew older, he grew increasingly isolated and paranoid. He became obsessed with finding a cure for death and spent vast sums of money on what his advisors would tell him was pseudoscience.

The Mashgool came to our planet in peace. They offered us a partnership among the stars and exchanged scientists with us. Robert Tanner was among the first scientists to meet with the scientists of the Mashgool. When he saw their fuel, called Termiculum, he immediately knew that his cure for death was in his grasp. He did not care about the rest of the technology or even sharing any earth technology with the Mashgool. He took the Termiculum and designed a life support suit. When he announced his discovery to the world, he offered the suits for sale at two point five billion dollars a piece. There were twelve takers: a Saudi prince, Abd al Rahman Faisal ibn al Saud; an Internet Search Company founder, Dmitri Szrin; a billionaire financier, T. Prescott Perry; a home cooking conglomerate owner, Sally Witherspoon; a German Chemical Conglomerate owner, Wolfgang Piers Schaftberger; a Chinese media conglomerate owner, Xiao Xiang Zhou; Retail Heir, Meyers Zarfin; billionaire investor, C. Tippet Sanders; Dictator of South Central African Republic, Maose Mfabo; Narcotics Trafficker and Opium Prince, Hajjibullah Mafsaranjani; King of England, King Charles X; and eccentric American Playboy Steel Magnate, Anderson Quigley.

Robert Tanner did not stop there. When public outcry erupted he defended himself and his immortal compatriots. He hired mortal men to kill and die, defending immortality. He paid them magnificent salaries, as did his compatriots. They banded together to defend their new ideal. Then Tanner launched a Public Relations campaign where he blamed the Mashgool for tricking him into accepting the life support suit. All the blame was placed on the Mashgool who hovered over the planet earth in their space cruisers, oblivious to the dangers brewing below.

Robert Tanner succeeded in convincing many governments of the world to launch an attack on the Mashgool to drive them away from the planet. Others did not believe Tanner and attacked him and his confederation. Several Mashgool cruisers were

314

destroyed in acts labeled as terrorism. The Mashgool's retribution was swift and absolute. The bombardment of the planet's surface was to continue for one month until nearly all traces of the pesky race were destroyed.

Robert Tanner sued the Mashgool for peace. He implored them that humanity deserved a better fate than annihilation. After twenty days, survivors were given the option of traveling to Moojtema, or facing swift death. Those that resisted were annihilated with Mashgool weaponry. Moojtema was seen as the best hope of mankind in a cruel universe.

Robert Tanner was driven out of Moojtema after it was revealed that the Termiculum he sold the other twelve immortals was adulterated, designed to last a tenth of the time as normal. Of course, in his dealings with the Mashgool, he took the pure Termiculum and kept it for himself, giving the other twelve remainders that did not power their life support units for more than a year.

XXXXXXXXXXXXXXXXXXXXXXXXXXXXXXXXXXXXXXXXXXXXXXXXXXX
XXXXXXXXXXXXXXXXXXXXXXXXXXXXXXXXXXXXXXXXXXXXXXXXXXX

"Why should I believe this?"

"You were sent on your mission with someone, right? And they died?"

"Yes. My friend betrayed me."

"Don't worry. All of us were put in similar circumstances. None of us brought any Termiculum with us, though. It's quite strange that he would give his enemies a share in the booty. Jenkins here was forced to kill his friend who thought he was trying to kill him. I had to kill my own brother who turned against me. The man is full of tricks."

"Why did Tanner do that?" Isaac asked.

"We don't know."

"What's going to happen to me?"

"Unfortunately your spectacle was covered on the Random Rotten Robbie Showcase. There isn't much we can do for you. We'd ask you to work with us, but unfortunately your profile is too high. You'll have to go to trial. You may be able to bargain with the Circle of Twelve perhaps. Tell them the truth."

"I only came here to get my wife," Isaac said. "That's the truth. I could care less about Robert Tanner and his ambition."

"Your wife?"

"Yeah. Deer. The Beauty Perfumes Girl."

"She's safe. She's working in the nursery."

"How do you know?"

"We know where everybody is in Moojtema. We wish you had come to us sooner. We could have saved you some trouble. In fact, had you been inserted into the lower levels it would have been easier to find your wife. Being the richest man in Moojtema really marks you."

"It's almost like Tanner wanted me to fail."

"You inserted a virus into the GOD, didn't you?" Ridley asked.

"A DNA copy of the Holy Bible. Why would they have me do that? It didn't do anything."

"No. It did. Don't you see? It's a work of humanity: a fundamentally human book."

"It's totally unlike anything else on the GOD," Jenkins said. Their silent third partner just nodded along.

"What's happened?"

"Among the lower levels, there is quite a degree of dissent brewing. Ultimately, this dissent had its root in the Bible virus that you put on the GOD. The stories are more appealing to them than the Mashgool's Holy Book. The base levels have been reading it. The virus you introduced has gone viral amongst them. They have been organizing. It is unable to be stopped now."

Isaac looked off in the white distance past the men. He stared for maybe ten seconds but it felt like a lifetime.

"After my trial," he said, "what is going to happen to me?"

"You may be executed, Isaac. We don't know."

"Can you make sure my wife comes to see me in my cell?"

"Yes. We will do that for you."

Isaac was paraded in front of the cameras for the Random Rotten Robbie Showcase when he entered the courtroom. It was plain, with silver walls and looked like something inside a ship. There were no spectators inside the courtroom; the cameras were enough to beam the show trial all over Moojtema. Citizens were glued to videoscreens inside their homes and public establishments; they stopped in corridors to watch. The evidence from the Random Rotten Robbie beat down at Isaac's party was played over and over. It was edited so it looked like Rotten Robbie kneed him in the testicles at least sixteen times before succumbing to Isaac's choking him.

Isaac's attorney argued that Isaac had not signed the contract to allow the Random Rotten Robbie Showcase into his home. As counter evidence, the prosecution called the Tangerine haired woman to the stand who called Isaac a horrible wrongdoer who insulted her personally and claimed he said, "If I ever see Random Robbie, I'll kill him."

"You see, the man has planned his crime in advance; it smacks of pre-meditation," said the prosecuting attorney, a man who slithered around the room like a snail with squinty eyes, taking every little detail in.

His defense attorney cringed as they played the tape from the retail office back and Isaac did, in fact, say those things.

"Worse! The defendant introduced a harmful virus into the Graphical Operating Database. He did this attempting to subvert the security of our fair city."

Isaac's defense attorney did not bother to answer those charges because Isaac admitted to them in the pre-trial briefing. His attorney told him that the book was so popular among the first fifteen levels of Moojtema that calling Isaac a criminal for introducing it into the GOD would only make the public angry.

The prosecuting attorney next called Butler to the stand. Butler swore on a copy of the *Cantos of the Mashgool* to tell the truth. As Isaac knew, the truth was often borne on the backs of different vehicles, packaged and conveyed for different purposes: one truth with many interpretations.

Butler told a story about how he met Isaac and how Isaac gave him employment in a time when he was unemployed. He then went on to say that he wanted to leave his employer and go on a pilgrimage to serve the Mashgool, but his employer made him stay pursuing an insane quest for his wife, who he said was the Beauty Perfumes Girl. Butler said that Isaac scared him on a daily basis and he only went along with Isaac's requests because he was afraid. Butler told the judges that he asked his employer several times to let him go on pilgrimage but his employer refused his requests saying that he didn't trust anyone else to live in his home and take care of it.

"It is the right of every citizen of Moojtema, at any time, to ask to go on pilgrimage!" the prosecuting attorney noted for the record.

"Objection. My client was unfamiliar with the laws and bylaws of Moojtema," his defense attorney said. Isaac was sure that the objection would stand and looked at his well-paid lawyer with pride.

"Overruled," the judge said. "Ignorance of the law is no excuse, counsel."

The prosecution introduced video evidence of Isaac staring at posters of the Beauty Perfumes Girl. There were at least one-hundred and fifty clips that surfaced of Isaac talking to posters, looking at them with his head cocked to the side in awe. Transcripts of messages sent to her PERSON PAGE were introduced into evidence and the president of the Beauty Perfumes Girl fan club testified that some of the messages that Isaac sent were the most shocking displays of fan obsession she had ever witnessed, including a fantasy where the Beauty Perfumes Girl had grown up in the woods and married him in a ceremony.

"Obviously," the Fan Club President said, "he got that fantasy from her late fall posters selling Deep Sylvan fragrances."

Dr. Sickwell came to the stand next and was asked his professional opinion of Isaac's state of mind at the time of the commission of the crime.

"The patient was in an advanced state of delusional psychosis. He was extremely suicidal and needed to act. I am just glad the only thing he did was attack Robbie. The subject is highly intelligent, and things could have been far worse."

The prosecutor interjected, "You also profiled his diary entries, right, Doctor?"

"Yes," Sickwell replied. "The man has a classic messiah complex. He seems to think he's on a secret mission, or at least he alludes to it in several instances. I think what we have here is a profile of a very wealthy man who became mentally imbalanced through lack of social interaction, specifically sexual interaction. He is also most likely homosexual and trapped in the closet."

The defense attorney questioned Sickwell, asking if he thought it was improper that a doctor should testify against a former patient, under whose care the patient was when he committed his alleged crimes.

Sickwell laughed, "I am only trying to protect the good citizens of Moojtema."

Isaac was asked if he had anything to say in his defense. He took the stand reluctantly and stared at the blank panel of lenses of cameras thrust into his face.

"I came to Moojtema to find my wife," he said. "I know you may not believe that because in the four years that we were separated she grew famous here because of her looks. You could not believe that she was not created here. I knew her in the Forest before I ever came to Moojtema. I married her there. I made a horrible decision that separated us. Had I found her, none of this would have happened.

"I apologize to Robbie for attacking him. I do not apologize for his show, which I think is vile. I never participated in his show. I suppose it was a mistake inviting him to my party, but Doctor Sickwell encouraged me to invite him. He also convinced me that I needed to be a patient of his at that time. If I had only trusted myself more, I would have found my wife. Instead, I listened to that madman, and now look where I am.

"I am not delusional. My wife is here somewhere in Moojtema. You all know her as the Beauty Perfumes Girl, but I know her as Deer, the love of my life. If you would kindly let me, I will take her with me and depart Moojtema forever. I will split up my assets among the lower level peoples of Moojtema if they will only heed the message of *The Bible* that I delivered to them and aid a fellow brother on the path of righteousness. I would suggest they read Exodus for strength. I am ready for anything, even ready to die for my love."

The prosecuting attorney looked at Isaac shocked. The judges sat with mouths gaping open like baby birds waiting to be fed. It was the first time the accused had ever admitted any crime. Usually they blamed someone else. They blamed their lot in life. One man had even screamed, "It is because I was born a damn Barber! A meager Barber!" This man admitted he did wrong.

The judges announced the verdicts to each of the charges. One judge, a young woman who the prosecuting attorney ogled throughout the proceedings read each charge and the other two judges announced their ruling.

"Attempting to incite a riot," she said.

"Guilty!"

"Guilty!"

"Attempted murder of a celebrity."

"Guilty!"

"Guilty!"

"Covetous behavior towards a clone."

"Guilty!"

"Guilty!"

"Rabble Rousing."

"I didn't even know I was being tried for starting that riot for covering over the Beauty Perfumes Girl posters," Isaac lamented.

"Do not speak unless you are spoken to! You are the one here to answer for your crimes. You planned a party for the proletariat. You instigated them and made them feel downtrodden. You adulterated the youth. You thought too much in general. You tried to find meaning in the meaningless. That's what you do, Isaac. You're a damn spear jabbing me in my side, reminding me of my humanity."

"Guilty!"

"Guilty!"

"Espionage."

"Guilty!"

"Guilty!"

"Treason."

"Guilty!"

"Guilty!"

"What is the worst punishment we can give him?" one judge asked with a wry grin on his face.

"We must decide. Give him two months in solitary. We will come to a sentence. Jailer, take him away!" the female judge said.

The third judge sat there with a dumb look on his face, waiting to echo the other judge. When he heard no opportunity, he just twiddled his thumbs.

Isaac waited in agony in his cell. He did not care about his fate. He wanted to see his wife. He held out hope that the former agents of the Institute would deliver her to him. He waited for days, perhaps a week. He did not know if time was passing slowly or quickly. He measured the time, when his meals came. A gloved hand passed him a gray gelatinous cube, about four inches by four inches that tasted like salted filth. He ate it because secretly he hoped it was poison.

For all he cared, they could bring him a clone, as long as she could talk and he could lay his eyes on her once more. He tossed on the cold metal floor. He shivered away the time naked, all the time he thought he should be sleeping. However, he could not sleep.

In the morning the guard did not bring him the gelatinous cube. Isaac waited. There was a shuffling and an argument. His door swung open.

"You've got five minutes with her, so make it last," Ridley said. Deer walked in like a fireball singeing out the darkness. Isaac fell to his knees sobbing with his hands over his face. Ridley backed up and bowed, he closed the door humbly.

"Is it you?" Isaac bawled.

He crawled forward on his knees and held his head to her hips and sobbed squeezing her, trying to transfer his soul to her own.

"You aren't a clone?" he said between gasps for breath.

"No. We met outside my mother's dugout. I told you that I would wait for you until the Earth was smashed into dust."

"And you waited."

"I did, husband. I waited. My wait was not torture. I knew you would come."

"Seeing your posters was torture for me."

"No. Those aren't my posters. Those are all the clones they made from me. They found me to be disagreeable. They could not make me smile, or make that fishy face model pose, so they stuck me in the nursery, up to my elbows in baby shit everyday."

"Enough talking wife, kiss me," Isaac said, and rose to her level, grabbing her to him. He kissed her like there would be no tomorrow. She pulled her clothing down in heaps around her ankles.

Isaac slammed the door to his cell with his leg and made love to his wife. It was a hurried affair, caught on camera. They did not care who saw them. If there was one genuine act of human expression in the corridors of Moojtema that day, they were engaged in it. If there was but one particle of love, they produced it. When Isaac finished, he whispered into his wife's ear.

"I am going to have these men smuggle you out of Moojtema. You must go to the Forest and wait for me. Go back to your tribe. Please, honey, do not stay around here."

"You will die for what you have done, husband."

"If it means getting you out of here, I will die one thousand deaths. You must go, Deer. You must go and try to be happy."

Deer wept. Bitter tears streamed down her face. "Happiness is not possible for me without you."

"It is," Isaac cried.

The agents opened the door again. Ridley proclaimed, "Before your sentence, we will bring her back to you."

He pulled Ridley close, "You must get her out of here, after you bring her to me again."

Ridley nodded and did not say a word.

Isaac slept with a smile on his face. Her smell was firmly imbedded in his nostrils. His thoughts were fixed on her. He fixed his gaze on the ceiling. Everywhere he saw her face.

At the end of the month the agents returned with Deer. Ridley notified Isaac that they made plans to get her to a shuttle. After Ridley departed, offering them some privacy, Deer told Isaac the news.

"I am with child husband. Your child."

Isaac wept. He embraced her. The words flowed from his mouth like a holy hymn.

"If you bear a daughter, you will raise her just as you have been raised. You will bid her to marry the strongest and wisest man she can find. This is the oath of a woman on the Earth. You married me when I was weak, because you saw in me a lion. I have become that lion. If you bear a son you will tell him to trust his fellow men and seek to be trustworthy. These are my two highest hopes for my children. If I die, you must remarry."

Deer wept. "No, I will wait for you, Isaac. I will wait until the Earth is smashed to dust again."

"Deer, you must do what I tell you. They will surely kill me for my crimes. You cannot wait forever. If after one thousand days, I do not return to you, you must remarry. Do what I say. Promise me."

She cried, small sounds creeping from her throat. She nodded her head to him in silent concordance.

"Time is up. I am sorry, Isaac," Ridley said, opening the cell door.

"Ridley, you must get her out of here. You must do this for me."

"I promise you Isaac, I will do my best. Most of the exits are blocked by the Zero Levelers. They are rioting something fierce. Screaming for Exodus. There's really no stopping them now. Level by level, people are joining them."

"What will you do?"

"We will get her to a shuttle. You have my word I will get her out of here."

"I trust you, Ridley. I barely know you, but I trust you."

The female judge entered his room on the sixth day of his confinement.

"You have come to deliver my sentence," Isaac said.

"No. You have been granted a reprieve."

"I'm free to go?" Isaac asked, with elation in his voice.

"You are free to go from this court, but a higher court wishes to sit in judgment of you."

"Who?"

"You will be taken to the Circle of Twelve immediately. They will decide your fate. Enjoy your minutes as an innocent man."

He was allowed to walk freely from the jailhouse down a corridor. On the floor lights pointed the way to an elevator with only one symbol on it. On the silver mirrored door, there was a sign that said, "All who pass, look inside yourself."

Isaac could see his reflection in the mirrored surface. He thought he had seen better days.

The elevator was totally undecorated except for a jewel-encrusted button: a circle of sapphires inlaid around a disk of platinum. The number 12, in diamonds, formed the center. Isaac looked around the elevator and down the hallway. No one was coming. He pressed the button and the doors closed suddenly.

The elevator jerked upwards, sliding like a stripper on a sensitive pole. Upwards for an eternity of pointed pondering, "What will my fate be?"

At what was the halfway point the voice shot into his head, what seemed a pre-recorded message, but what was a private at the Tanner Institute.

Isaac if you hear this please say YOU ARE CLEAR TO ME.

Isaac if you hear this please say YOU ARE CLEAR TO ME.

Isaac if you hear this please say YOU ARE CLEAR TO ME.

Isaac sighed in annoyance and said, "You are clear to me!" It ricocheted off the silver elevator walls like a bullet.

Oh dear God, sir he responded!

There was the sounds of fumbling and broken glass in his head.

Isaac this is Commander Jacobus we have been trying to reach you for months.

"You're the one that told me I wouldn't be able to send a message. Your little ploy for the Bible Virus didn't work, Jacobus. The GOD is still up. Its power influenced the people to rebel. The lower levels are rioting now."

What's your status?

"They found me out. I'm probably going to die soon. I've got a lot to tell you about your boss there. I hope he's somewhere you can apprehend him."

Paraclete Tanner?

"Yeah Paraclete Tanner. He's responsible for this whole mess. He sold humanity for a chance to be immortal."

He always said he was forced into it.

In his head there were more sounds of fumbling and sounds of metal rods being snapped in half.

Isaac, you don't know what the hell you're talking about, boy! You're a damn fool.

"Dr. Tanner, I respect your work as a scientist. You were an awful human being in life, and an even worse one in your death. You're a damn fool."

I am not a human being, Isaac. I am an immortal -- immortal like God would be if he existed. But he doesn't. I am God, Isaac. Well, at least the closest you'll ever get to one.

"Commander Jacobus did you pick up that transmission? I hope you heard that Jacobus," Isaac said.

Isaac, we keep losing you.

"Tanner is jumping on the frequency. Can't you stop that psycho?"

Private, hold this frequency open. Override any attempt to listen in.

"No. Let him think he's overriding the frequency and listen to what he's saying," Isaac said.

Can you do that private?

Ehh. I can try sir.

In his head, there were the sounds of breaking glass, the crumpling of plastic like the breaking of a seventh seal, and a trumpet blaring.

Isaac winced at the sounds in his head.

Isaac. You are just a goddamn fool. Your whole mission has been a sham. I sent you because I'm bored, Isaac. I'm bored to the core of my very being. Do you know what it is like living for five-hundred years? Death would be a gift, a welcome relief. But I can't bring myself to do it. You've been very entertaining to me though, Isaac. I've watched your every move. Don't you know I can see through those eyes of yours? You've made me so happy, son. I'm very surprised you even made it this far. You've served your purpose though. You can go die now.

In Isaac's head, he heard the sounds of cutting onions and fire burning.

Damn you, sir! I trusted you! I devoted my life to you! Your cause, sir! I devoted myself to your cause! Enlightening the world!

Jacobus don't be so silly. What would an immortal want with a pesky cause. The world is for me. Good and noble causes are pursued by men who want to leave the whole world a better place for their children. Evil causes are pursued by men who want to leave the world a better place for their children. It's really all the same, Jacobus. Why leave any world at all?

Dr. Robert Tanner, I am ordering you to be placed under arrest for planning the murder of Isaac. You are under arrest for the murder of Major Nathanael Hardoak. You are under arrest for the killing of countless human beings.

You bastards will have to find me, Jacobus!

"Count all the diamonds on the ground and you'll see his handiwork. Now be quiet! I have to think!" Isaac said.

The elevator doors peeled away into the floor like an infinite strip from an orange and collapsed into the floor. The air in the new room hung musty like a crypt. Isaac stood in the center of a circle surrounded by the Twelve, enfeebled, their gray faces stretched and contorted like addicts longing for painkillers. Nearly all were dead in their seats, twitching. It looked like they had been slaughtered and left to rot. Isaac choked back vomit at the dead, preserved faces.

"The Christ," the old surviving sniddler, said coughing dust, "what made him special? And don't tell me he was the Son of God."

Isaac thought. He stood in front of him, wary to speak, waiting to be judged, expecting the death sentence.

"Time is up!"

"What then?" Isaac said, bowing mockingly.

The immortal smiled widely.

"He was a new type of man. There were no men like him before him and no men like him after him, just followers. He was a new type of man, just as I am a new type of man. You, too, are a new type of man, I believe. It's just a pity that you won't be able to share any of your wisdom with the rest of your fellow men."

"I already have."

"Your book? That old rag? The Christ never would have signed his name to that one. The rabble that you shared that with, they can't understand it. Those piss ants really got up in arms after your trial. They're still rioting. I want you to call them off."

"They're not rioting because of me. I didn't tell them to do anything. They're rioting because they no longer believe all of this. They realized it's all a fiction."

"Your book. Your *Bible* is a fiction."

"Could be. It doesn't matter. It's ours. It's human, something you gave up a long time ago. *The Bible* is not my book, just as it's not their book. They can use it however they want. It inspires them, I don't. I can't stop them."

"Emmm. Perhaps that is so."

"It is. I can't stop them."

"You're certainly an agreeable little pet for Robert Tanner aren't you?" the lone immortal asked, sneering.

"I care nothing for that creature. He's as good as dead. We found out about his charade."

"Just like we found out about it. I certainly hope he's good and dead. Sending that one pure Termiculum crystal up here. Not enough to share. Pure genius on his part! Then again, he is a genius. You are his tool. You did his bidding well."

"I didn't do it for him. I came here for another reason."

"Your wife?"

"No."

"Yes you did! Don't lie. I watched your little display in your cell. How sweet. Saucy."

He pressed the button on a videoscreen. Ridley and Deer were entering a shuttle.

"This brings us to the question of your choice."

"What choice do I have?"

"You have to be punished for what you did. Aiding in destroying something so beautiful cannot go unpunished."

"You should punish yourself then. You helped destroy the world."

"Pfahh. This big old ball of madness and folly? We just changed it. Gave it a new order."

"You have a choice, Isaac. Do you see those two elevator doors? One will take you to the outside. One will take you to your doom. Which do you choose?"

"I'll go outside."

"When you get there, look to the sky. Your wife's shuttle will explode in front of your eyes."

Isaac smiled. "Then I choose my death."

"I never said death. It will be painless. You'll be sent on a pilgrimage. With no return."

Isaac walked to the door that the disgusting creature pointed out. He turned to the immortal and held up his hand. He clicked his fingernail slowly. He smiled at the immortal.

Roger. We have your coordinates fixed. Bombers are enroute. Get out of there.

"I am leaving," Isaac said.

"Don't tell me. Begone!" the immortal cackled.

Isaac smiled to him and turned into the elevator. It went up.

The elevator went up against the force of gravity for minutes. Isaac felt nothing. He did what he must.

The doors opened. The temperature was stifling inside. Thousands of hairless sweaty men lined the walls, sitting on wooden benches, facing forwards, their bald heads glistening in the low light.

Attendants in white approached him. He palmed the diamond so they couldn't see. They shaved his head while another attendant helped him out of his clothing.

"All pilgrims must be decontaminated. You must be hairless, and free of bacteria," they said.

The washed him with sponges that stank of chemicals. It burned his skin briefly, like stepping into the hot sunshine. His body hair peeled of when they washed him with cool water like a baptism. All the hair from his body, from his genitals, his chest and armpits, even his eyebrows ended up a sopping mess on the floor that an attendant mopped into an open vacuum sucking drain. They hosed him down with cool water again, like a bath in the river Styx. One attendant dried him and bade him to sit on the bench with one of the other thousands.

"I am to die," Isaac told his comrades.

"We will become servants to the Mashgool," the men said.

A woman in white with great breasts barely visible under a form fitting muslin handed him a small, orange pill and a glass of water saying, "Pleasant tidings on your journey. It will ease your mind."

The men swallowed the pill with water. Isaac faked taking his pill and palmed it. She passed by again to see if everyone had taken it. He placed one hand under his buttock quickly and shoved the tiny pill and diamond into his ass. He hoped it would not melt.

He looked at the men next to him. They seemed to drift off into a torpor and stare straight ahead. He looked at the men across the square from him. They were all staring straight ahead. Isaac mimicked them. He recalled a verse from the *Cantos of the Mashgool*: "…and the Mashgool are served by the faithful. The faithful are taken up by the Mashgool and held close to their bosom. Blessed are the faithful to the Mashgool. They shall know no fear, no pain, and no loneliness. Death shall have no victory over them…."

The elevator doors opened. A voice overhead, nearly inaudible to Isaac, bade the men in soft tones to enter. They stood in unison. They filed into the elevator and all stared blindly straight ahead. There was no fear in any of them. Isaac screamed inside.

The doors closed. He felt the elevator lift. They went upwards for what seemed minutes. The time passed slowly. One of the men farted audibly. There was no reaction from anyone, not even a snicker. It smelled of caramelized onions with a touch of swamp gas.

Isaac tried to control his breathing and mimic them.

The elevator crept upwards, retracted by spider silk nanotubules. Isaac's heart began to pound. It was all he heard in the elevator: A sick *thump thump*. A slick of sweat broke out in the claustrophobic elevator car that held thousands.

The elevator ground to a halt. Oxygen canisters in the ceiling leaked their contents. An airlock whirred into place. A clank of bolts tightening shocked Isaac from shitting himself.

The elevator doors opened. The voice called them peacefully. The men filed into a narrow corridor. Steam occluded Isaac's vision. When it was his turn, he followed.

They walked down the corridor and turned the corner, disappearing into the steam. Static played in Isaac's head. He could barely keep from running. Where would he go?

He turned the corner. The man in front of him disappeared into the misty spray. It smelled and tasted of alcohol. More disinfectant.

Isaac heard a loud pop and a whoosh.

Four laser intercrossing laser beams quartered the man who did not cry out. The fine bloody mist hung in the air like a silk burial shroud. His bald head and shoulders flipped in the air end over end, spraying blood. Robotic arms caught the slaughtered man's head and shoulders and a frosty blast froze them. They chinked onto the conveyor belt and moved forwards. Robotic brooms swept the legs and arms to the side. Thousands of limbs twitched randomly at the shock.

Isaac screamed and jumped onto the piles of twitching limbs. Detached arms squeezed onto his warmth, clinging to a desperate sense of life or nervous impulse. A bolt of blue lighting zapped from the wall and struck Isaac like a bee sting.

*

Fifteen strike fighters, guided by Isaac's coordinate to the Immortal's location, pounded the metal onion with missiles. This bombardment weakened its hull enough for a bomber to drop a single nuclear warhead inside. It bounced twice and landed at the feet of the Immortal, who yawned. The nuclear warhead exploded with a blinding flash of heat. The onion dissolved in an instant and the massive space elevator tottered and fractured. It hit the ground inside the middle of Moojtema and began splintering.

*

Alarms sounded in the ship. It lurched downwards violently. Isaac splayed on the cold metal floor. He looked up and saw *them*.

Small creatures, jellyfish with tentacles, floating on metal disks, flooded into the room. The Mashgool. They farted past him, belching high speed like pig squeals.

Isaac stood, and one of the creatures crashed into him. Isaac punched into its jelly flesh, digging his hands as far as they would penetrate, screaming, "Damn you!"

He was stuck. The Mashgool dragged him, as he tried to extricate his hand from the mess. The Mashgool flew into a small chamber and flung Isaac, arm and all against the wall. Isaac squeezed his arms against the jelly and cried out.

*

Institute whirlybirds under the command of Paraclete Jacobus McCrimmin circled Moojtema as the space elevator crumpled and rained into the vast chromosomal structure, starting fires. The Mashgool protein extraction spaceship loomed above on a collision course with Earth like a great asteroid blotting the sun.

Institute strike teams descended from ropes and aided in evacuating the populace from the burning hulk. They trickled out under the shadow of the wreck dropping towards them. Flaming from the atmosphere, the Mashgool ship arced across the sky, screaming protests to the winds. Thousands poured from the wreckage, dazed like cattle leaving the pen for open pastures. All night long the survivors walked out.

At daybreak, Deer watched the flames billow and the ship streak across the sky from a hillside. Ridley brushed his hand over the top of hers and let it linger. She pulled it quickly away.

"Do you think old Isaac made it?" he said with a hint of hope in his voice, though she didn't know if it was for Isaac's hope or his own.

"I don't know. I told him that I will wait for him until this earth is smashed to dust," she said crossing her arms. Not a hint of a smile broke on her face.

"What did he tell you?"

"He told me that if he does not return in a thousand days, that I should marry the strongest and wisest man and have many children. He told me to teach my daughters to do the same. He told me to tell my sons to trust and be trustworthy."

They walked down amongst the tattered people making their way from the destroyed wreckage of Moojtema. The blackened humans cast suspicious frightened glances, unsure of the dawn they were seeing for the first time. Ridley looked at Deer. She was beautiful. Her gaze seemed far off as she stared at the crowd of men and women -- Holy almost. Above the torn and humbled masses, two butterflies flitted in an eager tease, dancing a dance of eternity.

The ship erupted into a fireball as it crossed into the upper atmosphere. It traced a sick burning streak across the sky as shards of outer shell peeled away and ignited.

Isaac brought his hands to his face as the Mashgool struggled to wrap its tentacles around his throat. Its skin was cold and the air filtering through the vents on its plastic bubble smelled like heavy crushed garlic. There was no distinguishable face, and the tentacles undulated rhythmically with each belch and fart that formed words Isaac could not distinguish. It seemed to be telling him something. He did not let up his grasp even as the tentacles withdrew.

The door had closed behind them with a metal chunking, and an airlock whirred into place, grinding like torture, until it slipped and seized into position. Two seconds followed, then the explosion sheered the pod from the doomed ship's hull like a billowing orgasm. The pair bonded duo struggled and fell freely, wrapped together arm and tentacle for a moment with the rest of the fiery mess, before the thrusters hurtled them out of sucking orbit towards infinity. When Isaac and the thing slapped against the wall they fell unconscious, with Isaac wrapped in a tentacle embrace.

The small pod no longer operated under a power of its own. No one piloted the small star craft as it hurtled into the black distance. It passed the earth bound moon and accelerated.

Isaac was the first to come to. He stared at the beast and peeled its tentacles from his neck.

I must kill it, Isaac thought. He looked around the cabin for anything to strike, or bash, or pierce, or crush the Mashgool's body. The walls were shimmering smooth, strangely warm to the touch. In an indentation, he saw a black device similar to the one Hildebrand used to deliver the *Cantos of the Mashgool* to the faithful. Isaac pressed it hoping that it would reveal a space that held a weapon. The black button went further inside its housing but nothing happened.

Isaac sat shaking the stars from his eyes and stared at the thing. The Mashgool was miniscule, even when anchored on its floating disk. It was about as tall as Isaac's arm. Angry, Isaac slapped its plastic dome. The Mashgool did not stir. He slapped it again and the sound echoed off the walls of the chamber. How are these things capable of enslaving and butchering men? He slapped it again so hard his hand hurt, trying to pound his way through the bubble. He reached back to slap its dome again when the Mashgool shot to life and hovered menacingly over him. It burped and farted staccato patterns that crescendoed to an enormous guttural blast.

From the walls, the translation came, "You foolish man, just what are you doing? Do you realize what you've done? How am I going to explain this to the Sector Governor? An answer will be demanded! Just who the hell are you?"

Isaac stared at the Mashgool. He tried to find eyes to stare at. It would be hard for him to intimidate this thing. Isaac stood up so he was at the Mashgool's level. The Mashgool floated upwards until it was near the ceiling.

"I'm just a man," Isaac said. The walls burped and farted his response. The Mashgool descended downwards floating in front of Isaac's face. Through the plastic dome bubble, Isaac could make out thousands of tiny blinking red stalks. He figured they were eyeballs. What he did not know was that the Mashgool could not see his skin. The Mashgool eyes were not capable of picking up that wavelength so it appeared as invisible. Isaac was just a bag of bones and more importantly, meat.

"I've never talked to a man before. I did not know you could talk."

"Because you've been busy slaughtering us."

"The process is automated. I'm just here to repair the machines if they break."

"I'm glad you want to reason with me," Isaac said.

"There is no sense in me fighting with you in here. I can't use my weapons in this confined space. It will blow the craft apart and I'll die, too. Besides, you're in for a world of pain when we get to the Sector Governor's Station."

"I don't care anymore."

"We were told you were unthinking, useless creatures. I did not know you could care."

"Who told you that?"

"Our leadership. They say that about most of the inhabitants of the planets we vanquish."

"Well, I'm not useless. Most of the human beings I know are not useless. We're capable of art and science and feats of engineering and love."

"What good is your science? You're trapped on your little blue planet, your strange blue sphere. You know, I read about your planet as a child in a famous Mashgool book called *On the Blue Planet*. We teach our children the way to not do things in this book. Your race is an example of stupidity to us. We think you're the most despicable species we've run across. Most of our subjects put up a remarkable fight. They battle us for years. They struggle and die but at least they are worthy of being our opponents. You despicable humans did it to yourselves. We planted the seeds and watched. We came in and cleaned up the mess."

"No. You manipulated a man who was a monster. He's responsible. Not all of us."

"You mean to tell me you think one man can be responsible for the demise of your species? You were that weak? Anything that weak deserves destruction."

"We are individuals. Each man and woman decides for themselves to create something or participate in the destruction of the Earth."

"Most just live in that holding pen down there. Despicable existence. You know that many of your kind would much rather be sheep than men?"

"No. We can always think for ourselves. The only way you can do that is through fear."

"Yes. It's a shame you didn't remove that section of your tasty brain from your DNA. It's quite pathetic. It turns you into servile little creatures."

"You're a servile little creature. Look at you. You're just fixing machines on some slaughter ship. You aren't important."

"That's where you're wrong, *man*. I'm part of an organism more enormous than anything you can fathom. I'm one sensing node in this organism. What I see, we all see. It was one of our nodes that discovered your little planet after your famous scientist, whom you call a monster, did his experiments that would have, if the stupid people of your planet didn't get all up in arms about them, enabled your puny civilization to become a star power."

"We're born, we live, and we die. That's the way of man."

"Pathetic. Even more pathetic than the way you value your individuality. All those rights you bitch and complain about all the time are just a hindrance. Mashgool says that the way of the universe is strength. You see it everywhere in nature man. The weak species, as your own is known to us, are subsumed. The strongest species, the Mashgool in this particular universe of the multiverse, will always triumph."

"What's the point? What's the triumph?"

"Again with your human want for meaning. Mashgool have no such hindrance. You wonder how you fit into the whole. The Mashgool are the whole. You fill our bellies. We thank you."

Isaac leapt to his feet and slapped the Mashgool from its orbit with a balled up fist.

"Don't talk about that!" Isaac screamed. The walls delivered the message in a high-pitched whine coupled with three short toots.

The Mashgool floated back to its orbit saying nothing. Hours passed. Isaac had the urge to pee. He looked to the Mashgool floating above him near the ceiling.

"Where is the bathroom on this thing?"

"Filthy animal. Just go. I have no need for that disgusting endeavor. We control unfortunate aspects of our metabolism. We have one up on nature."

Isaac glared at the Mashgool and turned his back. He pissed into the corner but it trickled down the path of least resistance, pooling on the floor.

"Disgusting creature," the Mashgool farted.

"Ditto, sicko," Isaac said.

More time passed between them. The urine began to pickle and stink.

"How much longer before we get there?"

"I'm fairly certain you'll have starved before we arrive. This pod is designed for a being with a Termiculum power source. Oh there's water, but no food."

"I've been hungry before," Isaac said.

"You don't know real hunger," the Mashgool said.

"How long to get there?"

"Whether you know it or not, we're being pulled along at a speed approaching, but not quite reaching, the speed of light. Still, we have about 4.5 dominions to cross. It will be some time. I don't think you'll make it."

"Looks like I'm in for a fast," Isaac said gritting his teeth.

"You're in for a death," the Mashgool responded with an ignoble belch.

"I'll eat you if I have to," Isaac said.

"Sorry. My heart pumps cyanide, enough to kill you with a drop of my blood."

"I'll risk it."

The Mashgool laughed. After nearly four weeks Isaac discovered its laugh was high pitched and brassy, declimating fiercely then ending with a whimper like a trumpet blown by a withered old man.

"Sick," Isaac said scratching the beard forming on his now gaunt face. He lay in the corner barely able to move. He endured weeks of the Mashgool's taunts and jibes.

He asked the Mashgool, "Can you die? Are you one of the immortals?"

The Mashgool laughed again and said, "An immortal man would surely die of boredom. No I'm not immortal. See here's how your foolish species operates, it's a pity that you did not realize it before we did. Having beaten all your natural enemies, your species set up obstacles for itself. You overcame these obstacles but then boredom sets in and you have to invent new obstacles. You're always creating and vanquishing monsters. We don't get it. You are an absurd bunch of creatures."

"Just what does your species do then?" Isaac said barely able to hold his head up without it drooping down towards the floor.

"We busy ourselves. That's the only way to survive in this Universe. We stopped walking in circles long ago. Your planet has gotten a taste of our business. When we made contact you fools were still burning the plant material of your planet for warmth. Pathetic."

"There is no talking with you. Everything I do, everything humans do is pathetic to you."

"It is."

The pod yanked out of its elliptical path. The walls became translucent. They were at the coronal edge of a giant red sun dotted with small white stars. In the distance, Isaac saw the Mashgool Deep Station. It glowed bright red, reflections off the metal surface. The Mashgool began flying around the pod, zipping back and forth like a bottled gnat.

"I thought you don't get nervous," Isaac asked.

"I'm not. I'm the only one reporting back from the expedition."

"What will they do to you."

"They already know what happened. It wasn't anything we could do. I am returning with the culprit."

"You think I did that? How can one man be responsible for all that?"

"Four-hundred and ninety expeditions and not a single incident. Then you come along and all this destruction comes with you. Yes. I'm placing the blame on you."

"Good. I'll take that blame and I'll double it two fold. I would gladly do it again."

"You're an uppity little beast," the Mashgool burped.

Isaac met the Mashgool's derision with silence; it was the most powerful weapon against arrogance.

The pod drifted towards a docking station on the massive Mashgool Deep Station. Isaac could see Mashgool wearing metal suits, flying in the empty space around the station. Two Mashgool approached the pod and fastened what looked like big snaking hoses to its exterior. The hoses contracted and pulled the pod into position with a protrusion on the station's surface. Isaac stared through the translucent panel at a wing of the space station that projected outwards for a distance at least the radius of the Earth's moon.

A circle spun down in the center of the floor and Mashgool entered, flying on floating disks, wearing shimmering robes. Their silver and blue tinged robes dragged the ground underneath their floating disks giving them the appearance of being at least five feet tall.

"What is the thing doing here?"

"He stowed away," the Mashgool said.

"It looks nearly starved. Hairy. Disgusting. What is that smell?"

"The smell is the man's biowaste."

"Disgusting. Is it contagious?"

"I've kept my virus shield on."

"What happened to the extraction ship?"

"It was destroyed. We don't know how."

Isaac spoke weakly. "I did it. I pointed out where the Circle of Twelve resided and some of my friends destroyed the onion on your space elevator. I guess that brought the whole mess down."

"This freak needs to go to quarantine."

"Send the isolation team."

The Mashgool in the bubble floated past the brilliantly robed Mashgool. It turned to Isaac and said, "You are most interesting. Your bravery is beyond reproach. Had you have been a sniveling coward like the vast majority of your species, I would have ordered your immediate death. I believe we have something to learn from you."

Isaac tried to nod, but he was barely able to lift his head.

"I will see that you are taken care of and restored to health," the Mashgool said.

"Why?" Isaac asked, but the Mashgool had departed.

The robed Mashgool left the pod soon thereafter, unable to take the stench. As they departed, one inquired to the other why they shouldn't just launch the pod onto a course with the giant, red sun.

The isolation team entered the pod and immediately began sticking various probes in Isaac's body. Some of the probes burned. Some pinched. Still others sucked up samples of his bodily fluids.

"What delegation are you from?" one of the Mashgool asked as it stabbed Isaac with a silver instrument.

"Can't you tell? He's from the blue planet," another Mashgool snapped.

"I've never seen one full grown before," the Mashgool said.

"Nor alive," the other one said.

A third Mashgool approached with an instrument that looked like a weapon to Isaac. Shiny and cylindrical like God's Crucible. Isaac screamed weakly as the Mashgool fired it. A blob of goo surrounded Isaac and expanded, foaming at the edges to form a sphere. Isaac could still breathe. The Mashgool Isolation team rolled Isaac, in his ball, toward the hole in the floor. Isaac fell for what seemed like a minute. The ball then came to rest on a cushion of air and lowered gently to the floor. The isolation team followed him, hovering downwards on their floating disks.

When the Mashgool began rolling the ball, Isaac did not move, but rather stayed still. It was as if the foamy goo he that trapped him was only one sphere within another larger sphere. Isaac could not see where he was going. He could only see the shadows of his captors on all sides of him.

The ball began dissolving around him, letting the full light in. Gaseous vapors surrounded Isaac, choking him, swirling blue and purple against the overhead lights. Isaac stood up. One of the Mashgool put a Universal Translator around his neck. It fit snugly.

"Another prisoner!" screamed a creature with a single eye on a stalk that met with shoulders hunched back, running to the floor where two spindly feet wide like garden rakes shuffled across the floor. A Universal Translator dangled around the stalk and its eye blinked furiously.

"Quite strange, this one is! All upright and hairless, fair skinned and squinting."

Small cells lined the concave walls in levels up farther than Isaac could see. Creatures poked their heads out like animals in a zoo, curious at their new compatriot. Furry beasts, slimy beasts, beasts with arms radiating like starfish, beasts like bears with hairy smashed in baby faces hooted and yelled like a monkey house in a zoo at Isaac. Isaac stood in the center with his arms folded, looking upwards as scat rained down on top of him. Purple scat. Yellow. Green. Bright red billowy cloud-like scat that descended to the floor like a feather settled into the crevices. Chunky scat. Liquid scat. Creatures from across the universe shit their protest from their tiny cells.

"Nim, have this mess cleaned up immediately!" the Mashgool yelled to the one-eyed creature and departed in disgust. Nim shuffled to within a few feet of Isaac and began using his feet to pick poo flecks from Isaac's clothing.

"Apologies, apologies," Nim said staring at Isaac with his single eye, blinking it copiously. "The bombs were not aimed at you. They were aimed at our captors."

"I was told this was a medical quarantine," Isaac said.

"I suppose it is, but many of us have been waiting forever for our chance to have our case before the Governor. Xzzlit, how long have you been waiting for?"

A triangular head on a long neck, which gave Xzzlit the appearance of a snake, shot from a first floor cell. "For three-hundred-twenty-five revolutions of the Xlatian Sun around Star Cluster Z."

"How long is that?" Isaac asked.

"You look to be able two-hundred revolutions old," the snake beast said, glaring at Isaac.

"About twenty-five of our years, then."

"Just where are you from?" Nim asked blinking with his pupil dilating to its fullest aperture and shrinking at regular intervals.

"Earth," Isaac said.

"Never heard of it," Nim said.

"It's a beautiful place, well, was."

"We all come from beautiful places. What is your name?"

"Isaac."

"And Isaac, why are you here? Were you captured? Are you here to negotiate a treaty with the Mashgool? A trade agreement perhaps? You requesting right of passage for a ferry? What's your rank in your society? You look like royalty, my boy. I'm royalty. Takes royalty to recognize royalty," Nim said not breathing. As far as Isaac could tell, he spoke through his eye, too, because Isaac did not see a mouth moving.

"I'm just a man. I'm here because I helped destroy one of the Mashgool farms."

"Oh' I bet they're not happy. You're here to be judged a criminal by them?"

"No. I don't know. I was in the farming ship when it started falling out of orbit and I got into an escape pod. It brought me here."

"What were they farming?"

"Us."

"What?"

"The ship was set up to butcher us. Just like I'm sure you have animals that you eat."

"Oh. Dear. How? How did it happen?"

"Best I figure some people thought they could sell the rest of us to them in exchange for living forever."

"Are they still living forever?"

"No. I think they're all dead."

"Good. Let me tell you something, Isaac. The Mashgool value resistance above all else. I do not think they will fault you for destroying their ship. They may praise you. Weird, I know. In their eyes, if a species resists them, then that species is worthy of continued existence. If a species offers their science, no matter how weak it is in the Mashgool's eyes, they will cooperate with them. If a species kowtows to them in exchange for their technology, many times that species ends up in your species' situation: as food. Well, I guess that's only if they are tasty. Sick, I know, but it is how they operate."

"They're bastards, the whole bunch of them!" Xzzlit screamed from his cell.

"Xzzlit there is the Chairman of the Neobin Commonwealth of Trade Planets. They tried to compromise with the Mashgool over the mining rights to the Azz'han Asteroid System. He's here to make a universal declaration of war against the Mashgool to get the bastards to leave the Trade Planet Commonwealth alone. All the prisoners here are either royalty or nominated by their civilizations to negotiate or flat out refuse Mashgool proposals."

"What are you, Nim?"

"I'm an Emperor of a minor civilization spanning four stars. The Mashgool made contact with us and realized our baby's feet would make excellent decorations and headdresses for their Mashgool ladies. I'm here to humbly ask that they stop or face war."

"And they'll stop if you do that?"

"Oh yes. Either way they've established themselves as the most powerful force in this segment of the Multiverse. You bow down, they wipe you out or make you irrelevant. You say you'll fight them, they laugh and leave you alone. They're a strange creature. But it's all in accordance with their lust for strength. You know they believe that the primary goal of the Multiverse is strength? Strange, right? To them it's only intelligent species with their free will, that can choose weakness and lassitude."

"What of their religion?"

"What do you mean?"

The Cantos of the Mashgool?

"Never heard of them. I've been dealing with the Mashgool my entire life."

"It's a book. They say it's their holy book. The tome of their religion."

"They say that for all the planets and all the creatures they come into contact with. They study the civilization for a while and design a book that will appeal to the masses, cause divisions, and insure their control."

"Sick," Isaac said.

"No. Brilliant," Nim said. "The Mashgool are very fond of operating principles. You could say that their way of life is all about refining their operating principles. They're very willing to discard the old in favor of the new. They're very adaptive. They don't cling to any beliefs. In fact, they consider that is the ultimate weakness: the resistance to change core beliefs even in the face of overwhelming evidence to their falsehood."

"The Mashgool I was in the pod with told me they all think with one mind."

"True," Nim said. "What one sees, they all have the capability of seeing. They are individuals in that they each occupy a certain time and space, but they are all linked together via massive neural nets. This way, the refinement of their operating principles goes without any painful transition. They all agree simultaneously. They are all capable of independent thought, but when something makes sense to them, it makes sense to all of them."

"They have agreed upon a logic," Isaac said.

"Or it just works," Nim said.

"Their logic is a bunch of trash and nonsense!" Xzzlit screamed from his cage.

"Never mind him. If you were here for as long as him, you'd be angry, too. Let me see you to your room."

Isaac's room was situated between two slender white-colored creatures with silver eyes like teardrops beneath a vicious mouth of teeth that fit together like a zipper. They bowed humbly to their cellmate and introduced themselves as the Fallorian brothers, vicious rebels against the Mashgool and co-creators of the now destroyed and disbanded Fallorian Promised Guild. Emperor Nim bowed deeply to Isaac and bade him farewell for now but promised to keep him up to date on the status of his trial.

"We almost beat those Mashgool bastards back at the Battle of Third Zibbit," Eek, the more stout of the Fallorians said.

"Did you fight well?" Isaac said.

"Yes. They resorted to dirty tricks. They always resort to dirty tricks. Don't ever trust those Mashgool bastards."

"What are you two here for?"

"Inciting a rebellion against the overlords of the universe, what else?"

"What is your punishment."

"Oh, we'll be let go after we have our little talk with their governor."

"It's so strange. They just let you go? How many of them did you kill?"

"Hundreds of thousands. Old Peek here got quite adept at destroying their small battle cruisers."

"Aye, I did," Peek said humbly.

"And they're just going to let you go?"

"I guess they're going to give us ribbons."

"An award?"

"Aye," Peek said.

"After they captured us, they said they were going to give us the highest honor awarded to any enemy of the Mashgool."

"Aye. The Crimson Star of Gloop. Quite an honor," Peek said.

"And what are you going to do after you leave?"

"Raise another Guild and keep fighting them," Eek said.

"I'm retiring," Peek said.

"Oh, no, you can't. We have plenty more Mashgool to kill, Peek."

"Its getting old, Eek. Them giving us this medal and releasing us makes me think they just don't care if we fight them."

"Isn't that what you're supposed to do? Fight them?"

"Aye," Peek said.

"But it's pointless. But you're earning their respect."

"They have weapons which can destroy an entire galaxy. They don't use them. It's like we're just toys for them. Amusements."

"Aye. They love fighting, these Mashgool. They love opponents. They love conflict. That's why they're letting us go."

"You know they're letting you go?"

"Aye. We've been captured going on five times now."

"And you keep fighting them?"

"When in doubt, fight it out."

"Aye. That's sound advice. Don't want to end up like the Pylori."

"Who are they?"

"Despicable creatures. You'll see them when you go to your trial. There's no sense even wasting my time talking about them."

Peek shuffled back and forth on his feet. "You want to know the easiest way to kill a Mashgool?"

"Sure. That could come in handy," Isaac said.

"The thought transducer. Located in its head."

"The brain?"

"The bastards don't have a brain. Well not like you or me. It's a hunk of metal. That soft body they have is just a sort of support jelly. Gotta use something hard, dunno like those carbon crystals. That's what we use. Superheat them and let them fly, right through that damn thought transducer. It will drop."

"The carbon crystal," Isaac said, thinking. "You mean a diamond."

"Aye. Sure. They're plentiful enough. Just none here."

"I've got one."

"Where?"

"Umm, well, I hid it."

"Really? Let us see. Be quick."

Isaac squatted and pulled the diamond from his ass.

"What'd you store it in that pocket? How did you get that by the guards?"

"Yeah, I put it in my jail wallet. I was never searched. They probably didn't think their food could get something past them."

"Food?"

"Yes. The Mashgool use my people as food."

"Dear. Well it's time for you to start fighting them."

"Aye, make him a member of the Promised Guild," Peek said.

"Right! What a lovely addition he will make. What are you a prince of your people? How many of your kind can we expect to join us?"

"I'm just a man. I guess I could start recruiting when I return home."

"Peek. Do we have enough materials around here to make a one shot wonder?"

"Aye. I'll have to barter with the Sazian clowns upstairs. We should be able to do that."

"How much time will it take, Peek?"

"Maybe a day or two. Aye. A day or two."

"When is your trial?"

"I don't know. Nim's working on that. Why you want me to do it?" Isaac said with astonishment.

"Of course we want you to do it. Don't tell Nim anything. Nim is an idiot. Don't trust him with anything. He'll report right to the Mashgool. He's too stupid to even breathe."

"He's just an idiot. He doesn't mean any harm by it, Eek."

"We should kill him before he gets one of us killed," Eek said.

"We couldn't possibly kill him, he's an emperor. We need all the friends we can get, Eek. And to think that I'm usually the hot-headed one," Peek said.

"Fine. Fine. Stick to the plan. Make that one shot wonder as soon as you can."

"Aye. I've got an idea. You can get your trial sooner if you try out for their orchestra."

"Right. Make the orchestra and stay here forever."

"Aye. You want to try out for the orchestra, kid?"

"I don't play an instrument."

"It's okay. You'll only blast one note out of it. Right into the Governor's thought transducer."

"What's the point of killing the governor?"

"The point is that it will be a statement of your resistance to them."

"There's no way I'll get out of here alive."

"Quite to the contrary. You'll probably get a medal."

"This is insane."

"You've never dealt with the Mashgool before."

"Aye. He hasn't. We know all about them."

"Right. We do," Eek said. The two brothers began talking in whispers to themselves. Isaac went to his cell. Food waited for him in a simple bowl: the same gray ooze that was so popular in Moojtema. He drank it in gulps, and the cells in his stomach sang psalms to glory.

#

Three-million, five-hundred-thousand, six-hundred, and fifty-three years before the first human being walked on the savannahs of Africa the Mashgool composer Pfft Boo Boo introduced the notion that the Mashgool should preserve, more than anything, the musical traditions of their conquered subjects. He formed the first universal orchestra, composed of all the musical instruments discovered by the Mashgool up to that point in time. Many of the instruments were from worlds that the Mashgool devastated. The performers were only just learning how to make sounds with their instrument. The sound was cacophonous--utter rape to the refined Mashgool ears. Pfft Boo Boo was warned that his project would be canceled and all the instruments catapulted into a tiny white dwarf star if he failed again. Pfft Boo Boo tried again. First, he sectioned the orchestra into their various sounds. Next, he made sure that all of his players were the absolute best to be found in the universe. Finally he spent three-thousand, six-hundred, fifty-five years, three months, one week and four days composing a symphony that if it were a mathematical equation instead of music could describe the basic structure of the universe.

It began with a single Xlorian cawet string plucked in 4/4, pulsing the heartbeat of the universe. To its bassy resonance, all other layers were added. Jaunts and forays echoed and rolled over each other playfully telling the tale of the first Mashgool expeditions into the vast, unknown universe. The final crescendo caused at least five heads to explode as the ecstasy caused thought transducers to overheat and catch fire to the protoplasm.

The current conductor of the symphony orchestra represented the seven thousandth "passing on" of the thought transducer of Pfft Boo Boo. Seven-thousand biological bodies housed his genius and became dust. The metal brain was the ultimate reservoir for musical art in the universe.

The orchestra was at the space station for repairs and to see if there was any musical genius among the convicts and ambassadors waiting for audience with the governor. Pfft Boo Boo held tryouts daily. Most of those who performed for a seat were sent away. Every night before the feasting, Pfft Boo Boo's orchestra would play the symphony that caused heads to explode for the governor. In two weeks earth time, they would leave to continue their grand tour of the cosmos.

Isaac woke in a haze. A servant, a spherical creature with tough gray skin that bounced for locomotion, set a bowl of the salty gray ooze out for him. Isaac drank the slime greedily.

Nim popped his head in Isaac's door. "I've heard that you have some musical talent," he said.

"Who told you that?"

"Eek Fallorian, I was talking to him this morning. He says you play the Melancanthian Trumpet like a dream."

"I picked it up about five years back," Isaac said groggily.

"I'll arrange a tryout for you then, but you shouldn't disappoint."

"I won't," Isaac said.

Nim bowed and shuffled away on his oversized feet.

Isaac stood from his hard bed and stretched. Peek Fallorian jumped into his door.

"Got your trumpet."

"Good. Do I have to learn how to play it now?"

"Aye. You have to learn how to release its surprise."

"What do I do?"

Peek held the golden trumpet up. It had what looked like six valves connected to a large bell shaped protrusion. A small piece of metal jutted to the side. Peek pointed to it.

"That's how you aim the thing. Put it to your lips and aim that metal at the Governor's head. Then you press this fourth valve here and the one shot wonder will fire. If your aim is true, it will send a molten diamond through old Governor's thought transducer."

"What's the point of that? The Mashgool I rode with over here said that they are all equal. They'll just find another Governor in a few seconds."

"No. Mashgool can access the contents of one another's thought transducers, but once one is gone, the data can't be recovered. This Governor here was once a famous Mashgool Admiral. His knowledge of deep space battle tactics is priceless."

"They will kill me."

"No, they won't. They'll applaud your bravery. They may give you a medal. Trust me."

"I have to do something. They are eating my kind."

"That's awful."

"The strange thing is, we resisted them. We fought them. I was told after we brought down one of their battle cruisers that the Mashgool began a surface bombardment of our planet."

"Aye. But that's highly unlikely. Something else happened," Peek mused.

"Before I shoot the Governor, I'll find out," Isaac said.

Peek handed Isaac the trumpet. It felt heavy in his hands.

"That is loaded and ready to go," Peek said.

"I guess I can't practice," Isaac said.

"No. You get one shot."

Isaac put the trumpet on his shelf, so that the bell was facing the wall.

Nim shuffled in excited, the stalk of his body jibing back and forth. Peek Fallorian had displeasure on his face.

"You will have your tryout tomorrow! This is great news. I've heard there is to be a very special guest in attendance."

"Who?" Fallorian asked.

"None other than the Emperor of the Mashgool will be here. He's making an inspection of this outpost. Glorious news!"

"Glorious news indeed," Peek said with his zipper mouth gaping in a strange smile.

"Well, you'll play for us, right?" Nim asked.

"Eh, I don't want to ruin any surprise," Isaac said.

"Why, it won't ruin it! You could put on a small concert for the prisoners. Increase morale!"

"No one wants to see him play, Nim!" Peek blurted out.

"Why, that's not true. I want to see him play."

"Damn you, Nim. Just get out here if you know what's good for you."

"That's no way to treat an emperor!"

"You fool! You're not an emperor anymore. Just like my brother and I are no longer leaders of the Promised Guild! You're a damn prisoner! Don't you see that?!"

"I'm here to declare unconditional war on them," Nim said sheepishly.

"You're their little pet, Nim," Peek said.

"Isaac, why don't you want to play for me?" Nim asked.

"My mouth is sore right now, Nim. If you want to see me play, attend the tryout."

"They won't let me," Nim said. His big eye started to well up with tears. "I am just a prisoner here. Just like Xzzlit. Just like you Fallorian brothers. Just like everyone else."

"You're not special, Nim. They make you think you're special. You're nothing to them."

Nim walked from the room staring at his oversized feet.

"If that bastard comes around again, I'll kill him," Peek said.

"I don't think it's necessary. I think he'll be moping around for quite some time," Isaac said with his arms crossed at his chest.

Eek entered the room carrying a pair of clothing in his spindly hands. "We're all set, then?" he asked with his silver eyes gleaming.

"Yes, I'll be ready," Isaac said.

"You'll want to look your best tomorrow. I got this suit for you from those Sazian gangsters upstairs. Cost me a great deal, you know, concessions for weapons when we get out of here."

"Aye. Try her on," Peek said.

Isaac disrobed. Their silver eyes burned through his body. He turned his back to them in shame. The suit was made of fine purple cloth, and it was so sheer it felt almost wet to the touch.

"Nice," Eek said. "You need any adjustments?"

"No. It fits well," Isaac said.

"Hang her up. I'd get plenty of rest today. You'll need your concentration to be at its maximum tomorrow," Eek said.

"Aye. Can't take a shot without concentration," Peek said smiling. His zipper mouth stretched to its widest. Isaac could nearly see the dark pink tunnel of his throat.

The Fallorian brothers talked with Isaac about their struggles with the Mashgool. They spoke about the foundation of the Promised Guild. They talked at great length about comrades in arms that they lost throughout the vicious battles in every corner of the universe. Isaac lamented privately that all the bravery seemed for naught because the Mashgool treated the other intelligent species of the universe like playthings. It seemed to him that it was not the outcome of the fight that was important to them, but the fight and struggle itself. After hours of stories of adventure and bravery complete with showing off scars for proof, they bade him goodnight. Before Peek Fallorian departed, he made Isaac tell him how the one shot wonder operated and run through the exact steps he would take to assassinate the new target, the Emperor of the Mashgool.

The Mashgool Emperor did not stay in a fixed location. He constantly moved with an enormous fleet of flagships and small fast moving battle cruisers. His path was completely random and he visited installations when he saw fit. It was a miracle that Nim was able to glean the information from one of the guards. Apparently they saw Nim as not being that much of a threat.

The flagships surrounded and dwarfed the station. The orchestra took its places in the massive parabolic pit, the expansive of which was large enough to seat over fifteen thousand instruments. The harmonics of the arena surrounding the dining platform were perfect and one could hear the musicians clearing their throats as they took their places. A metal column projected from the center and the orchestra director took his place there. Music projected in front of him, glowing in the ethereal air, as he cleared his throat and adjusted the fit of his golden robes.

The Emperor entered surrounded by a retinue of hundreds of guards. On his shoulder stood a Pylori, a furry creature with a sunken face, large saucer ears, and bright, blood red eyes. Its head darted uncontrollably in fear, taking in all the threats in its environment. They were once mathematicians and philosophers of the highest caliber. They spent all of their time pondering questions of being and the nature of time and space. They never bothered to create technologies based on their equations; simply establishing proofs of the nature of the universe was the ultimate end of inquiry for the Pylori.

The Mashgool found them early in their campaign season. They sent representatives bearing gifts to the Pylori Overcademy, the governing body of Pylori science. The Mashgool advisors were haughty and unimpressed with the proofs the Pylori demonstrated, though secretly the Mashgool coveted it all. It was a Pylori physical proof on the independent non-sustainability of matter that allowed the Mashgool to manufacture their precious Termiculum. This proof also caused the Mashgool to disbelieve anything they described as being tainted with the supernatural.

When the Pylori laid eyes on the Mashgool and viewed their battle cruisers and sophisticated weaponry, they immediately acquiesced to all the Mashgool demands. They handed over all of their science for nothing in return. They reasoned that they could still practice mathematics and science at the Overcademy. The Pylori deeply offended the Mashgool by not threatening open warfare. In the course of three turns of the planet Pylorus, the Mashgool quickly appropriated all of the nearly ten billion documents housed in the Overcademy Library, and burned the rest with a bombardment by battlecruisers. All but the most stupid Pylori were massacred. They devolved under the Mashgool's careful breeding program to the pitiful creature they were today.

The Mashgool emperor sat to the right of the governor. His robes were electric pink: the color reserved for Mashgool royalty. The emperor was not part of a dynasty; as a species, the Mashgool were too smart for that. The thought transducer was selected at random to serve for a period of one year. Serving as the Emperor greatly increased the administrative knowledge of the particular Mashgool selected and ensured that it was evenly distributed amongst the hyperlinked Mashgool neural net. Eventually given enough time, all of the extant Mashgool would become Emperor for a year and the cycle would repeat itself. Prior to being named Emperor, Zubb Aswad was a mining foreman in the Termiculum precursor mines located in a sector of the Milky Way Galaxy that no one cared to visit, as it was cold and dark and lacking in tourist destinations.

Isaac, holding his golden trumpet, was seated in a chair facing the black waxen wood, semicircle table. He dared not move. The orchestra, to his rear, began warming up their instruments. The sound drowned out the farted and belched chatter of the Mashgool ministers, advisors, and honored guests. Mashgool ladies gossiped, farting in wild high-pitched squeals, batting their headdresses made with the baby's feet of Emperor Nim's people to and fro as they laughed in gay unconcern of the suffering of others around them.

The Mashgool Emperor, Zubb Aswad, floated upwards. The entire room fell silent.

"We are here for four reasons, some more important than the others," the Mashgool Emperor said.

"The first is a performance, the second a feast, the third a trial, and the fourth is a tryout. The same creature being tried is the creature trying out. Strange, but it has never happened this way before. In the billion-year history of our empire, this is the first time that a criminal mastermind has also been revealed to be an accomplished musician. I am an emperor, but also a poet, so I don't think it's that strange. We have assembled a panel of competent judges. We know this creature's crime is great, but we do not yet understand the gravity behind it because we have no idea of this creature's intent. In order to discover his intent we will put him to question. If his intent was pure, he will be free to go. If it was tainted he just may have to stay."

The Emperor floated downwards. The Conductor Pfft Boo Boo ripped one audibly, Isaac heard the translator say, "Places!" and the single Xlorian cawet string plucked in 4/4 like the opening of a massive funeral march for the universe. What followed made Isaac want to weep with joy, if he was not worried about what the Emperor was thinking.

The Emperor stared at him for the entire two hour duration of the symphony. Isaac tried to look away. He felt the eyes, buried in protoplasm, burning through him. Isaac looked back at the pink dressed jellyfish, and it was as if the thing could see through his soul, seeing exactly what he had planned. Isaac traced the line of the Emperor's dead eyes and saw that he was staring at the trumpet.

Isaac squirmed. The emperor bobbed up and down to the music. One of the ladies screamed and her coxcomb fell from her head onto the table. The Emperor looked at her. Guards picked her up from the table and carried her from the room. Isaac thought about taking the shot, but he would have to wait until it was time for his tryout. The trumpet did not depart his white knuckled grasp.

The symphony came to an end and the Mashgool applauded by making a sound with their mouths like the squeaking of mice.

The Emperor floated upwards again and the room went silent.

"Now, the feast!" he farted with the strength of a blowhard hippopotamus.

Tray after tray floated into the room, unaided by any servants, and parked at the appropriate spot on the table. The covers lifted. The beautiful smells wafted and made Isaac's mouth water until he saw what was on the table.

On the trays were human baby heads, little cooked ears and all, round little heads, browned and coated in sauce. The Pylori leaped from the Mashgool Emperor's shoulder and grabbed a tiny head in its hands. The Mashgool Emperor attached a harness to his shoulders that supported a tiny stand on his chest. The Pylori jumped from the table onto this stand. It grabbed a tiny mallet and whacked the head, opening the soft skull. It took a bite and chewed. The Mashgool Emperor salivated impatiently, rocking the Pylori back and forth.

The Pylori leaned forward and spit the chewed up baby brains into the Mashgool Emperor's open mouth. He swallowed greedily. Isaac could see the pasty substance move through his translucent gullet, before it was covered with the plush robes. Isaac looked to the trumpet.

"It's delicious!" the Emperor announced.

Other Pylori dashed to the table, bringing their masters back their selections. The table was soon a feeding frenzy of Pylori politely bowing to each other as they darted to fill the mouths of the Mashgool with their wishes.

Isaac sank in his chair. Each baby head the Pylori grabbed, his stomach turned.

"Enough," Isaac shouted.

The Emperor floated upwards. The rest of the part froze. Pylori locked into position on the table.

"What did you say?"

"I said enough. You can't eat those any more!"

"Who are you to tell us what to do?" the Emperor said.

"I'm Isaac. I'm a *man*."

"You're the rogue in charge of destroying our farm. Is that right?"

"I did. I destroyed it. I'd do it again."

"Look at the bravery on this one. Why, I'd say if he cooked this meal our precious Pylori would be dead of poisoning by now."

One of the Pylori stumbled into a plate of what looked like giant red crabs with enormous crushing claws. It hid between the two specimens with their shells cracked open and bits of savory crabmeat stinking out, exploded like the crabs had swallowed hand grenades.

"It's wrong," Isaac said.

"Why is it wrong? You did the same thing on your planet. Things that were tasty, you ate. Things that weren't, you killed. It was written in your book. Let me see. That obscure tome. Yes here it is. Right on my mind. I quote, 'have dominion over the fish of the sea, the birds of the air, and all the living things, that move on the Earth'...blah blah blah...'have them for food.' We follow the same dictum as you, except our domain and our dominion is the entire Universe."

"It is still wrong," Isaac said, his trumpet in his hand.

"Please, you are interrupting our meal. You will have your chance to speak at your trial."

"I am speaking now, Emperor. I will not hold my tongue any longer."

"You insolent little worm. You are as devious as your leader was. The one that sold your kind into our dominion."

"Our leader? Who was that?"

"The Earth Scientist Tanner," the Emperor said.

"He wasn't our leader!" Isaac yelled.

"He was your most brilliant scientist and the reason that we discovered your planet. He said he was your leader. He wanted us to install him as governor of the Blue Planet."

"You believed him? You're fools."

"It made sense to us," the Emperor said.

"Not everything that makes sense is true," Isaac said.

"Who...who was he?" the Mashgool Emperor said.

"Just another man, with a talent for science," Isaac said.

"We assumed he was your leader. That is what he told us at least. He said that he was having troubles with a breakaway faction, a faction that threatened to hold humanity back from its true potential. He called these people religious."

"What did he want your help with?" Isaac said, as the creeping chill moved down his spine.

"We begged him to declare war on us, but he would have none of it. He asked us to help him in his plans."

"You went along with him?"

"At that point we knew that there was no getting him to resist. The power we offered him was too great. You could see it in his eyes. They glowed with lust when we showed him the properties of the Termiculum. He wanted us to help him wipe out these religious ones so that humanity would have a future. He said they were the cause of all the disorder in the world. We thought he spoke for everyone. Everyone but these religious ones."

"We are all human beings. We can all think for ourselves. We are all individuals. He didn't speak for anyone but himself. Tanner did everything for himself," Isaac said holding the trumpet to his chest.

"He made the suit that cured death for himself. We saw it before in our own civilization. The war started. It started small at first. It happened underneath our cruisers and no one even fired a shot at us. We just watched the explosions. We watched him cleanse the world of his opponents."

"How did you lose that battle cruiser then? Wasn't it shot down?"

"It just crashed. It happens sometimes. Not even the most advanced civilizations can plan for accidents," the Mashgool Emperor said.

"That man, Tanner, he is at war with everything, but ultimately at war within himself," the Emperor said.

"He's immortal, but he hates himself. It's worse than being in Hell," Isaac said raising the trumpet slightly.

"So, he isn't your leader?"

"No. The farthest thing from it. I think he's dead now."

"How can you be sure?"

"When I return, if he isn't dead, I'll do it myself."

"How will you return? Are you prepared to fight us?"

"I am."

"You're going to fight our empire? You know that we could destroy your entire galaxy with the push of a button, right?"

"I do. Still, we will fight you."

The Emperor laughed, rising high above the table. His Pylori lost its balance and fell to the table, landing with a splat and scattering the baby heads on the ground. The Mashgool ladies joined, and it sounded like a farm of hogs on a spit.

The Emperor fell to his chair. "Get the button, damn it!" he screamed.

Soldiers pushed a floating metal box, the dimensions of an office desk, beside the Mashgool Emperor's place at the table. The Emperor floated to the button greedily. It glowed as red as blood.

"Are you ready to be responsible for the destruction of your species and the entire galaxy?"

"You won't do it."

"I won't?"

"No. You want me beg you to stop. You want me to get on my hands and knees and beg you to stop. I won't. Go ahead and do it. Push the damn button. Just let me play a song for my people first."

"On your trumpet?"

"Aye, on my trumpet. It has a mournful sound."

"When you're done, I push the button!"

"This song will be my resistance," Isaac said.

"Get on with it. It had better be a fitting ode," the Emperor mocked.

Isaac put the trumpet to his lips. He aimed with the mock spit valve about an inch above the Mashgool's face at the pulsating thought transducer. He smiled, and pressed the fourth cylindrical valve.

The diamond that was Jesse heated to over 10000 degrees Kelvin in an instant and shot spinning around a central axis line true towards its target. In less than a nanosecond, the projectile found its mark. The Emperor slumped forward and the Mashgool ladies screamed like demon crazed swine. The Emperor's thought transducer fell from the gaping hole where his face was and split in half onto the dinner table. Soldiers stood frozen. They had never seen an act of such blatant aggression and were only used to intimidating people. The Pylori jumped from the platform of its decapitated master and picked up both sides of its brain, jostling the volatile metals enough to cause an explosion that shot out both sides like a shaped charge. Pieces of tentacle flung in the air into the orchestra. Pfft Boo Boo called the orchestra to attention but the chaos had spread to their ranks. Yells of horror dumped in from the Prison Wing.

Eek and Peek Fallorian, at the head of thousands of quarantined prisoners began to trickle and then pour into the massive room from the attached hallway. They carried crudely sharpened implements, but the bloodthirsty captives wielded their rage as their ultimate weapon. Screams of every pitch followed them. The Mashgool soldiers turned and tried to float away towards the airlock and the flagship but the captives cut them off, hacking and ripping tentacles with fury.

Peek Fallorian ran ahead killing Mashgool with a horrible precision, whipping triangular shards of metal the size of dinner plates that crippled the Mashgool until he could rip their thought transducer from their heads with his bare hands.

A clamor rose from the orchestra pit. Pfft Boo Boo kept calling the orchestra to attention but they did not listen. Instruments clanged and dumped death knell sounds into the air as musicians hurled them at the conductor. A brass cymbal knocked him from his floating disk and he slopped to the floor, useless like an octopus fallen from its tank. The musicians climbed the podium to his lectern, some with instruments in hand, and pummeled Pfft Boo Boo until he stopped his spasms. He shrieked, "Death! And for such and artist!"

"To the flagship!" Eek Fallorian yelled to the troops to rally them.

"Aye! Seize the arms room!" Peek echoed. The ran towards the open airlock. The prisoners followed. The orchestra joined them.

"We are certain to get four Crimson Stars of Gloop for this one!" Peek screamed.

"No, brother! From this day forth we dream up our own medals!" Eek shouted to his brother over the wave of collective rage behind them.

They stormed into the ship like locusts. Mashgool tried to run, struggling to reach the control room. They careened into walls and off each other, panicking. The freed captives of a thousand civilizations forced one of the Mashgool to open the arms room. They seized into it, picking up the strange contraptions, unused for lifetimes, and quickly putting them into action. Peek and Eek Fallorian took up the vanguard, racing ahead to cut the Mashgool from entering the control room where they could destroy the flagship. Peek Fallorian blasted the Mashgool with their own weaponry, taking aim for the thought transducers only. The orchestra members sprayed and prayed, ricocheting rounds and plasma bursts randomly off the walls, blackening them. Tentacles calamaried on the floor squirming where they fell from Mashgool arms, bodies, and faces.

The control room door whirred, slowly closing. Isaac thrust the trumpet in the seam and the door held. Eek and Peek Fallorian concentrated their fire and ordered the Tellurian Bassoon players to hurl grenade after grenade in the door. They exploded one by one, coughing smoke and billowing from the slender gap. The door strained against the trumpet and finally snapped it. It shut with a empty thud.

"Blow the door! Everybody back," Eek Fallorian ordered.

The mass pressed back against itself. Isaac aimed a long metal cylindrical object at the door and was about to activate it before Peek Fallorian grabbed his arm. Peek took the weapon and turned it around.

"Get down!" he yelled.

Isaac covered his head and put his hands to his ears.

The shockwave hit the door and only bent it. At any moment they expected to be vaporized in a giant explosion when the Mashgool countdown ended.

"Get another one up here!" Peek yelled to the crowd. The masses passed up three more, careful not to activate them. Peek launched the shockwave round at the door in rapid succession. On the third explosion, the door collapsed back into the fiery control room.

Isaac and Eek rushed forward. Peek tossed the canister to the ground and loaded another magazine into his weapon, his finger ready in the trigger well. The trigger stood taut but able to be depressed with minimal tentacle pressure. Eek was in the door first. A single Mashgool, knocked from its floating disk, and dressed in tattered and scorched silver robes, slithered towards a central control panel and slowly crept its tentacle upwards towards a prominent button. Eek took aim and fired, missing. Isaac shot the Mashgool in its gelatinous body, spraying protoplasm on the control. Peek fired. The thought transducer split in half and burst into flame.

Gunshots and plasma bursts erupted randomly throughout the ship as the former captives cleared its bowels of any remaining Mashgool. A pocket of fierce resistance erupted near the engine room where several Mashgool had holed up trying to blow the reactor. Several martyrs lost their lives trying to flush the Mashgool from their barricade.

Peek Fallorian monitored the Mashgool farting coming over the radio waves.

"They're on to us!" Peek shouted to the battle worn rebels.

"Does anyone know how to drive this thing?" Eek screamed.

A miniscule voice from the crowd, barely rising over the labored breathing answered, "I can."

"Let yourself be seen!" Peek yelled.

A Pylorian stepped from beneath the feet of Emperor Nim.

"Nim? You can drive this?"

"Not I! Him!" Nim said picking the Pylorian up with his feet and thrusting it forward.

"Ack," Peek said, turning his face.

"I know. I've seen them drive it hundreds of times," the Pylorian said in a meek voice. Its lip quivered, testament to its life of chewing food and testing food for poison.

"Let the Pylorian try!" Isaac said.

"How do we know that he won't just destroy the ship?" Peek said.

"I won't. The Pylori were once great! Through out my service, I wanted this as much as every single one of you. No one was willing to act until this human came along. He inspired me to the former greatness of my people," the Pylorian said. He looked to Isaac and said, "I am sorry for tasting your kind. I had no choice."

Isaac nodded grimly to the little creature with the flattened face of a hairless cat.

"Then fly, Pylorian, fly! Get us out of here before these bastards blow us to pieces." Peek yelled.

The Pylorian leapt up the control panel, pulling levers and pushing buttons. It looked through scopes and its bright eyes glowed like the fires of the sun.

The ship began to list and finally move forward out of its dock with the space station. The crew of prisoners and Mashgool orchestral slaves cheered.

"Hold on!" the Pylorian flagship's captain ordered.

The ship gained speed.

"They are on us! Battle stations!" the Pylorian yelled to the much bigger creatures around him.

They ran to the guns. Those that could fly, manned starfighters, launching from the bays through the wall of Mashgool interlinked fire. They dropped into space, champions of the desperate day, took massive damage from plasma hits and exploded into soundless supernovas.

The Pylorian activated the flagship's heavy weaponry and obliterated one of the pursuing flagships with a single heat laser that cut the ship in two, sending tiny freeze dried Mashgool floating into the fray.

The small starships strafed another Mashgool flagship, unmercifully harassing it until its hull failed and a fatal hole punctured in the supposedly indestructible metal. A plasma bolt fired by a Xenea flutist penetrated the engine fuel core and ignited, exploding into space fatally. It listed burning and crashed into the space station. Vital gases sucked into space, ripping sleeping Mashgool from their floating disks, sending them farting into the freezing void.

The remaining flagships turned from the captured ship in full retreat. Their inexperienced crews hid in the ship's corners, terrified of dying.

"Hold on to something now!" the Pylorian Captain shouted.

His small hands coaxed the lever controlling the warp flux and then pressed it into gear.

The ship paused then lurched forward faster than light.

The flagship, a Mashgool 97 Series Galaxy Smasher, with a dual quad Termiculum core capable of indefinite power generation and life support capabilities, cruised through the Bacchus asteroid field at the edge of the galaxy known to humans as the Milky Way. They came across several ships on their month long journey, many joined the fleet after hearing the news of the crew's destruction of the Mashgool Deep Space Station for the sector. Ships that did not join the fleet were charged a toll and allowed to pass. Those ships that did not pay the toll were boarded and seized and their crews were press ganged into the service of Captain Atrius of Pylorus, who now wore a magnificent Navy Uniform with the dual Order of the Crested Phoenix medals, the Promised Guild's highest military honor. Isaac's gray uniform, as appointed head of the fleet intelligence division, was decked with a single Order of the Crested Phoenix medal and Expert Marksman badge. Peek Fallorian, the Vice Admiral and Chief Weapons Engineer, thought that Isaac deserved that honor.

Eek Fallorian guided the fleet to its destination: the outer worlds of Fallorian where it would join with the waiting Fallorian fleet to combine forces against the Mashgool Third Fleet and another Deep Space Station. Finding the home galaxy of the Mashgool was their top priority as they needed to take the offensive as soon as they gained enough numbers. Each member of the United Worlds Pirate Promised Guild pledged their civilization's undying gratitude and steadfast support to the enterprise. Isaac lamented that his world was all but destroyed and would be unable to contribute anything. He thought of his beautiful wife. She surely was thinking that he was dead. The galaxy was still extant, and she had made him a promise that she would wait for him until the universe was smashed to bits, just as he had promised her in turn. When the flagship neared the apex of its approach and a straight path to Earth, the blue planet, was finally possible, Isaac approached Admiral Eek Fallorian and begged to be relieved from his duties.

"I need to go and find my wife. It has been far too long that I have been pursuing other men's adventures in neglect of her. She's also going to have my child," Isaac said to Admiral Eek Fallorian, who watched the map with a vague fascination.

"You never told us you were married. The life we're embarking on is not the life for a family man. It's going to be hard and bitter and will only end in death. Hopefully, it will ultimately be the death of the Mashgool. We're going to teach them their place, but it will be bloody."

Vice Admiral Peek Fallorian butted in, "Just let him go, brother. Can't you see that this man has suffered enough?"

"You must promise us, next time our fleet is in the vicinity of your solar system, that you will join us again," Eek said.

"I cannot promise anything. I can only tell you that it was an honor having served with you both."

"You are fascinating to us, Isaac. We have never met a species that the universe has given such a hard shake to. You are the only creature we have ever met that absolutely refuses to be held down."

"We can be held down for a while but once one of us does what everybody else is thinking, I'd hate to be on the receiving end of our fury," Isaac said.

"You are a true individual, Isaac. We couldn't have asked any of those other creatures in that horrible jail to do what you did. They were all cowards. Do you think Engineer Nim ever would have done that? No. I doubt even my brother or I would have had the courage to do what you did."

"You told me that the Mashgool respected resistance. I resisted them."

"They respect token resistance. They fight and crush real resistance. It gives them as much purpose as turning the kowtowing civilizations of the universe into a miserable bunch of slaves and servants. Obviously, when we really resisted them, they showed themselves to be horribly out of practice."

"Oh, believe me, they're planning now to fight back. It is a good thing we destroyed that space station, but those flagships that escaped will be carrying the news of their defeat back to wherever their home world is," Peek said.

"You told me they'd give me a medal. You told me they would applaud what I did."

"We had to provide you the motivation to go on a fool's errand. You succeeded, Isaac. You're the reason for the success of this resistance."

"You both used me then," Isaac said.

"We did not use you. If you would have missed, we would have still fought by your side. Though we probably wouldn't have been as successful," Peek said.

"Things happened for a reason, Isaac," Eek Fallorian said.

"You really believe that? You really believe that things happen for a reason?"

"I do, Isaac. If you believe in yourself and you have ambition in this universe, you will make things happen. You will write your own destiny," Eek said.

"Have a fanatic belief in yourself," Peek said.

"Yes, Isaac, remember that talent is ambition smashed through a sieve of doubt. This doubt enforces your discipline to practice to gain in skill. Both you and your species are capable of greatness. We see it in you. You are humans, the much maligned creature of infinite possibility. Have a fanatical belief in yourselves. Imagine the universe you want to live in and realize it."

"I will do my best," Isaac said.

"Captain Pylorian, program one of the hyper speed escape pods for a course to the *Blue Planet*, Earth."

"Who would want to go there?' the Captain asked.

"Just do it, Captain!" Admiral Eek Fallorian said.

"Aye," the miniscule Captain said. He pressed a series of buttons in sequence and a door to an escape pod opened.

Isaac went inside and strapped himself in. Admiral Eek and Vice Admiral Peek, the Engineer, and all of Isaac's other friends he made on his fantastic journey stood at the doorway wishing him farewell and good luck in finding his beloved wife.

As the door closed, the escape capsule filled with protective foam that swelled around Isaac. The capsule detached from the body of the flagship, drifting for a moment in empty space. As the warp core engaged, a terrible sadness tugged at his being. As the capsule flung towards the blue planet, the sadness filled with a tinge of sweet joy. He drifted off into dreamless sleep as the capsule hurtled into the void toward its destination.

Isaac slept as in stasis as the capsule hurtled past stars and planets, ripped past planetoids, and narrowly missed asteroids at the belt of wobbling boulders separating Mars and Earth from the outer planets of Jupiter and Saturn.

The capsule tilted, following its program, and atmospheric entry plates rose to cover the surface as the teardrop shaped capsule made contact with the gaseous ocean surface of the Earth's atmosphere. It streaked across the northern sky. Men and women of the forest looked overhead, thinking it some portent of doom from the heavens. Children gasped as it buckled the sky behind it and boomed against the surface.

It smoldered over the continents, taking an angle of approach oblique enough not to completely burn up. The foam protected Isaac against cooking. Its edges withstood temperatures of up to 4000 Kelvin.

*

Men driving camels through the shifting sands past a small nomad encampment in the large peninsula known to the ancients as Arabia, shuddered as the thunderclaps approached, beating the sky like a the massive heartbeat of a monster Djinn. The capsule left a white-hot vapor trail and burned the sky over them, illuminating their shamagh covered faces. The camels grunted and spit, pulling against their tethers. The capsule impacted, shooting sands hundreds of feet into the air, raining down on them like a sand storm.

They froze, thinking a giant, black meteorite had collided with the Earth.

*

The women in the tents screamed at the commotion. An old man peeked his head out of the tent, followed by his grandson. They looked alike: the old man a parched and desiccated, taller version of the little boy.

They walked hand and hand to the edge of the crater and saw the black capsule smoking. The foam evaporated, forcing the outer door open. Isaac awoke and stared at the bright blue sky.

He stood up and dusted himself off. His muscles were tired from the journey. Isaac heard the sound of the women yelling and camels struggling against their caravan masters.

He looked to the top of the crater and saw the old man and young boy standing, staring at him. He waved to them. The old man pulled his grandson close, hiding him beneath his robes.

The old man walked to the very edge of the crater and reached his hand down for Isaac to come up the side.

Some of the younger men, sensing their grandfather's bravery, aided in helping Isaac to climb up the side of the crater. The sand burned pinholes on the underside of his hands, and felt like thousands of fiery suns.

Isaac stood to his feet. His grey uniform was marred with the yellow sand and foam particles.

The old man was the first to speak. "Min wayn enta?" he asked with wide eyes. Isaac looked to the boy. His eyes were as wide as two moons.

Isaac pulled the Universal Translator from around his neck and held it up for the man.

"This will translate between us, so we can speak," Isaac explained. The Universal Translator spit out his dialogue in perfect Arabic.

The old man laughed, cackling with his head pitched back. The young men joined in with their elder.

"Min wayn enta," the old man said with a smile.

"Where are you from?" the Universal Translator said.

"I am Isaac. I am from here, Earth."

"What happened to you?" the old man asked.

"I have been on a journey across the heavens. I have been gone for a long time."

"You must have seen amazing things," the old man said.

"I have."

"Come, let us go to the tent. We will have a feast and you can tell us all about your journey."

"I cannot stay long. I must find my wife," Isaac said.

"You can rest and enjoy our hospitality and then you can find your wife," the old man said.

The old man said to the young boy, "Mohammed, run to the tent and tell your mother and the women to prepare some food for us and our special guest."

The boy dutifully ran off. His feet cut furrows in the sand, little imprints that the blowing winds covered as soon as they formed.

*

Isaac sat as the guest of honor and told them his adventures. They cried during the sad parts. Laughed during the happy parts. The women sighed when he talked of his love for Deer. Late in the evening, Isaac became very tired and could not continue. The old man showed him to his tent, and Isaac curled up amongst the pillows.

*

With his belly full of spiced camel meat, he drifted off into sleep, snoring as the desert winds buffeted the leather flap of the tent like a drum. He dreamed a dream of man, the creature of infinite possibilities and awoke when the boy Mohammed nudged him in the morning. Mohammed laid a bowl of camel yogurt next to Isaac's bed and scampered off. Isaac tasted it. The yogurt was tart and creamy. He mixed it with honey to palate it. He opened the flap to the tent and stared at the thunderstorms on the far off horizon. Rains swept across the valley in the distance, black streaks pierced with flashes of lighting. He looked in the opposite direction, to the west. The bright red sun crested over the distant dunes. He yawned with the warmth of the sun on his face. He would head off in the direction of the desert in search of his wife. He breathed deeply. It was a new day.